CW01084423

This book is dedicated to all of life's misfits, eccen
who has never picked up a book before… oh yeah a

old belly laugh.

Enjoy.

1

Six Inches for the Holy Spirit

Chapter one

Like every other day, I woke up with existential angst and a hard-on. The same thought popped into my head. What is the point of life when one's life is so utterly shit? Proper shit. Well not proper, proper shit like those starving Ethiopians on the tele sat out in the searing heat of the midday sun with pot bellies covered in flies while earnest but well fed journalists and camera crews ran all over the place. Or little Indian beggar kids who'd had their arms and legs chopped off by criminal gangs shit. But still shit. Oh well, there was fuck all that I could do about any of it so mechanically, I reached under my bed for my jar of Vaseline, rubbed some all over my cock and balls and closed my eyes. Some of those Ethiopian mums on the nine

2

O'clock news last had their tits out. Within no time I had a picture in my head of Kim Wilde, Samantha Fox and Debbie Harry somewhere out in Africa presenting a hard hitting documentary on poverty or famine or something. This quickly escalated into an inter-racial lesbian orgy and within less than a minute I was done. A picture of a scowling Kate Adie then popped into my mind so I decided that I might as well get up and go to school.

It was Monday October 5th 1987. Just another ordinary day of mindless tedium and casual violence. I'd managed to get to first break relatively unscathed. I have to admit that I was in quite a buoyant mood up until then because I'd just had double French with Miss Higgins. Miss Higgins was one of the hotter teachers in our school. She wasn't Linda Lusardi or Maria Whittaker or Kathy Lloyd or that other page three bird with the small tits and didn't come anywhere near Bo Derek or Kim Basinger or Demi Moore or even Kylie Minogue and miles away from being a sexy as Cait O'Riordan, the bassist from my beloved Pogues. The latter was constantly in my top five list of celebrities I'd like to fuck before I die. Miss Higgins was still very shaggable though.

As she wrote conjugated French verbs on the board I spent the whole time staring intently at her VPL. Her visible panty line. With one hand in my pocket I fantasised about what colour they were and what they'd look like around her ankles. What's that miss you want me to stay after the lesson and help you tidy up? I bet you do you sale salope! As soon as the last kid left the room she'd be on me like Gerard Depardieu on a frog and snail baguette full of drugs. I would have emptied my bollocks into my pants right there and then if it hadn't been for some cunt at the back of the class throwing an empty can of coke at my head and putting me off. It was a good image to store in the old wank bank though so I was still pretty chipper at that stage of the day. I'd always had the same two preoccupations. Sex and death. The only way I thought that I could ease the dark clouds that persisted in following me around was to have sexual intercourse with every beautiful woman in the world and then die. Only then would I be happy. It was immediately after French, while still pondering my putrid existence, when the inevitable occurred.

As I skulked across the school playground, eating crisps one at a time from my pocket, head down trying not to draw attention to myself I suddenly felt a short, sharp, shocking pain to my left ear. I tried not to outwardly react but in a situation like that one's brain goes into overdrive. Blood is rushed to the affected area, one's inner voice yells, what on earth was that!?' And, 'Golly gosh that ruddy well smarts a tad! How the blazes can I stop this excruciating pain?!' Or something like that, mine did anyway but with a lot more expletives. I don't know the science behind it but I do know that my legs buckled and I staggered about clutching my ear lobe. Eventually I managed to extricate it. It was a bulldog clip. At the time I didn't know what a bulldog clip was, but it didn't take me long to find out. An empirical example was given to me on that fateful day and it's one of the few things I learned at that school that I have managed to retain. It's basically a clip on a spring and when attached to a person's extremities it smarts, to say the least. So anyway, I un-clipped it from my ear and looked around for the culprit, glaring menacingly at anyone within bulldog clipping range. At first glance nobody seemed obviously guilty of this heinous and unprovoked act of unprovoked cruelty. Nobody was laughing and pointing, nobody was looking particularly gleeful or walking about with exaggerated strides, looking up to the skies and whistling with their hands behind their backs, or nudging their mates and sniggering or any other obvious tell- tell signs of having performed a recent misdemeanour. I scanned the yard from left to right trying to look as fierce as possible while scrutinising the plethora of adolescent faces who for all intents and purposes were going about their business. The more I inspected my peers the more I thought they could all be culpable. With very few exceptions I hated every one of them. Pupils, teachers, caretakers, and dinner ladies, the fucking lot of them. Fuck them all. I contented myself with the thought that all of these outwardly innocent looking, mouth breathing, shit kickers will soon be paying dearly for messing with the soon to be legend that was Johnny McQueen. All I need to do was figure out how.

But in the mean time I decided to take this cruel and uncalled for, and not uncommon, incident as a sign from above to bunk off early and have a discrete, medicinal wank at the back of the bus on the way home. An image of Miss Higgins sat at the wheel wearing nothing but a bus driver's hat and a coquettish smile confirmed this, so I fucked off.

Later that day and suitably refreshed I was out in our back garden oiling the chain on my beloved Chopper bike when out of nowhere, my dad, accompanied by Brian, this week's family social worker, walked up to me. My dad then inexplicable put his hand on my shoulder which made me flinch and I nearly shit my pants in fright.

4

'Johnny darling, although Mummy and Daddy still love each other very much… and please remember that it's not your fault (dramatic pause) we've decided to separate.' I stopped mid squirt.

'Johnny darling'?

'Mummy and Daddy'?

'It's not your fault'?

'We still love each other very much?'

'Separate'?

What the actual fuck?

My initial thought was that my dad's head had finally popped and he'd actually gone mental. My father was not the sort of person to call me or anyone else 'darling.' Furthermore I was 15 years old and hadn't heard my parents refer to themselves as Mummy and Daddy ever. Not one single time. I'd never heard either of them say that before. My father traditionally addressed by my mother as bitch and my mother always addressed my father as cunt.

Okay let's move on to, "it's not your fault." Why would he even bother to say that? I knew perfectly well that if they were splitting up it certainly wasn't my fault. Well I did until he'd mentioned it. I knew for a fact that it had absolutely nothing what so ever to do with me so why did he say that? I bet he read it in some book, probably called something like, *How to tell your kids you're separating without scarring them for life but at the same time hinting that it's their fault.*

Chapter one… 'blah, blah, blah children are delicate little souls so if you call them nice words like darling and refer to yourselves as mummy and daddy and say it's not their fault as you give them the sad news, they might not blame themselves and the chances of them turning into criminals, psychopathic killers, drug addicts and or up to and including, child molesters at a later date might well be minimalised, perhaps.'

This was the best bit though, "we still love each other very much". Well that was a lie. When he first uttered these immortal words I had to stifle an involuntary snigger. I tried to hide it with an unconvincing cough while turning my back and for some reason ringing the bell on my bike. This in turn had the unintentional effect of sounding like a drummer hitting a cymbal right on cue like when a comedian has just told a really bad joke. In any other circumstance this would have earned me a severe

5

slap across the head for being, and I quote, ' a cheeky little cunt' or for having a 'smart mouth' - which I always took as a compliment - but as there would be a witness, aka Brian, thankfully daddy had to let it go unpunished.

Chapter two… 'as you're telling your children this unfortunate turn of events try not to hit them, as this may undermine the words 'darling' and 'love' and it's not your fault'. This was the only silver lining to an otherwise very dark cloud.

As far as I was aware my parents had never, ever loved one another or even liked each other for that matter. For as long as I could remember anyway. As I listened to them bickering away over the years and throwing punches and plates and knives and whatever else came to hand – one time mid-row, my dad actually threw our dog at my mum, literally picked it up and hurled it across the room at her. I don't know what breed it was but it was certainly not one of those fun sized, toy dog, put it in your hand bag and go clubbing, type of ill-tempered and camp little yappy ones. It was a full sized, good old fashioned proper dog sized one and as it flew through the air it gave my mum a real, Giant Haystacks-esque, ITV sport, Saturday afternoon wrestling smack down, and she instinctively tried to catch it she staggered backwards and fell right through our glass coffee table. If she hadn't been so morbidly obese it could quite possibly have killed her but fortunately for all concerned her fat arse cushioned the blow and within no time she was back on her feet and striking my dad with the poker. It was one of the few highlights of my formative years and mercifully the dog was fine.

I often wondered if there was ever a time when they were actually in love. I never knew exactly how they'd met and my mind boggled as to why they were together when they clearly hated one another. I sometimes amused myself, or more accurately, distracted myself from the horror of my family with delightfully romantic scenarios of how they first got together and their first tentative attempts at courtship. Had my dad ever bought my mum flowers for example? Had they ever gone out to dinner and then off to the cinema? Did they ever take an evening stroll along the canal, hand in hand making moon faces at each other? Was there ever a time when my mum had secretly slipped heartfelt love letters in my dad's lunch box before waving him off to work? Had my dad ever worked? Had they ever kissed or hugged each other while sober? Had there ever been a time when my dad had tenderly kissed my mum's fingers or nuzzled her neck while quoting some of her favourite sonnets? Then, inevitably, my

6

fifteen year old furtive and over developed imagination would take up the helm. How long into their courtship before my mum gave my dad a blow job? I always tried to supress these images but I had no control over them. I tried to subdue an image of my dad performing the intimate act of cunnilingus on her. I'd be picturing them doing every sordid, sexually explicit act I'd ever heard of. I never thought too much about why my mind would go from one extreme to the other like this but it always did. One minute I'd be picturing the two of them passing shy, furtive glances at each other as they passed along some Dublin street back in the 60's and before long I'd be imagining them violently fisting each other and snarling covered head to toe in their own faecal matter. The bottom line was that I saw myself as a romantic and I saw them as two depraved sub-humans and I hated the pair of them with a fury. My brother Wayne and I were living in a waking nightmare because of those two and there was nothing that we could do to escape. We hated them and they hated us.

We were all good God fearing Catholics and as kids I guess one just accepts that one's life is horrifying because it's all part of God's great plan. We were all sinners and therefore had to suffer. It was as simple as that. We were poor because we deserved it and our parents reviled us because we deserved it. So we just got on with it. As a young boy I'd prayed with all my might that if my parents would stop fighting each other and beating me and our Wayne that I'd be the best damned Catholic He'd ever made. But my prayers were never answered. As I got older, I began to question God's plan a bit more in depth and eventually came to the conclusion that if He did exist at all He was definitely a bit of a sadistic cunt.

The way I saw it, any religion that let you behave like my parents did all week and then confess it all on a Sunday morning to an alcoholic paedophile, goth, transvestite who would then magically absolve you of your crimes was taking the fucking piss. I did enjoy going to church though and even from an early age found the whole thing a extremely sexy. Prior to my balls officially dropping, that heady concoction of incense mixed with guilt and sin and wickedness had always given the place an undercurrent of seedy depravity which never failed to my cock hard.

Obviously the actual service itself was constantly mind numbingly dull and because you always had to receive the Host on an empty stomach I was always

7

starving hungry and on the verge of passing out but looking back, even as a kid, I found it to be a very sensual place. As the priest droned on and all about how shit we all were compared to the man Himself I used to cast my eyes along the church walls at all the paintings and religious iconography and concoct my own less than holy scenarios of those biblical tales just to keep myself awake. Our church was chock-a-block with sexy statues of pious looking women with big tits reaching up skywards to the big man and once I'd convinced myself that I was definitely going to burn within the fiery gates of hell for all eternity anyway I might as well enjoy my short time on this earth. Thus I became content just to let the old guy waffle on and on while I was imagining myself giving all them alabaster pious slags a right good seeing to. We always used to take our place along the same row every week which gave me a clear and unrestricted view of a large, life-sized statue of the big man aka Our Lord and Saviour, Mr Jesus Christ himself. All through the service I'd be fixated on Him and why he was portrayed the way He was. That crown of thorns embedded into his long, tousled blonde hair, His pleading eyes, that athletic build, His hands and feet nailed to a cross, helpless and naked except for his tiny loincloth that only just about covered his modesty. I'm definitely as straight as they come, no doubt about it, but He was beautiful and to be frank pretty much asking for it. The saucy little minx. No wonder so many women turned up. Mrs O'Reilly who lived down the street from us used to go three times on a Sunday and also during the week, the dirty cow. Catholicism is basically a sadomasochistic cult and it's never been a surprise to me that even we Catholics are all fucking perverts. I really don't know why I stopped going actually.

Inevitably I became an altar boy and Christ only knows how I got away without being buggered senseless by any of the motley crew who ran the place. Looking back at old photos of me I was clearly a very shaggable little boy. I would have tested the resolve of even the most God fearing Christian let alone your average sex offender. But put me in one of those little altar boy frocks and you would have had to be the most restrained of holy moly pious mother fuckers ever not to have wanted to bum my little bottom hole all to fuck. Or at the very least wank me off into the font.

Being an Irish catholic my dad had also been an altar boy back in the old country. I'd always toyed with the idea that the reason why he was such an arse hole might possibly be due to the abuse he must have suffered at the hands of all those old priests. Maybe that was the reason my parents hated each other? Dad had been

8

buggered senseless as a boy and inevitably, like so many other victims of abuse, soon became the abuser. Dad now craved the back door and my mum wasn't so keen. I'd figured that his mind must have got all twisted and bent out of shape during his formative years due to the Catholic Church using him for their own sexual gratification. Rather them than me though. The mucky buggers. I was sure that if these dirty fuckers could time hop into the future and see what all their victims ended up looking like they'd think twice. My dad was proud of the fact that he began smoking roll ups from the age of five and had his first pint at six years old. Nicotine and alcohol and all the drugs and fighting over the years had left him looking like the elephant man's ugly brother.

I spent a great deal of my childhood wondering why our parents hated us and also each other. Eventually I settled on the idea that due to his suffering at the hands of the Catholic church he'd become a sexual deviant who could only be satisfied by emptying his load into the arsehole of my own dear mother. I bet he was a nonce too. I bet he'd molested me as a kid and I've repressed it. Pretty little thing like me, big round eyes, innocent smile. I was like a character in one of those Japanese animations but even more sexy. Jesus, I didn't stand a chance. I'd have tempted the most sexually normal of folks when I was younger, both men and women. I bet Sally Holmes next door spent every spare moment sucking me off and forcing me to orally pleasure her when she was supposed to be babysitting me, the filthy cow. And who could blame her? Not me.

I bet my parents were all like, 'Thanks awfully for agreeing to babysit at such short notice Sally darling it's just that my boss gave us tickets to the opera for tonight and we simply couldn't refuse as it's Volvos production of Nissan Dormouse don't cha feckin' know!?'
And Sally would, no doubt be licking her lips and be all like, 'Oh that's okay Mr and Mrs. McQueen, it will be my bloody pleasure! ... And what's that you say? Little Johnny is already in bed and Wayne's staying with his aunty Joan? Oh good I'll just sit here and watch tele then… like a good girl.'
Yeah sure you did Sally, sure you did babe. I bet as soon as that front door slammed shut it was up the stairs two at a time and straight in to poor, little, innocent Johnny's room. I'd be lying on my back dreaming sweet, blameless biblical dreams of Jesus and Mary and all the saints as she crept in, slowly undressed, pulled off my bed

clothes and climbed up onto my innocent face. 'Oh Johnny.' she must have gasped, but not loud enough to wake me up, 'Your cock is so big and hard! 'I can't help myself Johnny, you're so handsome I've just got to put that huge thing in my mouth!' Then I bet she'd suck it until I shot my load right down her beautiful throat. 'Shush, shush Johnny go back to sleep it's all just a lovely dream.'

I'd wake up the next morning and be all like, 'Mummy why is my face so shiny? And are we having kippers for breakfast?'

It'll take years of therapy to bring to the surface all the sex I've had without even knowing it. She's only a few years older than me though and she's never been in our house to my knowledge. I've watched her sunbathing in their garden enough times to know that she is an insatiable, horny little slut though, and I bet she spends all her spare time with her fingers down her knickers thinking about gobbling me off and I don't blame her.

Now I'd thought about it I wouldn't be surprised if I'd been farmed out to the whole town back in the day. Father O'Connor definitely wanted a piece of me. The mucky old sod. His hands were always shaking as he placed the Host on my tongue on a Sunday morning. 'The body of Christ'? The body of fresh faced jail bait Johnny McQueen bent over the altar more like. I bet he got me drunk on communion wine then metaphorically coveted my oxen from behind before shuddering to a satanic climax, wearing a vibrating crucifix up his knackered out Derek. He's proper old too. I bet he was the one who bummed my dad when he was a kid. Then my dad bummed my mum and when she said, 'No John no more bum games! I know all about your past and I feel your pain but it's all too sinful so it is! But Lord forgive me if you have to do it bum the kids!' Yeah that's probably when he turned his attention to me and our Wayne. That's what happens. I've read about that in the paper, all paedos blame being bummed as kids when they get caught rummaging around in their pockets near a playground or trying to drag a child into their Ford Capri. I'd be very surprised if he'd bummed our Wayne though. You'd have to be pretty messed up to go anywhere near our Wayne with any sexual intent. I find it hard to eat if he's even in the house, God love him.

On a day to day basis it may not have been what the chattering classes would classically call, 'making love' but my mum and dad, despite their differences, definitely enjoyed the sacred act copulation. Up until very recently our Wayne and I used to hear them doing it through our bedroom wall pretty much constantly. For two people who couldn't bear the sight of one another during daylight hours, come nightfall they were, if anything, overzealous in that department. They were at it like rabbits. And these weren't the cute, cuddly bunny rabbit type of 'rascally rabbits' either. No sir. My parents made up in the bedroom like, oh let's see...two big, sweaty, hate-filled, foul-mouthed walruses who'd had a bottle of own-brand whiskey and a gram of meth amphetamine blown up their arseholes. Honestly, how they managed to get so fat while taking so many drugs is a medical phenomenon. I'm not going into too much detail here because by now I'm sure that anyone who is so inclined can probably guess what sort of wrongness went on behind our far bedroom wall. Maybe mum eventually did draw the line at bum love but anything and everything else seemed to be on the menu. Nothing surprised me in our house anymore. Sex toys, rubber sheets, adult nappies, golden rain and, due to me slipping on the evidence one fine morning, evidently the insertion of frozen stools enveloped in prophylactics and shoved up the wrongun. And that was just our Wayne's bedtime routine.

He'd always had night terrors and often woke up in a pool of his own blood, sweat and tears and usually a good amount of spunk too. He was a nervous wreck and who could blame him? Nobody knows the exact date or even year of his birth but he's certainly a good three or four years older than me so he's had to endure our parent's for all that extra time on his own. He was pretty much a lost cause before I even came into this world. The poor cunt. Day after day they'd be continually fighting and hurling insults and accusations and counter accusations at one another and in order to save myself from going mental I like to slip on the head phones from my stolen Walkman, press play and enter a reality of my own choosing.

This is a world in which nothing was ever vicious or scary or violent or cruel and entering it had saved my own sanity.

In this reality nothing was ever thrown or torn or broken and I could pretend that we were just a normal family and I was just a normal kid. A kid who was loved and cared for and wanted. When I'm watching my parents going at each other in my head I'd change the words I knew they were screaming to something less toxic. This way their arguments became less traumatic for me. Instead of the angry domestic slanging match I saw before me I could transform it all into any scene from the latest film I'd watched or book I'd read. These over dubbed plays could range from anything I'd

11

memorised by Dickins, Hemmingway or Shakespeare to scenes from any of the Carry On films or Hollywood musicals I'd watched on TV. Even cartoons like Scooby Doo or Bugs Bunny and my all-time favourite Mr Daffy Duck. My dad was a first class prick and the last thing I wanted was to grow up like him so I was desperate for alternative role models even if they were clearly insane animated poultry. Daffy Duck was my hero because he was sarcastic and didn't give one flying fuck. Daffy and Bugs Bunny, The Marx brothers, Jack Nicolson, Woody Allen, Chevy Chase, Mel Brooks, anyone who I felt was cool at the time I tried to emulate. I didn't want to be a hard man because my dad was a hard man and as I said, he was a prick. I wanted to be a funny man. I wasn't all that keen on school and, as my parents could not have cared any less about us, rather than attending that mental asylum more often than not I'd usually bunk off and sit in front of this magical box that was saving my life. It didn't matter to me what I was watching either. It brought me peace and I just needed it to be on all the time. The only time our TV was ever off was if we had visitors. Official visitors. If I ever walked into our house and the television wasn't blaring I'd instinctively know that something was up and I'd immediately turn around and walk back out again. No television meant that in the living room sat either the police, social workers or the priest and none of them ever brought good news.

Alternatively if I was in a more playful mood, rather than snippets from the mainstream media, I'd give them a few choice lines from the plethora of porn videos I'd seen. I'd overdub my parents' vitriol and give them clichéd German accents, amusing myself no end as I'd pretended that they were quoting dialogue from some of the best ones I'd recently wanked off to.

 'You're a fecking cunt John so yas are and I curse the day I ever set eyes on your stupid fat fecking face' might become,

 'You vill take me up the dopple ganger mine hare yah? Witt unt cline unt ubber Flaubert vessel nien?' 'Yah mien hairs! Yah vole oh yah Viv unt spatula snail! Snail Eat Liebert dick!' We didn't learn German at my school so used I had to ad lib obviously. I was fully aware that these words were not actually in fact real German words but that was beside the point. All I wanted to do was block out the horror of the situation in which I'd found myself during the many times my parents went toe to toe. We didn't have a lot of food in the house or wear the latest fashions and designer brands, but at least my dad had his priorities right and we had a TV and VCR and

12

where there's a VCR there is always pornography not far away. I'd found my dad's porno films a couple of years before and some of my friends had VCRs and their dads had porn too. Some kids swap stamps, or tea cards or top trumps but me and my mates swapped porn videos. However bad my days were, I knew that sooner or later I'd get the living room to myself and be able to bash one out and that fact kept me sane. I lived in a world of total fantasy in which television and pornography were my saviours and, when added to my bizarrely overwhelming misplaced confidence, imagination and razor sharp wit, and if you erased my parents from the equation, I sometimes didn't actually think my life was too shabby at all. Relatively speaking anyway. However much other kids and, even more cruelly, adults, made fun of us or looked down on me and our Wayne's circumstances I always knew instinctively that they were the ones to be pitied and not us. I had somehow developed a plethora of tricks to keep me from going bat shit crazy amongst the chaos and mayhem and I think that this is why I remained normal in the loony bin that was our home. Unlike my poor brother who was a real whack job.

Every time that my parents were having a furious row, kicking and punching and throwing stuff around I'd be sat on the sofa watching them go at it with a gleeful look on my face as they acted out my own ad hoc script or were simply accompanied by the sound track booming into my ears and blocking out the actual reality of the situation – the Smiths, The Pogues, The Pistols, Echo and the Bunny men, Jesus and the Mary Chain, Pixies, Velvet Underground, The King himself of course and thousands of other artists could free me from the hell that were my parents. Our Wayne, by contrast, would just be staring blankly into space and who knew what the fuck was going on in his mind as he tried unsuccessfully to shield himself from the horror that was day to day life in our house. He was just an ordinary, run of the mill type of boy and he had no tricks up his sleeve to defend himself from the psychological damage that our state of affairs brought with it. As we grew up my brother had little choice but to absorb and thus be forever scarred by the years of torment and abuse we'd suffered at our parents' hands. Life had turned his brain into a big bowl of mush and it looked like there was fuck all anyone could do about it.

So anyway, me and my old man and Brian the social worker are all in our back garden and I'd just been told that mummy and daddy are separating like I was three fucking years old or something.

'Is there anything you'd like to say Johnny?' Says my dad. 'What the actual fuck is happening here?!' I thought to myself. He'd never spoken to me like this before. It's that bloody book again. Why was he being so polite all of a sudden? It was really giving me the creeps.

'Chapter three… give your child a chance to voice any concerns he or she has, even though this will shock the shit out of them because you've always been a cunt and never ever asked your children's opinion about fuck all. Ever.'

Maybe I should ring my bell again? Yes, maybe I should pretend to be traumatised by my parents' separation and from now on only communicate by ringing this bell like a modern day Harpo Marx? Maybe they'd be nicer to me? You can't slap a retard. Surely that's illegal? Well unless you work with retards on a full time basis of course. That seemed to be the norm in those particular establishments. I had many experiences of this. My own dear mother frequented them on a regular basis. There was fuck all wrong with her and she only went for the free food and happy pills and to have a break from us and our dad. And also to keep the social off her back so she could keep claiming. Mental institutions always seemed to attract people who were built like brick shit houses who seemed to be permanently very angry. Not so much the doctors who always seemed to be seedy little Joseph Mengle characters but definitely the staff. These were the sort of labourers who have to clean the patients and take them to the canteen for their meals and down to the shops and that. I've watched enough BBC2 documentaries to know that there's always an undercurrent of malevolence in those places. Malevolence and sexiness. I bet the sexier patients get a good seeing to as soon as it's lights out. Why else would you want to do that job? There must be some perks.

'Okay Mr Smith we can't pay you much but I see from your resume that you're a fucking angry psychopath and a sexual pervert so feel free to give any of our clients a proper kicking if they get out of hand and sexually abuse anyone that takes your fancy. And of course please don't forget to help yourself to anything from the medicine cabinet."

I remember watching one particular documentary in which there was this really fit looking teenage girl who was totally paralysed from the neck down. She was totally helpless and could only communicate by blinking one eye and I distinctly remember bashing one out about her that night. All the boys at school did. Nothing

14

was specifically said but as we discussed the programme the next day we all knew what we'd shamefully done. I still have the odd tug about her to this day to be honest.

So yeah, I contemplated pretending that the imminent divorce of my parents had dragged me into the dark, eternal abyss of depression and mental illness. I'd get time off school at least or maybe get to go to a special school for spazzy kids. That would be okay because I'd have the advantage of not actually being a real header. Maybe there would even be nympho girls there, I surmised. Beautiful, sex crazed girls locked away for their own safety due to their unbridled passion and lust for cock. I looked at my dad and Brian and tried my best to look all learning disabilities. I opened my mouth, dribbled and rang the bell again.

Then my dad scowled at me and muttered, 'Aww fuck it.' and he was just about to give me a back-hander when he suddenly remembered Brian was standing next to him and thought better of it. I knew he couldn't keep up that pathetic charade for very long and order was restored. Brian gave me a kind of pitying sort of look and said, 'If there's anything I can do for you or your brother Johnny just let me know okay? I'll always be here for you okay?'

'Oh I bet you will Brian you saucy old hippy I bet you will. I said and I winked at him but he just looked bemused like he always did. My dad stared at me contemptuously and asked if Brian fancied a pint down the pub. Brian said that he didn't drink alcohol which shocked the shit out of both of us. My dad then threw his hands up in the air, muttered something unintelligible and then stormed off in the direction of The Dolphin. Brian just stood staring at the ground until I said, 'I think Glastonbury festival is that way dude' and pointed in the direction of our garden gate. After a few seconds he seemed to have come round and eventually bad me farewell and fucked off. I went upstairs and had a furiously energetic wank about sex-crazed girls with disabilities into one of Wayne's socks before throwing it under his bed with all the others.

Chapter two

I wondered what the future held for me and our Wayne now. I couldn't help but feel that this might be for the best as it couldn't have gotten much worse. It's not like we were suddenly going to be thrown on the scrap-heap like Kevin Davis. Kevin was in my class at school. He was one of those effortlessly self-assured little middle class twats with everything he could ever have wished for until the day his dad fucked off with his mum's sister and left them with fuck all. Then his privileged life instantly collapsed. When his mum became a single parent his life suddenly became all about free school meals and second hand clothes. Goodbye to cinema trips and after school activities and hello to getting his head stuffed down the toilet and getting beaten and bullied and robbed. Poor Kevin could no longer pay off the school hard men and had to fend for himself like the rest of us. When you're poor it seems to ooze from your pores for everyone to see and invites in all kinds of abject misery. Within the blink of an eye Kevin changed from a cocky little extrovert to a timid little introvert who seemed to perpetually smell of toilet cleaner.

'Welcome to the club Kev, take a fucking pew.'

I had never been a bully but even I had to quash an urge to kick him in the nuts. Suddenly he wanted to be my friend, safety in numbers I guessed, but I told him to fuck off and fend for himself, the cheeky cunt. Poverty to Kev was all shiny and new, but I'd always been poor. I can't remember what my dad did in relation to work because it's been so long since he had a job but if he was ever on Mastermind when it got to the bit where they say, "occupation?" He would have to say, 'professional scrounger'. I'm not being hard on him, that's what he was and he was good at it. He got disability benefit, plus a few more handouts here and there because he had kids. I can only assume that they had children just for the extra benefits. He put a lot of effort into what he thought he was entitled to and was richly rewarded by the state.

If he'd have put his talents to more of a legitimate use I have no doubt that he could have been very successful. He was a brilliant method actor for example. One day, due to pressure from the social, out of the blue, he got himself a job on a building site. Me and our Wayne were delighted and went to school for two solid days with our heads held high. On day three he'd fallen from a scaffold and hurt his leg, his neck and his spine. X-rays revealed no broken bones but for years that fucker walked with a limp and wore a neck brace just in case the benefit squad were still monitoring him. Everybody knew he was taking the piss but he ended up with an out of court settlement from the building company, a cash sum from the scaffold company, the aforementioned disability allowance, a disability badge for his non-existent car which he used to hire out to his mates in the betting shops and pubs and a whole host of other benifits too numerous to mention. This was before everybody else was doing it. He was a pioneer of sorts, he knew what he wanted and went after it; a go-getter and if there was anything to be got, as long as he could get it without getting out of his chair for too long, he'd be sure to find a way to get it. A lot of people round our way regarded him as a hero. He was an inspiration to all the other shiftless twats who could think of a lot better things to do during the week than go to work. '…here mate let me buy you a pint, you're working'. Often I'd come home to find him holding a seminar on the intricacies of government handouts and how to claim them. If they ever held the social security Olympics my dad would most certainly have come first in the one hundred meter benefit fraud.

A few days later my mum came into the lounge while I was watching the tele. It was a Wednesday and I didn't like Wednesdays at school so I didn't go in. It was around 11 am and Mum, or Julie as I called her, was already half cut and so was her best mate 'Aunty' Joan. Aunty Joan wasn't my real aunty just an 'honorary' one, as she liked to call herself, although she'd never actually done fuck all for me except offer me discounted drugs on occasion. She always had an assortment of pills and medicines which she got from a mate of hers who worked in a pharmacy. Aunty Joan herself was addicted to painkillers and steroids, a heady combination indeed. Her face was very masculine which gave her the appearance of a very ropey drag act but her body was in my opinion anyway, superb.If you were into that sort of thing, which, along with many other sorts of things, I was. She looked like Conan the barbarian but with a perpetually pronounced camel toe between her powerful legs. She loved to parade about the place wearing all this tight Lycra showing off her rippling muscles and to all intents and purposes, her very masculine physique. Her arms and legs were huge and she had a beautiful six pack of abdominals bulging across her belly and I'd spend many a happy time fantasising about shooting my load all over them. Her arse cheeks looked like two boiled eggs in a hanky and it drove me crazy thinking about all the ways I could give her one. She knew it too and would always be teasing me and trying to make me blush.

My mum staggered up to me and put her big ugly face into mine and said, 'Johnny babe has your da given you the talk yet?' She laughed into my face and I could smell her putrid alcoholic breath. Oh God I hope it wasn't 'the' talk! I thought to myself. 'And what fucking talk would that be then Julie?' I asked, trying to remain nonchalant, even though I was bricking it. We seldom exchanged pleasantries and I was always a bit disappointed that she never asked me why I wasn't at school. 'Please don't let it be the birds and the fucking bees one because I think that ship has long since sailed by now mother!' I chortled trying to remain calm. 'I certainly don't need any advice on how to shag birds that's for sure!' I laughed a tad unconvincingly. 'Oh my God have you lost your virginity at last then son!? I thought our Wayne was walking a bit funny earlier!' She replied, after which they both cackled and screeched as I went bright red. 'Fuck off Mum I've done it loads of times with loads of different birds!' My mum delved into the front of her leggings, rummaged around for a bit then pulled out a small, folded up piece of paper and threw it onto the table. 'Feckin' name me one bird that you've shagged Son, just one and I'll give you this gram of feckin' speed right now for feckin' free so I will!' Then they both laughed again as I squirmed. Fuck me I was only fifteen but round our way that was late and it wouldn't be long before the local neighbourhood would be questioning my sexuality. 'I've shagged loads of girls from my school if you must know!' I blurted just wanting to curl up and die.

'Aww don't be cruel to him Julie look at his bright red face' said Aunty Joan, as she slowly made her way towards me. This wasn't going to end well. She came right up to where I was laying on the couch and then in one quick motion straddled me. She pinned down my arms and clamped her enormous thighs around my waist. I closed my eyes tight shut in order to postpone the inevitable but I could still feel her gyrating and writhing up and down me like she was riding a fucking bucking bronco. 'Tell me all about these school girls you've had your wicked way with then Johnny you dirty little bastard' she breathed into my ear and I could smell the familiar mix of cheap alcohol and cigarettes, fake tan and stale sweat. 'Get off me Aunty Joan you fucking paedo!' I yelled not meaning to sound quite so high pitched. 'A paedophile am I now Johnny? You're the one up to your little nuts in all these innocent little

18

school girls now aren't you son?' She replied in mock disgust. 'Can't you handle a real woman like your Aunty Joan Johnny? I could show you a trick or two' she said as she bit down on my ear. 'Ow! Fuck off Aunty Joan you're crushing me and I can't fucking breath!' I said this as I tried to wriggle out of her grip but she had me pinned down tight on the sofa. I opened my eyes and looked up to see Aunty Joan's gruesome face staring into mine. The gaudy makeup, the wrinkles, the almost full moustache and the wild look in her blood shot eyes almost made me scream with fright. 'Please get off me Aunty Joan I've got to go to school! I'll get in trouble! The authorities will come round and I'll be put into care! I'm underage! You'll go to prison and end up on the nonce wing and be everyone's bitch and have to eat ass just to survive!' I screamed in desperation. 'Do I look like I'd be anyone's fucking bitch to you Johnny?' Replied Aunty Joan. Then, still riding me she flexed her arms and then kissed them both theatrically. 'Everyone would be my bitch and they'd all be eating my arse!' she laughed as she climbed up onto my face and ground her fanny and arse all over it. This was my actual first taste of pussy and it wasn't at all as I'd imagined. Far from being some subtle 'musky' scent like I'd read about in the porn mags, this one smelled like a rank cocktail of herring, deep heat, piss and body odour. Fuck me, if that's what pussy smells like then I'm out even before I'd really begun. I decided there and then that if they all smelled like that then I'd have to become a homosexual. I couldn't help but retch which made Aunty Joan very upset. 'Fuck me Julie he's a little bum bandit look at him! I've given him his first taste of minge and the ungrateful little poof is dry heaving! You'll need to take this one to the fucking doctor because he's a fucking ferret!' There were many things wrong with what she'd said, but now wasn't the time for a discussion about sexual politics. 'Just fucking get off me Aunty Joan. I'm not a ferret but I am going to fucking faint if you don't release me!' Her thighs now clamped both sides of my head and I was talking directly to her camel toe. I couldn't breathe in because I knew that if I did I would puke right on her Lycra clad rotten old clopper. Grudgingly she slid back down to my crotch area and started getting herself at it again grinding herself into me. This was much better because the smell abated somewhat and If I didn't look at her grisly face the rest of the show was pretty good if I were being honest. She glanced around at my mum who was too busy racking up lines to give a shit about her son being raped by her best friend. Aunty Joan looked at me wild eyed and crazy then forced her tongue deep into my mouth.

19

My initial thought was that I hadn't realised how few teeth Aunty Joan actually had left in her mouth. My own tongue, looking for a place to hide as hers darted about in a drugged-fuelled frenzy, kept catching on her gnarly old stumps and it was a job not to cut it all into slivers. My cock was getting hard though so I grabbed her tits and squeezed them with all my might then started pulling frantically on her nipples. 'That's a good boy Johnny I knew you were a dirty little bastard' She whispered urgently into my ear while biting my neck and drunkenly slobbering all over me. 'I can feel your hard little cock against my tight little wet kitty cat Johnny. I bet you want to stick it right up me don't you, you filthy little rotter!' She breathed, while rubbing herself coarsely up and down the length of my increasingly stiff knob. For some reason the word 'rotter' made me laugh which nearly ruined the whole thing but I managed to stifle it just long enough to climax into my pants. I groaned as I came. 'Is that it you selfish little shit bag!?' Aunty Joan looked down at the increasing wet patch forming on my jeans. 'Fuck me gently you self-centred little bastard now I'm half cocked. She grabbed my hand and stuffed it down the front of her shorts. 'Finish me off you bloody little prick!' She hissed. It was all wet and hairy down there and I did my best to do what I was told. I'd obviously never done this before so I relied on all my previous pornography experience which was extensive to say the least. I rammed three fingers up her and she gasped while at the same time looking around to see what my mum was doing. Those lines must have been Valium because she was half comatose now and slumped head down on the table. 'That's it Johnny frig the fucking fuck out of my tight little cunt hole!' Any sexual desire I'd had for my aunty Joan had left at the very moment that my balls emptied and I now found her sex talk extremely cringe worthy.

Her 'tight little cunt hole' didn't feel that little or tight to me but now wasn't the time to tell her my thoughts on it so instead I shoved my whole hand up her like I'd seen James Herriot do to a cow once in All Creatures Great and Small. 'Oooh good boy that's it!' Luckily her head was resting over my shoulder now so I couldn't see her face or smell her breath which made the whole thing a lot easier. I screwed up my eyes and tried to imagine I was finger banging Sally from next door. Meanwhile Aunty Joan was starting to pant and her breathing was getting more erratic so I guessed that mercifully she was about to climax 'nearly there Johnny that's it frig it, fucking frig it, frig it…' She was now guiding my hand with hers and using it as one

20

might use a dildo. I suddenly felt that I was being used but I was also glad because my hand was starting to ache and I was getting tired of the whole thing. I'd just come myself and I really couldn't have cared less and the quicker it was over the better. Then suddenly she let out a series of gasps and it was all over. She pulled out my hand and brought it up to my face. 'Lick your fingers' she said. I looked at her big bulk and realised that I had no choice but to do as I was told. I took a deep breath and put my fingers in my mouth. Then I puked all over her tits and she punched me in the head and must have knocked me clean out.

Chapter three

When I came to, I was lying back on the sofa with a coat over me. Aunty Joan must have shoved me back on the couch and covered me up so I wouldn't be found unconscious and covered in spunk. She had fuck all to worry about though as I wasn't going to go to the police and say I'd been sexually molested by my fake aunty. That would have been the dumbest thing I'd ever done. Who else but a drugged-addled old hag would want me?! Her sordid little secret was safe plus she wasn't really anything to boast about either so I decided that I wouldn't tell anyone what had happened. If I was going to be traumatised by that little incident in the future then fuck it, I'd just have to wait until then because now I felt fucking fantastic so it would be a price worth paying.

My face felt sore so I staggered to my feet and went up to the fireplace and looked at myself in the big mirror. I had a nice big shiner, but nothing as bad as I'd had many times before. Result. I was over the fucking moon. I hadn't exactly lost my virginity but it was good solid start on the road to sexual maturity. I stared back at myself in the mirror and grinned. Fingered a bird and basically got wanked off that'll do me. Happy days. Then I went to the kitchen to wash off the smell from my fingers before I yakked up again. I also gave my cock a quick swill too just in case I got lucky again that day. Suffice to say that I need not have bothered. I went upstairs and lay on my bed. Jesus, surely all bird's fannies didn't stink to high heaven like Aunty Joan's I pondered. I'd seen plenty of films in which the man, or indeed woman, ate pussy for ages and I'd always fancied having a go myself; but if they all tasted like my aunty Joan's smelled then I'd have to have a rethink. I hoped that hers was rank because she was so old and full of drugs and this had tainted it over the years. I hoped that Sally's didn't smell anything like that fucker because as much as I loved her I wasn't going to lick her out unless she had a darned good scrub down there first. Beggars can't be choosers though and I still thought that in the grand scheme of things I'd had a result. I looked down at my fingers that had now been right up inside a real woman's minge. They were red raw from all the scrubbing and there was still a faint whiff of decay coming from them however much I wiped them into our Wayne's pillow. Finally I went back downstairs, found some Vim under the sink and scrubbed my hands once more until I was sure that putrid smell off Aunty Joan's dirty old box had gone. Then I had a nice long wank about it all.

The very next day, just as I got home from school, my dad, without taking his eyes off the tele said, 'Hey Wayne, is there a fucking library in this town son?'
I suddenly thought to myself, why is this cunt still here? I distinctly remember him telling me some time ago that he and Julie were separating so why doesn't he fuck off? I was really looking forward to him not being here as he was a fucking useless piece of shit and I hated him. Bang goes my chances of getting put into care with a load of sex crazed nymphos if this lazy prick won't even get his fat arse of the sofa let alone get the fuck out of our house, the selfish arse hole. I took a deep breath.

'I thought you and Mum were getting a divorce Dad? I asked him outright.
'What are you fucking talking about Son?' he replied seemingly oblivious to a conversation we'd had that was possibly life changing for everyone.
'The other day you came up to me in the garden with Brian the hippy and said to me something along the lines of me and your mummy are fucking separating and it wasn't my fault etc. etc. ring any bells Dad?' I asked.
He was silent for a bit then replied, 'Oh yeah that was going to be a social security scam I was going to move out and move into your uncle Terry's spare room until your mum got it all sorted out but then me and your mum had a row and she told me that she wasn't going to go through with it all which we both found very ironic don't you think?' He laughed a long rasping cigarette-stained, lung cancer laugh until he started coughing and then the effort of the coughing brought up a good portion of one of his lungs by the look of it because he spat it into the fireplace and it landed on a piece of unburnt coal and slowly slid off into the hearth giving me a good long mesmerising look at it. I wasn't even disgusted because I'd seen both my parents do this a million times before.

'Why the fuck did you get me involved then?' I was trying to obtain some sympathy for all the heart break this might have caused me if I'd actually given a fuck. 'I've been worried sick since you told me! I've been off my food! I don't want you and Mum to split up. I love you both very much and anyway who would get custody of
23

me and our Wayne!?' I said in mock despair. He shot me a weary look and was obviously not fooled by my bullshit.

'I told you so that because that Feckin' Brian cunt was there wasn't he? I needed to convince him that it was all real and not just another scam because he's a disbelieving bastard. I needed to make him think it was the real deal so he'd go back and tell his superiors that it was all legitimate so we'd get the extra benefits. Are you really as dumb as you fucking look son?' He yelled.

We'd had many social workers over the years but they'd all eventually given us up as a lost cause or quit in despair or had nervous breakdowns.
'I didn't even get time to tell our Wayne because me and your mum had a row after I came back from the pub after telling you so we just forgot about it. I meant to tell you but must have forgotten but you know now, so no harm done. And to answer your second question about what would have happened to you and our Wayne if me and your ma parted company then I can only presume that you would both have gone into care and been raped to death. Except Wayne obviously. He would have probably been doing most of the raping knowing that prize cunt.
 But it's all academic now son because, due to a falling out, me and your mum are back together and never happier.' He chuckled. And that was the end of that.
 'Now then Son if you would be so kind as to give me directions to the library you can get the fuck on with whatever you were doing which I hope was fucking leaving this room. No offence but Daddy has a splitting fucking headache and would like to be left the fuck alone. Do you or do you not know the way to the fucking library?'

'Yes I do Dad' I replied. I didn't even bother to ask him how come he didn't know whether or not there was a library in the town he had spent most of his life in. I was just happy for the intellectual stimulation of the lively conversation that I knew was about to take place.
'Where the fuck is it then?'
'Well it's in town.' I reply
'Fuck me Son!' He cried, 'Where a bouts in town!?'

I declined to comment on his sexual proposal - did he actually on some level want me to make sweet, passionate love to him right here in the living room while watching Countdown? On this occasion it would have to be a no so I simply replied, 'Opposite Safeway's.'

'Where the fuck is Safeway's?' He shouted at me all exasperated. Now you might have thought at this point I would have said. 'Opposite the fucking library you dumb ass paddy cunt', but experience had taught me that this would have resulted in visit from 'Dr Tickle' or to give it its formal name, 'Doctor John's tickling stick', which although it sounds like my dad's nick name for his gnarly old cock, was actually the hilariously ironic name my dad gave to his belt. Dr Tickle was not someone who I looked forward to giving me my medicine in any shape or form. All through our childhood if we misbehaved my dad would undo his belt and we'd have to go through the same old charade. We'd have to wait on the stairs terrified until he called us into the living room which was now the doctor's surgery slash confessional. 'Next!' he'd shout. Me and our Wayne would look at each other in horror having to quickly decide which one of us would have to go first. We were both shitting ourselves equally, but each time our Wayne would go first so he'd get the brunt of my dad's fury so that my 'medicine' would hopefully be marginally less. I loved him for that. We would have to knock on the door and wait until we were let in. My dad would be sat at the kitchen table with his belt in his hands. 'Ahh Mr. McQueen what can I do for you today?' He would always ask. Then we would have to say that we were ill due to being cheeky or dirty or clumsy or whatever the fuck it was that we'd supposedly done to deserve Doctor fucking John's tickle stick. It wasn't even a stick anymore. It used to be, but he broke that across our Wayne's back one time so had to replace it with his leather belt. Our medicine aka the cure aka penance was always a belt across the legs or back or on our hands or wherever the mood fucking took him depending how angry or pissed he was. During all this my mum would always sit in her chair watching TV and ignoring the whole thing. Our cries and screams and pleadings would have no effect on her. Rather us than her I guessed. Bum the kids and hit the kids but leave me alone! Even the neighbours were too scared of my dad to do anything to help us and it just became the norm.

'It's about a two minute walk from the bus station' I replied

'And where the fuck is the fucking bus station Wayne you little cunt!?' I couldn'y even be arsed to explain to him that my name was actually Johhny. His face was contorted and getting very red and I hoped that the prick would suddenly clutch his chest and do us all a fucking favour and have a heart attack and die.

'Fuck me, are you taking the fucking piss you old cunt?' I said, but only inside my own head. I could hear the fury starting to bubble up through his veins so I took a deep breath and said, 'The Library is on the same road as the Bell, about a hundred yards up towards The Standard if you're starting from The Dolphin.'

'Oh yeah Okay, cheers Son. Now shut the door on the way out.'

And that was the end of the conversation.

The morning after our stimulating discourse regarding the whereabouts of the town library, I was sat in front of the tele eating a packet of Space Invaders before packing myself off reluctantly to school, when who should I see staggering down the stairs at 8am on a weekday, but my dad. Instinctively I looked at my watch, shit I've overslept and it's now 4.30 in the afternoon. I looked again; nope it was 8 in the morning. I gave him the once over, He wasn't wearing his suit so he couldn't be going to court, but he'd combed his hair and was wearing his going out jeans and a clean shirt not jogging pants and a stained t-shirt so he was definitely leaving the house. He wasn't going to the job centre for his six monthly review either though because he was wearing aftershave.

Today's benefit scrounger Seminar: The Significance of Aftershave.

 'If you go for your interview wearing aftershave, those cunts from the dole will think you've still got some self-respect and furthermore, money to burn; because aftershave signifies that after the interview you will be going down the pub and the bookies and, as they've got to work all day, they will try to cut your allowance purely out of jealousy and spite. You've always got to be one step ahead lads and try to see yourself through their eyes.'

This was intriguing. Maybe he'd shit the bed? It wouldn't be the first time. Oh well, fuck it. I had better things to do than sit about pondering what that fat fuck was up to. I had things to do and people to see. Well hopefully one person in particular. Ten days before, to the minute, I'd been in the kitchen scratching about looking for something to eat when I spied Sally from next door walking down her garden path on her way to college. My stomach did a kind of back flip every time I saw her. And so did my cock. She was beautiful. She was skinny as a rake with long black hair, green eyes and pale skin. My parents were Irish. 'You two cunts are Celts, your blood is green and white and don't you ever forget it!' This was a familiar Saturday night theme in our house. 'Oh Danny boy the pipes the pipes are calling, from glen to glen and down the mountain side …' '…I'll tell me ma when I get home the boys won't leave the girls alone, pulled me hair and stole me comb but that's alright till I get home…and of course the fields of Abhenry.

I'll tell me ma, one coming from my dad's mouth always made me and our Wayne piss ourselves due to the gayness of it all. I'd never been to Ireland or anywhere else for that matter - my dad came over when he was 17 years old and there's no cunt more patriotic than an ex pat - but sometimes we'd have our extended family over for the weekend and most of them, and all the other Irish fuckers I knew, were usually pale, ill-looking with either jet black hair or gingers with strong jaws and freckles who all looked like their cock's stank

Anyway, the point is, did I fancy Sally because she was Irish looking? Was I genetically pre- disposed to find her attractive due to my green and white blood or was it because of her long skinny legs, green eyes, pert little ass cheeks and unfeasibly large tits? I ponder this now but at the time I just wanted to give her one. Wanted to fuck her brains out. I wanted to fuck her so much it was all I could ever think about. It was fucking torture. So anyway, I'm stood there gawping, trying desperately to take in her every detail in the ten second slot that I knew from experience that I'd have before she disappeared down the street. Mondays and Wednesdays she was usually gone until late afternoon, around 5pm and nearer six on a Thursday. Tuesday she has off and Fridays sometimes she doesn't get home until one or two in the morning. The dirty, no good stop-out. Honestly, sometimes it's so late I feel like ringing the police. Once it was gone three and when she did eventually turn up I had to stop myself from screaming out of my bedroom window, 'for fuck's sake Sally do you know what the fucking time is?! I've been worried sick!' But I let it go because I don't want her to think that I was weird. So there she was, the girl of

27

my dreams striding down her back garden path in a short black skirt, green Harrington jacket, bare legs and ten holed, black Doctor Martens. I instinctively un- zipped my fly. Fuck me I wonder how much she'd charge me just to put my hand up her skirt for five seconds. Actually I'd given this an awful lot of thought and I was trying my best to save up enough money to do all the things to her that I'd spent so long dreaming of. I'd worked out that all my sexual fantasies regarding Sally Holmes should come true for about seventy five to eighty pounds cash. My plan was to pluck up enough courage to talk to her without going bright red and getting a hard-on. Then, as time went by, we'd become good enough friends for me to make her an offer she couldn't refuse. For the last year or so I had become a connoisseur of that family's laundry hanging on the line in their back garden. Well obviously it was Sally's underwear that I was primarily interested in but of course this was mixed up with the rest of her family's. From me and our Wayne's bedroom window I had a clear and uninterrupted view of its day to day contents and mild curiosity quickly turned to a casual obsession. One can tell a lot about a family from the clues hanging from four meters of plastic encased string and by the state of it one didn't have to be Colombo to know that they were probably even less well off than us. My plan was to take advantage of their economic situation and I couldn't really imagine it failing. Basically I was going to offer Sally cold hard cash for sexual favours. After we'd been friends for a couple of weeks I'd be round hers listening to records and drinking coffee or whatever and after we'd just had a play fight and I was lying next to her on her bed just wearing a t shirt and underpants and I'd casually start playing with her hair then I'd look her straight in the eye and say, 'Hey Sally, as we're such close friends now and you're so poor I was just wondering if you'd let me sniff your knickers and then finger bang you for five quid?' 'You would!? Cool! 'Then she'd shyly giggle as I lifted up her skirt and buried my head between her legs while inhaling deeply before expertly sliding my hand up her leg, between her soft, cool, milky white thighs, into her knickers (the little black lace ones probably, (I think they're her favourites because they're on the line two or three times a week) and then eventually I'd slip my fingers inside her tight, wet minge. Then as the situation gets steamier and steamier I'll whisper in her ear something like, 'Oh Sally I'll give you another twenty if you'll suck me off while I manipulate your breasts and pull on your nipples until you are stimulsted.' I'll say breasts rather than top bollocks or norks because I don't want to

28

be too vulgar because I know that birds don't like that rough talk. And then she'll probably say something like, 'Oh Johnny I've watched you from my bedroom window so many times and you always get me so wet and I've wanted this for so long, just give me thirty all in!' Then after we've had a bit of a rest I'll tell her about my abused childhood, chuck her a few more give her one up the Derek, like-father-like-son. But I'm hoping that by that time I'd have given her such a good seeing to she'll waive the fee and we can spend the rest of the money on chips, white lightening and an engagement ring.

Suddenly, mid-gawp, she tripped over Ziggy, their cat. (I'd learned its name off my mum in a rather cynical bid to get to know her, and planned to use it as soon as the right situation arose, 'Oh Sally wow, your cat Ziggy is acers! Named after the alter ego of David Bowie that's such a cool and radical name…please will you sit on my face for seven pounds?'

So she's tripped, stumbled and, as she's tried to regain her balance by grabbing hold of the washing line, it's snapped and she's fallen backwards, legs akimbo onto the grass still holding on to the washing line, bringing it all down on top of her. The next moment was probably the happiest moment of my life thus far. As she fell her legs opened I caught a glimpse up her skirt and had my first real life, albeit fleeting, glance into the heady realms of the Holy Grail. Up until now her black lace panties were my favourites, and sure I'd seen these white ones on her line with the sun shining through the damp gusset and I'd idly thought about slipping them off her ripe little bum cheeks before putting her to the sword, but now they'd taken on a whole new erotic meaning. As she went down, due to the colour of her underwear and the angle of the sun I could see both the form and shape of her bush that, enveloped by those oh so tight little dung hampers, resembled a beautiful, puffed out dove's chest. Albeit one with loads of jet black pubic hairs sprouting out of it. Furthermore I got a nice shot of one bare, muddy, succulent bum cheek. As she lay there flailing about on her back like an upturned beetle on that bright sunny morning clutching a washing line full of her own damp underwear, I frantically bashed one out into the kitchen sink and came into a mug that said, 'World's Best Dad' which I found to be beautifully poetic in an ironic way. I think he must have nicked that for himself because neither of us boys bought it for him. The prick.

29

Anyway since that most auspicious of days I've been looking out of our kitchen window at precisely 8.05 am every day of the week, just in case of a repeat performance. This morning I scurried to the kitchen still full of anticipation for another glimpse of Sally's panty encased pussy but although I saw her, which was once good enough, it now seemed a little disappointing; she looked pretty firm footed as she sauntered down her garden path with a bowl of fresh washing. I gave my knob a squeeze more out of habit than sexual desire, but my heart wasn't really in it and I even thought about going back to the living room to ask my dad what the fuck he was doing up at this hour because it was starting to bug me. Just as I turned away I heard a high pitched scream coming from the direction of what I could only assume to be Sally's demure little gob. I spun round towards the garden and saw Sally looking up in the direction of our house, wide eyed and mouth contorted with, which I now know to have been, utter disgust.

'You dirty, fucking, RETARDED CUNT!'
Retarded cunt? Ahh she must be referring to our Wayne and thankfully not me. Phew. That was a relief. Guilty conscience I guess.
Brilliant. I rushed to our back door, threw it open and ran outside.
'You filthy, little, fucking, wanker!'
Yep, that'll definitely be directed at our Wayne.
Sally was now hysterical, screaming and shouting obscenities at the top of her voice in the direction of me and my darling brother's bedroom window.
I looked up expecting to see a cowering Wayne trying to hide his big bulk inexpertly behind the bedroom curtains, perhaps peeking his head out now and then full of guilt and shame like a good Catholic boy or even better, just a pair of closed curtains. Nah, not in the McQueen residence, not a chance. That would be too normal. What I actually saw was our Wayne standing up there behind the glass, obviously bollock naked and evidently still having the same wank he was having before he was caught by Sally having it. I looked at our Wayne, then I looked at Sally then back at our Wayne, then back at Sally.
Sally suddenly noticed me. 'Fucking hell you little prick! Tell your fucking brother to stop fucking looking at me and wanking his fucking cock for fuck's sake!'

What else would he be wanking, I thought to myself? But that was me just being pedantic so I didn't mention it. I was dazed and confused and also mesmerised by this whole turn of events.

I stared at her. God she was so beautiful. Even with her now bright red face, bulging eyes and little flecks of spittle in the corner of her mouth, she was still drop dead lush. Hang on. Oh God! She was actually talking to me! I blushed. I could feel my whole body turn deep crimson. I had to act fast. What would the Fonz do in this situation? 'Heyyyy!' I gave her a cheeky wink and a double thumbs up. Nailed it. I pressed on. 'Sally isn't it? We've never actually been formally introduced, my name is Johnny.' For some reason I then bowed deeply. I then offered her my hand even though she was far too far away to have been able to have shaken it so I put it in my pocket where I hoped it would be safe from any more hiccups. 'A little background. I live next door to you… in there.' I pointed towards our house. Bearing in mind that I'd never actually spoken to her before I thought that I'd come across as pretty damned cool especially as I was sure I was on the cusp of passing out.

Sally looked me dead in the eye and said, 'What?'

She looked puzzled and her head turned to one side like a quizzical puppy. I could see that she was trembling, hopefully with sexual excitement.

'I live here' I continued waving my hand majestically in the general direction of our hovel. 'well up there most of the time with our Wayne' I pointed up to our bedroom window which focused both of our attentions back to our Wayne who was still frantically going for it hammer and tongs. His face was also bright red and contorted, and there was also spittle coming from his mouth, but his eyes were screwed tightly shut and he did not look in any way what one might describe as beautiful.

We both stared at Wayne transfixed.

Once when I was at primary school our class went to visit a zoo and even though I was a kid I could tell that for most of the animals they had found themselves caged inside a living hell. The elephant for sure was definitely suffering from depression and the monkeys had clearly all gone insane. When we got to the monkey enclosure Tracy Brenan started to jump up and down grunting and beating her chest like King Kong. Standard practise for a ten year old I guess, but the monkeys had probably seen this a few times in the past and one sauntered over to the fence where we all stood, shat into its hand and threw it at her. Fortunately for Tracy, it missed her and hit our rather

31

nice, but ineffectual teacher, Mrs Clipson, square in the mouth. This was amusing enough but it got better because this act seemed to encourage all his monkey pals. The next thing we knew they were all at the fence screeching and running up and down hysterically like planet of the fucking apes, but with monkeys and a much tighter budget. It was all quite threatening to most of the kids I guess, judging by the screams and tears and general panic from the human side of the fence but for me it reminded me of a normal Saturday night at ours, and the only difference I could see was that these cheeky little monkeys had better manners than my family and their shit smelled better.

As I stepped back out of harm's way in order to enjoy this bit of theatrics at a safe distance out of the corner of my eye I saw one of the cheeky little scamps climb up on to the fence and start furiously beating his little monkey lipstick to within an inch of its life. Within a few moments all eyes turned to this little fella and, as one, we all seemed to have become hypnotised by the sight of this particular monkey wanking off with such concentrated anger. It was captivating, and we all stood there enthralled by this welcome interlude to an otherwise unexceptional day out. All of us except Tracy Brenan that is. She was too busy goading the shit throwing one.

'Oi you missed me you hairy little cunt! Is that all you've got? Wanka!' -This rather course language was de rigueur at our school at the time and it's only as I reflect that I can see how frightfully crass this must have sounded to the uninitiated- As she said the word, 'wanka' she made the universally recognised sign of being a wanker by shaking her fist up and down several times in quick succession in the monkey's direction. The rest of us were still transfixed by the actual wanking monkey and stood there open mouthed, which in hindsight wasn't a good idea in that kind of situation. On cue, the wanking monkey shot his not inconsiderable load into its little hairy palm and flicked it expertly straight through the bars towards our dear Tracy. I can still see those two beautiful arcs of monkey spunk flying through the air like two squirts from a child's water pistol. Spurt one hit the right side of her face and as she instinctively turned her face to see where the first load came from shot two hit her right smack in her open mouth and then continued its journey by slipping down her throat. Three girls puked simultaneously and Tracy burst into outraged tears while simultaneously sticking her fingers down her gullet in order to retrieve it. But alas it was long gone and she now was the proud owner of a belly full of primate wrigglers. The wanking
32

monkey went over to the shit throwing one and I swear I saw them high five. The rest of us pissed ourselves laughing and as I glanced at up at Mrs Clipson I noticed that she too was in hysterics and furthermore I could tell that she knew that she'd had a let off that day because monkey cum swallowing trumps monkey shit in the face any day of the week. I remember trying to convince Tracy on the way home on the bus that there was a very high likelihood that she was now pregnant. She looked fucking petrified and the last time I heard about her was that she was now a semi-professional lesbian. I don't know if that incident had any bearing on her eventual sexual orientation, but looking back she did cut her own hair and clothes shop at Millet's but we all did back then so fuck knows.

Wayne had the same expression on his face as the wanking monkey from the zoo which could only mean one thing…WE were nearing the end of this delightful show and very soon it would be Torra! Torra! Tally Ho and bombs away.

'Fucking what? You weedy little cunt!?' said Sally in a tone that could not in any way be be described as jovial.

'Fucking language on it though.' I thought to myself. We Irish do indeed enjoy a good old swear up. Sure there has been some fantastic writers and poets and artists from that Emerald Isle but what we are really known for is foul language, racism and good old fashioned homophobia.

'I was just saying my name is …' I stammered as my Fonzy impression faded quickly out of sight and I became more like an even camper version of Frank Spenser.

'I couldn't give a flying fuck what your name is you scrawny little spastic! Just go up there and stop that mong from fucking wanking off while looking at me!'

Should I tell her the wanking monkey incident? Maybe it would calm her down? Ease the tension, a bit of light relief, the calm before the storm?

I decided against it.

Instead I just stared at her. She was wearing a t- shirt and tight blue jeans. I tried not to stare at her tits. Oh God her nipples were so hard. I tried to speak but I couldn't concentrate on anything else apart from her hard nipples underneath her tight, white t-shirt. On the t-shirt was a picture of David Bowie and his face had become distorted due to the poky- outiness of her amazingly pert tits and rock hard nipples. Somewhere in my head I heard a voice say, 'Pull away Johnny. Take your eyes off her tits. Look away Johnny' but then I heard another voice saying, 'Don't move Jonny do not move

33

a muscle just keep very still.' This time I was definitely going to faint. Sally brought me round with the immortal words,

'What the fuck do you think you're looking at, PERVERT CUNT!?'

'Excuse me?' I replied trying to appear indignant.

I was now firmly back in the room. Back to my senses. Back in my garden looking at Sally. My throat was dry and I couldn't speak properly and when I did I couldn't stop. '.. I was just admiring your t -shirt I really like Bowie. You have a cat called Ziggy, it shits in our garden…My dad says if he ever catches it he's going to skin the little cunt and throw it back over your fence, or cut off its feckin' head and put it on your mum's fecking pillow. I don't mind it though cats have to shit somewhere don't they? At least they bury it not like dogs they just shit and walk off. Have you seen the Godfather? Once I was at a zoo and a monkey shat in its own hand … is it shit or shat? Anyway this monkey threw it at this girl called Tracy Brenan, she's a lesbian now but I don't know if that's just a coincidence but yeah anyway it missed her and hit our teacher, Mrs Clipson, right in the fucking mouth then while everyone was looking at this another monkey began this angry power wank and …'

Sally cut me off mid flow, which in hind- sight was probably for the best.

'What the fuck is that?!' Sally pointed in my direction, just below my belt.

I looked down at myself. Oh God..

'Now YOU'VE got a fucking hard-on! What the fuck is wrong with your family!?'

Was this one of those rhetorical questions? I didn't know what to say. A mental image of the wanking monkey popped into my head. Maybe I should pull out my cock, wank into my hand and with a quick flick of the wrist throw it at her then go back inside, murder my family and calmly phone the police. 'Hello Police? I'd like to report a crime please, yes I've just spunked all over my next door neighbour and murdered my family. What's that? You'll be round in a jiffy to take me to the nut house? Cool, ok see you soon. Quick question, any hot nymphos there at the moment? In wheelchairs? No? Okay well let's hope I at least get raped by some of the hotter orderlies then, see you in a bit! Caio for now!'

Could the memory of Sally's jizz stained t -shirt sustain me for the rest of my life in a mental asylum? Probably, but luckily for everyone my train of thought was interrupted as Wayne's now gruesomely contorted face hinted very strongly that he was just about to have his moment in the sun. Sleeping in the same room with him for

34

all these years I'd seen that look a thousand times and one could be in no doubt that he was just about to blow his stack.

'Look! Our Wayne's just about to cum!' I shouted, pointing back up to our bedroom window. Good save Johnny son. Good save.

We both looked up and at that exact moment my brother Wayne pushed his mashed up face against the glass and let out a primeval kind of howl as he ejaculated all over the inside of our bedroom window. Horribly mesmerized, we witnessed the whole climax to this, even by our family's standards, rather sordid show. The two muffled thuds, one after the other that literally shook the pane as the force of his load hit the glass like two birds flying into it, one after the other. Then there was a slight pause before Wayne's body slumped forwards and rested his forehead against the window. Gigantic beads of sweat popping out of his skin and rolled off his head as his massive bulk heaved itself up and down in post climatic recovery. With mouths agape, Sally and I dragged our eyes away and looked at each other, then back to Wayne just in time to see him tap his cock on the window sill a couple of times. He then gave it a squeeze, wiped it on a curtain and grinned at the pair of us. This performance climaxed with a double thumbs up and a clear and distinctive, Heyyyy! With a flourish he then drew the curtains and the show was officially over.

There was an awkward silence.

Sally Holmes and I looked at each other for what seemed an eternity. Then eventually she said, 'Why do mentals always have such massive knobs?'

'I know! And you should see his bollocks they're like two fucking scotch eggs! My cock is really tiny compared to his fucker! ' I blurted.

Sally looked me up and down and replied slowly, 'Yes I know.'

I blushed.

'Don't worry about it Johnny I've seen smaller ones than that my six month old nephew for example. And there was this one time when I was at the fair and we watched this freak show and one of the women in it had a clitoris that looked a bit like yours but it was a bit bigger to be honest, and thicker.'

Then she laughed. Fuck knows what a clitoris was but I thought I'd better laugh too and once I joined in we couldn't stop for what seemed like forever but in reality was probably about a minute.

'I'm sorry about all that beastly, nastiness just now.' I said, glancing up at our house. 'It's a compliment really.'

'Oh yeah a real compliment! Well, I'm flattered kind Sir' Sally said as she did an exaggerated formal curtsy.

'Oh fuck it, don't sweat it Mate it's not really your fault your family are all...'
She stopped herself.

'Wow what an eventful morning already! Being objectified, degraded and reduced to a mere piece of meat for the sexual gratification of you and your brother is a fantastic way to start the day so thank you both for that. Anyway all this cock action has made me late. I've got to go to college, see you later Johnny. Please thank your brother for making me feel so special.

'See you later Johnny!' That's what she said! 'See you later!' Well it seemed like after a shaky start ole Johnny boy had managed to somehow pull it off, no pun intended. Miraculously I've come out of this rather fucked up situation on top! She's seen my bulging cock and now she's gagging for a taste of it! When she gets back from college I'm going to knock on her door and she's going to drag me in and use me like her very own fucking fuck slave! 'I'm not even going to go back in for a wank now' I thought to myself. No, my next batch of duck butter would not be headed for an item of our Wayne's ragged old clothes or down the sink. Nope. This time my dirty concrete was heading for my beloved, destination, face and tits.

Okay let's get the order straight now so I don't look like an amateur. I mused. Excluding probably getting banged off my dad, the local priest and God knows who else in our town when I was a kid, and even including getting tops and fingers off aunty Joan before coming into my jeans, to all intents and purposes I was still a virgin. But if I got my moves down now she'd never guess. Although my experience with Aunty Joan had put me off oral sex I was still going to give it a go for Sally's sake as birds in those pornos I'd seen always seemed to enjoy it. Plus I wanted nothing more in this world than to please Sally. Okay, okay I quickly came up with a fail proof strategy. I'll fuck her mouth first then her bush, then mouth again, both arm pits, backs of her knees, bush, mouth, bush, then mouth again then empty my balls right up her tight little brown …

Sally stopped in her tracks and spun around again to face me.

'Oh yeah and Johnny darling, there's just one thing'

This is it! She's going to ask if I'm free to slosh one up her tonight! I try to remain calm.

'Yeah Sally babe what's up?' I say, cool as fuck and leaning nonchalantly against our outside toilet wall my only regret being that I wasn't wearing my donkey jacket and monkey boots and chewing gum.

'If I ever catch you perving at me sunbathing or hanging out the laundry or following me home from college or wanking off into your kitchen sink while I'm scrambling about in the fucking mud like a helpless cunt I'll cut your fucking balls off and choke your fucking brother to death with them okay?'

'Yep, okay Sally yes, yes that's understood. Can't argue with that. Won't happen again. Sorry Sally, harsh but fair, okay have a nice day, bye Sally see you later, or not, I don't mean spy on you again…or follow you home…or watch you get home in the wee small hours …Okay bye.' I babbled, feeling the blood rush to my ears again as I tried once again not to faint or have a stroke. And with those last devastating words she skipped out of her gate and up the road. Fuck it. Fuck it. Fuck it.

Chapter four

I went back inside to lick my wounds and sulk my polyester socks off. My dad was in the living room smoking a cigarette. His whole body seemed to be in shock. I could see his hands shaking and his eyes were the dictionary definition of piss holes in the snow, if they have definitions for that sort of thing. It's not like me to kick a man when he's down and I'd be walking a very fine line but fuck it, I needed cheering up. I decided to push his buttons for my own amusement.

'Good morning Father what a beautiful day!' says I, knowing that my overt cheeriness would compound his sullenness thus making me genuinely more cheery and him more surly.

'Fuck off Johnny you sarcastic cunt' he replied. He remembered my name, what a turn up. I could have cried with joy.

'Pray tell me sire, why are you up at this hour? Have you found yourself gainful employment at last?' I continued with wide eyed innocence, while gleefully striding up and down. 'Oh we're a proper feckin' comedian today aren't we? Why don't you make yourself useful and make your dad a cup of tea Son there's a good boy?' says he.

'I would but I don't know who the fuck he is!' says I triumphantly.

'Well it certainly ain't me ya ugly little cunt' he came back with.

'Touché Papa touché' I replied. Honestly there's nothing like a bit of familial banter in the morning is there? Fuck me it was like being in the fucking Walton's sometimes in our house.

'Go on son I'm feckin' parched. I'll give ya a fag so I will! He's pleading now and trying to look hurt. I'd nicked most of his fags the previous night so this rather paltry offer did not appeal to me. I hated myself for it but it was still a thrill for me when my dad was being nice to me even if it was because he wanted something. I obviously knew that he was still a real arse hole but sometimes I played with the idea that deep down he really did love me and our Wayne. Sometimes I'd picture him on his death bed where he'd beckon us over and tell us how sorry he was for being a fucking cunt to us all our lives. Then we would all hug each other and cry and I'd say that I forgave him. Then I'd give our Wayne the nod and he would put a fucking pillow over his sorry face and suffocate him while he kicked and screamed while begging for mercy.

'Fuck that Dad I'm already late for school and you know how important education is to me! Why don't you ask our Wayne I know that he's just got himself up, or more accurately, off, I chuckled to myself. 'I'll see if he'll come down and make you a nice cup of tea with extra cream. I'm sure if he knows you want something warm down your throat he'd be happy to oblige. See you later, love you, hugs to mama, bye!' And with that I scooted out of the room and through the front door narrowly missing the glass ashtray that hurtled towards my head. 'One of these days that smart mouth of yours is going to get you into real trouble Johnny you fecking little gob shite!'

'No, I Love YOU more!' I yelled as I slammed shut the front gate and ran out of harm's way. 'Johnny you cunt come back 'ere!' He called me Johnny twice in one day, things were definitely looking up. There's nothing like taking the piss out of the old man to recharge one's batteries.

Now then what to do to fill up this glorious sunny day? School was out of the question as it was a Tuesday and that meant double music with Callahan first thing and to put it bluntly he was a condescending cunt and a bully. Like they all were. I'd never met a teacher who I didn't want to punch square in the face or set fire to. Even now, all these years later, if I'm out and somebody introduces themselves as a teacher I look them up and down and think, 'hmm which one are you? Bully, psychopath, nonce or inadequate bed wetter?' Usually they are a combination of all four. My primary school was a convent and run by nuns. They were a vicious bunch. Lucky for me I was a Catholic so in the scheme of things I got off lightly. Unlike my unfortunate class mate Adrian Tucker who had the misfortune to be a proddy. He was going to hell anyway, but the nuns made sure that his life on earth wasn't too rosy either. The poor soulless cunt couldn't put a foot right. He was beaten for all sorts of tiny misdemeanours; Fidgeting, not paying attention, not sitting upright, top button undone etc. but mostly for not being one of us. I saw him get smashed against a wall by Sister Mary Joseph for having scuffed shoes once. His shoes were a lot less scuffed than mine, but regrettably he was wearing proddy shoes. Adrian's main crime though was not being a Catholic and as much as I felt sorry for him I was glad it was him and not me getting beaten for a change. To this day I'm yet to have a wank about a nun so I think I was damaged too in some way. I do remember that once when I was about

39

twelve I had an English teacher who told me that I had potential but I thought that he was taking the piss or trying to groom me. He was a nice enough guy so maybe he was just being kind. Too late now. Then there was Miss Travis who was my art teacher. She was cool and hot and let us smoke fags in class if we wanted to. She was huge, like a big sexy Amazonian wearing too much eye shadow. I've had many a tug while thinking about climbing up her legs and giving her one over by the turps table. Can women really be sex cases? I guess it's all about context. My Aunty Joan certainly used me for her own sexual gratification that's for sure, but apart from when she stuck her tongue down my throat and the smell of her fanny hole I didn't mind that at all.

If Miss Travis had sucked me off while I was throwing clay or forced herself upon me in any way, shape or form I don't think I would have been traumatised by it or blame myself or go running to the headmaster or my head of year or my parents or burying my shame deep down inside me until it eventually manifested itself in some God awful way in the future. Oh no I'd be shouting it from the fucking roof tops and selling the smell from my fingers to the highest bidder. 'Smell that! But is it art?' Anyway apart from those two, all the teachers that I've had the misfortune to have met have all been proper bell ends.

I decided to go over to the kids' playground and have a smoke. An upside of having two chain smoking, alcoholic, prescription addicted parents, is that it's fairly easy to pilfer from them and I always had an abundance of cigarettes and other assorted drugs.

From the top of the slide I had a clear view of our front door. I climbed up the slide bit, turned around, made myself comfortable and sparked up. Now then, what the fuck was my dad up to? Three fags later our door opened and out came my dad. He was hunched over and cowering from the morning sun like a retiring old pit pony on it's first day on the surface. Honestly I'd seen healthier looking corpses. He looked to his left and then sharply to his right like a spy from some B-Movie and shuffled off towards the bus stop. I finished my fag. I was in no particular hurry because I knew where he was going. I waited until he was out of sight and went back to our house. I went around the back in order to get my bike. Instinctively, I glanced towards Sally's back door even though I knew she wasn't in and then looked up at me and Wayne's bedroom window. Wayne's spunk was drying on the window pane and glistening in the reflected morning sun. If I was that way inclined I'd have reached for my quill and rattled off a romantic poem about its beauty but instead I involuntarily started to dry heave. How does he produce so much? I pondered. 'It must be those massive bollocks. Lucky he'll never get laid because he'd drown a bird from the inside out with that amount of sex piss. I grabbed my bike and headed off into town towards the library.

My dad thinks he's a clever cunt but he wasn't fooling me. I entered the library, grabbed a broadsheet, hid behind it and waited. I was confident because I knew my prey. We are all creatures of habit and my dad's goes something like this: get up, get fucked up and then go back to bed. If he ever leaves the house it has to be for a very good reason. Today he had to take a ten minute bus journey, buy some fags and a six pack of extra strength lager, drink two cans in quick succession in the park for a bit of Dutch courage in order to deal with the general public and then smoke half a dozen cigarettes. He'd have a bet after he'd read the racing pages in the library for free so no more distractions en route. It had taken me about twenty minutes to cycle here, so if my calculations were correct he should be arriving in about an hour. Two hours later he skulked in through the front doors. I peered over a copy of the Times. I hoped that he was not really my dad. In the cold light of day I could see what a strange looking man he was. All twitchy and awkward and nervous. He walked up to the information desk, and by the way the lady on the desk reels back in abject horror, my educated guess about the booze and fag intake was correct. Plus I could see that there were only four cans left in his plastic bag. The poor, pathetic old sod. I should feel sorry for him but I don't. He nodded and made his way towards the lift. Such laziness it's only two floors. I bounded up the stairs two at a time. I spent a lot of my days here so I knew where everything was - well anything that might have a bit of wanking material betwixt its pages anyway - I slipped into the 'Education' booth. Safe as houses and with a good overall view of the place. Like a rabbit caught in headlights, my father staggered about. Books were like kryptonite to my dad. He stumbled around tripping over things that weren't there and eventually found, and stared for a long while at, the information board. Running a trembling finger down the list of subjects then back up and down up and down until finally it came to rest. He wandered away, stumbled about for a bit then came back to the board. The same thing happened twice. Eventually a member of staff came up the stairs and I saw the relief on my dad's face as he collared him.

'Fank feck for that son! Now then would you have any books on mentals?'

'I beg your pardon Sir?'

He did a sort of loud exaggerated whisper

'I need a book about being a feckin' head case. He then glanced around sheepishly and then he put a filthy finger up to the guy's mouth, grinned and said, 'Shush this is a library. He then fell about laughing at his own pretty obvious joke.

The man abruptly brushed away my dad's finger from his face and said, 'I'm sorry Sir? Are you looking for a book on psychological disorders?

'Yeah Mate, psychological disorders! That's the feckers!' My dad shouted gleefully before putting his finger up to his own mouth.

'Um, please follow me Sir'

I crept closer to remain within earshot.

'Which type of disorder are you particularly interested in Sir?

'Depression'my dad confidently replied.

Bingo.

My dad stared at the kindly old librarian.

'Will that be all Sir?'

'What? Um yes, yes that will be all my good man, now if you'd be so kind as to feck off and leave me be I'd very much appreciate it and keep the feckin' noise down this is a feckin' library don't cha know!' He's all pleased with himself and let out a raspy, cancerous laugh.

My dad turned away to scan the shelf as the librarian walked off incredulous as to my dad's lack of social etiquette and generous use of the F word.

My work here was done. I didn't even wait to witness my dad steal whichever book he chose. This had dole scam written all over it, and he wouldn't be as stupid as to leave any kind of evidence such as a librarian's stamp in a book on depression leading to his details should he ever be investigated. Plus he was a thief and didn't pay for anything.

I wandered into town. I nicked a cheese and ham sandwich, crisps, chocolate and a drink each for me and our Wayne from Marks and Spencer - one has to maintain standards – I ate mine in the park, nicked a Pogue's album from Acorns record shop and headed for home.

I cycled through the park, head down going as fast as I could, trying to break my record of nine minutes and 47 seconds on my digital watch. Apart from my Chopper bike, my digital watch was by far the best thing that I owned. My dad's brother, Uncle Sean had given it to me one night when he was round our house and fucking steaming. He was telling me how much he loved me while crying and blubbering all over me, which to be honest I didn't really mind because even though it was drink and drug fuelled as it was still some degree of affection and I was always after a bit of that regardless of the source. It was gold coloured and had the time and the date and a stop watch on it and I fucking loved it. I'd just got to the lake when my front wheel suddenly jammed and I flew through the air and crashed face first onto the concrete path and used my face as a brake. My Pogues record had snapped but on the bright side the sandwiches in my coat cushioned the impact and, apart from picking gravel out of my face, I appeared to be okay. But this particular adventure had only just begun.

'Well, well, well if it's not our little Johnny McQueen,' Fuck's sake it was an ambush. I dragged myself off the floor. The Oakhill Gang. Main members, Mickey, Debbie, Kenny, Matty, and Benny. These five cunts always hung around the park mugging little kids and smoking and selling weed and whatever else they could lay their grubby little hands on.Mickey grabbed me by my coat hood and swung me around violently. 'Empty your pockets you little bitch' said Debbie. Although this was a bit emasculating, part of me still found it also a bit sexy. From previous experience I knew better than to give in to any bravado because this would only make matters worse so I meekly emptied my pockets.

'You pathetic little pikey cunt' said Mickey 'Is that it!?' thirty pence, two sandwiches and a broken, fucking record?'

'Well there's nothing wrong with your eyesight you lanky cunt' I replied. Well I didn't actually say that out loud but I did say it inside the safety of my head. On these occasions it's best to let nature take its course. Least said, soonest mended and all that. So I just nodded. I'd been robbed so many times by this lot I knew how it was going to pan out so I just went into damage limitation mode. 'I saw your retard brother yesterday and gave him a slap' said Mickey as his little gang of wankers

43

sniggered and laughed. 'You two are fucking pathetic It's not even worth robbing you cunts' he continued. 'From now on I want five quid a week off the pair of you and if you don't pay up I'm going to beat the shit out of you. Is that clear?'

For fuck's sake. How on earth was I was going to be able to pay this cunt five quid a week was beyond me. I never had any money ever and neither did our Wayne but I just nodded and kept my eyes firmly fixed on the ground.Benny sauntered over and slapped me around the head and then kneed me in the bollocks. If they let me go now I would have considered that a result. 'Okay Johnny get the fuck out of my sight' said Mickey. I sighed with relief as I'd had much worse in the past. 'Hang on a minute we can't just let him off that lightly He needs to be punished for being a poor little pikey cunt! We don't want to be seen as soft touches...that'll be bad for our reputation' piped up Debbie, the ugly fat cow.

I have always blamed the Godfather films for this type of behaviour. Everybody wanted to be a gangster and it was all about the culture of fear and intimidation and fucking respect. 'Okay, Okay' replied Mickey 'Let's have a think.'

'Make him eat dog shit!' Chimed in Benny. Fuck's sake that old chestnut. I wasn't even bothered about this as I'd eaten dog shit many times at the hands of the various gangs around here. It was admittedly an acquired taste, but after a while one gets used to it. If that was all I had to do I would still call this a result. 'No I've got a better idea' Kenny suddenly said. 'He can suck my dick'

Ohh the fucking little bender. Kenny was always a bit suspect with his feminine fucking traits, always brushing his hair and wearing outlandish clothes and mincing about the fucking place like Larry fucking Grayson. At least he was the cleanest of them all and at a push if I had to suck one of them off I'd have to say that his dick would probably have been the cleanest. I would certainly have preferred that than going anywhere near Debbie's toilet parts, I wouldn't have been at all surprised if that putrid slag had a bigger dick than all of them.

'Fuck's sake Kenny you fucking little poof!' Replied Mickey.

'I'm not a poof! It's all about humiliation Mickey! Humiliation and respect!' Replied Kenny indignantly.

'No Kenny it's all about you being a fucking chutney ferret and wanting me to suck your gay little cock.' I thought to myself, but thought it best not to voice that opinion out loud.

44

'To be fair you are a fucking little bender boy though Kenny' says Debbie.

'No I'm not!' Cried Kenny. 'Just because I like to dress nice and have nice hair doesn't make me a poof!'

'No you're right Kenny' replied Debbie 'It's every time we mug some boy you always, fucking always, suggest that they suck your fucking little cock. That's what makes you a fucking little bender Kenny.' She had a good point.

Kenny was almost in tears with outrage now. 'I'm not a fucking poof!' He protested.

'Okay, okay, let's just get it over with. Johnny, suck off Kenny and not because he's a fucking poofter but because it's humiliating and commands respect, get on your fucking knees fella. Said Mickey.

For fuck's sake, I thought, here was me expecting my first real sexual experience to be hanging out the back of my darling Sally and in fact it will be down on my knees in the middle of a park sucking off this little queer. Well you've got to start somewhere I suppose. Surely spunk will taste better than dog shit though, I mused. Benny and Matty shoved me to the ground and onto my knees as Kenny walked over to us while unzipping his flies. He was shaking and trembling with anticipation as he came closer and closer. Did he want or expect me to swallow his load or should I spit it out? What about a finger up the arse? I read somewhere that a finger up the arse adds to the pleasure. Sometimes I do that while having a wank. Would that be spoiling him? I didn't want to be known as someone who's really good at giving blow jobs and end up sucking off every Tom, Dick and Kenny in town. I made up my mind to try and be really bad at it, just in case although also thinking how good at it I would be in different circumstances.

His crotch was now level with my face as he leaned back and pulled it. I couldn't help being delighted to find that it was a *lot* smaller than mine. 'Open your fucking mouth Johnny' demanded Kenny, doing his best to look triumphant,

'Fuck me it's really very tiny isn't it Kenny?' I blurted out. Kenny's petite little hard-on immediately shrivelled to nothing and he quickly zipped it back up and slapped me across the face.

'Oh for fuck's sake let's just get some dog shit' said Mickey as Kenny burst into tears. 'Oh and I'll have that watch off you too Johnny.' What a cunt.

One needs to find little victories in the face of adversity and all things considered I think in some tiny, pathetic way I handled the situation with as much dignity as I could have hoped for considering the circumstances. As I cycled home with the familiar mix of blood and dog shit in my mouth and no watch, I considered myself to have gotten away lightly. Happy days.

Just in case I bumped into Sally on my way home I decided to freshen up in the local public toilets. Even though I had to admit the chances of me bumping into her seemed rather remote I couldn't take the chance. Always be prepared for any unexpected occurrence was my motto. What if she came home from college early to try and 'accidently' bump into me in order for her to force me onto my knees and command me to eat her sweet, hairy pie only to find me covered in dog shit and my own blood? I couldn't take the chance. I parked my bike up against the toilet wall, entered and walked up to the wash basin. I pushed down on the tap and covered my face with the lukewarm water before swilling out my mouth. I glanced up at the wall to the old familiar graffiti, phone numbers and homoerotica. Then something in my peripheral vision caught my eye.

An old man was standing at the far end of the communal urinal and was studying me intently.

'Hello young man' he said cheerily.

'Alright Mate?' I replied politely.

'You look positively filthy young sir! What have you been up to eh? A bit of rough and tumble with your play mates I shouldn't wonder. I was young myself once a long time ago and I used to love to get stuck in with all my pals. I bet you like to go in hard eh? Do you like to get physical with all your little pals? I bet you do!' He chuckled. He was looking at me intently and he had one hand obviously on his cock but I couldn't hear any sound of pissing.

'You're a lovely looking young man, why aren't you at school? Bunking off eh? Don't worry I won't tell your teacher.' He continued.

'Listen Mate I don't mind you watching me clean up while you have a wank into the bog but I want at least five quid' I found myself saying. I must be giving off some sort of homosexual magnetism today and thought I might as well make the most of it.

'How dare you suggest such a thing you ruddy little bugger?! I'm doing no such thing. I was just passing the time of day!' he replied in fake shock.

46

'I'll wank you off into that bog for ten quid' I replied. The guy was old and posh and obviously a fucking nonce so why beat about the bush. I evidently gave him the horn and he clearly had a few quid, so why not just get fucking on with it was my thinking. He sputtered his indignation and professed innocence and gave me an affronted, almost hurt look but as he was definitely still pulling his pudding, I disregarded his protests. 'Listen Mister, do you want me to wank you off or not? It's already been a rather tiresome day so if not I'm leaving and you'll just have to finish yourself. I told him, rather pleased with my business-like attitude.

'Okay you little sod but I've only got two pounds and for that I want to kiss you and for you to stick a finger up my bottom!' he suddenly blurted out.

I fucking knew it!

'Fuck off I'm not fucking kissing you or putting anything up your dirty old arsehole, you decrepit old cunt!' I said disgustedly.

'Okay I'll give you three pounds to masturbate me into this urinal while I stroke your bottom, play with your hair and nuzzle your neck!' He replied.

'Mate you've got to stop wanking because I can't think straight. Four pounds and I'll wank you into the urinal but no fucking kissing or touching but I will stick my finger up your ass through your trousers. Final offer.' I replied and stuck out my hand instinctively to seal the deal but then quickly retracted it.

'Four pounds, a peck on the mouth and a finger right up my bare botty as I orgasm into this delightfully sordid trough! He shrilled.

'Five pounds, no kissing or touching except my finger rammed up your wrinkly old hoop and that's my final offer, take it or leave it you dirty old ponce. I countered.

He suddenly became very red in the face and I realised that I'd been had, or rather he'd just had himself, the cheeky old bastard. He lurched forward and I couldn't help but see a tiny little drop of spunk on the end of his tired-looking old knob. He groaned and glanced at me shamefully but then let out a defiant little laugh. I was fucking furious. He'd played me for a fool and obviously had no intention of ever giving me anything at all. I'd just been a visual and verbal aid to his sordid little bout of self-abuse. A part of me actually admired that to be honest, the devious little queen. 'Be on your way now Sonny, there's a good boy' he chuckled as he wiped his geriatric old cock into what looked like an embroidered hanky. I was fucking livid that I'd been scammed by this old duffer.

'Listen here you cheating old cunt give me my fucking money!' I shouted.

'What for Old Boy? You never earned any money. I did it all by myself!' he replied gleefully.

'Give me my fucking money you old poof!' I screamed in frustration. I ran towards him and kneed him in the nuts. He crumpled to the floor. 'Give me my fucking money!' I started to beat him around the head. 'Give me my fucking money! Give me my fucking money! Give me my fucking money!' Suddenly I came to and realised that I'd beaten the fucking shit out of him and he lay bloody and bruised on the tiled shithouse floor. His trousers were down and I realised that his cock was still out and he'd pissed himself in fright.

'Good boy' he said. 'You're a very good boy, thank you my dear, dear little boy.'

What the fuck was wrong with this cunt? With a trembling hand he reached into his back pocket and pulled out his wallet. He opened it and inside I could see two crisp five pound notes. He handed me one and told me again that I was a good boy. I kicked him hard right in the cock and helped myself to the other five pound note and threw his wallet into the stinking urinal.

'Yeah cheers mate, nice doing business with you' I said as I made my way out.

'Same time next week young man?' He shouted after me.

'Yeah fuck it, why not?' I called back.

That old nonce was the first person that I'd ever hit in my entire life and I must say I liked it. I liked it a lot. Not being on the receiving end of a kicking felt fantastic. I'd often wondered what the fuss was all about and now I knew. What a fucking buzz. I looked down at my own cock and it was raging hard. So some people like to beat other people up and some people like to get beaten up and there was money to be made in either scenario. By the state of my own cock right now I knew which one I preferred. I also knew I needed to get home and treat myself to a right royal wank, which I felt I'd thoroughly deserved.

My mum was up by the time I got back.

'Hello Johnny darlin' have yas got any fags love?'

'Morning mum, yeah here you go.' I threw her a fag from a packet that I'd nicked from her earlier.

'You're a feckin' angel babe honestly you are. God feckin' bless and save ya' said my mum as she lit the first fag of the day and coughed up something into a tissue.

'What time is it darlin?' She enquired. I didn't know because I no longer owned a watch. Why the fuck did she ever bother to ask about the time anyway? She never had anywhere to go at any particular hour. Her life was simply a heady cycle of waking up, getting off her tits and then going to bed, ad infinitum.

'Dunno, about one I think, why?' I replied.

'WHY?! Never fecking mind why! Who are you the fecking police!? Mind your own feckin' business ya cheeky little cunt that's feckin' WHY' she suddenly screamed. Fuck me that escalated quickly. She's fucking Lady Di when she wants one of her own fags back, the cunt, talk about psychological disorders, my parents could write their own book on how to be mental.

'Oh sorry Love, it's just that I've got such a splitting headache and I've got to meet your Aunty Joan later about a bit of business and I really don't feel well. I think I'm coming down with the flu or something. Is there any beer in the fridge?' She continued.

Fuck me mixed signals or what? She's up and down like a whore's drawers. If I was a head teacher and wanted to put my pupils off experimenting with drugs I wouldn't invite some knackered out old ex junky carrying a dog to the school to give a boring old lecture on the evils of addiction, I'd bring them round here and let them witness what it's like to live with a couple of the fuckers who are still bang on it. Unpredictable mood swings, domestic violence, listlessness, physical and emotional neglect, laziness, general cuntishness and that's not even scratching the surface or mentioning the indescribable smell or the fact that the house could do with a light dusting to say the least.

'I don't know mum why don't you get off your big, fat fucking ass and walk the two yards over to the fucker and take a fucking look for yourself, you lazy old bag of bollocks?' I shouted. I didn't actually say that. I just looked at her. The sun was shining in through the window right onto her face and it was not doing her any favours whatsoever. Some of my friends had hot mums. My mate Billy's mum for example was well fit, and Boner's and Squint's and Cum Face's too, in fact the more I

49

thought about it, all my friends mum's were fit as fuck and I'd do them all right now given half a chance. Nobody would want to shag my mum though. You'd have to be a proper sex case to want to bang my old lady. Niche to say the least. Our Wayne would though. He's a real sick fucker with no discernible standards to speak of. Bless his heart. I stare at my mum and picture the two of them going for it and involuntarily burst out laughing.

'What the feck are you looking at me and laughing for you cheeky little cunt!?' Screamed my mum.

Her expression was a mixture of anger and hurt. I felt bad, so instead of saying, 'oh I was just imagining you and our Wayne having sexual intercourse,' I said, 'Oh sorry mum I was miles away and just thinking about the time when you pushed Dad down the stairs and he broke his ankle.' That cheered her right up and then we both started laughing.

Chapter five

Up until now you might have gotten the impression that my father was pretty much a solid gold prick but sometimes he could be quite amusing. Get a bottle of scotch down him, a gram of sniff and a win on the horses and he could be quite the entertainer. He'd laugh and sing and do his, 'I'm fucked but too fucked to care' kind of Irish jig in the living room and twirl my mum around the settee to a bit of Elvis or Buddy Holly or The Dubliners then collapse exhausted in his chair. My mum would pretend to be cross but I think we all appreciated a bit of light relief every now and then and counted our blessings. He could also command a room with his endless stories and vast array of filthy jokes and, if it was a special occasion, he'd get out the guitar and give us all some good old Irish rebel songs. If I wasn't his son and I didn't know what a horror of a man he was ninety nine percent of the time I'd probably have liked him myself. Most people liked my dad because, when he was on form, he was the life and soul of the party. So it came as a bit of surprise to everyone around him but me when she suddenly started to become inexplicably depressed. It was a textbook case, quite literally. It didn't take me long to find the book he'd stolen from the library tucked into his (rather impressive) porn collection. After having a massive three hour long power wank I took it and read it. The book in question was "Cheer up you sad cunt: *Depression, a pop up guide"*. Not really it was called "Clinical Depression: A Doctor's handbook". It was a good choice, concise and to the point.

My dad became what you might call a 'classic case' and within a few weeks he had all the main identifiable symptoms. I'd read the book over the course of a few days when he was asleep or comatose and could tell what page he'd got up to by each new symptom. Eventually even our family and friends started to notice subtle differences in his behaviour. He played a blinder and if I didn't know what a scamming bastard he was I might even have fallen for it myself. The benefit squad were clearly back on his case and about to review his circumstances.

'Mr McQueen we've studied your notes and we do believe that you are without a doubt the laziest, most good for nothing mother fucker we've ever come across and therefore we are stopping all your handouts with immediate effect. Now get the fuck out.' But if he could convince them he was clinically depressed then he'd be exempt from any enquiry or even having to trundle down to the unemployment office once every two weeks just to lie his fat arse off.

"The symptoms of depression can be complex. If you are depressed, you often lose interest in things you used to enjoy. Depression commonly interferes with your work, social life and family life. There are many other symptoms, which can be psychological, physical and social

- Psychological symptoms include: continuous low mood or sadness, feelings of hopelessness and helplessness
- low self-esteem
- tearfulness
- feelings of guilt
- feeling irritable and intolerant of others
- lack of motivation and little interest in things
- difficulty making decisions
- lack of enjoyment
- suicidal thoughts or thoughts of harming yourself
- feeling anxious or worried
- reduced sex drive

Physical symptoms include:

- slowed movement or speech
- change in appetite or weight (usually decreased, but sometimes increased)
- constipation
- unexplained aches and pains
- lack of energy or lack of interest in sex
- changes to the menstrual cycle
- disturbed sleep patterns (for example, problems going to sleep or waking in the early hours of the morning)

Social symptoms include:

- not doing well at work
- taking part in fewer social activities and avoiding contact with friends
- reduced hobbies and interests
- difficulties in home and family life"

- "Some symptoms are easier to spot than others." No shit Sherlock.

Fuck me he was on the cusp anyway and it didn't take a lot of imagination on his part to push himself into the abyss of perpetual darkness and despair and try to claim a few more government handouts along the way. I picked out a few classic symptoms and studied his case. 'Feeling irritable and intolerant of others.' This one is hard to gauge as he's always been a miserable old cunt. Having depression seemed to me like having a continuous hangover or coming down off amphetamines so it took a bit longer to spot the signs in him than on someone who had started out as a fully functioning and relatively normal human being. Anyone who had any dealings with him knew he was a sullen fucker with frequent and violent mood swings. He was hard as nails and basically fought his way through life and the only person who had any control over him after his own mum died and that was my mum.

'Not doing well at work' Hmmm that's a difficult one as I can't remember him ever having a job apart from the building site one that lasted three days, although he's not bad at drug dealing I guess.

'Changes in menstrual cycle' well I'd often seen blood in the toilet bowl after he'd been in there but couldn't be sure if it came from his vagina and had to concede that due to the accompanying smell it more likely came from his arse. 'Constipation' tick.

As I said, he'd already got the majority of these symptoms so it was just a matter of sign- posting them to the relevant authorities in order to make some profit out of them. If his plan worked, he'd be getting happy pills from the doctors and extra benefits from the government. I decided to just sit back and let the whole sorry story unravel and see how it all panned out. It was no skin off my nose what he did, plus if he was going to play that card it might turn out in my favour. I fantasised about what might happen if he took it too far, got sectioned and ended up getting raped to death himself. I'd have paid good money to watch that.

A few days later I came home from school expecting, as per usual, to find a… I wonder what the collective noun for dickhead wasters is. A horror? An abomination? A parasite? A full colostomy bag? Let's go with parasite, so yeah I expected to find a parasite of wasters hanging around our house smoking weed and drinking cheap cider while listening to the latest ramblings by my dear father on how to be better off on the old rock and roll than if you were actually working full time. But the place was dead quiet. This was very unsettling as our house was seldom if ever silent. I looked at the clock on the mantelpiece. Elvis' left hand was pointing to the number eight. I did a quick mental calculation, hmm still not sure. It's been eight o'clock according to the King ever since I could remember. It still burned me that Mickey and his crew had stolen my watch but there was fuck all I could do about it. I saw my dad's on the kitchen table. School boy error, I should have pawned it but his mum gave it to him and I was feeling virtuous for some reason, so I just looked at the time and put it back down. Just as I suspected it was indeed four o'clock in the afternoon which has always been breakfast time at the McQueen residence. The only trouble was nobody was home. This was unheard of and at first this felt quite disconcerting. I had a quick scan of our entire estate and took advantage of this once in a lifetime opportunity to have a nice long power wank while sitting in the silver back's chair. I ran upstairs to my parents' room, grabbed a tub of granny grot's moisturiser - a mental image of someone shutting a barn door after a horse had bolted followed by someone pissing in the wind flashed through my mind - gathered a plethora of pornographic wrongness at my feet and, after a disappointingly short period of time I came into one of my dad's discarded underpants. Nonchalantly I threw these rancid things over my shoulder and, glancing at the broken clock on the wall, mumbled in my best Elvis, 'Thank you very much' then did a few karate moves to distract myself from that self-loathing, empty, and guilty feeling one gets immediately after pouring oneself a hand shandy.

I pulled up my jeans and glanced around for any skid marks, sweat and or cum stains or any other tell- tell signs of masturbatory activity. I'd become something of a writher and grinder as I went about my filthy business recently. This was in preparation for the real thing - should that day ever come - and, as our shower had been broken for months, I'd become somewhat hygienically challenged. I'd been trying to cover my tracks a bit more since the time I'd casually used a pair of my mum's tights to mop up my shameful bollock nectar and when I'd finished, rather lazily, shoved them back in her 'unmentionables' drawer. I thought no more about it until a few weeks later as I was sitting down one evening eating my tea which, tradition dictated as it was a Wednesday, was a Turkey Twister sandwich dunked into a pot noodle. Just as my darling mother shuffled past to plonk her fat arse down on the sofa I couldn't help noticing the overwhelming and unmistakable smell of rancid, clearly past its sell by date, spunk. Looking up towards the source of this acrid aroma I stared in horror and utter disgust as my own dear mother flopped down, legs akimbo, directly opposite me displaying for the entire world to see, a massive cobweb of dried semen stains running from her black, be-netted double stitched crotch to her gnarled, corned beef coloured knees. Although one couldn't help but be impressed by the sheer volume of baby gravy that I'd produced on that particular occasion considering the amount of times I bashed one out during an average day, I couldn't help but be a little disappointed in my mother's attention to detail in relation to her wardrobe. Honestly, what a filthy old bag she'd turned into. Fortunately nobody else seemed to notice or care and after a few days I got used to both the sight and the smell although I did make a mental note to be a bit more discerning as to what I used as a wank rag in the future. To this very day I can't eat a Turkey Twister sandwich without thinking about my mum's marbled crotch and getting a slight twinge in my nether regions.

But where was everyone? Mad they gone out on a family trip? A picnic perhaps? Maybe they'd joined the National Trust and gone to visit a stately home? Could they possibly be, right at this very moment, inside one of our country's fantastic art galleries or museums? Maybe they'd all hopped on a train and gone to the seaside. I felt a strange pang of jealousy before coming to my senses and giving an involuntary snort of derision. No, I would be very surprised, dismayed in fact, if any of those scenarios were actually the case. We never did anything as a family apart from sit around the television or watch wearily as my parents got fucked up and had a bit of a sing song which usually resulted in somebody getting a punch in the face. I'd been on the receiving end of numerous beatings over the years but any attention is better than none I'm sure you'll agree. Apart from when we were a lot younger and they'd taken us to the shops as decoys while they were on the rob. We'd never gone anywhere together. This was probably for the best though. You know when you're walking down the street and see a whole family out together that are just so fucked- up looking you want all your mates to be there so that you can all point and snigger and make cruel jokes about them and thank your lucky stars that they aren't your family? Well that's my family you're taking the piss out of. My family were all what the experts would call, dysfunctional, to say the least, with me being the only exception.

Now that they've closed all the loony bins, if you want to have a peek into the world of the down trodden or mentally deficient, pop down to your local bus station. If you're feeling particularly brave saunter into the nearest café. Here I guarantee that you if you're looking for cheap holiday in other people's misery you will not be disappointed. Order yourself the cheapest cup of tea in town, sit down, feast your eyes and take it all in while thanking your lucky stars that you're only visiting. As condensation pours down the windows take a good look around. Here you will find the town's 'characters.' The heady mix of grisly old pensioners, pregnant teenage mums smoking fags while bickering with their skinny, grey faced other halves. Ex-cons biding their time until inevitably going back inside, down and outs, child molesters and junkies, the unemployed and the unemployable. And also many people that at one time would have been kept under lock and key for their own safety and for the safety of anyone that they might bump into while having a bad day. Or even a good one. The fucking retards. Here you will typically find my brother aka our Wayne. Our Wayne is, and don't get me wrong, I have a lot of time for the poor cunt but our Wayne is to all intents and purposes, a fucking Benny. A retard.

When our Wayne wasn't sat in the bus station café with a lump in his trousers while harassing big Sue who ran the gaff our Wayne spent most of his days wondering about town grinning like a cunt and saying sexually inappropriate things to any remotely pretty girl that happened across his path. If you've ever read "*Of Mice and Men*", well he was similar to the big lumbering dip shit one that killed that mouse by loving it too hard. Underneath though he was really just a gentle giant and harmless, unless you looked remotely like a human female, then there would be a fair chance that sooner or later you'd see his genitals. To be honest our Wayne should have been locked up in the nut house or holed up in a halfway house for sex cases wearing a tag and getting followed around by tabloid journalists, but back then he was left to wander the streets flashing his massive cock and balls to anything that looked remotely like it might have a vagina. Maybe this might have worked in caveman times and perhaps this act was, in his own fucked up way, a kind of courtship; as if to say, 'Listen girls. Yes sure I'm not the most intelligent, articulate, sporty or handsome of chaps but fuck me look at the size of me and look at the size of my fucking cock. If you want big strong babies, I'm your man.' Either way I think the most common response was usually shock and awe because one would have to admit that the lad was blessed in the trouser department to say the very least. Sure he'd get a handbag round the head or threatened with a sawn off stiletto or the like but so far he'd never actually been arrested which was quite remarkable considering the amount of times he'd got his knob out in public. He had the bollocks of a large bull. I bet if one of those old Nazi doctors or a mad scientist had got hold of him, by now there would be an army of super human mongs doing all sorts of sub-human shenanigans for their governments and the world would be deluged in hot, salty monster spunk.

Fuck only knows where they all were. I tried to think rationally. I guessed that my mum would be round Auntie Joan's house smoking fags and taking prescription drugs and drinking own brand vodka while flicking through cheap weekly magazines and telling everyone within earshot what a useless cunt my old man was. My brother would be in the precinct flashing his unmentionables and my dad would be either slumped in the park fucked up on value cider, or in a holding cell waiting to be charged with a plethora of minor criminal offences. It was a bizarre coincidence that they were all out at the same time though so I decided to make the most of it.

Now then how should a young, carefree buck such as myself take advantage of this once in a lifetime situation? Maybe I could have had a tidy up or baked a Victoria sponge cake as a lovely surprise as they all trundled in weary from their endeavours? I decided against those options and started searching the place for drugs. I ran around the house looking for illicit booty and in five minutes I was back in the living room with half a packet of fags, a bag of weed, a bag of a white substance (possibly coke but more likely speed mixed with baby powder) and a half bottle of own brand whisky. Call me an old romantic but in a situation as rare as the one that I found myself in it will come as no surprise to anyone that I thought to myself, that I might as well get royally fucked up and then, as far as I'd be able to under the circumstances, indulge in a right royal power wank.

I opened the little bag of white powder, wiped a space on the table, emptied the contents of the bag onto the table and without even chopping it up or having a little test dab, bent over it, pressed one nostril closed and snorted the contents of the bag right up my fucking hooter. The searing pain travelling up my nose and into my brain suggested it was indeed speed. Fucking hell. My eyes started to stream as I staggered about trying not to scream. 'Mother fucker! Fucking mother fucking cunt fuckers!' - I just had to hold it together for a few minutes until the effects of the drug kicked in. I took a large swig of the whisky and instantly felt better. I started to chew my lip. Smoking weed would be a waste now as the effects of the speed would override it but fuck it I liked the taste. It was all free anyway so with trembling hands I did my best to roll a joint. Fuck me I was whizzing off my tits. Sure it wasn't coke - even my parents weren't that fucking stupid as to leave the king of all drugs lying about for a shitty little no-mark like me to find - but it also wasn't the shit padded out with baby powder gear that my dad serves up to his mates and I was whizzing off my fucking nut. First things first I took the now empty bag of Billy back upstairs and into the bathroom, filled it with talc and put it back exactly where I had found it. Always cover your tracks when it comes to the big stuff. My dad wouldn't miss a few fags, but a bag of speed is a bag of speed. Hopefully he'd just think he'd been conned by one of his dealers and I wouldn't be a suspect. I went back downstairs, picked up the joint and deeply inhaled. I didn't need it because I already felt great to be fair, but any rational feelings had long gone and I just wanted to get mullered.

Among the multitude of thoughts I was having one came to the surface that involved the cultural differences between the British and the French. The latter, it was commonly thought, being a lot more sophisticated than the former; whereas a French man might change his glass of wine between bottles, your typical Brit would quite happily lick alcohol off a dog's dick if that's all there was. If you are careful I think that you can do drugs your whole life without it really being an issue, everything in moderation as they say. I'm not like that though. I'm the opposite.

I was flying now. I was gurning and twitching like someone having a fit. I also felt very horny. I walked into the kitchen just on the off chance that Sally might be doing naked lunges in her back garden. Nope. Fucks' sake now would have been a good time for her to be in her garden semi –naked. The only problem here was, as I instinctively squeezed my cock at that thought, I realized, that although my mind was telling me to yank myself into oblivion my body was not equipping me with the necessary tools. It was four thirty in the afternoon and I'd only had four wanks thus far today: one in the morning before getting out of bed-I'm very loyal and also a hopeless romantic so my first wank of the day is always about Sally- one while standing on a bog seat with my mate Black Clint while looking out through the infamous broken pane of the boys' east block toilets at my English teacher Miss Whitehead as she patrolled about on playground duty- White blouse, big tits and those sticky out nipples got me every time- once again at lunch time in the school library over a picture of some African bird's tits and hairy fanny and one half an hour ago, into a pair of one of my dad's discarded underpants. So it must be the speed keeping me so tiny and soft, because I'm usually at least a ten a day man. I decided to go sit in the garden and wait for Sally to get back.

'Oh hi Sally.' I'd say all wide eyed and innocent 'Good day at college? What's that you say? You can't stop thinking about me and now your fanny is dripping like a broken fridge and you just want to ride my cock to paradise and back then take a load to the face? Well you're just going to have to fucking wait until the effects of these drugs have worn off babe because I can't even piss out of it right now.' I took a long drag of my joint and opened the back door. I heard whimpering coming from the shed. 'What the fuck is that?!' My whole body went into shock. Satan? Maybe Satan has come home! Poor old Satan. He was our dog until he'd obviously got tired of being used as a missile in the domestic disputes between my parents and fucked off. Tired too of all the drunken beatings from my dad. A dog will put up with a lot of horrible shit - unlike a cat who will leave at the earliest sign of household standards dropping 'Dear humans, I've noticed that you now buy me own brand cat food and that dry stuff rather than caviar and foie gras so I'm off next door. Goodbye forever. Kind regards, Tiddles.' - 'Oh my God' I thought, 'Satan has come home and has somehow got trapped in the shed!' - He was the dumbest dog you could ever meet so this wouldn't have been a surprise at all - I twisted the door knob and swung open the door. 'Satan is that you boy!?' My voice came out a tad hysterical, more to do with the drugs in my system than real sentiment, as I couldn't really give a shit about him to be honest. He was a lot more popular in the family than I ever was, and all he did all day was flop about and lick his balls and arsehole. The lucky bastard. I peered through the darkness waiting for my eyes to adjust. 'Satan? Is that you boy? Are you hurt boy? Satan you mangy mutt is that you?'

Gradually my eyes became accustomed to the dark and I could just about see a crumpled heap in the far corner. Satan was a kind of whippet type thing but this shape was a lot bigger than that. I instinctively took a step back. I felt a tingle in my cheek which is my body's sign of being shit scared. 'Who the fuck are you and what do you want?!' I stammered. I was really getting hysterical now, all high pitched and shaking like a nonce at the fairground. 'I've got a gun!' I shouted. Why the fuck did I say that? "Oh Hang on did I say gun? Oops excuse me, what I meant to say was that I think that I've shat myself." Instead of going on the attack shouting yippee ki yay mother fucker while doing a theatrical forward roll in its general direction I decided to fuck quietly retreat. Sometimes the best form of attack is to fuck off back into the house and lock all the fucking doors and then take a big shit.

I ran back inside, locked the back door behind me and stood in the centre of the kitchen hyperventilating and trying to collect my thoughts which were now going a million miles an hour. Then it suddenly dawned on me. It was obviously my fucking dad. He'd blatantly gone into the shed hoping to get found by one of us, all crumpled up and whimpering and generally being depressed, so we'd think his head had finally popped which, under interrogation from the benefit chaps, would add weight to his claim that he was now incapacitated and thus never able to work again. Well, he could fucking well wait until someone else found him because I wasn't in the mood to deal with his shit right now. As I walked back into the kitchen I heard the front door go.

Well that was my afternoon of self-pleasure ruined before it had even begun. I'd always found it more difficult to have a good wank with someone else in the house as it curtailed my sense of sexual abandonment. I deftly ran through the hall and up the stairs to our bedroom and jumped on my bed. The familiar and somehow comforting stomping up the stairs suggested that it was our Wayne. Moments later he skulked into our room sporting a black eye, swollen face and various cuts and bruises about his person wearing the saddest expression I'd ever seen.

Chapter six

I loved our Wayne. I felt sorry for him and I pitied him but he was my older brother and rightly or wrongly I really loved him. He was a brute to look at but deep down in his bones he had a kind heart. Sure he was always on the verge of rape or serious sexual assault but he really was a gentle soul once you got to know him and I always regarded him as a victim of circumstance. Wayne had a long history of being bullied. Wayne was bullied by my parents, most of his teachers, many of his peers and sometimes by random mother fuckers who took one look at him and saw him as an easy target. As a young kid I vividly remember my brother coming home with black eyes and swollen lips and a plethora of injuries on a daily basis. He would never discuss it or comment on it but he had the look of a hunted animal and was constantly on his guard. I could never understand how such a brute could take so many hidings without reacting but he just seemed to regard this as his lot in life.If he thought about it at all.

I was in a heightened state of mind to say the least. All sorts of emotions were bubbling to the surface. None of them, at this point, sexual for a change. I looked into his eyes, and I suddenly became furious. Maybe it was my own frustrations or the hopeless look in his puffy eyes or more likely all the drugs coursing through my body but the red mist came down. Enough was enough. The fucking buck was going to stop right here and now. I shot off of my bed, got up and bounded over to where my brother was now sitting on the edge of his.

'Fuck me Wayne what the fuck happened to you this time?' I yelled. 'Some cunt down the Level punched me for being a thick cunt' he replied.

'Well what the fuck did you do?' He looked at me with a puzzled expression on his daft face.

'What do you mean?' He replied.

'You're the size of a fucking house for fuck's sake, with fists the size of fucking spades! How big was this cunt?'

'I dunno...normal size' he replied.

'So you let somebody half your size punch you for being a thick cunt and you just took it? Fuck me Wayne you really are a fucking dip shit why didn't you hit the cunt back? You are the biggest cunt I've ever seen and you're constantly having the fucking shit kicked out of you! What the fucking, fuck is fucking wrong with you!? Do you enjoy it? Or are you just a cunt?' I exploded, rather exasperated by the whole situation and charged all to fuck due to the amount of drugs in my system.

Now one might think these words were a touch unkind but even though my brother was indeed a fucking evolutionary throw back and shot all to fuck in the head, he was still my brother and this shit had to stop. Plus I'm a weedy little runt and I had my fair share of beatings and they had to fucking well stop too. My defence was humour and sarcasm which, on occasion, could be quite cutting on a theoretical level but it couldn't physically stop a head lock or a dead leg or a kick in the nuts or a punch in the throat. In my experience that type of behaviour only exacerbated the whole situation but it was the only defence I had. I needed to call into action the one thing we had in our collective armoury, and that was our Wayne's brutal strength.

I took hold of both his shoulders and looked him square in the eye.

'Wayne mate, you're the biggest and hardest cunt I know. Why don't you stick up for yourself and start kicking the fucking shit out of these cunts for a change?' He looked back at me with the vacant stare of the mentally challenged and I was just about to punch the cunt myself.

'Fucking stand up!' I commanded. I ran over to our bedroom wardrobe and swung open the door that had a mirror behind it.

'Now then bruv come over here and look into that mirror and tell me what you see' I yelled, all wild eyed and hysterical. Thankfully on this occasion I was glad that our Wayne was used to doing as he was told. We both stared into the glass and to be honest I didn't know which one of us looked the bigger cunt. Wayne still had is coat on which didn't help him at all because for one it was too small for him, two it was fucking filthy and three he was wearing his coat inside like a fucking mental case.

I on the other hand was all wide eyed and twitching like someone suffering from Tourette's syndrome. I suddenly thought to myself that maybe I did actually have Tourette's and briefly thought about cocking my head to one side and spitting and shouting out the word cunt but then thought better of it because it would be too distracting and I might lose the momentum that I was trying to build up.

'Do you like what you see Wayne?'

'No'

'And why is that?'

'I'm fat and I look sad and this coat is too small and I'm wearing it inside.'

This was a good start because there was clearly nothing wrong with his sense of self awareness.

'Will you be content to live like that for the rest of your life?'

'yes.'

'Wrong answer Wayne. Please try again.'

'No?' he meekly replied.

Correct! I shouted while patting him on the back enthusiastically.

'So what are you going to do about it?'

'Take my coat off?'

'Fuck me Wayne. I mean in the long term'

'Dunno. Go on a diet?'

Fuck me I was losing impetus, 'take his coat off and go on a diet?' for fuck's sake.

'No Wayne, you've got to take a good long look at yourself and decide to make real changes in your life! Do you want to be a victim forever? Do you want to be bullied for the rest of your life? Do you want to come home every day and sit on your bed and feel like a piece of shit or do you want to change your life and become a winner!?'

I was coming out with a stream of consciousness amalgamation of all the motivational clichés I'd heard from those daytime chat shows on TV where fat, lazy mother fuckers would come on to moan about how shit their lives were. Then Trisha or Oprah or my favourite one to wank off to, Ricky Lake, would bring on an expert to try and get these lazy fuckers off their sofas and become upstanding citizens or whatever. I'd usually come by the end so I wasn't entirely sure how it all finished.

'You need to start living your best life our Wayne! As the great John Lennon once sang, 'Life is what happens to you while you're busy making other plans!'

'It's not the number of breaths we take but the number of moments that take our breath away!'

'Live for the nights you'll never remember with the friends you'll never forget!'

'I don't have any friends Johnny.' Said Wayne forlornly but at least he was listening.

'Shut up Wayne I'm your friend and we will go out and find you some I promise, now...where the fuck was I?'

'Something about breasts I think Johnny' Wayne grinned.

'Breaths it was breaths you fucking pervert.' That was quite amusing though. For our Wayne anyway.

'Live, laugh, love!' I continued. Fuck me there was hundreds of these fucking things and I was firing them off like a machine gun at our Wayne hoping some of them would land. For me they were all bollocks and instantly forgettable but Wayne seemed to be getting inexplicably inspired by them so I pressed on.

'You have to look through the rain to see the fucking rainbow! Sing like no cunt is listening. Love like you've never been fucking hurt and mother fucking dance like no cunt is watching!' I'm aware that to the untrained ear all these expletives might sound a tad crass but we have Irish blood and it's in our DNA to enjoy a jolly good swear up and I've always thought that they add a certain je ne sais pas to a motivational speech..

Where were all these sound bites all coming from? I couldn't stop. All those days off from school wanking off while watching daytime TV had somehow paid off it seemed. The speed in my system had obviously opened a door in my brain that up until now I didn't know existed and these pearls of wisdom were just tripping off my tongue.

'Yesterday is history, tomorrow is a mystery and today is a gift. That's why they call it the present!' Boom!

'Keep calm and carry on!'

'Shoot for the moon even if you fucking miss, you'll land among the stars!'

'You have to kiss a lot of frogs before you find your prince!'

Wayne looked at me via the reflection of the mirror quizzically.

'Not actual frogs Wayne. Frogs in this case are metaphors for ugly birds until you find a proper sort but I think that one is aimed more at the birds and homos although it still works for normal guys. You've just got to swap prince for princess and possibly toads for frogs.'

Wayne seemed content with my explanation so I pressed on.

'Everything happens for a reason!'

'If life gives you lemons make some fucking lemonade!'

Wayne at this point laughed and shouted angrily at the mirror, 'I love lemonade!'

He was breathing deeply now and starting to get himself at it.

'You'll find love when you stop looking!'

Wayne starred right into his own eyes through the looking glass and shouted 'I want to be loved!'

At one time I would have laughed at this and called our Wayne a soppy cunt but in this context it was all rather emotional because I'd never heard our Wayne express himself ever before. Plus I had to admit that being loved wasn't such a bad idea to me either actually and I could also do with some of that.

Suddenly I saw the fog lift for a moment and some glimmer of enlightenment dawn in those big unhappy eyes. I could almost see his befuddled brain trying to turn over like a car engine that's been left too long without firing up. His usually slack jaw tightened, his tongue came out of his mouth and his dull eyes suddenly became, if only for a fleeting moment, alive and alert. Fuck me, Wayne was thinking. I pressed on in case we started bawling our eyes out and hugging like two raving eggs.

'Live everyday like it's your last' I blurted.

'Dream as if you'll live forever. Live as if you'll die today!'

Wayne was lapping these up and couldn't get enough of them. I didn't understand most of them myself so fuck knows what he was making of them. To me they were mostly just meaningless words cobbled together to give losers a few seconds of hope before they continued on their desperate and meaningless way into the bottomless pit of their shitty, dull lives. Wayne was standing up straight and smiling and nodding along though, hanging on to my every word and this was the happiest I'd ever seen him so I dug deep.

'Real eyes realise real lies!' What did that even fucking mean? It didn't matter at this stage because with every new sentence our Wayne was becoming more and more animated.

'Too many cooks spoil the broth!' I threw in that one to see if it made any difference to our Wayne's enjoyment. It didn't.

'Broth!' shouted Wayne.

'You can take a horse to water but you can't make it drink!'

'I fucking love horses Johnny' Beamed Wayne. Retards always prefer animals to humans I thought to myself. Surely he must know I was taking the piss with these last two?

'You can't hurry love! You just have to wait!'

'Fucking love the Supremes Johnny!' shouted Wayne

Well fuck me that was a turn up. Who would have thought that our Wayne would have spotted that one? He didn't even say Phil Collins. Good lad. I decided to stop being a prick and dredge up some more chicken in a basket inspiration.

'Life is not about waiting for the storm to pass. It's about learning to dance in the rain!'

This one brought back a memory of Ricky Lake talking directly at the camera at the end of one of her shows and saying exactly this as I was pressed right up against the TV screen and trying to get my dick in her mouth. I remember it so well because as I came the camera cut to the audience and I emptied my load all over a close-up of the pixilated face of an old black woman wearing an ill- fitting wig and I was fucking furious. But as the old adage goes, 'everything happens for a reason' because our Wayne was now having the time of his life.

'Everything happens for a reason!'

'You've already said that one Johnny.' Said Wayne suddenly looking crestfallen.

'I know that Wayne. I was just reiterating' I replied trying to cheer him back up.

'What's that fucking mean Johnny?
68

'It means if a thing is worth saying then it's worth saying twice!' I replied triumphantly, thinking that I may have made that one up myself.

'Oh Okay Johnny, good one.' Replied Wayne who was now back on board.

'You miss 100% of the shots you don't take!'

Wayne acted out taking a penalty and cheered as he scored an imaginary goal. He was actually happy for the first time in his life and I wasn't in too bad a mood now either.

'Life is like a game of two halves but at least you get to eat an orange!'

'Wayne looked unimpressed with that one so I decided not to make any more of my own up.

'You do one Wayne!' I shouted at his reflection in the mirror.

He paused for a bit then shouted excitedly, 'One up the bum, no harm done!'

I laughed out loud. 'Yes Wayne perfect! Do another one!'

'Have a break… Have a Kit Kat!'

'Again!' I shrieked excitedly

'Because I'm worth it!' Shouted Wayne and comically tossed back his hair. I'm in bits now and laughing hysterically.

'Just do it!'

'That's Asda price!' He shouted and slapped himself twice on the arse.

'Gillette … the best a man can get!'

'Maybe she's born with it.' Both of us together… 'Maybe it's fucking Maybelline!'

'I can't believe it's not fucking butter!'

Wayne was getting all the limelight now so I butted in again.

''Your limitation is your imagination!'

'Push yourself because no-one else is going to do it for you!'

'Great things never come from comfort zones!'

Wayne was hopping from one foot to the other and grinning again. We were back on a roll now.

'The harder you work for something the greater you'll feel when you achieve it!'

'Sometimes later becomes never. Do it now!'

It suddenly dawned on me that I must have unconsciously remembered these quotes while I was wanking off to the presenter as they were saying them at the end of their particular shows. Even Oprah. I decided at that moment to have an honorary wank about the three of them as soon as I could find the time. Maybe I'd take the three of them from behind while they were banging on about inspiring and empowering women of colour or fat birds or something along those lines but for now I was busy trying to inspire and empower our Wayne.

'Dream it! Wish it! Do It!' I continued.

'Success doesn't find you, oh fucking no Wayne, you have to fucking well go out and get it!' I was adlibbing around a few now just for added emphasis.

'Dream bigger. Do bigger baby!'

'Don't stop when you're mother fucking tired Wayne. Stop when you're mother fucking done!'

'Wake up with determination bitch! Go to bed when you're done!'

Each sound bite one was an orgasm. Fuck me even I thought that was an awful lot of wanks. How did I ever find the time?

70

'Do something today that your future self will thank you for!'

Suddenly I got a flashback of trying to smash one out all over the face of Trisha as she was summing up about domestic abuse, when I over -shot and came all over the back of the TV. Most of it slid down between the grooves into the bits with all the wires and stuff and it started to smoke and give off a very peculiar smell. At least I didn't have to bother to clean that particular bout up because it got cooked.

'It's going to be hard but hard does not mean impossible!'

Their contexts were now all coming back to me. This last one was Oprah, trying to get house bound women to start exercising with household items. I came while watching a group of clinically obsess women dancing around the studio unconvincingly while holding a tin of baked beans in each hand.I think that was also the time I tried to, unsuccessfully, train our Satan to lick my spunk off the television screen to save me doing it. Not lick it off obviously. I meant clean it off. I ended up smearing cheap dog food all over it and he still wouldn't go near it so I ended up grabbing our old table cloth, giving it a quick wipe around then putting it back on the table. It was summer and after a few days even mum noticed the stench and eventually threw it out.

'Don't wait for opportunity. Create it!'

'Success is not final! Failure is not fatal! It is the courage to continue that counts!'

I think that one was actually Winston Churchill but I don't think I've ever wanked off about him. I have over Margaret Thatcher though. A lot. Especially during the Falklands war. What is it about old women in hair nets driving tanks?

'We know what we are but not what we may be!'

That one was William Shakespeare. I know that because I was in English once and Maria Barnes was stood at the front of the class quoting some bird off Hamlet and when she spoke her face went all red and her nipples poked through her school blouse and I think the whole class got a hard-on including Dinky Doulton, our English teacher. Prior to that I'd always assumed that he was bent like the rest of them. He was definitely a paedo though, the dirty bastard getting off on that poor girl's embarrassment.

There was a sudden moment of hiatus.

'I could hit the cunts back.' Wayne suddenly muttered, almost to himself.

'I could hit all them cunts back and then they would be the sad cunts and I would laugh at them and they would be the fucking moron, spastic, cunts.' My immediate thought was that even though that sentence was grammatically fucked it was the longest one I'd ever heard him say. Although if I was being brutal I also thought that if he did hit them back he would still be a moron, spastic cunt as he so elegantly put it, Bt at least some progress was being made and this was no time for pedantry. Or the time to correct his appalling sentence structure. He stood up straight and stared at himself in the mirror. To me and I think, also to our Wayne, he now somehow seemed twice his usual size.

'Sieze the fucking day, ain't it Johnny.' He muttered. A gauze seemed to lift from Wayne's eyes and they became clear and even sparkled. He definitely looked different. He took off his coat, then his jumper and then his T-shirt, flexed in the mirror theatrically and started doing strong man poses. He stunk like fuck and he was still a fat bastard that much was true but he also had a lot of muscle going on under it all. I decided to keep my clothes on.

He then began to get more and more animated and hyperactive. He stared at himself long and hard then began to pace up and down punching the air and doing theatrical – really bad - karate kicks and shouting, 'Whaaaa! Hi yah! Jackie Chan! Hong Kong Phooeychop! Honk Kong phooey chop! Jackie Chan! Whaaaa!' I thought that he'd actually flipped his lid. I thought that all the beatings and bullying and turmoil in our Wayne's shitty life up until now had pushed the fucker over the edge and he was never coming back. I looked at him working himself up into a frenzy and thought to myself that anything could happen from here on in. And the best part was that I was already relishing the unpredictable nature of it.

72

I guess that maybe I should have calmed him down or tried to reason with him, but I didn't. Fuck that shit. I was loving the whole spectacle and at that moment I realized that the best thing I'd ever done up until that time was never to lay even one finger on him. There were many, many times when he was such an annoying cunt I could have happily kicked the shit out of him and he would have just taken it. But that day never came and on this auspicious of days my restraint had paid off.

He stared deep into my blood shot eyes. My head was fucked and a million thoughts were whirling around it but I knew that at that moment he was going down his hit list to see if I was on it. His was an extensive list and it took, what I perceived to be, a hell of a long time to go through it. Fuck me Wayne please don't find a reason to kick my head in. My life flashed before me. Had there actually been any occasions when I'd given him a slap or belittled him in any way like most of the people he'd come into contact with over the years? Eventually he looked at me with kind eyes, smiled and drew me in for, what to my relief, was a bear hug. He held me for what seemed like an eternity but was probably less than a minute. In all our childhood years I realised that we'd never hugged each other or anyone else for that matter. Neither had we ever been hugged. Once I'd realised that he wasn't going to crush me to death it felt good and whether it was the drugs or just the fact that someone was holding me for the first time in my life my body relaxed and I began to cry. Then Wayne began to cry. I put my arms around him and we hugged and we sobbed. Big, heaving, guttural sobs. I didn't give a fuck what we looked like because it felt so fucking great. Wow what a rush. Wayne smelled so putrid and I undoubtedly did too but we didn't care. I'd never in my whole life felt so fucking wonderful. To be held was the best feeling in the world. At that moment I felt that I would never want to let go. We were holding each other and sobbing and sobbing and holding each other and snot was pouring out of my nose and mouth and I didn't give a fuck. I felt what could only be described as love for the first time in my life and it was fucking awesome. I could feel Wayne's huge bulk but he wasn't just fat he was just huge and powerfully strong. Then I felt his cock get hard and pushed the cunt off me. 'Fuck me Wayne you massive fucking bender! Then we were both laughing and crying and I had tears running down my face and, to be honest, if I wasn't full of amphetamine I'd like to think that I would have had a hard-on too.

73

Wayne got dressed and put on his coat. He looked at me wild eyed again and the moment passed. He was psyching himself up again and becoming more and more manic. 'Jackie Chan' he whispered and grinned. Wayne lunged towards me. If I hadn't emptied my bowels earlier in the day I know that I would have literally shit myself. 'Jackie Chan!' His face was inches from mine. I could smell his breath - pickled onion monster munch and Rola Cola- and also his spittle hitting me. He grabbed me in a headlock and I seriously thought he was going to snap my neck but he didn't he just ruffled my hair and let go. Fuck me I could have cried with relief. Jesus Christ, talk about mixed signals.

'Hey ho let's go! Shoot 'em in the back now! 'Said Wayne 'Johnny Go! Go! Go!' He yelled excitedly and I, trembling for all sorts of reasons, grabbed my coat and shouted my favourite quote from Johnny Rotten, 'Let's go to war!'

Chapter seven

We ran down the stairs. 'Where the fuck are you two cunts going?' My dad had clearly got bored of whimpering in the shed and was pissed that I'd ignored him. He was in our living room looking hung-over and sullen and patently looking for a fight.

'Was that you lying in the corner of the shed earlier?' I said to him, ignoring his question.

'I said, where the fuck are you two ugly little shit cunts going!' He stood up and stumbled over to where we were, eyes all bloodshot, scowling and automatically taking off his belt. Before I could say anything our Wayne sauntered over to him and head butted him. I heard a loud crack as my dad's nose broke and sprayed his blood all over the place. He fell backwards onto the floor.

'One! Two! Three! Wayne was standing over him and giving him a boxing count. 'Four! Five! Six! Seven! Eight! Nine! Ten! 'Aaaand he's out! He's out! ' Wayne was dancing around the living room and showboating like Mohammed Ali. 'Floats like a butterfly, stings like a bee!' he shouted while throwing punches in the air and doing a very passable impression of the Ali shuffle. Fuck me, my dad was unconscious on the floor. I went to the kitchen, emptied all the cups and plates out of the washing up bowl, filled it full of cold water, came back into the living room and threw its contents in my dad's face. Even though the shock of the icy water revived the fucker I slapped him a couple of times liked I'd seen in films and he opened his eyes not quite knowing where the fuck he was.

'In answer to your question, dear Papa, I can only think that we're going down to the park.' Then, utilising Karmic law as I understood it coupled with, what I thought under the circumstances was a valiant attempt at the 'crane' as seen in *The Karate Kid*, I kicked the cunt as hard as I could in the nuts as I, in my best Kung Fu voice, screeched, 'Jackie Chan!'. Which was lost on my dad but made our Wayne laugh for possibly only the second time, up until now, in his sorry life.

'I'll do time for the fucking pair of you and I'll do her too. I'll take my belt to the feckin' lot of yas.' My dad muttered this almost imperceptibly but we both heard it. Wayne was already heading for our front door but then he turned and stared at my dad. I guess if it was a film, once I'd understood what was about to happen I would have said something like,' No Wayne, stop! He's not worth it! He's had enough! Or some old shit like that but I knew exactly what was about to happen and I couldn't fucking wait. Wayne came back into the living room and slowly walked towards our father.

'Fuck off out Wayne you stupid little fucker before I really hurt you and that sarcastic little runt of a brother!' Said my dad but I could tell by his tone and the pleading look in his eyes that he also knew what was about to happen.

'Sarcastic little runt? Well that was hurtful. Now Dad, would you like to say your last confession or shall we just let our Wayne get on with it?' We heard him literally shit his pants and I suddenly wondered if it was the pair that I'd had a wank into early. It's funny what pops into one's mind on occasions like these.

'FUCK you TWO CUNTS!' replied my dad but with no real conviction. The belt was already unbuckled so as Wayne tugged at it, it flew out of the loops with that dreaded whoosh sound that we were all so familiar with. Wayne triumphantly waved it around his head repeatedly. I looked at my brother who was having the time of his life and relishing this new found freedom and then I looked at my dad lying in his own shit and now curled up into the foetal position.

'Don't Son, please don't I beg you Son. I promise I'll never lay a finger on anyone in this family ever again! I'm sick; I've got cynical depression! I'm sorry boys I'm sorry for everything! Please give me a chance to redeem myself and make everything right! Please boys!' pleaded my father.

Cynical depression? I laughed out loud. Well this was a change of tack to say the least. He was now begging for mercy when two minutes ago he was threatening to murder the fucking lot of us. What a pathetic little man he really was. All those years of abuse and now look at him lying on the floor in a crumpled mess. What the fuck had we been afraid of for all these years?

'It clinical depression you've got you stupid cunt, not cynical' I say. 'Anyway you don't have clinical depression at all because I know all about your little benefit scam. You're just a fucking lazy fat fuck and I fucking hate you' Then I leaned down and spat into his face. There wasn't a lot of spit that came out though. I think I was very dehydrated and whizzing off my tits didn't help but anyway it was more of a gesture.

'You fucking little cunt you've always been a cheeky little bastard wait 'til I get my hands on you I'll fucking kill you!' rasped my dad. Fuck it, in for a penny, I kicked him in the head. I'm not the biggest of lads and it didn't seem to do him too much harm but it made me feel a lot better. I pretended to give him a second one and he flinched and cowered and cradled his head in his hands which made me feel great because he'd done that to us so many times over the years. He was too lazy to even beat us properly. I didn't really think about the consequences of all this at the time of course I was just caught up in the moment. My dad uncovered his head and turned his attention to Wayne who was still gleefully waving aloft my dad's belt like a prize fighter who'd just won the biggest fight of his life, which of course was actually true.

'Wayne Son please don't! You might accidentally kill me and they'll lock you up in prison for the rest of your life, or put you in Borstal with some real nasty fuckers and you'll be beaten and raped every single day!' My dad was almost grovelling now. Wayne stopped waving the belt and looked quizzically down at our dad lying on our living room floor covered in blood and shit with tears streaming down his worn out face. He suddenly looked very old and weak, all his former strength and power whether real or imagined had now deserted him. Wayne smiled at my dad and in a very chilling and cold manner simply said, 'Next!' He then brought down the buckle of that infamous belt into my dad's face. Time after time he lifted up that symbol of fear and control all through our childhood down on to the face of our father. The first blow cut him deep across his cheek, opening it up revealing bone and tissue and an awful lot of blood. The second blow literally embedded the buckle into my dad's left eye socket and Wayne had to stop and pull it out which pissed us both off as it interrupted his rhythm. It was anyone's guess where the next blow would land and a
77

couple of times he missed all together and nearly hit me so I took it off him and had a go myself. My aim was even worse though and I ended up bruising my own leg really quite badly. Wayne took it off me again and started swinging it with two hands, a bit like an axe, which worked okay but to my mind had less romance to it. My dad was now cut to ribbons and I started to worry about the mess on the floor. Our mum would go fucking mental. Then I suddenly thought fuck it who cares anymore? This time tomorrow we would be in Borstal getting raped anyway so she'd have to clean it herself, the lazy cow.

'Do you want a drink Wayne?' I was suddenly parched.

'Yeah go on then' he replied. 'Fucking exhausting beating the shit out of one's dad isn't it our Wayne?' I said and he laughed. I handed him a mug full of water as Wayne never touched alcohol and got myself a beer from the fridge. Wayne glugged down his water and suddenly became preoccupied. His head suddenly shot up like a Meer cat.

'I need to go down to the park' he said, almost to himself.

'Yeah fuck it, drink up and let's go. It stinks in here anyway.' I replied, and looking down at the shattered remains of our father continued, 'You don't live here anymore Dad. Your reign of terror is over. The McQueen is dead long live the McQueen. If you're still here when we get back I'm going to kill you.' Then I jumped on his head, drank the rest of the beer, racked up and snorted another line and then we both left our house to continue our teenage rampage.

We bounded down the street full of fucking beans to say the least. This was the beginning of a brand new dawn for me and our Wayne. We were finally going to get the respect that we had deserved around here and, more importantly, all the rewards that being feared and respected would bring. Lots of money and lots of fanny. An all-day, all you can eat, full English of prime gash. Well I would anyway. Our Wayne had finally found his strength but a lady would still have to be mentally ill or blind with no sense of taste or smell to ever want anything to do with him in any sexual way. Who knew for certain though? Either way things were certainly going to be a lot different for us now, I could feel it.

Wayne was like a man possessed by a man on a mission as he thundered down the street with me barely able to keep pace. 'Fucking hang on Wayne you cunt!' I shouted suddenly remembering his new status as a hard man and making a mental note not to ever call the cunt a cunt ever again. He barely acknowledged me and just continued to jog down the road with his eyes fixed straight ahead. I wondered if we should stop and make a plan.

'Wayne! Wayne, hold up! Let's stop and make a plan!' I shouted.

'I've already got a plan Johnny' replied Wayne.

Well fuck me I didn't know what which more shocking, Wayne actually formulating a plan in that thick head of his or him actually stringing coherent sentences together. I could not wait to see Wayne's strategy come into effect as I bounded eagerly after him. I'm not a hero or much of a fighter. I'm more of a, run like fuck, or hide behind some kids or birds kind of guy. I'm in the self-preservation society and I'm the only member. I'm not a coward. I just think that if there's going to be a fight it should be evenly matched and fair. You don't see bullies picking on guys that are bigger than them or look harder do you? That would be fucking ridiculous. Except little guys. They would. But generally speaking people starting fights are usually fairly sure that one way or another they're not going to lose and end up looking like a cunt. Out of all the times I was bullied it was never a fair fight. Usually there was a ringleader, typically short and angry or from a dysfunctional family. 'Fuck me bruv, so your uncle bummed you on a drunken Saturday night and your mum is a crack whore? So fucking what? Write shitty urban poems about it and become a counsellor you cliché and take your boot off my fucking neck.' Then you've got the henchmen, usually big fat, thick-necked cunts who are essentially bodyguards for the little Hitleresque pigmy leader. If there was ever a time when there was the chance of a fair fight I'm sure I would have taken it. It hadn't happened so far though.

They say that for girls the bullying is more of a psychological nature and much more harmful and long lasting. That that may indeed be so, but if you've ever been kicked in the nuts and then winded and punched in the nose by three guys all at the same time it really does hurt like fuck and is also rather humiliating. I can't help thinking getting called, goofy cunt, or fat ass or slag or not letting you hang around with them during play time might be a tad preferable. We all like to see a good punch up if it's a fair fight or involving two cunts that you don't like but even as kids, if it's too one sided there's no real thrill in watching. Unless it is on the very rare occasions when two fit girls are going toe to toe then that's entirely different. That's a fucking wank fest and fuck the morality of those erotically charged clashes.

Julie Simpson and Vicky Flanagan had a tear up one lunch time and I think that kept the third year boys, and I'd like to think, some of the fitter girls, wanking for the rest of the term. Mr Swann (Science) and Miss Ryder, (P.E) were on playground duty at the time and seemed to take a hell of a long time to break it up. And who would have blamed them? It was sexy as fuck. I still have the odd tug over that one even now. There are certain unspoken rules when two lads have a fight. There's always a certain protocol one has to follow, especially if there is an audience. Typically, and of course there are a plethora of exceptions, you have the fighter and the fightee, attack and defence. The instigator circling its prey, fists up like they've seen on the tele and throwing insults, 'Come on then you cunt, let's have it!' the fightee usually doesn't want to say too much in case it provokes and escalates the situation and is just praying for divine intervention or spontaneous combustion. I've been on the receiving end of many a beating as I may have mentioned, so I'm speaking from experience here. The perpetrator plays with its prey like a cat with a mouse, goading and toying. The whole thing usually lasts for less than five minutes in reality but at the time it feels like an eternity. Because of the crowd one must try not to beg or plead for mercy and in my case I used my only form of defence and that was sarcastic humour. I knew that eventually the chances were I was going to get fucked up but if I could get a few laughs in on the way to accident and emergency then for me that was a small, if some might say, pathetic, victory. I'd glance at the crowd and say things like, 'Give my brain to medical science if I die today guys!' Or, 'not the face! I'm modelling at the weekend!' Sometimes if I was friends with someone in the crowd I'd give them a name check, 'Danny if I die today I want you to have my porn collection and tell my mum I died a hero!' One time the guy who was fighting me actually laughed out loud and said,' Johnny you're a really funny fucker' but then as I was taking a rueful bow I let down my guard and got punched in the jaw and went down like a sack of shit. I mean it wasn't Saturday night at the London Palladium material but I'd usually get a few laughs and that would give me some kind of comfort before the inevitable pasting. More often than not though, it would be a few groans and someone would shout out, 'Fucking get on with it!' which would thankfully speed up the whole process and I would get kicked and punched to the ground and that would be it. At least in a one sided fight, the spectators would usually get a bit of a spectacle, a confident display by the favourite, a few witty asides from the underdog and a knock down.

The worst kind of fight was between two amateurs. These types of fights usually happened by accident. Someone pushes in at the dinner queue or bumps into someone in the corridor which leads to verbal insults and pushing and shoving... and the next thing these poor cunts know, they've been encircled by a baying mob clapping in unison and shouting the immortal words, 'Fight! Fight! Fight!' Happy fucking days for everyone except the two poor mugs who now have to, at least half-heartedly, have a scrap. In this scenario both participants give it a lot of verbal but it's a lot less threatening in case of escalation, neither cunt wants that. In this situation both combatants are subtly trying to give the other one a get out. 'You pushed in!' 'No you pushed in!' 'You shoved me as you ran by!' 'No I was pushed into you by someone else!' 'Ahhh so it was just a case of a misunderstanding! Well let's shake hands, forget the whole thing and be on our way then shall we?' Yeah, not a fucking chance. The gathered crowd will not let that happen. We've come to see a fight and a fight we shall have. 'Fight! Fight! Fight!' It's on bitches. Whether you like it or not, there's going to be a fight. Typically one of the older boys will usually say something like, 'if one of you two cunts don't start hitting the other one I'm going to hit the fucking pair of you!' The die is now cast and from here on in it's about damage limitation, both to one's reputation and to one's face and or bollocks. In the unlikely event that one of the two would be a boxer or martial art expert and plucks up enough courage to actually throw a punch or some kind of karate chop in the vague direction of their

81

opponent this adds an extra dimension to the proceedings. Once I saw a boy try and do a roundhouse karate style move and get it completely wrong, lose direction and accidently kick Vicky Brennan right in the tits. He ended up beaten to fuck by her and her gang of hatchet faced slags. I was wanking for days about that one and kind of envied him, especially the bit where he got punched in the bollocks because, however you dress it up, that's still a female hand on the gonads. Lucky cunt.

Usually though it's pushing and shoving and name calling and a bit of wrestling on the ground until it's either broken up by a teacher or everyone just wanders off due to apathy. Then both participants get up, brush themselves off and go off in different directions with their respective mates bullshitting that they won the fight but knowing that they've both been humiliated and their reputations, already non-existent, have now become less than fuck all. They are usually good at maths or English though so at least they can cling desperately to that, although at that moment they'd both trade academic ability for physical strength and a massive pair of bollocks. Nobody remembers who got the top marks in the science exam but everyone remembers who the two poofs were dry humping each other for ten minutes in the playground that time. For ever and ever.

'Alright Dave I haven't seen you in thirty years! What's that you're a multi-millionaire married to a Russian super model and you've got a fleet of classic cars? That's great mate! What a female super model? The last time I saw you, you were bum fucking that other kid in the east block playground. I naturally thought that you two would have made a go of it? Do you still keep in touch?'

'No'

'Shame because you looked good together. Anyway see you around.' It never goes away. The best thing one can do after that is move to the other side of the country and keep your head down for the rest of your life. Or just die.

So anyway, there I was chasing after our Wayne on this bright sunny afternoon and we were heading full pelt towards the park. For a big lad our Wayne was a spritely thing and he was miles ahead of me even though I was still very full of amphetamine.

I wanted to stop and reflect and formulate a plan. There were always fucking loads of kids down there and they were a lot older than me and even Wayne. My plan was to creep up on them and do a stealth attack mainly using Wayne as infantry with me a safe distance away throwing bottles and stones. Like in those films where the main protagonist is fighting his way through a crowd of bad cunts cutting and slashing as he goes and just when it looks like he's going to triumph all on his own one of the bad guys catches him unawares and just as he's about to kill our hero a bottle comes flying through the air and knocks out the villain. I'm the cunt who threw the bottle from a safe distance, the hero of the piece. Simple.

Our Wayne wasn't aware of this plan though and as I turned the corner leading into the park I witnessed him nonchalantly pick up a brick from a nearby garden and casually walk over to the bench on which sat five of the biggest cunts in town. The infamous Oakhill Gang. I don't mean they were physically big. I mean that, on a scale of cuntishness, these cunts were as far to the right of the scale as one could be without falling into the abyss of eternal cunt hell.

These were the same pricks who had robbed me and humiliated me for as long as I could remember. You had the ring leader Mickey Smith, a tall, stringy mother fucker. I guess he was the brains, although I always thought he was thick as pig shit personally. Then you had Debbie something or other, fuck knows what her second name was, but she was a fat cow and even I would have thought twice about giving her one, that's how ugly she was. Well okay I would have fucked her but only from behind and on a pill. When we were very young I remember that we had two cats, Puff-Puff and Specko. Specko was the silverback. The Daddy. He would be off all day fucking other cats and fighting and generally behaving like a fucking Don while Puff- Puff stayed close to home and didn't do very much at all, apart from fart like a cunt and sleep. They both lived in our shed and every day, when my mum wasn't such a lazy drunken fuck, she would put down a plate of food for them, but Specko would always eat both and to be honest I didn't blame the cunt because I figured he needed it more than lazy bones because he was using more energy bowling all over town giving it the large one, so I never intervened. Plus fuck it, they were only cats so fuck them. Well the point being that even with traipsing around town hell raising and carrying on he still became fat as fuck while Puff-Puff looked positively skeletal and when I ever saw Mickey and Debbie together I always thought of those two cats and always smirked at the thought, which wound up the pair of them no end but I truly couldn't stop myself, especially when I thought of the time when I put a banger up Puff-Puff's arse hole and lit it. Listen, I didn't know at the time how fucked up that was, every kid used to torture animals back in the day and plus it didn't even die. In fact I think it must have eventually starved to death so if anyone is to blame it was Specko, God rest his soul.

Mickey came up with this classic after which they say that Bob Dylan and John Lennon gave up writing, 'Wayne, Wayne he's got no brain. Where is it? It's down the drain!' I mean it wasn't exactly fucking Shakespeare now was it? But every time they saw our Wayne everyone would start chanting it and then eventually one of them would give him a slap. Also there were the three runners or prospects as they would have preferred to be called. Benny Whitehouse, Kenneth Davey and Matty Bell. Who the fuck calls a kid Benny or Kenneth for fuck's sake? I can't help but feel that this could have been part of their problem. Giving a kid a shit name is child abuse.

Benny though? Benny and Kenny sound like a shit double act that you'd find on ITV. Matty Bell was obviously called (behind his back because he was a spiteful little shit cunt) 'Bellend.' These three used to run around on their bikes dealing daughters and Henrys, which Mickey would hand over to them and they'd distribute all around town. (Oh yeah a daughter is a 'quarter' of an ounce of weed or hash, and a Henry is an 'eighth'...Henry the eighth, get it? Subtle I know and I'm certain that to this day the cops never cracked this code). Say one thing for my dad his gear was a fuck of a lot better than the shit these pricks were selling mostly to school kids and single mums. Mickey more than likely bought it off my old man to be fair and I didn't dislike him for dealing shit drugs at inflated prices I disliked him for constantly beating the shit out of me and our Wayne and also that he was a fucking knob end. If you wanted to be a drug lord you needed to surround yourself with henchmen and that's what Mickey did. He'd pay them in drugs and booze. As Mickey was 21 he could go into pubs and off licences and buy cheap cider and beer and this was what he did and that's fair exchange I guess. I'd seriously thought about doing it myself since

I had a ready supply at home anyway and my parents were usually too fucked to notice if I had any of it away. I'd dreamed of starting out like Mickey then building my empire slowly but surely like any self-respecting gangster. Of course I did, we all did around our way. Nobody had any legal ambitions, the chances of any cunt around here becoming doctors or high court judges or fucking rocket scientists was remote to say the least and it didn't even occur to any of us that this could be possible. We didn't even think about that possibility. He sporty kids wanted to be professional footballers and the rest of us wanted to be drug dealers. The girls all wanted to either get pregnant as soon as possible in order to secure a council flat or if they were ambitious, work in a hair dressers. And if the odd kid did have aspirations of bettering themselves in any legal way they had their fucking head kicked in.

My ambush plan went out the window as Wayne strode up to Mickey with a brick in his hand. 'What the fuck are you going to do with that then retard?' Said Mickey, all full of bravado as he looked at the brick and glanced around at his mates. 'Wayne, Wayne he's got no brain…' Bellend chimed in with a sneer on his face. I'd caught up now and was standing there empty handed, scared shitless and full of drugs. Mickey looked at me and said, 'Fuck me he's got back up!' and they all started laughing.

'Fuck you Mickey, you lanky streak of piss' I replied, and it suddenly occurred to me that I was shaking like a shitting dog. We needed a plan and fortunately for me our Wayne had one.

From that moment on everything became slow motion and high definition Technicolor. Wayne stood toe to toe with Mickey and with the immortal words, 'Shoot dem balls,' Wayne lifted the brick and brought it down on the top of Mickey's head. Fuck me the sound of brick on bone is a sound I'll never forget, like a spoon cracking an egg but with more bass. Thud. Blood pissed out of Mickey's skull like a firework, it was really quite beautiful to be honest. Wayne caught a face full of it, and as Mickey stared at him in utter disbelief, he smiled and licked his lips, 'Mother's milk.' Said Wayne. It was a surreal moment and I remember wondering whether he'd have a different little sound bite every time he fucked someone up. Mickey's legs buckled from under him and he went down. Wayne, still with the brick in his hand (well to be accurate it was now a half brick), smashed it into Mickey's face with a
85

satisfying crunch. Mickey's nose flattened itself against the brick resulting in a torrent of more blood. Mickey was now choking, and as he struggled for breath, I could see that most of his teeth had gone.

'Harsh but fair our Wayne, harsh but fair' I heard myself say and was impressed by my own calmness. I think in retrospect I'd retreated into my own head and convinced myself that it was all a dream so I might as well enjoy it. The next thing I heard was Debbie scream. A blood curdling scream of such a high pitch I heard a dog bark instinctively in the distance.

'Debbie you seem upset. What's wrong?' I enquired.

'Get the fuck off him Wayne you mental cunt! You've killed him!' she screamed as she stared at her beloved with utter disbelief.

'Now Debbie, that's a serious allegation to make towards my brother, please apologise and we will say no more about it' I replied.

'What the fuck is wrong with you?!' She shrieked back.

'Now Debbie you're getting yourself at it now aren't you? You're not thinking straight. It's obvious isn't it? Mickey here' - I nodded in the direction of Mickey who is now barely conscious lying on the floor with Wayne standing over him getting his breath back still clutching what was left of the brick - 'and Benny and Kenneth and young Bellend, and to be honest Debbie, you too; you've all been very rude and disrespectful to our Wayne over the years, and I've got to say, and to me too, so what the fuck did you think was going to happen? Debbie,' - I walked over to her and held her by her shoulders - 'look at me Debbie' – I held her head in both my hands - 'Debbie, please look at me. Did you, for one second, think about the consequences of your actions? Hmmm? Debbie? How did you think it was all going to pan out in the long term? Did you think about it at all? No? Did you think that we'd all just get old and you cunts would be beating the shit out of us day after day for ever and ever amen? This day was bound to happen now wasn't it? If you'd thought about it for even one second Debbie this day was bound to happen, I mean look at the size of our Wayne... isn't he a big, fine, strapping young man? Look at those hands all covered in

Mickey's blood. Aren't they like two shovels Debbie? Say yes Debbie, please Debbie...say that our Wayne's hands, that are covered in your boyfriend's blood, and I think I can see teeth and bits of bone too, are like shovels and also say sorry for all these years of bullying him and me too while you're at it, you ugly... fat... cunt.' Debbie looked at me with what I can only describe as utter disregard and contempt in her eyes and spat in my face. I felt a strong urge to head-butted her. So that's what I did. Considering that this was my first head butt, I was rather pleased with it. I brought my forehead directly down onto the bridge of her nose and split the fucking thing in half.

'Debbie, I want you to walk over to our Wayne and say sorry please.' I said this in my best telephone voice or what I imagine would be my telephone voice if I'd ever made or received a telephone call. Debbie seemed more preoccupied with holding her nose together at this point, so I grabbed her by her hair and marched her over towards Wayne and Mickey.

'Benny, me old sparring partner, question...do you have any parents or siblings?' Benny looked like he was going to try and make a run for it and this would have no doubt inspired the rest of the remaining gang to do the same. Benny looked very pale, almost grey and I suddenly saw what a pathetic little outfit they truly were.

'Benny, have you gone deaf?' I said to him.

'What?' he stammered. I laugh out loud even though I'm sure that Benny didn't mean that little joke.

'Good one Benny. Now do you have any parents or siblings, or pets?'

'What's a sibling' he replied. I think this is the first real conversation I'd ever had with Benny and I wasn't exactly over stimulated by it.

'A sibling is another term for brothers or sisters. Do you have any brothers or sisters, parents, grandparents or fucking pets you cunt? And bear in mind that before you answer I know most of these answers already, although I'm not sure about grandparents. I know for example that you have a sister because I've had quite a few

87

wanks about her and to be honest quite a few over your mum too. Mother and daughter stuff.' - I mimed myself ejaculating over the pair of them - Anyway I digress, answer the fucking question Benny'

Don't ask me why, too many violent movies perhaps or for the theatricality or fucking this and that but at that moment I thought it would be appropriate to enforce my question by kicking Mickey in the bollocks. It was hardly worth it because he was barely alive by the looks of him but I think I got my point across because Benny immediately got the gist.

'Yes I've got a Mum and a Dad, Nanny and Grandpops, Aunty Sue, our dog, and two older sisters. He replied meekly.

'I didn't ask about aunties and uncles but I know you've been under a lot of stress recently so we will let that slide. Now then if you three cunts move one inch we will kill your mums and your fucking nans and any fucking pets you have and all your brothers and sisters and even Aunty fucking Sue and then we will kill you.

So fucking keep still. I think it's better for everyone if we can all just get through this in a civilised and gentlemanly manner. What say you Guys?'

I gave Debbie a very hard dead leg right between the muscles of her somewhat bulky thighs. At this point I think her head had popped and she just let out a disappointing groan.

'Tickles a bit does it Debbie? Have you never had one before? I've had one nearly every day for years Debbie and a great many of them off you and these cunts.' I said while looking around at a lot of sorry fucking faces.

'Right then, if you three nice lads would be so kind as to all sit down quietly on that bench and behave yourselves, Debbie here is going to apologise for being a cunt - and might I add, a fat ugly one too - to me and our Wayne, you then you three can decide in which order you'd also like your fucking heads kicked in okay?' Kenneth literally shat himself at this news.

'Oh for goodness sake Kenneth why did you have to go and do that? Wayne and I do not want shit all over us. Blood is one thing, but we draw the line at shit. Debbie, you're a lady do you have any tissues on you? You know for when you're doing your wardrobe and that? Debbie? Tissues?' I pulled her head sharply back and looked into her broken face.

'Debbie, just answer the fucking question before this whole situation gets out of hand' She slowly put her hand in her coat pocket and pulled out some crumpled toilet paper and tried to hand it to me. 'See, I was right. You ARE a lady!' I said gleefully. 'Now then be a good girl and wipe Kenneth's bottom for him.'

'Fuck off!' said Debbie defiantly.

'Oh Debbie there's no need for spicy language. Where are your maternal instincts? I thought you lot were all friends? Kenneth has done a big uh oh in his pants and as you're the only female here, you've got to fucking clean the cunt up and quickly please, time is of the essence as we have still got a lot to get through'

'Johnny I swear I will kill you, you fucking cunt' she muttered.

'Wayne please be a dear and kick Debbie in the face for me.'

Wayne deftly kicked her in the face.

'Now Debbie let's get Kenneth cleaned up shall we? There's a good girl, we don't have all day.'

I dragged her over to where the boys were patiently sitting.

'Bellend oops, how rude sorry mate, Matty I mean, Matty would you be an absolute angel and help Debbie out here by pulling down this little poofter's jeans please?

'Fuck you' said Matty with little conviction.

'Wayne, is there much of that brick left?'

'A bit' replied Wayne matter- of -factly.
89

I took it from him and smashed it into Matty's face, knocking in his two front teeth.

'We really should have brought along some more weapons, this is getting embarrassing. Wayne could I ask you to please pop off and find some more bricks as this one has seen better days and we've only just got started.'

'Not a fucking problem Johnny' replied Wayne. I felt quite safe by now as Mickey was slipping in and out of consciousness, Debbie seemed a lot more subdued, Kenneth was sat in his own shit, Matty was crying like a fucking baby while looking for his teeth and Benny was silently rocking backwards and forwards on the bench muttering something or other that I didn't catch, although it might have been a prayer.

'Matty I really need you to listen now okay? I want you to pull down Kenneth's jeans and pants so Debbie can clean his little bot bot. Will you do that for me Matty? Say "yes Johnny".'

'Yes Johnny' he replied through blood and snot and tears.

'Brilliant, that's a good Bellend, stand up Kenneth please.'

He got up and Matty undid his belt, unbuttoned his fly and pulled down his jeans and pants.

'Ahh so we meet again!' I said, directing my gaze at Kenny's little cock.

'Fuck me Kenneth is that a vagina?!' I shrieked with mock delight. His cock was fucking ridiculously small and his bollocks were hairless. 'If we had more time and it wasn't caked in shit I'd ask Debbie here to lick you out! A nice bit of girl on girl action for the lads eh guys!?' This didn't get the laugh I was hoping for even though it was hilarious.

'He's all yours now Debbie, get stuck in and be thorough we don't want Kenneth getting a rash do we?' Debbie was a broken woman now and she did what I asked trying as best she could under the circumstances.

90

'That tissue is too dry Debbie, you're just smearing it everywhere! Get it wet! Use some of the blood coming out of Benny's mouth!' I advised.

Debbie duly took the shitty tissue from between Kenneth's legs and dabbed Benny's mouth with it. Benny retched and added a bit more fluid to it which I thought was a touch, and then she began trying to clean up Kenneth's shitty arse which if anything looked worse. 'I think we are going to need some more tissues Debbie, it's worse than I thought. Use your coat.' Said I, helpfully.

Without question she took off her coat and began rubbing it between Kenneth's legs and arse crack. This all seemed quite normal to her now, and Kenneth was patiently letting her do it. She wasn't really getting anywhere to be honest and it wasn't even that sexy so after about five minutes I told her to stop and asked Benny politely to pull up Kenneth's pants and jeans so we could continue proceedings.

'Please, Benny will you pull up Kenneth's pants and jeans?' immediately replied Debbie without a hint of fuss this time.

'Soooo we can continue with proceedings' I whispered in Debbie's ear as I gave her another dead leg but on the opposite side which is a classic and, when it's not being done to you, is hilarious as the recipient tries to walk away. I do love keeping up traditions.

'So we can continue with proceedings' said Debbie. She didn't even react to the dead leg which I found a little disappointing, but I guess she was a little preoccupied.

'Okay then where were we?' I said to no one in particular.

At this point Wayne returned with two more bricks, a large stick and inexplicably a hammer and a screwdriver. Perfect.

'Who's next Johnny?'

'Ahhh that's right. Now then you three, who wants to be next? I'm going to give you a couple of minutes to discuss it amongst yourselves and now as we seem to have an abundance of weaponry you can also discuss which weapon you'd like to see used on
91

the other two. Here's your choices. Brick to the face, Benny I'm counting you out of that one as it doesn't seem fair. Hammer to the knees, ankles, feet and elbows, I don't want to influence anyone but I think that's got Kenneth written all over it but no more shitting yourself Kenneth please as we are all out of tissues and Debbie's coat is already pretty much ruined. Finally, we have a screwdriver through the hands and feet. That one has a certain religious element to it. Is anyone religious here?' Nobody replied.

'Oh I nearly forgot about the stick! Okay a simple stick up the arse inserted by my good friend and Brother Mr. Wayne McQueen. Take a bow Wayne, you're doing a great job.' Wayne solemnly bowed to what I thought was a rather unenthusiastic crowd.

'Okay let's say, two minutes of heated debate then we will crack on as we are rapidly losing light.

Mickey darling I seem to recall that you have a rather splendid watch. Can I have it? Groan once for no and twice for yes.' I said as I kicked him twice in the nut sack It's wasn't even that much fun anymore but he did groan twice so I took my watch off his wrist and put it back on mine.

'Thank you Mickey. You, my friend, are a gentleman. Okay guys you have two minutes to decide each other's fate. Oh and if you don't decide I will, and you won't like that at all. On your marks, get set, wait… wait …okay… Go!'

Within ten seconds the heated debate rapidly turned into a fist fight as they argued as to who should have what done to them. I couldn't help but think if I were them I would have made a run for it and fuck the family's consequences but they didn't and they argued and fought each other for the full two minutes. What I could gather from all that tiresome squabbling was that nobody wanted the stick up their arse and everyone wanted the brick in the face, even Matty. Imagine being in a competition where that was the best option.

'Right time is up, put down your pens and pencils!' I said light heartedly but once again no real laughter came forth. Tough crowd.

'Let's have it then.'

Benny said, 'We all want a brick to the face.'

'That's not an option' I replied. 'At least I'm giving you options, me and our Wayne weren't given any options when you were torturing us now were we?'

Silence.

'Listen you've wasted my time and your own time and also Wayne's and these two need to get to hospital by the looks of them so I'm going to let Wayne decide as it's his special day.'

'No! No!' cried out Benny. 'Kenneth gets the hammer, Bellend the screw driver and I'll take the brick! '

'Okay great now is that your final answer as I'm running out of patience?'

'No fucking way! Cried the other two in unison and Kenneth gave Benny a smack in the mouth.

'Right fuck this. I'm going to have a fag and while I'm doing that our Wayne here is going to decide your fates. Mickey, please can I have a cigarette? Groan once for yes...' I kicked him in the head and took out a packet of fags from his inside pocket, wiped the blood off them and took one out.

'Mickey please can I have your lighter? Groan once for … oh fuck it' I kicked him in the stomach. 'Cheers Mate you're a very generous man.' I found his Zippo and lit the cigarette.

'Use your imagination Wayne' I said.

Wayne immediately sauntered over to where those three cowering fuckers sat and smashed Benny and Kenneth in the face with a brick, breaking noses and splitting lips and smashing in cheek bones.

'Aww they look like triplets!' I said gleefully.
93

'Okay Wayne, that'll do I think they've learned their lesson. Let's go home '

Wayne looked at me almost hurt like he'd been short changed. The four who were still conscious, namely everyone but Mickey relaxed their shoulders and blew out a sigh of relief.

'Oh don't look at me like that Wayne...I'm JOKING! As I said, it's your special day, so fill your fucking boots Dear Brother.' I laughed as I exhaled a large and, what I considered, impressive puff of cigarette smoke to emphasise the cruelty of that last remark.

The bench became a hive of activity, wailing and sobbing and pleading but still nobody thought about running the fuck away. I would have given my parent's names and address and insurance numbers and also those of everyone I knew right at the start. Dick heads

'Happy days our Johnny!' grinned Wayne. He then produced a handful of what looked like 8 inch nails from his pocket.

'Right then. A new proposal has been put forward, any takers? Who wants their legs nailed to this bench that you all seem to fucking love so much?'

'Benny!' shouted the other two in unison.

'That makes a lot of sense to me as Benny tried to fuck you both in the arse didn't he? And if there's one thing that really grinds my gears it's disloyalty. Boys hold the cunt down'

Benny at last tried to make a run for it but Matty tripped him as he ran and he went flying arse over tit. Then without me saying anything, he and Kenneth dragged him back to the bench and held him in place. Wayne may not be the brightest student academically but those nails went into Benny's legs and then into the bench like a knife through butter, straight and true. He would have made an excellent chippy if things had turned out differently. Benny passed out during the second one which was a bit disappointing but, give Wayne his due, he still pressed on and finished the job.

94

'Good lad Wayne, you've done a fine job of that. You should be proud.' Wayne looked very pleased with himself and even blushed with pride. It was really was great to see him smiling.

'Right then you two little pricks who wants to go next?'

'What? What do you mean?' gasped Kenneth in disbelief.

'Sorry was I mumbling? They say that the British eat their words. I'll try and enunciate a bit more. I can only apologise lads, please forgive me.'

'Which. One... Of... you... two... little... cunts... wants... to... go next?' I said pausing on every word in order to make myself crystal clear this time.

'Pricks' said Wayne.

'Correct. Yes they are our Wayne, I don't think we are going to argue about that.' I replied.

'No. I mean pricks, Last time you called them little pricks but now you've called them little cunts.' Countered Wayne.

'Bravo. Bravo that means you were paying attention. Yes, sorry, okay for the final time...which one of you two "pricks"'- I glanced at Wayne who nodded back approvingly - 'would like to have their legs nailed to this bench next?'

'Fuck off Johnny! Fuck off ! We helped you with Benny for fuck's sake!' said Matty.

'Oh and you thought that was enough to let you go? I see. I thought that you were just being agreeable. I was about five the first time you cunts set about me, and now I'm fifteen so you do the maths Matty, that's give or take...Matty how long is that for five points?'

'Eight years?' he mumbled with his head down.

'What!? Eight? No you cunt, it's fucking ten! Fifteen minus fucking five equals fucking ten for fuck's sake! I mean fucking hell Matty, it doesn't get much simpler
95

than that me old mate. So to reiterate my point, you cunts have been beating the shit out of me and our Wayne, you can add another five years or so on to that but in your own time because you're clearly mentally impaired, no offence. So it's hardly fair that ten plus years of torture and humiliation should be boiled down to a simple brick in the fucking face now is it? Kenneth, you've been quiet, what do you think? Give me your honest answer.'

'I don't know'

'You don't know? Okay so Kenneth doesn't know. Matty now you've had time to reflect, what do you think now? Matty? Bellend? Matty?! Wayne, Matty seems to have gone deaf! Now I'm not a doctor but I think he's got blocked wax in his ears. Do you have a syringe full of warm water about your person?'

Wayne actually looked down at himself and fumbled around in his pockets then looked back at me, shook his head and said, 'No Johnny.'

'Fuck it. Okay, take that brick that you've got and take my brick and smash both sides of his fucking head with them and let's see if we can't dislodge some of this pesky wax.'

'No, No! Please fucking no!' pleaded Matty.

Wayne strolled over to him and coolly smashed the two house bricks into both sides of his head like someone banging a cymbal.

'Name that tune!' I said gleefully, but got no response except Matty passing out as blood drizzled out of his ears.

'Fuck it, now we don't know if that worked or not. Can't help thinking that we might have made it worse by the looks of that claret coming out of them. Don't worry Wayne it's not your fault it was my idea, but I think we both had Matty's best interests at heart so fuck it. Plus he's a fucking cunt, so fuck him. Agreed Wayne?'

'Agreed Johnny'

'Now then Kenneth it looks like it's only us three left.' I looked around at the blood soaked bodies of Mickey, pretty much dead now, Debbie, still breathing but unrecognisable and Benny, nailed to the bench but slumped down like one of those ventriloquist dolls but without a hand up its ass. Matty was slumped next to him looking like the elephant man.

'Now then Kenneth I guess out of you five you are the less disagreeable and with those boyish good looks of yours, and if circumstances had been different, we could have conceivably been friends, even wing men if you get my gist. You're a lover not a fighter am I right Kenneth? Although you were off to a poor start by being given the name Kenneth but that wasn't your fault. Anyway I'm starting to bore myself now so let's crack on, long story short I'm going to leave your fate to chance.' I dug into my jeans' pocket for a coin. Nothing.

'Wayne do you have a coin I could borrow?'

Wayne searched his pockets and didn't find anything either.

'Ahhh, so the thing is Kenneth when you've been bullied as much as we have over the years there's certain precautions one must take before leaving the house, one being not carrying any money as it will invariably get robbed off you. Now Kenneth, do you have any money on you?'

'I think there's some change in my front pocket actually.' Replied Kenneth, who'd perked up a bit at this news of a possible reprieve.

'Wayne, be a dear and have a delve into Kenneth's front pockets will you please?'

Wayne strode over and plunged his giant hands into both Kenneth's front pockets simultaneously. He was rummaging about there for a good while and I couldn't help but notice that his mind had wandered away from the subject.

'What the fuck?!' Cried out Kenneth.

'What's up Kenneth?'

'Your brother is touching me up for fuck's sake. Get him off!'

'Our Wayne will get himself off in due course. Sorry Kenneth no can do, you see he's locked on and when he locked on there's nothing you, or I, or anyone can do until it's over.'

'Until what is fucking over!?'

'You really are fucking stupid aren't you Kenneth?'

Wayne had a manic grin on his face and even if you'd have hit him with a truck at this point there was no stopping him.

'Ahhh my cock! He's pulling my cock off!' screamed Kenneth

'Don't exaggerate. Anyway if you don't like it, why is it getting bigger? Are you a homosexual Kenneth? Are you enjoying that? I think you are and so does our Wayne by the size of that thing bulging out of his trousers.' Wayne had an enormous erection and I think it was safe to say that he'd forgotten all about the coins.

'I think at this juncture the best thing to do would be to do nothing. Just lay back and enjoy it. I mean getting wanked off in the park on a lovely sunny day? It could be worse Kenneth it could be a lot, lot worse my dear boy.' I went over to him, held up his head in my two hands and kissed him hard on the mouth. I liked to think it was all part of the humiliation but even with all those drugs inside me I still felt something move in my own jeans. Kenneth, still covered in his own shit with a smashed in face and swollen lips getting ferociously wanked off by my brother was - apart from the tongue lashing from my Aunty Jean - my first kiss. Swoon.

'Kenneth, the quicker you come the quicker we can all move on Mate. If Wayne isn't doing it for you then I don't know, focus on Debbie or something. Shall I lift up her skirt? Give you a bit of titillation? It's a bit of an insult to our Wayne but there's no accounting for taste. No cunt is going anywhere until you've emptied your bollocks into our Wayne's hand.'

I lifted up Debbie's skirt with my foot revealing her underwear which was also now covered in shit.

'Well that's just wrong. I think Debbie should really think about re-evaluating her hygiene routine. I mean that's fucking niche right there isn't it? Maybe that's what Mickey is into? What do you think, Kenneth?' Does Micky have any German blood?

But Kenneth seemed to have taken my advice and had a very determined look on his, once handsome but now destroyed, face.

'That's the spirit Kenneth, focus!'

I lifted up my t-shirt and danced around as erotically as I could.

'There you go Kenneth fill your boots you mucky little queen'

Time seemed to stand still. A moment of calm descended upon the park as the three of us concentrated on Kenneth's imminent orgasm. Our Kenneth must have dug deep inside his wank bank to pull out his ultimate 'go to' fail safe masturbatory fantasy, and hats off to the cunt because after a lot of internal struggle and writhing and groaning he eventually shot his desperate load.

'Well done young Kenneth good boy now that wasn't too bad now was it? Cigarette?'

I put a fag in his mouth and lit it.

'I envy you Kenneth, how was that for you?'

Kenneth didn't reply.

Wayne took out his hand, brought it up to his face and sniffed his fingers. Then put his fingers into his mouth. He swallowed.

'Yukky yukky! Not for me Johnny.' Said Wayne disgustedly.

'Oh no what a shame!' I replied, 'maybe it got mixed in with his shit? That's bound to take the edge off. Bring some over here and let's have a try. It's not every day that you get to taste another man's jittler. Not that I've ever tasted my own of course. Although I've seen a lot of yours over the years am I right our Wayne?'

Wayne gave me a proud smile. He sauntered over to me and held out his hand. I sniffed his fingers then tentatively licked one that had Kenny's spunk on it,

'Creamy, salty, bitter and shitty!' I declared. And looking over to a crest fallen and somewhat humiliated Kenneth said, 'It's a no from me.' What a day for firsts though! Now then no more Tom foolery and fun and games, let's get back to business. Wayne, please can you check Kenneth's pockets for coins and this time try and focus on the job in hand, if you'd be so kind.' I said.

Wayne delved back into Kenneth's jeans and pulled out a handful of change.

'There we go! Fantastic! They were there all along! It pays to be thorough doesn't it?' I said, as I walked over to Wayne and took a ten pence piece off of him. Keep the change Wayne, you've earned it.'

Wayne looked delighted.

'Hang on. While you're there check his back pockets too please Wayne. No, actually, would you be so kind as to stand the cunt up and pad him down?'

Kenneth suddenly looked terrified, and to be honest I didn't blame him. But Wayne simply stood him up and I have to say, frisked him in a very professional and thorough manner. Very thorough.

In Kenneth's back pocket was a wallet and inside his coat was a plastic bag.

'Ooh what have we here then, your fucking packed lunch?'

Wayne handed it all over to me. I opened the wallet and there was about fifty quid in it plus about ten wraps of white powder. Inside the plastic bag was nearly a kilo of weed and numerous other bits of drug paraphernalia.

'Jesus Kenneth, don't you know that drug dealing is illegal? What the fuck would your mother say if she could see all this? She'd say Kenneth you're a very naughty little boy and you should be punished, wouldn't she? Or words to that effect.'

'Fucking hell Johnny, Mickey will kill me if you take that off me!' cried Kenneth.

I look over at Mickey who is still unconscious.

'I think Mickey has got more important things on his mind right now to be honest Kenneth, trying to stay alive for example. I replied and Wayne laughed. It really was great to hear our Wayne laugh and I tried to remember the last time I'd seen him so happy but come up blank.

'The spoils of war mother fucker, heads or tails? *Continued.*

'What?' said Kenneth.

'It's fucking pardon you cunt, not fucking what! Kenneth, fuck me were you dragged up? Say fucking pardon.'

'Pardon' he meekly replied.

'Why? What have you done?' I gleefully replied. And Wayne laughed again. Best. Day. Ever.

I opened one of the bags of white powder, tapped out half of it onto the back of my hand and swiftly inhaled it.

'Wayne?'

'No thank you Johnny' he replied. Wayne didn't touch alcohol or drugs which I admired in a way. He'd seen what it had done to our family and I couldn't blame him for not wanting to participate. I on the other hand loved it.

'Heads or fucking tails you little bitch! Remember we were going to toss your fate and then we got distracted by Wayne tossing you off?!' I continued as Wayne was now laughing hysterically at my admittedly weak material, but it's all about audiences I guess so I was still rather pleased with myself.

I flipped the coin high into the air with my left hand and unbelievably caught it with the same hand and smacked it down onto the back of my right.

I looked at Kenneth and raised my eyebrows quizzically.

'Heads.' Said Kenneth hesitantly.

'Right then, before we go any further, let's go over the rules so it's all fair and above board. If this coin has landed on our beloved Queen's head then you're free to go Kenneth. Free as a bird and no harm done. But, and I'd hate for this to happen because I think we've all got a lot closer during these last…' – I looked at my recently recovered watch - 'twenty minutes?! Fuck me doesn't time fly when you're having fun?! If the coin is tails then I'm going to hand you over to my dear brother because if anything he's taken even more beatings than me over the years and he's also been ridiculed and belittled and humiliated, and all he's done here today so far is give. He's probably put these four cunts that we see before us into four comas and he's wanked you off. He's selfless isn't he? He's selfless isn't he Kenneth?' I said giving him my best hard stare.

'Fucking say that our Wayne is selfless Kenneth. And also say sorry on behalf of you and your mates and every other cunt who has beaten up and bullied my brother over the years. And sound sincere, or that stick which still hasn't been used, which makes me feel a bit sad to be honest, is going right up your arse hole. Please do it now Kenneth. And also say that you love him' Even I knew that the last bit was childish even for me, but this new found power had gone right to my head and I felt like an emperor.

'Don't forget the last bit, as that's vital to the plot.'

'Pardon?' replied Kenneth incredulously.

102

'Fucking pardon! Brilliant Kenneth you really have come a long way today. Good boy! Just fucking say exactly what I fucking told you to say and say it without any sarcasm or I'll cut your fucking tongue out.' I replied, even though I suddenly realised that we didn't have a knife but thought if it came to it I'd try and pull it out using the screwdriver.

'I'll start you off because I'm nice like that.' I coughed twice. 'Ahem, Wayne mate, On behalf of me and my shit cunt gang…'

'Do I include the coughs?' said Kenneth who was rather petrified by now.

'Hmmm? No don't bother with the coughs or the, 'ahem' Kenneth. I like that you want to get this right as I think we all know the consequences of failure' – I wasn't so sure our Wayne was keeping up but that was beside the point under the circumstance. As long as Kenneth was paying attention that was really all that mattered and I could tell that he was - 'Right then crack on Kenneth old son.'

'You said at the start that I had to apologise on behalf of my cunt gang but then a moment ago you said, 'shit cunt' gang which version should I do?' Enquired Kenneth clearly terrified.

He was truly whipped now. I was genuinely starting to like this cunt. He was pedantic and I've always admired pedantry and attention to detail in a person and besides he was nearly my first kiss.

'Fucking hell bruv just fucking get on with it. My hand is going numb here. Okay just do your best but try not to leave out any of the main points, how's that? Just bloody well crack on Kenneth this is getting a bit boring now and I'm getting cold. Will you promise me that you'll mean every word please Kenneth?'

'Yes Sir' replied Kenneth.

'Sir?! Where the fuck did that come from?! That's fantastic that wasn't even in the script, you're redeeming yourself young Kenneth there's hope for you yet. Now get the fuck on with it.'

'Wayne mate, on behalf of our shit cunt gang and everyone else who has bullied and belittled you' - nice touch Kenneth - 'I want to apologise for all the beatings and humiliation and ridicule that you've suffered because of us over the years and I'm sincerely sorry for any upset that we may have caused you.' Said Kenneth paraphrasing but I had to admit his version was probably a bit better than mine. Which kind of wound me up a bit.

'"May" have caused? Fucking "MAY" have caused you cunt!? What the fuck? Does Wayne not look like he's been affected by all the shit that he's been the recipient of for all this time? You cunts, among many others I have to say, ruined the cunt's fucking childhood! Look at the cunt!' I grabbed his face and turned it towards our Wayne's.

'Does that face look like a face free from pain and anguish you fucking CUNT!?'

We both stared at Wayne and even though he still had spunk drying on his chin he didn't look like the most optimistic, devil may care or confident of human beings by any stretch of the imagination. Over the years he'd withdrawn further and further into himself and he looked broken and perhaps, irreparable. I made a pact with myself then and there that, after my own goals had been met obviously, I'd make it my mission to do everything in my power to give our Wayne everything his heart desired and get him to actually enjoy his life rather than just endure it.

I looked at the coin under my hand. It was indeed heads. I looked at Kenneth.

'Best out of three'

Kenneth, suddenly realised the reality and horror of his situation and instinctively made an attempt to escape. Wayne reacted swiftly by sweeping his legs from under him, pinning him to the ground and punching his arms and legs. Kenneth wasn't going anywhere now, except maybe to heaven. Or hell.

I bent down and put my lips to Kenneth's battered head. 'Tell our Wayne that you love him' I said quietly in to his ear.

'And don't you dare fucking pass out'

I dragged Kenneth over to the side of the lake surprised at my own strength which I put down to the previous amphetamine and the recent coke I'd just snorted.

'Fucking clean yourself up, look at the state of you for fuck's sake you're a ruddy embarrassment!'

Poor Kenneth couldn't really wash himself at this point so me and Wayne got into the lake with him and gave him an impromptu baptism by dunking him under the water a few times.

'You've been born again Kenneth! A fresh start! Please don't waste this opportunity! This is a chance to redeem yourself Pilgrim!' I cried, wishing I'd paid more attention in chapel, so I could have recited some apt part of the bible for added effect. I couldn't help but notice that our Wayne was making a very thorough job of cleaning Kenneth's bottom area.

We dragged Kenneth back to the bench just as Benny was coming to. Wayne immediately smacked him in the mouth and he went back under.

'Now that's better isn't it Kenneth?' I patted down his hair and straightened him up as best I could. 'Look at our handsome little boy Wayne! He scrubs up rather well doesn't he?' Wayne grinned at me and nodded and, rather disturbingly, licked his lips.

'Right then I think we all feel better for that. Okay best out of three wasn't it?'

'Yes best out of three, best out of three!' replied Wayne who seemed to be getting more and more agitated.

'Heads or tails Kenneth? And stop playing for time. It's fucking tiresome and it's upsetting our Wayne and you wouldn't like to see our Wayne upset now would you Kenneth?' I continued.

By now I think Kenneth had got the measure of the situation and meekly replied, 'Heads'

'Heads again eh Kenneth? Well it was lucky for you the first time so let's see if you can make it two in a row!'

I flipped the coin back into the air but this time I miss- judged the catch.

The coin landed by Kenneth's feet, and we all saw that it's another head.

'Fuck's sake, void!' I said rather disgruntled.

I threw it back into the air once again, this time expertly catching it and smacking it down on to the back of my other hand. I exaggeratedly took a peek at it. It was heads again. I looked at Wayne who'd read my face and looked disheartened.

'Fuck me Kenneth you're good at this aren't you that's unbelievable! Well done.'

'Best out of five!'

Wayne jumped up and down with glee but Kenneth didn't even really react. I flipped the coin five more times and caught them all.

Not showing the other two or really looking at the coin as I flipped it, I said, 'it's Tails! Three one! Tails again! Three two! Tails again! Three all! Tails again four three! You lose Kenneth! Aww that's a shame because you were doing really well at the start too. Hang on a minute what have you forgotten to say to our Wayne Kenneth?'

I look into his defeated eyes.

'I love you Wayne' he mumbled.

'I don't think Wayne heard you Kenneth please speak up and really enunciate your words this time as it's important.'

'I LOVE YOU WAYNE!' he shouted as best he could through his broken teeth and swollen mouth.

'Hang on was that a hint of sarcasm I detected there young Kenneth?'

'No! No! I really mean it. I love you Wayne!' Cried Kenneth totally exasperated.

'That's a bit gay isn't it Kenneth? Are you a homosexual? Didn't spot that one did you Wayne? Seems like you've got an admirer Bruv. What do you think about that? Do you reciprocate?'

'Pardon?' replied Wayne. Fuck me I should have been a teacher.

'Kenneth here seems to be deeply in love with you. How do you feel about that?'

Wayne looked at Kenneth bashfully and then started salivating.

He whispered in my ear.

I nodded at Wayne who smiled broadly back at me and I felt fantastic.

'Listen Kenneth you've lost the bet fair and square and now it's time to pay up.'

Kenneth made a rather pathetic attempt to flee once more but as all his limbs were numb it looked rather comical to be honest.

'Stand up Kenneth'

Wayne helped him to his feet.

'Wayne be a dear and escort Kenneth around the back of this bench please.' I said calmly.

'Please don't Johnny for fuck's sake, I'm sorry. I'm really fucking sorry for everything. Mickey forced us to do his running. He's beaten all of us too! If you let me go I promise I won't say a word to anybody! I'll say that Mickey started on you and you just defended yourselves!' pleaded Kenneth.

'Well to be fair that's what kind of did happen. We only came here for a friendly chat and things just got out of hand. I'm as sorry as you because I hate violence and so does our Wayne, don't you Wayne?'

Wayne looked at me quizzically.

'Listen Kenneth I appreciate your words and if there was anything that I could do at this point believe me I would but you lost the bet and I can see that you're an honourable man and furthermore Wayne is my brother and what Wayne wants from now on he shall get, if it's in my capabilities. So in short, me old mate, you're fucked, or should I say, about to be.' I winked at him and blew him a kiss.

Kenneth started sobbing at this point which made my cock twitch.

'Bend this cunt over the bench Wayne and pass me two nails'

'Put your hands out flat on this rail here Kenneth' pointing to the one nearest me.

'No! Please Johnny NO! For fuck's sake!'

'Wayne do you want to bother with foreplay or would you just like to get on with it?' I ask Wayne.

Wayne looked at Kenneth's body which was by now bent over the bench and said throatily, 'Just get on with it.'

'Your wish is my command' I said and smashed Kenneth's fucking face in with a brick and then nailed both his hands to the bench, stifling his fucking moaning with his big bag of shit weed.

I patted Wayne on the shoulder and said, 'Wayne, it's all about you now. You've earned this. Good luck' and then I kissed him paternally on the forehead. Two kisses in one day I surmised. Apart from all the ones I probably had as a kid without my consent that was a new record.

It's rude and distasteful to watch two people being intimate, so I busied myself going through all their pockets for drugs and money. I found about twenty little bags of coke, which if they were anything like the one I'd just put up my hooter were cut to fuck and basically only good for selling on. Three hundred quid. That's easily up the bum with Sally plus change. Three flick knives and a starting pistol. Happy days. I'm not a thief, although to be honest I am, but I did think it was the least they could do under the circumstances.

Meanwhile, judging my all the grunting and snorting sounds coming from the direction of the bench our Wayne was well under way.

I shouted over, 'Wayne, when you've finished, meet me back at the house and I'll rustle up something special for tea as we've just come into an unexpected windfall! Any preferences?'

'Fish and chips!' Replied Wayne without missing a stroke.

'Frozen or from the chip shop?'

'From the chip shop!' Replied Wayne excitedly.

It was true it had been years since we had fish and chips from the chip shop and even I started to feel hungry.

'That's a great idea Bruv. I'll get us large portions and mushy peas too, and fizzy pop!' I shouted back.

'Aww thanks Johnny! He shouted back as he banged away.

'Do you want salt and vinegar?'

'Yes please!'

'On just your chips or on your fish too?'

'Both please Johnny and the mushy peas!'

'I don't think that they typically put salt and vinegar on mushy peas because I think they come in a little cup but I'll ask okay?'

'Thanks Johnny!'

Well considering that we didn't really formulate a plan that turned out better than anyone would have anticipated.

Chapter eight

So it transpired that I was a fucking nut case. I felt okay with that and found the whole thing quite comforting. I mean it wasn't like I tortured animals as a kid apart from putting that banger up Puff-Puff's arse hole that time but I didn't really take any perverse pleasure from it. It was around bonfire night and I had bangers and the fucking thing was wondering about with its tail up and parading its ring piece for all the world and then one and one made two, simple. I even remember feeling a bit guilty about it afterwards. In the great nature nurture debate I believe that we are pretty much products of nurture. I couldn't be a proper certified psycho because I had feelings. I was in love with Sally. I loved my brother. I hated my parents. Giggling babies who waved at me in the street made me feel all warm and fuzzy. And shit like that. No I was just a bit of a cunt fair and square. I had empathy. Unlike your classic psychopath I was more of your vigilante, a Robin Hood type character but instead of stealing from the rich and giving to the poor, I stole from cunts like Mickey and pocketed the fucking lot for me and our Wayne.

It wasn't like I'd started out a loon. I'd become one due to circumstances beyond my control. Nurture not nature. And this fact made me feel okay about it all. I think we all have our breaking points and I'd reached mine back there in the park. A door had been opened and I'd burst through it and now there was no going back. It wasn't like I could stroll up to Mickey tomorrow, put my arm around him and say, 'Listen Mickey, I think we all said and did a few things back there that in the cold light of day we might have done differently but the past is the past yeah? Let's all just move on and forget about it all. Boys will be boys and all that?' and then we'd both give each other wry smiles and hug it out. No. Because for one Mickey was probably dead, and two I couldn't give a fuck about Mickey or any of his bitches and I was not seeking forgiveness. Mickey and his crew were a spent force. Mickey is dead. Long live Johnny McQueen. The way I saw it, attack was now the best form of defence and I had to build upon my recent, unprecedented success.

As I was leaving the park I casually wondered how long it would be before our Wayne had finished sodomising young Kenny because I didn't want his chips getting cold. Wayne was a brute with enormous sexual organs and I surmised as to whether this would have an effect on the length of time he would take. I could easily have fucked Kenny in the ass in under a minute I reckoned. Especially as it would have been my first time and they say that you never last very long the first time. I suddenly had a pang of jealousy knowing my brother - who, and I don't mean to be cruel, was if not an actual fucking retard, was at the very least a bit odd - was, at this very moment, losing his virginity before I'd lost mine. I thought about going back and having sloppy seconds so at least it would have happened on the same day but I didn't want to steal the limelight from him on his special day. Anyway, call me old fashioned, but I wanted my first time to be a bit more romantic than a homosexual rape in broad day light in the local park with a guy nailed to a bench. I had three hundred quid in my back bin and cheered myself up thinking that I could easily get a decent brass for that amount and still have enough change for some TCP, wet wipes and a rabies jab.

I caught my reflection in a shop window. It was safe to say I looked like a proper fucking mess. Apart from my usual, 'jumble sale chic' look I'd been doing my very best to carry off, I was covered in blood and dirt and other people's vomit. I decided that the prostitutes could wait because what I needed was a drastic change of wardrobe. If I was to become the new kingpin in town I had to look the part. I thought about Al Pacino in the Godfather, and the Kray twins, Jimmy Cagney and all those Hollywood gangsters. They all wore sharp, three piece suits and handmade Italian shoes and kipper ties and gold cufflinks and sovereigns on their fingers and what was good enough for them was certainly good enough for me. So I headed to a bespoke tailors' that I had passed many times but obviously never entered. I bowled in with my head held high and meagre chest puffed out as far as I could get it without hyperventilating and sauntered up to the counter.

A skinny twenty something homosexual man that looked like all of Duran Duran looked me up and down and said, 'Please sir could you be so polite as to get the fuck out of this shop before I have to summon that security guard over there?' I glanced around and saw an overweight, middle aged man sporting a black jumper and trousers wearing a peaked black hat who all together resembled a kind of own brand value copper. All my new found confidence was draining fast. 'I've got three hundred English pounds young man and I would like to view your most expensive suits and shoes, and any gold rings and cufflinks you may have and possibly a hat of some description.'

'Just fuck off son before I cuff you round the ear' replied the homosexual. If I'd also been a poof and he'd been a bit more friendly towards me I may have found him rather attractive. His haircut and clothes were all very trendy and also very tight especially around his genital region and judging by what I could see, he, like our Wayne, had been blessed. I toyed with flirting with him in order to convey that I wasn't homophobic, which to be frank was fucking rare back then. I also wanted to get some kind of deal on the suit and then maybe I'd let him suck me off or wank me into the socks to sweeten the deal. I suddenly found myself acting extremely camp. I knew by watching TV that gay men flounced about shrieking and being outrageous and acting like birds so I did my best amalgamated impression of all the ones I knew to put him at ease.

'Oooh you are awful but I like you!' I began. I arched my back and put one hand on my hip. With the other hand a wiped my fingers across the counter and in a high pitched tone, said 'Ooh look at the muck in here!' then I gave him a knowing wink.

A fist came flying towards me, which luckily with all my years of beatings I instinctively ducked from.

'Ooooh stop mucking about!' I shrilled making one last attempt at ingratiating myself to Mark fucking Almond.

'Security!'

'For fuck's sake I only want to buy a suit you bend cunt!' In retrospect I probably let myself down here but I was exasperated to say the least. I glanced around the shop, which fortuitously was empty apart from this Flock of Seagulls cunt and the security guard. I grabbed the former by his considerable fringe and slammed his head hard down onto the counter and heard a crunch as the glass broke at the same time as his nose exploded. With this he was immediately out of the game and I turned around just

113

in time to see the security guard lumbering towards me as best he could considering his size. With his arms out stretched he clumsily stumbled towards me like a zombie with diabetes. I could tell he was shitting himself but I guess he had to go through the motions or get the sack. 'Listen mate I only came in for a suit and this young man was rude to me, there's absolutely no need for anymore unpleasantness and besides the customer is always right!' I don't know why I'd suddenly adopted this holier than thou demeanour but at this stage I really didn't know what the fuck was happening to me. The day before I was just another pathetic little bullied child and now I was possibly a murderer and at the very least, a mental case who had aided and abetted the torture and sexual molestation of a minor and beating up a girl. However fucking gross Debbie was, she was still technically a female and that never looks good when it comes out in the papers or on the news. Oh well we're here now and we can't change the past, least said, soonest mended. I clearly remember thinking to myself.

'Listen my good man if you let me leave without further ado we will say no more of it.' If I'd have been wearing a cap I'd have doffed it politely and made my leave but the insecurity guard clearly had a point to make. I suddenly became aware of the security cameras dotted about the ceiling. 'If you like we could do a pretend fight, have a little tussle and I'll slip from your grasp and make a run for it and we'll both come out of this with some self-respect!' I pleaded, not wanting to go to prison just yet. The guard glanced at the cameras and said, 'Come on now Sonny if you don't try and resist arrest I'll put in a good word for you down at the yard' Down at the fucking yard? What did he mean the fucking farm yard? He couldn't arrest me! I didn't think so anyway I thought that they could only restrain you until the real police arrived. Maybe because I'd broken his boyfriend's nose he could have? Fucked if I really knew to be honest. Two can play at that game I thought to myself and yelled back, 'You'll never take me alive Coppa'!' and then kicked him as hard as I could in the nuts. He went down like a sack of shit and started moaning and groaning and clutching his bollocks. 'I fucking warned you Coppa'! I said in my best screen villain voice. I mean honestly I would have made a great actor if I hadn't chosen the thug life of a gangster. 'I fuckin' warned you dint I? But you wouldn't bleedin' listen!' I continued as I grabbed him by his jumper. 'No you didn't. You said we should have a rough and tumble then I should let you slip from my grasp and let you go!' he

114

groaned. 'Well yeah but what I meant by that was if you didn't cooperate I'd kick you in the nuts' I retorted. 'Well you should have led with that then shouldn't you son?!' He replied sounding almost indignant. 'Well fuck me mate you started banging on about arresting me and putting a good word in for me down at the fucking yard and I panicked! Can you even arrest me? Do you have that power?' I said.

'Well I can't exactly arrest you, but I can detain you until the real police arrive I think.'

'Well I can't allow that I've got enough on my plate as it is. I think I'm going to kick you again in the nuts and just leave actually as it's already been one hell of a day to be honest. I didn't plan any of this. I just came in to buy some new clobber then Boy George started getting himself at it.'

'No sir there's no need to kick me in the nuts again. I'll just lay here until you're long gone sir, I'm semi-retired and I don't need the hassle. Why don't you just leave and I'll wait a good couple of minutes and then I'll check on young Clive over there and then I'll phone head office. That'll give you plenty of time to escape.'

'Okay yeah that sounds reasonable but... I really do need a suit though so I think I'm going to have a quick look around first if you don't mind? That's a rhetorical question by the way because that's what I'm going to do. Don't you fucking move mate.'

I sped over to the entrance and flipped the sign on the door so it read closed and turned off the lights.

'Don't fucking move or I'm going to kick you in the fucking head okay?'

'That's fine by me sir I'll just lay here until you're done. I don't get paid enough for this shit anyway. Do what you like Son.'

Adam and the Ants was still out cold as I stepped over him and headed to the suits.

'What size would you say I was … um…what's your name mate?'

'It's Derek Son, or Del to my friends'

115

'Well Del, what size would you say I am?'

He looked at me and his eyes scanned me from head to toe.

'I'm not really an expert that's Clive's department really but at a guess I'd say you were about a 30 inch chest and 28 waist and 28 inch leg but as I say that's a guess and no disrespect but I don't think we have any suits that are that small.'

The cheeky cunt. But he was right. The smallest ones I could see on the rails were 38 inches across the chest. I picked out a white suit that came with a waistcoat, trousers and a jacket. Cool as fuck.

'I need a tie, cufflinks and spats! Where are the spats Del? '

I was suddenly aware that someone could try the door at any moment and wonder why the door was locked mid-afternoon on a week day, peer in and then try and get busy so I had to move fast.

'The shoes are over there son' replied Derek, almost casually now. He'd calmed right down and was now just sitting on the floor in quite a relaxed manner.

'What size feet are you Son?'

'I don't fucking know Del mate, five or six or seven I think, it's been a while since I checked'

Pointing, he replied, 'The kids' shoes are over there Son'

'Fuck off I'm not wearing kid's shoes I want a pair of fucking gangster spats like Al fucking Capone!' I replied indignantly

'I think they've got some two- tone dancing shoes over there, I quite fancied them myself, me and the missus used to go dancing all the time back in the day. That's where we met, up at the old ballroom. It's a bingo hall now, so even if I did buy them there's nowhere to dance anymore. It's all charity shops and coffee shops these days. I don't even get much of a discount here anyway…'

As Derek rambled away I busied myself trying on shoes. Everything was too big but I did indeed like the black and white two- tone spats that he was referring to so I took a pair of the smallest I could find.

'What size are your feet Del?'

'What do you mean?'

'Fuck me Del what size are your fucking feet mate? I'll nick you a pair and stash them somewhere for you to pick up later if you like?'

'What about the security camera?'

Fuck me that was easy, I thought to myself.

'Don't worry about the fucking cameras because I'm going to smash the fuck out of them and the video tape too so what would you like Del?'

'I want a size ten pair of those dancing shoes, that black suit over there - I've got the mother in law's funeral in a few days, she got knocked down by a bus while crossing the road coming back from the cemetery, it was quite ironic in a way…'

'Del we don't have much time you've got to focus Mate!'

Derek hauled himself up and went over to the suits and picked himself one in his size. He then went over to a rack of ties and picked out a few for me, some cufflinks and tie pins and a red cravat and stuffed everything into carrier bags. He stuffed his pair of shoes into another bag and also threw in a couple of pairs of trainers. He also looked me up and down and picked out two pairs of stone washed jeans and some white T shirts.

'Fuck me Del you alright there mate? How am I going to carry all that?!'

'Oh fuck off Son just go down the road to the Belcher café and see my old lady. Take out your stuff and leave mine with her. Tell her that I said it was okay for you to go upstairs to get changed and have a bloody wash because frankly you ruddy stink Son.'

He went to the till, pressed some buttons and it sprang open. He emptied it of notes, made a quick calculation, shoved some notes into his own pockets and pressed the rest into my hand.

'Give the missus fifty quid out of that to keep her gob shut and you keep the rest, now do me a favour and fuck off out of it Son. Please.'

Fuck me it seems like the whole world is at it. Oh well happy fucking days. In the corner of one of the walls was a pole with a hook on the end which was used to open the high windows of the shop. I grabbed it and smashed the two CCTV cameras to fucking pieces with it.

'Where is that video recorder Del?'

He showed me into a small office and pointed to the closed circuit camera's recording machine. I took out the tape and put it in a bag.

'Well Del it's been a pleasure sir. What's your wife's name?

'It's June son, say Del has a gift for you and she'll take you around the back and up the stairs. I was a bank robber back in the day, if you can do the time it's not a bad life. Actually all things considered I'd recommend it. Better than this shit. Pretty little thing like you wouldn't last too long in nick though so I'd think carefully about changing career if I was you.'

Derek and June. Master Criminals. Who'd have thought it?

'Alright Del I think we're done here. Nice to make your acquaintance but if you don't mind I'll be making my exit now.' I replied.

Before I left I frisked Clive and found his wallet. I took out his bank card and bus pass and surprisingly found his library card, what a sweetheart. I left his money because I'm not a cunt.

'Tell Steve Strange here that I've got his details and if he tells any tales about what's gone on here today I'll find him and cut his fucking head off.' I tell Del.

118

'I'm sure he'll keep his gob shut, now do one Son' replied Del

'Listen Del, tell the cops that a gang of kids came in and you think that the leaders name was Mickey and that there was a fat bird with them and three little skinny lads, one of which looked like he'd recently been sexually assaulted by an elephant, cheers.' I then shook his hand and made my exit.

I leave via the back door and in no time I'm striding down the back streets and heading for June's greasy spoon. I'm familiar with this café's location and in no time I'm inside. I bowl up to the counter and take an educated guess that the forty something, rather voluptuous lady with huge tits standing behind it was Del boy's missus.

'Morning June, remember me, it's Mickey, I just bumped into Del and he told me to give you this'

I discreetly place five ten pound notes on the counter and look her in the eye.

'Ooooh hello Mickey nice to see you again, Michaela take over for a moment while I see to this young man please'

Fuck me she was quick on the uptake.

'Gathering up the notes and putting them in her bra she says, 'Come round the back Mickey Son'

She ushers me behind the counter and into a hallway leading to some stairs going up to what I assumed was their flat. I follow her up the stairs watching her big ass swaying from side to side and I can nearly see up her skirt and I start to get a hard-on. At the top of the stairs she suddenly swings around and grabs me by the throat.

'Who the fuck are you son and how do you know my Del?' she snarls putting her face right up to mine. I can smell her breath and her perfume and try not to get too aroused but it's difficult as her tits are pressed right up against me.

'Well before I go any further remember that fifty quid that's stuffed in your bra okay? That's free money for you from Del that is.' I stammer.

She looked a bit concerned now and tightened her grip around my neck so I pressed on as quickly as I could.

'Del is fine, he's all good. Basically I've just accidentally robbed his work place and he got a bit involved through no fault of his own. He's perfectly fine except I had to kick him in the nuts because he tried to arrest me, or at least detain me but anyway he's got a nice new suit for your mum's funeral, sorry for your loss. I'm sure was a very loving mother, God rest her soul' – and I attempted to cross myself as best I could with June's hands still around my throat- 'and a pair of dancing shoes,' I continued, 'even though the old ballroom is now the bingo hall but I'm sure there are other places to go dancing if you do a bit of research' I blurted out.

'You've kicked my Del in the ruddy nuts!?' She clips me around the ear. It felt good and I liked it.

'Now June remember the fifty quid and the suit and shoes and that. He's perfectly fine and he said I could call him Del because we're now mates so calm the fuck down please as I'm starting to get a splitting fucking headache. He told me to come here and have a shower because I fucking stink and then get changed into my new threads.'

I show June the bags.

'These two are for Del and the rest is mine, he actually picked most of it out, he really does have a good eye for clothes and current trends to be fair June and he's wasted in that place. Especially for an ex bank robber.'

June seemed to calm down a bit and she began to compose herself. I don't know if she was aware but she was pressed right against my erection and she seemed to be rubbing her hip bone up and down it while looking at me directly in the eye. I was trying not to embarrass myself.

'You do look like a ruddy unmade bed son and it's true you don't half pen and ink! Follow me. But if you've hurt my Del I will ruddy well skin you alive son' She let go of her grip around my neck and moved back. Fuck me that was close. I liked Del and even though I'd kicked him in the bollocks I thought that we could eventually be friends, he could be like a father figure to me or something and I didn't want to compromise our relationship by coming all over his wife. Not just yet anyway.

'Focus on the fifty quid June, focus on the fifty quid and how smart Del will look at your mum's funeral, as I said, my condolences by the way. I'm sorry for your loss. I'm sure she was a great woman and a pillow of the community'

'It's pillar of the community and no she was a real cunt and we all hated her. She was nothing but trouble and I'm glad she's gone.'

Fuck me June had a right potty mouth and I was shocked and a bit disappointed to be honest.

'There's the bathroom. Pointing to another door she says, 'Go in there and take off your clothes and I'll bring you a towel.'

I entered what turned out to be their bedroom. Compared to our house it was beautiful. It had a big double bed with pristine white matching pillowcases and duvet. I'd never even seen a duvet set in real life. I'd glanced at them while wanking over my mum's catalogue and sometimes you'd see a scantily clad woman draped over one, but this was the real thing. It also smelled nice and fresh. Suddenly I felt very tired and wanted to just lay down on that bed and sleep. I looked at myself in their full length mirror hanging on the wall. In the cold light of day it was safe to say that I looked like a right sorry mess. I was dirty and scruffy in my worn out second hand jeans and a second hand t- shirt and a filthy old jacket that was once my dad's. I also looked very pale and ill. I couldn't remember the last time I'd had a proper meal. I stared at myself and appraised myself long and hard and then suddenly burst into tears. I sobbed my fucking heart out for what seemed like an eternity. I wanted so much to just crawl into that bed and sob and wail and sleep for a hundred years until everything was okay but I didn't want to mess it up so I just crumpled to the floor and hugged myself while I shook and sobbed with tears rolling down my face. This was no time to be crashing.

'Are you alright Love?' It was June.

I did my best to compose myself. 'Yes I'm fine thank you' I said unconvincingly. 'Are you sure Love? Shall I come in?

'No, No I'm not decent!' I said

'Okay Love well I'll put the towel on the handle on the other side of this door and when you're ready you can wrap it round you and pop into the bathroom I'll promise not to look okay?' She chuckled.

Well she'd certainly softened. Was that June's attempt at a coquettish giggle, the filthy old bitch? My libido kicked in again and I pulled myself together. I stood in front of the mirror and started gyrating and thrusting my hips back and forth imagining giving June one from behind while kneading and fondling those massive udders of hers. I started to rub my cock and balls. I then saw the door handle slowly move.

'I'll be out in a minute Jean I'm just undressing!' Don't come in!' I shrieked. I was trying to get my pants off over my hard-on and I tripped and fell onto the floor knocking over their laundry basket.

June suddenly burst through the door to find me splayed out with my pants around my ankles sporting an erection.

'Oooh you filthy little animal! What have you been up to in here!? She squealed gleefully. 'I hope you haven't been rooting about in my washing basket! Have you been pulling on that thing while sniffing my little panties you dirty little boy! Why, I should put you over my knee and give you a ruddy good spanking! I bet you'd like that though wouldn't you?! I hope you haven't spunked up on my best rug you dirty little sod!'

I was blushing profusely and dying of embarrassment as you can imagine but at the same time making a mental note to have some of these so called 'little panties' away with me before I left. Although none that I could see where what I'd have considered little.

She stared down at me as I covered up my cock and balls as best I could and threw me the towel. 'You're a right little tearaway now aren't you? Get in that bathroom and have a good scrub and I'll put these filthy rags in the washing machine.'

She gathered up all my clothes and theatrically picked up my underpants with two fingers with a look of horror on her face. 'I'm afraid that I can't put these filthy ruddy things in my washing machine they're only fit for the ruddy bin! I don't know why you didn't steal yourself some new underwear while you were at it Billy the ruddy Kid! You'll have to borrow a pair of our Del's even though he's twice your size' She stared down at me, gave me the once over and caught my eye… unless you want to wear a pair of mine you ruddy little pervert.

'I think yours will be too big too.' I said without thinking.

She gave me another long, appraising look as she continued to stare down at me. 'My, my, you really are an odd little boy now aren't you?' as she pretended to whip the towel off me, 'Want me to do your back son? She cackled with glee and fucked off back out the door. 'Don't take forever and try to keep your nose out of my laundry basket!'

I wrapped myself back up tightly and making sure the coast was clear I scurried along to the bathroom. That towel was pure fucking lush. It was big and fluffy and smelled fantastic and it felt great against my skin. I'd never felt such luxury. Our towels at home were all threadbare and thin and usually covered in shit stains.

 I opened the bathroom door to find a utopian dream for a scruffy little cunt such as myself. Everything was spotless. No piss stained carpet, no mould on the walls, a radiator that was giving off heat and a spotless bath that had an electric shower stuck to the tiled wall above the bath. It was heaven. The sink was spotless and gleaming and my mouth fell open in wonderment. 'These people must be fucking loaded' I
123

thought to myself. There was a thick fluffy little towel on a heated rail on one wall and I could actually see my reflection in their mirror. I'd never seen anything like it. It was straight out of a magazine or Dallas.

'Use anything you like but don't use all the hot water because Del likes a bath when he gets in!' Shouted June from the landing.

'Fuck me where did she come from?' I thought to myself, startled. Hang on, did she say hot water? I was in paradise.

I dropped the towel and stepped into the shower and pulled the shower curtain across the length of the bath. A shower curtain! A minute later I was lathering myself up from head to toe in shower gel. Not soap but this stuff called shower gel. It smelt amazing, like strawberries. 'Tesco's Luxury shower gel with extract of strawberries' was written on the bottle. I wondered if they'd adopt me. In no time I was lathering up my cock and balls and preparing myself for a luxury and well-earned wank. The next thing I knew I felt a wet hand on my ass. 'Now then little Mickey I'm here to make sure you wash properly in all your little special nooks and crannies that you'd find hard to reach all by yourself.' Murmured June in what I imagined was her sexy voice.

I jumped and slipped and fell into the bath pulling down the shower curtain around me as I went.

'Fuck me June I nearly shat myself! What the fuck are you doing!?' I screamed.

'Oh come on now Mickey I think we both know why you left the bathroom door unlocked now don't we?' As I was splayed out slipping and staggering around trying to regain my balance June began to paw at me with her big, soapy hands.

'Don't you like that Mickey? I'm sure lots of your mates would like to be where you are now so don't be such a precious little bitch and stand up and put the ruddy shower curtain back up because you're soaking the ruddy carpet.'

I did as I was told. 'That's better now where were we? She started rubbing the shower gel into my back and then my arse cheeks.

'June you've got to stop calling me Mickey that's an alias I was using but it's just putting me off now' I shouted over the noise of the shower. 'My real name is Johnny'

'Well Johnny, let's give those little bollocks of yours a nice good scrub shall we? Said June. Her face now very flushed. The next thing I knew a warm lathery hand was between my legs and her fingers were kneading my balls. Fuck me I must admit even though she was a fat old woman it felt amazing and she certainly knew what she was doing.

'That's better Johnny just relax and enjoy yourself.' In no time at all she had whipped off her top and bra and her big tits flopped out. They were fucking huge and really droopy and nearly came down to her belly. Blue veins crisscrossed them like the lines on a road map. The next thing I knew she was using her other hand to soap up my cock. 'There we go Johnny you like that don't you?

'Yes June' I gasped. 'Shall I go a bit faster Johnny would you like that?

'Probably not a good idea June' I said holding on to the two sides of the shower's tiled walls. My legs were just about to give way.

'Oh come on now Johnny baby it seems to like it now doesn't it? It's gone very hard! Shall I give it a little kiss on its little pink nose?

'Please slow down June! I gasped.

'Spray my face and tits with your dirty concrete Mickey Son! Empty those pods over me this instant!' She was very red in the face and one hand had disappeared up her skirt.

Pods? Dirty concrete? I had to stifle a laugh, the filthy old cow. It was doing the job though.

Just as I was about to turn around and give her old boat a facial, the next thing I knew she'd shoved a soapy finger up my arse hole and I shot my load all over the taps.

125

'Ohhh you naughty little boy! What about Mummy?!' June wailed. She let go of her grip, pulled her finger out of my arse hole and sat down grumpily on the toilet seat looking very disappointed to say the least. 'You're a very greedy little boy Johnny and Mummy is very upset' she sulked.

'What's this "Mummy" shit?' I wondered to myself. Where did that come from? My bollocks were now empty and my next thought was to get the fuck out of there as quickly as possible. Maybe June and Del couldn't have kids and this had turned June a bit mental. Perhaps she sees me as her own little boy that she'd never had or maybe she'd lost a child at some stage and I was to be the replacement? I'd heard stories of women who'd lost their own kid and went into hospital maternity wards and nicked other women's babies and brought them up as their own! Maybe June was like them but with a more sexy twist? Maybe she's going to try and kidnap me and use me as her sex slave!? I was up for that but I'd need my own room.

'Oh well Johnny, I'm sure there will be many more play times ahead when mummy gets to have her fun too.' She was still sulking but I was feeling fucking great. My first wank that wasn't performed by me! Score. Sure June was a bit ropey and old as fuck and more than likely mentally ill, but it still counted and by the sounds of it June was up for a lot more in the future. Now all I had to do was get the fuck out as quickly as I could without her sticking her finger back into my arse hole again. That was more date three stuff in my mind.

'Listen June that was lovely, really great and I'm sorry I spunked all over your taps and not your face and tits but all this has left me dreadfully late for an appointment so if you don't mind I'll just get dressed and be on my way.'

'Oh how can I be mad with my little baby boy' replied June. 'Do you promise to come back?'

'Absolutely!' I replied. I wasn't even lying. I couldn't wait to get proper stuck into June, she was as desperate as me and I was already thinking up all the things I was going to do with her in the very near future.

126

'You're a good boy my little Johnny' she replied trying to look all sexy and alluring. She helped me out of the bath and began to dry me. Her breath started getting very heavy as she patted me down. 'Here's a little taster of things to come my darling little baby boy' she said in a husky tone. The next thing she was on her knees, licking and kissing my cock and balls. I had to admit that it felt amazing. I looked down at the top of her head and her enormous tits that were brushing my knees. She wasn't that bad really and she certainly knew what she was doing. I stroked her hair gently and she looked up at me and grinned. My cock was getting hard again and this clearly impressed her. I began pushing my cock in and out of her mouth and groaning like I'd seen in porn films while using her head for leverage. I was going faster and faster until eventually, through my vast amount of experience, my legs began to buckle and I knew that I was just about to empty my pods again. I took June's head in both my hands and thrust my cock in and out of her wrinkly old mouth with all my might. 'Oh yeah your little baby boy is going to give Mummy her present right down the back of her fucking throat' I gasped, trying to get into the swing of this dirty talk. 'Baby going to come for Mummy!' I found myself talking in a fake baby voice and I nearly burst out laughing but didn't want to ruin the mood, plus I thought I owed it to June as I could see over the top of June's head that the first batch was now sliding down the bath and heading for the plug hole. I thought about scooping it up and smearing her face with it as I'd heard somewhere that spunk was good for wrinkles.

'Oooh don't pull my hair like that Micky love not so ruddy hard!

I wasn't really paying much attention to what old June was saying at this point as my mind was on coming up with the dirty talk.

'That's it Mummy you take baby's load you ragged old hag! Baby is going to bum your fucking old tits you slag!'

I'd got carried away with the theatre of it all and immediately regretted saying the last thing. I thought that the best thing to do was continue to fuck her mouth as hard as I could, cum, and then make my excuses and leave. She was saying something but I couldn't really make out what it was because her mouth was full of my cock.

'Not so ruddy hard or you'll …!' That was it! She was saying, 'not so ruddy hard and something else which I didn't quite catch.

Suddenly her hair came away in my hand and at the same time it was then that what turned out to be the top set of her false teeth popped out and flew into the bathroom sink. Time seemed to stand still as we both watched her plastic knashers spin round and round until eventually coming to rest forlornly in the plug hole. That's when I must have screamed.

'Oh my God Mickey I'm so sorry don't look at me!' She'd grabbed my towel and covered her head with it but it was too late, I'd seen.

She was almost completely bald apart from a few wisps of fine white hair dotted about on her scalp and it looked like the top of her face had caved in. I thought that I was going to faint.

I caught my reflection in the bathroom mirror. My mouth was wide open and I had June's wig in my hand and my once rock hard cock had rapidly turned into a rather pathetic looking maggot. I thought briefly about wanking myself into the wig and fucking off for ever but that would have been rude and anyway June quickly grabbed it off me, shoved it back on her head, scurried around in the sink and sobbing, retrieved her dentures and made a hasty retreat out the door.

'Not so ruddy hard or you'll pull my ruddy wig off!' that was what she was saying! Oh well, too late now.

I quickly dried myself off. Little did June know that once I'd gotten over the initial shock I wasn't that bothered about any of what had just occurred. June had showed me more affection in that half an hour than I'd ever had in my life and I wasn't going to jeopardise my chances of actually having sexual intercourse with her just because she was a fat, bald, toothless old bag.

'June please don't get upset! There's nothing to be embarrassed about! I've banged loads of birds who look a lot worse than you believe me! And many of them with even less hair! I shouted through the bathroom door. Trying to cheer her up. 'You

128

should see my mum's mate Aunty Jean she's even grosser than you! Ten times grosser than you! Or my mum for fuck's sake! She'd make a fly puke! Not that I've shagged my mum obviously! Although I did come in her tights once but that was more about convenience than anything sexual.

'For God's sake stop talking Mickey!' she sounded like she'd been crying and I couldn't blame her to be honest. She'd been trying to give it the Diana Dors, sexy older woman treatment and ended up looking like an Albert Steptoe. I could completely understand why she would feel utterly ridiculous and humiliated at this point in time. She was still better than a wank though.

'Listen June it's all golden but you've got to stop calling me Mickey June, it's really starting to get on my tits now. My name is Johnny June. It's ruddy Johnny.' I replied trying to change the subject, although that was indeed starting to grate on me. I didn't want word to get out that this maverick guy called Mickey had banged an older woman I wanted everyone to know that it was me. The notorious Johnny McQueen. The one and ruddy only.

Now she had me saying fucking ruddy too what the fuck was that about? I'd read that when two people fall in love they sometimes start mirroring each other. Maybe I was in love with June? I fucking hoped not. A picture flashed in my mind of me and June on our wedding day. I was wearing my new suit and spats and looked the business but she looked like how I'd last seen her, topless and bald and toothless. I laughed out loud. June and I could never work as a couple, unless she lost a bit of weight anyway. Plus there was Del. He'd have to be put out of the picture. I thought briefly about killing Del and setting up home with June. No, not today anyway. Too much had already happened today and it was all getting too much for me to take in.

'Listen June I really don't care if you're bald and toothless and fat!' I continued.

'Fat!' You cheeky ruddy sod! So you think I'm fat now!?'

She fucking was fat. I didn't know that it was a secret. Or maybe she didn't know she was fat. Maybe every time she asked Del if he thought that she was fat he lied and said no? Maybe Del liked her fat? Maybe Del was into fat, toothless, bald old slags?
129

The dirty bastard. I briefly wondered why people develop kinks and what incident might have sparked them off or whether it was actually innate. Nature or nurture. 'Yes well all the men in my family have always been into fat, toothless bald women right far back through the annals of time our Mickey.' fuck me now she's got me at it. Or maybe Del had a babysitter back in the day and she was a fat, bald woman and he'd developed a thing for them? Who gave a shit I just knew that I had to get out of there.

'Don't worry June I like my women with a bit of meat on them! Something to get hold of! A bit of purchase if you will' I'd heard men say this before, probably to their fat wives. Or to their mates as a way of explaining to them why their missus was so fucking fat.

'Just dry yourself and go into the bedroom and get changed! I've laid out some of your clothes. Please just get dressed and leave Mickey!'

Johnny June my name is ruddy Johnny!'

What was the point? The old dear has probably got Alzheimer's so fuck it. I thought to myself.

I tied the towel around my waist and scurried back to their bedroom. Sure enough, on the bed was a new pair of my jeans, a white T shirt and what could have only been a pair of Del's not too shabby underpants and a pair of his socks. Beggars can't be choosers and at least they were clean so I quickly got dressed pleased as punch with my brand new clobber. I couldn't remember the last time, if ever, that I'd put on brand new clothes and they felt amazing. Even Del's under crackers, which were far too big for me, felt fantastic on my skin. I put on my new trainers and admired myself in their full length mirror. My hair was slicked back still wet. I'd always wanted a Teddy boy quiff but I'd had my head kicked in enough without adding any more reasons. I did a quick Elvis impression and curled my top lip. It would be so much easier if people could all walk about like they wanted to without getting judged and laughed at. Big Ron who lived opposite us liked to walk about dressed as a bird with huge fake tits and a blonde wig and heels and carrying a little clutch bag. He was over six feet tall and built like a brick shit house and always had a five o'clock shadow and more often than not had holes in his stockings as he staggered, as best he could, down the street. He was always getting laughed at by kids but he didn't ever seem to give a fuck. He would sit in his garden on an old sofa smoking roll ups and drinking Tenants Extra dressed as his alter ego and when it was hot he'd wear his selection of bathing suits. I have to admit that when he was wearing his gold bikini one I would hide behind the curtains in my mum and dad's bedroom and unashamedly smash one out. I think that it was because he didn't seem to mind what people thought of him that most people round our way eventually just let him get on with it. He was hard as fuck though so maybe they were just too scared to take the piss. I'd known him all my life and he'd always been like that so it was never a big deal for me. Plus I'd always thought that it was none of my fucking business what he dressed like or how he acted he was just big Ron. All I knew was that he'd never been unkind to me and in my world that was very unusual and I was thankful to him for that. I'd also admired his strength to live his life as he wanted regardless of cultural conventions. I must admit too that I'd nicked a pair of his sexy panties off his washing line one night and put them on and had a wank. But that was the old Johnny. The new Johnny would probably not have to do that kind of thing anymore because he was most definitely going to be up sunk to his nuts in the guts of old June.

June had rather sweetly laid out all my illicit booty that I'd procured earlier in the day. She really was a keeper. It was a shame she was so fat and gross looking because apart from that she had all the traits of a girlfriend that I was looking for. She was a dirty, desperate hag with no self-respect. I gathered up all my things and bolted for the door. As I entered the landing June was waiting for me. She was now wearing a knee length see-through negligee. She'd also put on some bright red lip-stick, blusher and mauve eye-shadow. Her wig was back on and her teeth were in. The smell of whisky and perfume was overpowering and my eyes immediately started to stream but I could clearly see her tits and bush. Here we go again she was insatiable. I couldn't believe my luck.

'Not so fast Johnny' she purred. I could see lipstick all over her teeth but decided against mentioning it.

'You look stunning June' I stammered, pleased that finally she'd remembered my fucking name.

She sidled up to me and pressed her tits up against me while grinding her thigh urgently into my groin.

Even though June now made a startling resemblance to big Ron I told her that she looked both sexy and ravishing even though I wasn't sure what the last word meant but men always said it to birds in my wank mags so that's what I said. It must have done the trick because she giggled coquettishly.

'Oooh you little charmer' she giggled and slurred. I was pleased that I'd made her feel good about herself. And also pleased that my cock was getting hard again.

June caught my eye for what seemed like an eternity and through the wrinkles and possible cataracts I could see a desperation and longing. She was obviously once a good looking woman but the years had taken their toll. June wanted one more throw of the dice before the grim reaper finally took her and freed her from the vanities of life and she'd chosen me to be her swan song. Well she'd thrown a six with ole Johnny because I was more than happy to fuck her brains out however fucking ridiculous she looked.

The next thing I knew she'd shoved her mouth hard up against mine and her tongue was now down the back of my throat. I thought I was going to be sick. What if I swallowed her fucking teeth and choked to death just when my life was finally on the up? I decided to go on the defensive and used my own tongue to bat hers away. At first my sole purpose was trying not to die but eventually I got the hang of it and relaxed enough to get my tongue into her saggy old gob. I was soon whirling it around her mouth and flicking it over her teeth being as careful as I could not to dislodge the fuckers. June was making awful slurping sounds and grunting so I took her lead and did the same. We were like two pigs at a trough. I was really getting the hang of it and actually starting to enjoy myself. I started to experiment and began sucking and pulling on her lips with mine which she seemed to really like until I got carried away and started sucking on her nose. She pulled away and gave me a disgusted look or maybe she just looked at me, but anyway I decided against doing it again.

After what seemed like a hundred years June took her tongue out of my mouth and whispered something that I didn't quite catch. Was this what they called 'sweet nothings'? I was just copying everything that she was doing to me now so I whispered some incomprehensible bollocks into her ear too.

'I said drop the ruddy bags Johnny!'

Oh that's what she'd said!

I immediately dropped all my bags onto the floor and as I did so she took both my hands and put them on her tits. 'Wow' I thought to myself I was feeling actual women's tits again! They were warm and heavy as a squeezed them and I kneaded them and rolled them in my hands. I had to admit that even though they looked old and fucked they felt amazing. The next thing I knew June had pushed my face in between them as she pushed them together sandwiching my head. At that moment I was in heaven. It was so warm and lovely I felt like I could stay like that forever.

'Suckle Mummy' June groaned.

Here we go again. She definitely couldn't have kids.

Ignoring the madness of it all I did what I was told and through the flimsy material of her nightdress I took one of her enormous pink nipples and sucked it hard.

'Ooh you naughty little bugger Johnny!'

Why was I naughty? She fucking told me to do it! But I stopped anyway.

'Don't you ruddy stop now!' She gasped

'What the fuck? Make your bloody mind up!' I thought to myself.

June forced my mouth back onto her old nipple. Was that a hair?

133

'Ahh that's it my Baby, take Mummy's sweet milk.'

If any milk came out of these old udders I was definitely going to vomit. I was sucking as hard as I could now but thankfully so far nothing was coming out.

I soon realised that this must all be part of June's sick fantasy and relaxed.

'Baby like mummy's sweet milk' I said trying to get into the swing of things.

I looked up at June. She had her eyes closed and was smiling to herself. I was obviously doing a good job. I decided to up the ante.

'Baby needs his knob sucked' I said.

June opened her eyes, looked at me and said, 'don't you ruddy stop suckling mummy's fucking tits! You cheeky little cunt!' She hissed. Fuck me Joan was a pro method actor and could jump in and out of character in a bloody thrice.

Fair enough. I pulled back and started on the other one. She seemed to be covered from head to foot in perfume. It felt bitter on my tongue but I was really getting the hang of it now. I'd learned so much in such a short time. Sally would be well impressed with all my new skills and I couldn't wait to try them all out on her at our earliest convenience. Two birds! I thought to myself. One to practice on and a good one to take out and show off. Aunty Joan would be second reserve now. Who would have thought that my luck would have changed so rapidly? I decided to light a candle the next time I went to church. Which would be hopefully on me and Sally's wedding day. I was on fire now and I couldn't risk going near a church until then just in case I was set upon by a load of rampant clergymen bent on raping the bejesus out of me.

The next thing I knew June was unzipping my jeans and taking out my cock. Great, I thought, now for a quick nosh and I can get the fuck out as I thought I'd learnt enough for one day. Plus I was suddenly fucking starving.

June had other ideas though. She took one of my hands off her tits and put it between her legs. The first thing I felt was hair, lots of sticky wet hair. Had she pissed herself? I'd read somewhere that ladies of a certain age were pretty much incontinent.
134

Especially if they'd had loads of kids, and although June was obviously barren she was well past that age whatever that age was. 'Frig Mummy's foo foo Johnny!' She groaned.

Foo foo? By now this sort of thing didn't even phase me. I kind of guessed what she meant due to the circumstance we were in but 'foo foo'? That was a new one on me and I stifled a giggle.

Oh well it would have been bad manners to get into the semantics of it so I just pushed two fingers up inside her old growler and started to manically 'frig' it with all my might. It was big and wet like my aunty Joan's and also all saggy and once again nothing like the ones I'd seen in the porn mags but it didn't stop me having a good old go at it. June meanwhile was pulling hard on my cock and I knew it wouldn't be long before I was all done and dusted. Under my own initiative I took my free hand off June's tits and put it on her arse. I started rubbing and stroking with all my might. I grabbed a big handful and squeezed it hard.

'Do you like that June! Sorry I mean Mummy!?'

'Yes Johnny, Mummy likes that very much. Johnny good boy! Johnny good boy!' She gasped.

How do I know when she's finished? I suddenly thought. This could go on for days at this rate! It was obvious when I was done because there would be spunk everywhere but what about birds? This was an oversight on my part. I never really thought about that before now.

I slipped the hand on her arse between her ginormous buttocks and felt for her bum hole. I'd read somewhere that when it comes to sex your partner will do things to you that they would like done to them so I was going to ram my finger up her arse hole with all my might. When I eventually found it, it wasn't what I'd expected. First of all it was dry as fuck and also very lumpy. I made a few attempts to gain entry with no success. Then I had an idea. I would use June's incontinence to her advantage. If nature gives you a lemon use June's piss as arse lube! I took my finger from June's raggedy old knot and shoved it up her foo foo for a bit then jammed it easily up her
135

bum. Now we were really getting somewhere! Two fingers up her fanny hole and one deep in her arse and going like the ruddy clappers. This went on for a good few minutes until I thought I was going to sprain my hand - the one attached to the finger that was poking in and out of her tea towel holder due to the angle being a bit off.

'Oh Baby Mummy is coming! Mummy is coming!'

'Thank fuck for that' I thought.

'Frig it! Frig it Johnny my darling!' she cried as I tried to get her off as quickly as possible.

Suddenly I heard a door open from down stairs.

'June are you up there love?'

Fuck me it was Del.

'Don't you fucking stop Johnny' June hissed at me.

'But June it's fucking Del! He's back early!' I replied. I didn't know what time he usually got home and only said it because I'd heard that said in similar, usually less sordid, situations on the tele.

'I don't give a fuck if it's Rodney and fucking uncle Albert do not take those fingers out of my cunt Johnny!'

I didn't know whether to laugh or not, so decided to just crack on. Fuck me what happened to 'foo foo'?'

She was tugging furiously at my cock now so I followed suit with her 'cunt'

'Don't stop Johnny I'm nearly there!'

My hand was getting really tired so I took my finger out of her arse and concentrated on getting her off via her fanny hole. I didn't even know if it was possible to make a lady orgasm by frigging her bum hole and decided that this wasn't the time to ask.

136

'June love are you up there? Shouted Del

'Fuck me Del please do not come up the stairs' I thought to myself while franticly darting my fingers in and out of June's old clopper.

The good news was I was just about to come so there was light at the end of the tunnel. And heavens above as luck would have it so was June by the sounds coming from it. Then her whole, grotesque body shook and her knees buckled and she lent on me with all her considerable weight and she buried her head into my chest at the exact moment I emptied my load all over her fat wrinkled old belly. She stayed their gasping for what seemed like an eternity but all I wanted to do was fuck off out of it before Del came up the stairs and I'd have to kick him in the bollocks again.

June looked up at me and then down at her stomach which was all covered in my spunk. We both watched as it began running down into her belly button. She then scooped up a handful and put it in her mouth. 'Yum! Yum! Mummy like' she cooed.

'Rather you than me love' I thought but just stood there stunned.

Then she took my hand, which was still between her legs, and brought it up to my own face and smeared it all around.

That's when I retched.

'Baby got to go bye byes now June, fuck me, I mean Mummy, because Daddy is coming up the fucking stairs!' I didn't know whether to continue the baby mummy shit or not now it was clearly all over.

'Just take your ruddy things and fuck off you dirty little bugger' snarled June. Somehow she had me by the throat again. I knew this was supposed to be intimidating but I was distracted by the fucking smell on my hands.

'If you don't come back I'm going to the police and tell them everything okay' June continued.

'What that a grown woman wanked off a child and frigged the fuck out of his innocent little bot, bot? Fuck off June we both know nobody is going to say fuck all to any cunt now don't we but I really like you June so I'll be back soon I promise.' I replied. I should have kissed her hard on the mouth but it was more than I could do not to just keel over and start dry heaving at that point.

'You're a good boy Johnny' she said, her tone a lot softer now. And she tucked my cock back into my pants and zipped me up.

'Yeah and you're a very beautiful woman' I lied.

I grabbed my bags and made a run for it down the stairs.

'Oh so you found the place then son?' remarked Del as I sped past.

'Yeah cheers for the pants and socks and sorry for kicking you in the balls. June is nice isn't she? You're a very lucky man Del. Can't stop, gotta' go see you around. Oh and all your gear is upstairs with June.' I replied nonchalant as a mother fucker.

'They let me go home early due to the shock of the break-in! I said it was a gang of youths led by a fella name of Mickey!' He chuckled.

'Nice one Del I owe you one mate!' I shouted over my shoulder.

'Your wife's leathery old growler has seen better days Del and I've seen more hair on a dropped scotch egg!' I didn't say the last bit but I certainly thought it.

I burst through the café and headed for the door but not before Michaela looked at me and winked and said, 'Looks like you've been a very busy boy. I tried to stall him, best I could to give you a bit more alone time with June. Next time I see you I want my reward' and as she said this she squeezed my bollocks. Everyone in the café started to laugh and cheer and I blushed a deep red and I fucked off feeling like a fucking king.

Chapter nine

What a day I thought to myself, what an awesome fucking day it had turned out to be. Wayne's fucking chips! Shit I'd forgotten all about the chip shop. I glanced down at my watch. Ten past five in the afternoon. I'd robbed the Tailor's, had a shower, got wanked off twice and finger fucked June and got finger banged in the arse myself all in under an hour and a half. No wonder I was starving.

I got back to our house with my arms full of fish and chips. I'd also been to the shop and bought two big bottles of cola and bread and butter and mars bars and Twix and KitKats for afters. I couldn't stop smiling as I strutted down our road armed with all these goodies.

I opened our front door. 'Wayne! You up there?' I shouted up the stairs. Wayne spent all his time inside our house in our room hiding from the madness that was our parents.

'I'm in here Johnny!' Wayne shouted from the front room.

I walked in to find Wayne patiently sat up at the table knife and fork in hand. I didn't even think we had any knives or forks.

Wayne didn't ask me why I'd been so long and I didn't ask him how he'd got on raping Kenny.

'Did you get the mushy peas Johnny?'

'Yes Wayne, and I bought some salt and vinegar and ketchup and some packets of tartar sauce.' Neither of us knew what the fuck that was but Gorgeous George, the owner of the chip shop asked me if I wanted any and I didn't want to appear ignorant so said yes.

'What the fuck is tar tar sauce? Enquired our Wayne.

'Fuck knows' I replied. 'Gorgeous George asked me if I wanted some so I just said yes in case it was nice and they were only 5 pence each so I bought a quid's worth.' I'd already been corrupted by wealth.

Wayne looked at one of the little packets with the curiosity of a chimp with his head inclined to one side and then ripped it open with his teeth and sucked it dry.

'It's okay!' he then did the same with a handful of them and promptly ate them

I plonked all the food on the table and then produced the coke and chocolate. Wayne fucking beamed. 'Tuck in brother!' I said and winked at him. We were like two pigs in a trough grunting and snorting and burping and I for one didn't give one flying fuck. We had never eaten like this in our lives, and we were making the most of it. Wayne belched and I followed suit. Then Wayne belched again louder and I did my best to beat him. Then Wayne looked at me dead in the eye, lifted his leg and farted loudly. I kept his gaze and said, 'Wayne, can I ask you a serious question?'

Wayne looked back at me with a serious look on his face and replied, 'Yes Johnny' I reached over the table and held out my hand. 'Will you pull my finger?'

Wayne looked quizzically at me and replied, 'Yes Johnny.' And pulled. As he pulled I let out the most gigantic fart I'd ever produced and actually thought I'd shit Del's pants. There was a split second of silence and then we both fell about the place laughing our heads off. There then followed a cacophony of burping and farting and laughing until we'd polished off the fucking lot. Even though our parents were a couple of scum bags for some reason when we all ate together me and our Wayne had to keep quiet. If either of us made any noise during our meagre meals we would be shouted at and hit so we'd learned to keep our heads down. On this day though we were being as loud and as boisterous as we could possibly be and it was worth the rancid stench that had now filled the room.

When we'd finished we sat back in our chairs and smiled at each other. Neither of us spoke but we both knew that we'd never put up with anyone else's shit from this day forward. We had each other's backs and we'd had a taste of freedom that we'd never experienced before. We were never going back to those dark days when we were every cunt's whipping boys.

'Where's Dad?' I'd forgotten all about the cunt.

'Fuck knows' replied Wayne.

And that was that.

Just then we heard the front door open. It was our mum.

She came into the front room and stared at the two of us and then at the table.

'Look at this fucking mess! Where did you get those chips you little bastards? Get it all cleaned up or I'll leather the pair of you! And where is your fucking da?' She screamed, all red faced and obviously pissed as a fart.

I look at her up and down with a look of delight on my face and say, 'Aww there she is! Good evening Mummy and how was your day?'

'Fuck off Johnny you fucking sarcastic little shit. I'm fucking sick of you and your brother making a fucking mess all the time! Jean is coming over in a bit and I want this fucking house ship shape before then!' She replies, getting angrier and angrier.

'I've got an idea Mum, why don't you go fuck yourself?' I calmly say.

She's stunned for a moment. 'What did you fucking say?'

'I said, "Why don't you go fuck yourself?" are you fucking deaf you rotten old slag? Look at the fucking state of you standing there all pissed and filthy. You fucking stink too. You've never lifted one fucking finger in this house that's why it's so fucking filthy… you old cunt.'

'Get out of this house! And take your fucking retard brother with you! You're nothing but trouble and you've always been a burden to me and your dad!' she screamed, fists clenched.

141

Now normally in these kind of altercations me and our Wayne would try and make a bolt for the door while trying not to get a beating, then lay low for a couple of hours somewhere outside until we were sure that she'd fallen into an alcoholic stupor. We would then creep back in and go to our bedroom, safe in the knowledge that by the morning she would have forgotten all about it and life would continue as it always had. But not today.

'I'm not a fucking retard am I Johnny?' said Wayne to me with pleading eyes. This was no time for the truth so I replied, 'No Wayne you are not in any way, shape or form, retarded. If anyone is retarded in this family it's that fucking thing!' I smiled at my mum as I continued, I started at the top of her and worked my way down. 'Look at the fucking state of it Wayne, when was the last time it put a comb through its hair?! It's only got a few teeth and they're fucking manky as fuck! Why do you bother wearing make-up nobody is ever going to ever look at you except to laugh at you, you look like a cheap prostitute wearing all that slap. Look at its saggy old tits and that fat arse! And what's it fucking wearing?' I let out a snort of derision and threw a chip at her. 'It looks like the fucking Ethiopians gave her their fucking clothes! The cunt is wearing slippers on its fucking feet and it's just been out! No sane cunt would go out dressed like that! I was rocking and rolling now.

'Is that spunk stains on those fucking holey old tights?' I knew for a fact that it was. 'You are a fucking disgrace! Look our Wayne, it looks like it escaped from the fucking loony bin and has been sleeping rough in a communal fucking bin! Are you looking for the nurse dear? Are you lost? Is it time for your fucking medication you mental old fuck bucket? Look at the fucking state of it Wayne! Straight out of the funny farm! No wonder everyone laughs at us! It's because of you Mum, you fucking horror of a fucking person!' I couldn't stop myself and years and years of frustration came bubbling over the surface as let her have it.

'You're a fucking embarrassment Mum! I'm ashamed of you! You haven't ever loved us or cared for us and it's your fault that our lives have always been so fucking miserable! I fucking hate you Mum. I fucking hate you. You and Dad you are both terrible people and you should never have been allowed to have kids because you're a pair of selfish, fucking useless cunts. It was you that made our Wayne the way he is

142

because you fucked up his head with all your drink and drugged-fuelled rowing, and fighting and beatings. But that all stops from today because we are no longer two little frightened children that you can bully and boss around and beat up and you'd better get fucking used to it you nasty old piece of dog shit.'

My mum stared blankly at me. I wondered if my rant had had any effect on here or if she'd taken any of it in. Then she started to sob. Then she started to wail. We'd seen this side of her before and I for one wasn't falling for it again. Sometimes she'd beat the fuck out of us and then suddenly become all contrite and guilty and beg our forgiveness. This unpredictability was worse than anything else. Sometimes we'd fall for it and all her empty rhetoric but then a few days later she'd be back at us again.

'Oh my darling boys what have I done to you! I'm so sorry! It's the drink! It's your fucking father! My own childhood was so terrible! Please forgive me! Come and give your mum a hug I love you both so very much' she sobbed.

I was nearly convinced. Especially when our Wayne got up and slowly walked towards her. As far as I knew our Wayne had never been hugged by anyone in his entire life apart from me and he was desperately in need of some consensual affection. Maybe this time she meant it? Maybe this time she'd change her ways and things would be different? Maybe I was actually dreaming and this day had never actually happened at all? Maybe, due to all the drugs I'd taken earlier, I'd over-dosed and was now lying in a hospital bed in a coma and all this was occurring in my head as I lay there helpless while hot underpaid orderlies from the Philippines were sexually assaulting me.

'Oh my darling Wayne that's it come to your ma' She cried, one arm outstretched and beckoning Wayne towards her. 'Don't fall for her bullshit Wayne! She just wants you to do her dirty work for her and get you to beat the fuck out of me! I shouted hoping that this day wouldn't crumble into nothing.

Wayne ignored me and continued walking towards her. 'Fucking hell Wayne we've come this far together! Don't fucking ruin it by going back to our old lives! It's a fucking trap she hates you as much as me!'

Fuck sake if she gives him a hug Wayne's going to forget about all the bad times and forgive her everything just for a brief moment of fake affection and it'll all unravel. Back to fucking square one.

Mum, sensing her advantage, gave it everything she had and bent down on one knee, which, considering the fucking size of the brute and how pissed she was, even grudgingly, impressed me. She stretched out both her hands and theatrically cried, 'Come to Mummy our Wayne! Come to Mummy's loving arms Son!'

I think she was trying to look like Mary Magdalene, trying to manipulate Wayne by conjuring up some biblical scene from our Catholic upbringing but to me she looked more like Al fucking Jolson and I thought for a moment she might get too carried away and start doing Jazz hands.

'Come to Mummy? Fuck off you've never been a mum to us, ever! Don't you dare let her fool you Wayne or this day never happened and we're back to the beginning! For fuck's sake Wayne sit back down!' I pleaded.

Mum was crying now. Real tears. Fuck me she was good but I'd seen this all before. Every time the social services had come round or the police to take us into care over the years, she'd turn on the waterworks and she'd fool everyone. I knew from a very early age that for her we were just two more sources of government benefits and I fucking hated her.

'Wayne, listen to me, she doesn't give one flying fuck about you or me! She's playing you for the fool! Let's go out and spend some money! I'll treat you to whatever you like! More sweets! Some new clothes! Prostitutes! Anything you like Wayne, but let's just get the fuck out of here!' I was shouting now, desperate.

By now Wayne was about three feet away from her and I suddenly gave in and felt utterly hopeless and defeated. Mum glanced at me for the briefest moment and I saw triumph in her eyes. She knew that our Wayne had, for years, craved her affection and never once got any so she was playing her trump card. She was a low down conniving, manipulative cunt and would stoop to any lengths to get what she wanted.

144

'Give your mum a nice big hug and lets me and you go out on the lash and leave this little prick to clean up this mess our Wayne. You know you've always been my favourite.' She said, using her best soothing tone and looking triumphantly at me.

'I don't drink.' Wayne said, almost to himself. Then he brought his knee up suddenly to our mum's head, split her nose and knocked her out cold. Night, night Julie. Sleep tight.

Thank fuck for that.

'Good lad! I never doubted you our Wayne.'

'Prostitutes!' grinned Wayne.

Well then two for two. Down and out. Our Wayne had done the pair of them. It was touch and go for a while but he got there in the end. Bless his fucking heart.

Fuck it why did I mention prostitutes? Where the fuck are we going to get our Wayne a prostitute? I thought to myself. But a promise was a promise and I really did enjoy seeing my mum get kneed in the head and I also enjoyed the sound of her nose splitting. Might get myself one too while I was at it, I surmised.

Mum was out cold lying on the floor but still breathing. I couldn't really have cared less if she was alive or dead because she was already dead to me anyway. She'd done nothing for me or ever showed me any affection and I wasn't someone who loved their mum unconditionally like some kind of pathetic little cunt. My dad was a cunt too who hated us and I hated him. It would be a lot less hassle if they were both dead in my opinion. I didn't want our Wayne ending up in some detention centre for murder though because he wouldn't have lasted five minutes. Maybe Mum would come round and not remember what the fuck had happened and so would my dad and the whole thing would blow over. I doubted that very much but that was as far as my thought process went because I was getting horny again.

'Come on our Wayne let's get laid!' I said gleefully as we stepped over our mum and went out.

Chapter ten

With Wayne following in my wake I went straight across the road to big Ron's house and knocked on the door. After a few minutes I could see his big bulk tottering towards us through the frosted glass panel.

'Who is it?' he shouted through the door.

'It's me and our Wayne from opposite!' I shouted back.

'Oh okay, hang on Johnny while I unlock the door'

After about five minutes of bolts being pushed back and chains being released big Ron eventually opened the door.

'Alright there lads, how can I help you?'

Big Ron was wearing full make-up, a white blouse, a black knee length skirt, black tights and bright, high heeled red stilettos. He wasn't wearing a wig though so he just looked like a big bald man who was dressed in women's clothes.

Ron caught us staring at his outfit and tried to offer an explanation.

'Today is Friday and I call it, 'sexy Friday' where I make a bit more of an effort. Today I'm Alex the sexy secretary!' Explained Ron. 'I usually wear a long blonde wig and horn- rimmed glasses but I was getting too hot so I took them off. What do you think of these tits lads? They look real don't they? Double D's! Give 'em a feel they're very life-like don't you think?'

I was a bit hesitant but our Wayne was grinning like the Cheshire cat and immediately took up the offer with gusto.

'Fuck me they're fucking lovely Big Ron!' gasped Wayne as he squeezed and kneaded them.

'Alright our Wayne go steady Son, you'll have the buggers out! Cried Ron.

'Sorry Big Ron' Wayne looked sheepish but I couldn't help but notice the enormous bulge in his jeans.

'Look Wayne it's okay, you can stroke them but don't pull, you need to be gentle with us ladies.' Replied Ron.

Well this wasn't weird at all, two boys standing on the doorstep of an aging transvestite groping his tits like it was the most natural thing in the world. They were pretty life like though so I had a quick go myself.

'You're a very beautiful lady Ron' Our Wayne said shyly.

Fucking hell here we go our Wayne will be up to his considerable nuts in big Ron next. He's got a proper taste for it now and there will be no stopping the randy little sod.

Ron blushed a deep red and I thought the cunt was going to cry.

'Our Wayne, that's the nicest thing anyone has ever said to me'

'Yeah Wayne, why don't you get down on your knees and suck old Ron's cock right here in the fucking street' I thought to myself.

'I don't mean to be rude but can I interrupt your flirting for just a moment and ask you a question Ron?'

Ron was positively beaming now, 'You boys can ask me anything you like, I know that your parents can be a handful on occasion but in my eyes you two have always been good as gold. Fire away lad.'

He looked me up and down. 'Is it a question about your fashion sense because, no offence but you do look like a bit of a cunt dressed like that son.'

The cheeky fucker. The fucking irony of that statement was just fucking perfect but I was on a mission and pressed on.

'No Ron it's less a question of fashion but more a question of passion.'
147

Nobody laughed at my quick wittedness so I pressed on.

'Well you see Ron, me and our Wayne are getting to that age when we're thinking about sowing our wild oats, and as we know that you're a man or should I say 'woman' of the world we've come to you for some advice.'

Ron looked delighted. 'Well boys you've come to the right place! Just because I like to dress up as a bird and parade around my house touching myself and sticking things up my arsehole doesn't mean that I'm a poofter. I'm as straight as they come lads! Well pretty much straight in the scheme of things. I was a merchant seaman and I've been all over the world and I've shagged birds from every continent! I've shagged your black birds, your Asians, your tiddly winks, your nips, your wops, your spiks, and even a couple of conjoined twins from Singa ruddy por. Or should that be, just twins/ Anyway it had two heads and one fanny hole. You name it, if they had a brothel I'd be straight off the ship and sunk to the ruddy nuts in one before you could say all a ruddy board! It was only when I met and married my Brenda, God rest her soul, that I stopped shagging whores and became a faithful and devoted husband. After that I only shagged a few brasses from time to time like when I had a big win on the horses or on my birthday...or Christmas or when Brenda was at her sister's. You see Brenda's sister wasn't at all well and my wife used to go and visit her a lot. Well boys I don't need to tell you that I was a full blooded male and I had needs. Odd and bizarre needs that I'd picked up along the way from all me travels. It got to the stage when what you'd usually call normal sexual intercourse would no longer do it for me you see boys. I'd done things and had things done to me in those whore houses over the years that changed me as a man. Strange things, many of which still haunt me to this day. Dark things that I still sometimes wake up in the middle of the night screaming about.'

Ron was now staring into space and his hands were trembling.

'Cool' said Wayne staring up at him in awe. 'That's the sort of thing we're looking for!'

Ron suddenly came to.

148

'So yes anyway lads if it's whores that you're after you've come to the right man because I've slept with hundreds probably thousands of the buggers, all shapes and sizes. This one time I was off me bleeding nut in Egypt and this beautiful girl came up to me in the street and asked me if I was looking for a good time. Well, I didn't need to be asked twice and immediately said bloody too right I am love! She then smiled at me, took my hand and led me down all these back alleys. I was sure that I was going to be jumped and robbed but just as I was getting ready to kick her in the cunt and run off she knocked on this door. As we waited I was giving her the once over and counting my lucky stars because she was absolutely gorgeous boys. Eventually the door was opened and suddenly I was face to face with one of the most grotesque fellas I'd ever set eyes on. I'm not a religious man boys but when I saw him I immediately crossed myself. His face was just a mass of tumours and he had a hunched back lads! He really put the wind up me, I can tell you that!' Ron then began doing an impression of this man by bending over dropping one of his shoulders. 'Anyway he beckoned me in and when I turned back around the beautiful girl had disappeared! Well I thought that I was a goner then and it was all a scam but the hunchback beckoned me to follow him. I've always prided myself on being a curious man boys and I decided it was either shit or bust so I decided to go for it. He led me through this passageway and into a small room and in this room were two women lying on a bed.'

At this point our Wayne was hopping from one foot to the other with excitement.

'What happened next Ron? Tell us what happened next!?'

'Well I paid the hunchback a few shekels and fucked them both didn't I?! Ron replied triumphantly. 'What do you think I did?'

Well that was an anti-climax. Our Wayne looked crestfallen.

'Do you have any more brilliant sex stories like that one?' I asked him sarcastically.

'Well there was this one occasion where I was urinated on by an albino dwarf with three tits while I shagged her mother. It could have been her grandmother to be honest boys. She was a wretched looking thing, but she knew her way around a cock lads. Took both my bollocks in her mouth as well. She just dislocated her jaw like a bloody
149

python and the whole lot went in. Then she stuck a finger deep into my arsehole lads! Right up me back passage and started wiggling it about until suddenly I shot my bolt right down her bloody throat and when I looked down she'd taken a shit on my chest. For an old lady it was a very healthy looking turd to be fair. Then the albino one picked it up and ate it. And all for less than a pound in today's money boys.'

'Fuck me Ron, I would have lead with that one.' I said, and Wayne just stared at him with his mouth open.

'Well Ron that's fantastic and we'd love to stand here and listen to all your past sexploits but what we're really looking for is a kind of entry level prostitute to get me and our Wayne off the ground if you know what I mean?'

Then it was Big Ron's turn to look a bit crestfallen. I don't think he had many friends or even acquaintances due to being so fucking odd. Our family was odd as fuck too though and I'd always liked the fact that he had never looked down on us. My parents were drug addicts and alcoholics and more than likely both psychotic and most of our neighbours kept their distance and ignored us or worse, they pitied us.

'Listen Ron, what about if me and our Wayne pop over one night next week and you can put on some of your favourite frocks and parade about in front of us? You could do a sort of fashion show! We'll get a few beers in and a take-away curry or a Chinky and you can tell us all about your adventures as a merchant seaman! How about that!?' I offered.

'Aww fuck me Johnny that would be ace!' exclaimed our Wayne, visibly excited.

I suddenly realised that Wayne had never been over to anyone else's house or ever been to a party or ever had any real fun in his entire life. And neither had I.

Big Ron was rubbing his hands and hopping from one foot to the other in excitement. 'Oh boys that would be ruddy bloody brilliant! It's a date!' he trilled.

A curious and disturbing choice of words I thought to myself. I hoped big Ron didn't think this was a fucking date in the true sense of the word. I really hoped that he didn't think that we would all end up shagging each other. Although if push came to shove I wouldn't object to emptying my nut sack over those lovely big tits of his. It was no skin off my nose if he and Wayne wanted to get it on though and by the look on our Wayne's face I think he might be up for it. Wayne had been starved of affection all his life and he'd had a taste of it back in the park, over that bench. Sure it was one sided, brutal, non-consensual affection but closer than he'd ever been to getting some. I think that now that door had been opened Wayne was developing a taste for it. And so was I.

'Brilliant! It's a date then. Can't wait. Now then where are these prostitutes Ron? Wayne is chomping at the bit and I've got to admit that all this sexy chat has got me at it too so if you'd be so kind as to direct us to the nearest whore house we'll be on our way.' I replied, trying to hurry things along.

'Well boys the lady I go to is on Cromwell Road. She's getting on a bit but she certainly is experienced.' Said Ron.

Fuck sake I didn't really like the idea of shagging some old bird that big Ron had been up, but beggars can't be choosers. I just wanted to lose my virginity and I was more than happy to pay for that to happen. Sure it would have been great to tell our grandkids that me and Sally lost our virginities together one summer's evening as the sun set over a beautiful meadow or some shit like that but I was running out of time. I was nearly sixteen and around our way if you still had your cherry at sixteen you were clearly a bender.

'Excellent! What's her name and address and how much does she charge? I replied. I needed all the finer details so that we knew what to expect. I didn't want to get ripped off, even though at the moment money was no object thanks to me robbing Micky earlier. Over the years, after all the money and stuff that cunt had taken off me and our Wayne I figured we were still down and I reckoned he still owed us. If he was dead I decided that I'd gate crash his funeral, demand the outstanding balance from his grieving family then piss on the coffin. Then and only then would we be even. I might even try to shag his mum. Up the arse.

151

'Well her real name is Dorothy but her prossy name is Candice. I've been going there for years so I get a discount with my loyalty card. Although I think she does various deals like, two for one and early bird discounts. Plus it obviously depends what you're after.' Replied Ron in a very matter of fact way.

Dorothy? For fuck's sake it wasn't exactly inspiring me but Candice was a bit more whore -like I guess. Personally all I wanted to do was lose my virginity and practise for when I banged Sally so that she'd be bowled over by my sexual prowess and be mine forever. As for our Wayne who knew what sordid things were going on in his depraved mind? He was four or five years older than me- we never celebrated our birthdays- and I wasn't sure exactly how old our Wayne was. He'd had to live with my parents all on his own until I arrived and God only knew the sort of things he'd witnessed and internalised during that time and how it had affected his mental health. I was blatantly aware that I wasn't exactly what you'd call normal by any stretch of the imagination, but our Wayne was clearly psychologically fucked up in the head. Our Wayne had not been socialised and knew no boundaries especially when it came to sex. What depraved shit would manifest itself now he'd been freed from his cage and seen the light? The red light.

'Well I think to start with all we want to do is have some run of the mill, normal, everyday sexual intercourse just to get the ball rolling Ron.' I replied, while catching our Wayne's eye as a sort of warning to him not to do anything odd until we'd initially got our feet wet.

Wayne looked down at the ground and looked a bit deflated. To cheer him back up I continued, 'But I'm sure once we've got the hang of it we can progress to more adventurous sexual activity should we so wish,' at this our Wayne perked up a bit and shot me a wry smile. It was good to see him happy at last. I loved him dearly because he was my big brother and I was sure that if he's had a normal upbringing he'd have been just like everyone else but he didn't and he wasn't. Plus he'd just recently beaten the shit out of both our parents and that made me very happy and also extremely proud. If we went home to find both our parents were dead and the police waiting for us to take us to prison I was sure that I'd be fine about it because they'd got what they'd deserved. I didn't think our Wayne would cope very well in prison though so I

152

was determined to keep him out of it by any means necessary. Plus I'd be alone and vulnerable to revenge attacts without him. We needed each other.

'Right then Ron how much do you think it would cost for me and our Wayne, one at a time obviously?' I asked.

I loved our Wayne but didn't want to be going twos up on old Dorothy especially with his genitals being so much bigger than mine and showing me up. Plus I didn't want to be anywhere near him when he shot his load because there was always pints of it and we'd all be covered in the stuff. No, I planned to go first and get it all out of the way and then sit patiently in her living room sipping a complimentary cup of earl grey until he'd also done the deed and then we'd be on our way. I was thinking twenty minutes all in from start to finish. Then a bite to eat and off home to see the carnage. Another day another adventure.

Big Ron looked skywards and thought for a moment. 'Well boys I think with the pair of you and if you mention my name you'd be looking at around fifteen to twenty quid but as I say that all depends on any extras you'd be after.'

'We just want to fuck this bitch and get the fuck out Ron we don't want any extras!' I replied exasperated now.

'Now Johnny young man, have some bloody respect. Candice may be a lady of the night but she's still a classy woman and I don't want you going over there and being rude to her!' Big Ron replied while wagging his finger at me.

I was embarrassed by my behaviour. 'I'm sorry Ron I'm ashamed of myself, please forgive me. I just got carried away with it all. Of course we will treat Dorothy or rather, Candice, with the utmost respect. Won't we Wayne?' I replied while giving our Wayne a stern look and wagging my finger in a vain attempt to try to deflect my humiliation on to him.

Wayne looked at me with mock pity and slowly shook his head and tutted. 'Don't you worry Big Ron I'll make sure Johnny behaves himself.'

153

I was both hurt and dismayed. The cheeky fucking bastard. What the fuck?! Wayne taking the moral high ground? This from the man that had very recently beat the shit out of several people, one of those being a bloody bird and furthermore raped one of them over a park bench! Double standards or what?

'Listen Big Ron nobody is going to disrespect Dorothy aka Candice! We are just going to go over, give her one each, bung her a few quid and take our leave, simple as that okay?' I cried, just wanting the whole conversation to end now.

'Good lad. It's flat three, twenty five Cromwell road. Ring the buzzer three times on the bounce and wait to be let in through the main door'. Replied Big Ron and inexplicably shook both our hands. 'And don't forget to mention my name lads. Good luck and don't do anything that I wouldn't do' he chuckled as he waved us back down his path. 'See you next week! I'll shave me chest and legs and bollocks!' he shouted after us.

Jesus. "Don't do anything that I wouldn't do?" Fuck me what wouldn't he do? I thought that I was an oddball but Big Ron was the king of depravity. It was quite refreshing to be honest. I wanted to have a good go at everything before I settled down with my Sally. I needed to get everything out of my system before I settled down to a simple, no dramas, run of the mill, everyday life with my one and only. Getting pissed and shat on and all that other malarkey would have to wait for the time being though because all I wanted was to break my duck.

We marched on up the road and headed over to Dorothy's. Fortunately for us it was only two streets away. Who would have thought that all that available sexual intercourse was so close all this time? And hopefully for under twenty quid all in. I kept forgetting that I was now loaded. When you're poor you have to do everything on a budget and it was a difficult habit to get out of. I'd heard stories of self-made millionaires who were still tight as fuck and I understood it completely. I was going to have to get used to being minted and enjoy it, because I planned to become very fucking wealthy. Walking into that chip shop earlier and ordering what I wanted without calculating whether I had enough money was a first for me, and a revelation. Yeah I wasn't buying a fucking yacht or a Rembrandt but it still felt incredible. On

154

our estate everyone was poor as fuck and if we needed anything doing the first question would always be, how much? To live a life in which I never needed to ask that question was now my goal. I'd briefly witnessed how the other half lived. Nonchalantly handing over a fifty pound note to the bird behind the counter and seeing her face change from apathy to awe was like winning the lottery. I revelled in the moment when she passed it to her boss who looked at me then took out one of those marker pens, drew on it and nodded that it was legit. I smiled sweetly at her when she passed me all my change as I stuffed it into my pocket without even checking to see if it was correct. Walking back to our house with more food than even me and our Wayne could possibly have eaten in my arms felt like walking on water. I wanted everyone who I'd ever met to walk past me and see me on that day.

In a thrice we were standing outside an old Victorian mansion house that had clearly been converted into flats. The place had seen better days and looked shabby to say the least. It looked like a veritable palace compared to our gaff though and we bounded up the stone steps two at a time. So this was the place in which I'd lose my virginity. I took a deep breath. By the side of the main entrance door there was a row of names alongside a number going up from two to five. Number one I worked out must have been the flat in the basement. Beside the number three was the immortal words, 'Dorothy aka Madame Candice' hardly discrete I thought to myself. The first name was probably for her bingo mates and the meals on wheels guys. 'We've come to fuck you not feed you Dorothy!' I thought to myself.

'Press it Johnny! Press it!' Cried our Wayne excitedly as he punched me on the arm which nearly sent me flying down the fucking steps.

'Fuck's sake our Wayne! We need to be cool so she doesn't realise that we haven't ever done this type of thing before and over charge us or even worse, tell us to fuck off!' I replied. I whacked him with all my might on his arm but I don't think he noticed. I did notice that he had an enormous hard-on though. That thing seemed to be hard all the bloody time now.

I pressed the buzzer three times in quick succession with what I'd hoped would be all the flippancy of someone who'd had sexual intercourse with many prostitutes and wasn't at all out of his fucking depth.

After what seemed like an eternity a female voice answered via the telecom.

'Hello? Who is it please?'

I tried to picture her. She was definitely no spring chicken by the sound of her rather frail voice, probably even older than June. Suddenly the thought of the acrid smell of June's rancid old clopper came into my mind. But it wasn't just in my mind the smell was still on my hands from earlier. Or it could have been the cod. I suddenly thought that I was going to throw up but was fortunately distracted by Dorothy's voice again.

'Who is this and what do you want?' she shouted, suddenly getting all impatient and cross. 'If it's you bloody kids again I'll tell your parents you bloody little shits, you mark my words I will!' she continued

I panicked thinking that we'd already blown it and shouted into the speaker, 'Hello Dorothy it's Johnny McQueen and our Wayne! We're friends of Big Ron and we've come to make love to you! I paused. 'If that's okay?

Shit, I'd given our real names away! I'd even thought of some made up names on the way there too. Spencer and Travis. We were two travelling salesmen looking for a bit of light relief. Well that cover story was already well and truly fucked.

'Paddy McQueen's lads?!' she replied.

Fucking hell she knew our dad!

'I used to babysit for you two while your parents went dancing!' she continued.

 For fuck's sake it couldn't get any worse.

'Oh hang on I think we've got the wrong house actually' I replied. I was now ready to abort. Wayne hit me again on the same arm, the cunt.

He leaned into the telecom and said, 'Candice, Big Ron said we could fuck you for fifteen to twenty quid depending on extras and that's why we are here. Because we want to fuck you and give you money. We want to make love to you and fuck you and give you money. We want to get our ends away, with you... and pay you money. Fifteen to twenty pounds depending on extras.'

Oh my God. What a stupid cunt! It was over now for sure.

'Well why you didn't say that right at the beginning boys!? I'm up the stairs, first door on the left. Replied Dorothy in a very matter of fact manner and she pressed the buzzer to let us in.

Wayne looked at me triumphantly. Fuck me he was full of surprises today.

'Well done our Wayne! We're in!'

We pushed the door open and flew up the stairs.

'Now Wayne remember what Big Ron said, we need to treat Dorothy or Candice or whatever her fucking name is with dignity and respect. Yes she's an old whore but she's still a human being okay?' I lectured Wayne. 'Do not try to bum her or beat her to death okay? Not until I've had my go anyway. Are we clear on that?'

'Yes' replied Wayne meekly.

With trembling hands I knocked on her door.

Eventually, after about what seemed like ten million years, the door swung open and, out from a cloud of powder and cheap perfume, Dorothy stood in the doorway triumphantly. With legs akimbo and wearing a pink 'baby doll' nighty. I could already see that her nightie was strewn with various stains and what looked very much like fag burns. I'd seen similar ones in my mum's catalogue and wanked off to them many, many times. She was also wearing thigh high black leather boots and a long blonde wig. She stood there like a Goddess. A Goddess who had seen better days. A wretched Goddess dragged up from the depths of hell. A wizened old Goddess who was less of a Goddess and more of a frail old lady in cheap lingerie and an ill-fitting
157

acrylic wig that she'd patently purchased from the local joke shop. She looked as if a three year old child with learning difficulties had done her make-up. It wasn't exactly subtle. Her lipstick was smeared over the few yellow teeth that she still possessed and there was so much of that red blusher stuff on her cheeks that she looked like she'd got swine flu. Her skin was grey and almost translucent. She also had a deep scar across her belly and was covered in stretch marks and blue veins. She looked to me like she'd been dead for at least a week and then half eaten by her cats but nobody had bothered to tell her. I shuddered.

'Hi boys, I'm Candice. Pleased to make your acquaintance' said Dorothy in a low throaty voice. I think it was supposed to be sexy but sounded more like she had lung cancer.

I burst out laughing.

Wayne once again smashed his fist into my arm. It was really aching now and I thought that it must be severely bruised. I thought about hitting him back but didn't want to make a scene.

'Excuse my brother's manners Candice but he forgets himself when he's nervous. And may I say that I'm a tad nervous myself being in the presence of a beautiful lady such as yourself.' Said Wayne. Then the cunt bowed and waved his hand like some cunt out of King Arthur's fucking realm.

I did not know what the fuck had just happened. I thought that I was going to faint. Maybe all this was some big, fucked up dream brought about by all the drugs I'd taken. Maybe I was in a coma? Or was it me that was dead?

I tried to steady myself. 'Ah good day Candice, my name is Travis and this is my colleague Spencer.' - or was it the other way around? - I pressed on, 'We were in the neighbourhood on business and a casual acquaintance of ours, a certain, Big Ronald, told us that you were the classiest whore, sorry I mean, lady of the night, in town so we thought we'd give you a go as it were.' I stuck out a hand.

'Fuck off Johnny you rude little shit cunt you haven't changed one bit since I used to change your dirty nappies all those years ago.' Replied Dorothy full of scorn.

Trust me to lose my virginity to an old babysitter that had more than likely fiddled the fuck out of me anyway. And now I'm going to pay her to do it again. She looked nothing like all the birds in my sexual fantasies regarding this particular masturbatory theme and I was gutted. I stared at this anorexic voodoo doll with the shrunken head and could have cried. I'd naturally assumed that prostitutes all looked like Diana Dors or northern landladies, all tits and arse and come to bed eyes, not a stars in their eyes, happy shopper, mummified, Vera fucking Lynn.

I decided right then to take my business elsewhere. I glanced up at our Wayne to give him the nod that we were leaving but he was somehow transfixed with this peroxide walnut in boots. He was obviously seeing something that I was missing because the cunt was literally drooling at the sight of her.

'Listen Candice, we're dreadfully sorry but I've just remembered that we're late for a very important business meeting, sorry to have wasted your time. Maybe if it's mutually convenient we'll pop back later in the week. Come along now our Travis time is money!' I said, as I tried to push our Wayne back down the stairs. My plea fell on deaf ears as the pair of them seemed to be in another world. A world that did not contain me. Dorothy didn't even acknowledge me and continued,

'You on the other hand Wayne have changed rather a great deal now haven't you?' Her eyes ran up and down him then up and down him again until they came to rest on his enormous and rapidly expanding crotch area. She came towards him and ran her boney old hand down his chest. 'You were always such a lovely, little polite boy until…well, let's not go into that right now because you've turned out just fine now haven't you Wayne?'

Was she taking the fucking piss out of our Wayne? The cheeky old bag.

She continued to run her hand all over Wayne's body while paying the cunt compliments. Meanwhile I'm stood in the doorway like a prize prick. I gave in.

'Can we come in and slosh one up you then or what?' I sulkily said, while producing a handful of crumpled up five pound notes.

'Shut your fucking mouth Johnny. Can't you see that me and Wayne are getting to know one another?' she shot back like a viper. Albeit an old decrepit viper that had dried out in the sun about two weeks before.

She now had both her hands on Wayne's massive cock and balls and was kneading them rhythmically. If I hadn't felt so fucking affronted I might have found this all a bit sexy myself but I'd got the arse so turned away in mock disgust.

'Johnny darling will you do me a favour and get the fuck out of my house? Me and your brother here have a bit of business to attend to?'

'What!?' I gasped. 'But it was my idea and I set it up and I've got the money! I retorted.

Wayne put his hands out and I instinctively gave up the cash.

'What about a nosh after you two have finished then Doris? Or I could bash one out into your wig for a fiver?' I enquired.

'One my name is fucking Dorothy you horrible little runt. Two, no I won't be sucking your tiny, little knob off or wanking you off into my... hair...for all the tea in China and fucking three, if I ever see you around here again I'll personally cut your ruddy knackers off now get the fuck out of my house!' She screamed. The effort of which made her wig fall in front of her eyes which threw her off guard for a moment. Then Wayne, with the delicacy of a surgeon, gently and meticulously placed it back in place. The fucking bastard. They then looked at each other with such... well it burns me to say it even now, but they looked at each other with such love and mutual respect in their eyes that even in the midst of all the mayhem I didn't know whether to puke my guts up or cry my heart out. Then with a spindly old leg she kicked the door shut in my face.

'Well I know when I'm not wanted' I shouted through the door 'So I will bid you both good day and take my leave!'

'Ooh the treacherous little fucker!' I thought to myself as I made my way back out into the street.

I was a bit rude though I guess and probably shouldn't have laughed at her all made up like an Ethiopian coco the clown. I surmised. I probably wouldn't have been physically able to bang the decrepit bitch anyway. All that saggy, loose flesh. Probably got off lightly. I'd be better off saving myself for someone more worthy. I doubted that Wayne will be long anyway. I bet as soon as she gets his cock out he'll come all over the place and hopefully drown her in his dirty concrete. Or even if he does fuck her he'll probably snap her in half. The raddled old cow. Those boots and that wig were quite sexy though. And those little panties she had on with the pubes sprouting out the sides. Oh well fuck it plenty more prostitute fish in the sea for old Johnny. I assured myself.

I rolled a spliff and sat on the front steps and waited for our Wayne. I hoped she's got a shower because he'd had his knob up young Kenny all afternoon and even before that he's not exactly what anyone might call the most hygienic of lads. Once old Dot got his cock out into the open air I'm sure she'd vomit up her world war two rations and throw the cunt out. Suddenly I heard a dull thud coming from the upstairs window. I glanced up to see Candice's face pressed up against the pane. I could also see her saggy old tits squashed up against it and our Wayne's big spade like hands frantically rubbing up and down her emaciated torso, pulling and kneading her elasticated old skin. I watched transfixed as he took both of old Dot's nipples between his fingers and thumbs and rolled and pulled at them. For one horrified moment I thought he was going to lift her off the ground by them but thankfully no matter how much he pulled they just kept on stretching until they were about six inches long and I could see the veins and what looked like a tied mark under her emaciated old tits.

'Fucking please have the decency to pull the bloody curtains!' I shouted up but I don't think that easing my embarrassment was their immediate priority. I tried my best to avert my eyes from this macabre, sexual horror show but couldn't. It was like watching a silverback ape scuttling a dead spider monkey. Wayne, obviously trying to get a better purchase violently grabbed Dorothy's hair and her wig immediately came off in his hand revealing the old hag's head which unsurprisingly was completely bald apart from a few grey wisps of hair and liver spots. This gruesome revelation, rather than deter him, seemed to spur them both on and I thought at one stage our Wayne was going to push the bitch right through the window and I had visions of them on the pavement below covered in blood and still at it. The noise of their grunting and screaming was making a nearby dog start to whine and howl. They went out of view for a few minutes and to be honest I was a bit gutted because it was quite a show. Then suddenly they were back but Candice's wrinkly old arse was now pressed up against the glass and her wig was back on. Who knew that our Wayne was such a gentleman!? He now seemed to be wearing Dorothy's underwear over his head and was inhaling deeply, his breath fogging up a patch of window pane. At one point he noticed me and grinned and gave me a thumb's up. I couldn't help but feel proud for him. Then I saw Dorothy say something into his ear and he nodded and suddenly rammed one of his fat fingers up Dorothy's arse hole. Even I looked away in disgust as he took it back out, sniffed it and popped it in his own mouth. Then Wayne, still up her, turned his massive bulk and moved away from the window and I thought that this macabre and disturbing, although admittedly titillating, show was now at an end. How naive I was. A few minutes later just as I was getting my breath back and preparing myself for our Wayne to come out, the upstairs window was suddenly pulled up. Wayne lent out of it and waved at me grinning from ear to ear. 'Take that you little Bitch! You ruddy like that don't you Wayne!?' Screeched old Dot from behind him. 'Now I'm getting fucked Johnny!' Candice is fucking me with a big, fat plastic cock! It's really great!' Wayne shouted at the top of his fucking voice right into the street. 'She's got it attached to a sort of belt and it's black! There's all different sizes but I've got the biggest one and it's right up my bum hole Johnny!' He continued. 'You've got to try this Johnny it's the fucking dog's bollocks!'

Fucking hell Wayne, time and a place and all that. Behind Wayne I could just about make out Dorothy thrusting her arthritic hips back and forth with all her might, banging against our Wayne's ass cheeks. Say what you like about the old crow there was still a bit of life in her when it came to it and she certainly knew her trade. Well worth a tenner of anyone's money I thought. You go girl.

'Who is Mummy's little bitch then?' She screamed as her wig came off once more. 'I am Candice! I'm Mummy's little bitch!' Wayne groaned in between thrusts. 'I'm Mummy's dirty little bitch!' Then Dorothy put two bony fingers into our Wayne's mouth and stretched it from ear to ear. 'Do you like that you ruddy little Sod?' She screamed. I could see all of Wayne's teeth and gum and his tongue was sticking out like some grotesque gargoyle. I wondered to myself why she was asking him questions when he was clearly in no position to make a coherent reply.

Just then I heard a shout from down the street. 'Dorothy for goodness sake love I've got the kids in here, they've got the croup, and they don't want to hear all this! Close the bloody window!

Dorothy stopped and pulled her cock out of Wayne's arse, pushed him back inside, stuck her head out and shouted, 'Sorry Jean love I was getting carried away again! You know what I'm like when I've got the bit between me teeth!' Then she noticed me, frowned and said, 'I thought I told you to fuck off Johnny?'

'I was just waiting for our Wayne!' I replied, crestfallen. She obviously still held a grudge and all thoughts of me getting any of what Wayne was getting went out the window once and for all.

'Well I haven't finished with your brother just yet so I suggest you ruddy well do one before I come down there and tear you a new arse hole! 'She yelled.

Then our Wayne came to the window inexplicably wearing a little grey wig on his head which I took to be the one Dorothy wore going to the shops and yelled, 'I'll see you later Johnny! Me and Candice are in Love! I've got Chinese love beads up my arse hole!'

Well that explained everything didn't it?

Before I could reply the old trout pushed our Wayne back into the room and slammed the window down shut and locked it. Show over.

I had no alternative but to do as I was told and fuck off.

'For goodness sake!' I said aloud, surprising myself by my lack of profanity.

Our Wayne woke up this morning the same old retard he'd always been and now he'd fucked two people and - I tried to imagine the odds - he'd also been fucked himself. Yes it was only by that scruffy old skank but it still counted. Plus he was now laughing and saying proper sentences and really coming out of his shell. It's amazing what beating the shit out of a gang of bullies and getting your brown wings will do for a person's confidence. I was happy for the fucker though and I contented myself knowing that I was instrumental in our Wayne finally finding a degree of happiness. Maybe all was not lost with me and old Dorothy? Maybe he'd put in a good word for me and I could go back tomorrow with some flowers or boiled sweets or some powered egg or something and get my dick wet after all. Ron was right, she obviously knew her way around a cock and I sorely needed some sexual experience. If I was to make Sally my girl. I could always go back to June I thought. That smell though. Even now I could smell her on my fingers and if that was what all bird's fanny's smelt like maybe I should try and bat for the other side. I was quite prepared to wank off that posh old queen in the public toilets earlier before he mugged me off and even though he was an old cunt too, at least his jizz didn't smell like a tin of tuna that had been left out in the sun. I didn't get to taste it but it surely couldn't have been as bad as June's rancid fanny batter. So far in to my sexual journey I knew which one I preferred.

Just as I was having this internal dialogue, who should I see waltzing down the road but Andy Bennett. My stomach turned over and my cock started to get stiff. About six months before, when I was getting nowhere with any of the girls in my year - or anywhere else for that matter, obviously including Sally- I developed a bit of a crush on Andy Bennett. Well a lot more than a bit to be honest. I was consumed by him. He called himself 'Sandy' and he was obviously gay as a sequined maypole on the good ship Lollypop. He modelled himself on Madonna and used to sashay into class every morning belting out her songs and giving me a proper diamond cutter in my pants. As you can imagine he was ripped to fucking pieces by the boys in our class but he took the taunts and ridicule in his stride and even seemed to revel in it. I admired him for that. He'd always come back with some clever and cutting reply and eventually most of the other kids left him alone. He was also protected by his six loyal fag hags who flocked around him and hung on his every word. Collectively they called themselves the Fabulous Seven. Presumably because there were seven of them and their leader was a tranny bender. One time Steve Homer and Paul Tucker were giving Andy some stick in class and he just stared at the pair of them for a few brief seconds before suddenly clapping his hands, twice, in quick succession. On cue, the whole of his gang of bitches set upon them with an unbridled fury. They punched and kicked and scratched and bit those two little cunts to within an inch of their lives until Andy clapped his hands again whereby they immediately stopped. We were all getting flashes of their knickers and the odd arse cheek and bras here and there which, as you can imagine, was a right royal and unexpected treat for any red blooded bunch of dirty little school boys like us lot. For me it was the look of power Andy had in his eyes as he stood back and watched his minions setting about those two insignificant pricks which made me almost come in my trousers. During the next break I had to go to Miss Clipson's art cupboard - inside which I did most of my wanking at school - and tug off two in quick succession just to be able to concentrate on anything else until I got home and really went for it. It's still in my top five go-to wanks to this day.

It was on the final day of term just before we broke up for Christmas when I really fell for Andy though. As it was the last day and no teacher or anyone else really gave a fuck, we were all allowed to wear civvies if we gave 10 pence to the Africans or spazzers. This was the day when we could all show off our individualities and cultural allegiances. On these days the school was awash with an eclectic mix of bikers and skins and punks and trendies and Indies and goths all roaming around the school in their respective gangs. I was feeling very chipper because I was wearing a Ramones T-shirt, drain pipe jeans and Doctor Marten boots. All recently stolen by me especially for this occasion. I'd have liked to have worn a bit of eye liner too, but I was getting my head kicked in enough as it was. As well as seeing who liked what type of fashion or genre of music on these days you could also tell whose parents had

a few quid and who was poor as fuck. It was no surprise to anyone that I was poor as fuck but it was only then that I realised that we all pretty much were. As far as I could tell the posh cunts were in the minority and on this particular day it was their turn to get pushed around and humiliated. It was quite refreshing for me to see kids in expensive clobber get their clothes ripped and scuffed as they were thrown to the floor by the lowly and jealous hard nuts. My mum was a despicable horror of a woman but say what you like she was also a very good shoplifter and taught me everything she knew. It's fairly common these days but she was the first person I'd ever see to wear a full burka and go into any high street shop and stuff any item that she fancied up it, knowing that no security guard would have the balls to accost her. On the one occasion when she did get approached by a store detective in Marks and Spencer's she apparently flew into such a mock frenzy of indignation while screaming incomprehensible gibberish in fake Arabic the poor cunt had to apologise and let her go with a fist full of money off coupons. All my clothes that hadn't been bought from jumble sales or nicked by me were nicked by her so at least on days like this I blended in more with the other kids. So there I am sitting down at my desk trying to keep a low profile while looking out for any potential future wanking material when in walks Andy in skin tight gold hot pants, pop socks pulled up to his thighs, hi-top trainers and a white cheesecloth shirt tied up around his midriff. It was all I could do not to whip out my cock and start beating off like a caged chimp. As he passed me I was inches away from the enormous bulge in his pants and I could smell his heady perfume. I let out a groan as he passed me and he looked down at me with a knowing look in his eye. 'Do you have anything to say to me, you wretched little boy?' he pouted. Even though I was fucking terrified I took the opportunity to look him up and down and take in the full glory of his alter ego Sandy. I had a few options here. I could have said something horrible enough to have got a good kicking from his crew of slags which I'd fantasised about pretty much constantly since they beat up Tucker and Homer or I could tell him what I really wanted to do which was run my tongue down his belly and all over his cock and balls while wanking my own cock and then pull down those little hot pants, bend him over my desk and fuck him senseless in front of the whole class and then kill myself at the exact moment I climaxed into his lower colon. Instead I just stared into his eyes with my mouth open and sat there dumbstruck for what seemed to be an eternity. 'I didn't think so' Andy calmly
166

mouthed as he took one of his nail varnished fingers and slowly closed my jaw. He then inexplicably ruffled my hair, blew me an exaggerated kiss, theatrically flicked back his hair and sashayed away. I could feel my face go a deep red and prayed that nobody was witness to my utter embarrassment. The rest of the class were just gawping at him though and nobody was interested in me, thank fuck. I did my utmost not to turn around and watch what I knew would be that perfect little arse of his as he walked over to his desk but knew that regardless of the consequences I'd bitterly regret it if I didn't. I coughed and, accidentally on purpose, dropped my pen onto the floor behind me and as I went to pick it up took a good long look at him as he got to his seat. Those hot pants were pulled up tight around his arse and I feasted my eyes and wank- banked that image for eternity. I rushed home that night, made sure the coast was clear and prepared for the most important wank of my life thus far. I lay on my bed and put my legs over my shoulders, opened my mouth and almost instantly ejaculated all over my own face as I shoved a finger deep into my bum hole. I justified this by telling myself that I needed to experience what I thought it might feel like if Andy had thrown me on the bed, fucked me and then shot his load all over me like I imagined the gays did. The initial wave of spunk was warm and not that unpleasant to be honest and when the next wave went down my throat it wasn't the worst thing I'd ever eaten. I lay there for a few moments trying to decide if this was something that I could do on a daily basis. Then all the spunk started to get cold and congeal and I started to feel a bit like a cunt so I grabbed one of Wayne's T-shirts, wiped myself down, got dressed and tried to put it to the back of my mind. I was straight, I had determined, and was in love with Sally one hundred percent. Every time I thought about Andy (and his beautiful face and gorgeous thick cock and firm little bum cheeks and his defiant attitude and those soft thighs of his and what it would be like to have his tongue in my mouth while his hands ran all over my body and urgently undressing each other until we were both naked and my cock was buried deep in his ass) I'd done my utmost to suppress it and now here he was walking down the street and there was nothing that I could do to avoid him. He looked fucking stunning. Long blonde hair, white T-shirt and denim jacket and cut off denim shorts wearing black, ten- hole Doctor Marten boots on his feet. I groaned again. 'Come on Johnny even the straightest of straight men would want to fuck Andy to death, he has it all.' I said to myself trying to justify the ever increasing bulge in my jeans.

167

There was no way to escape him as he'd already seen me. He walked right up to me and stood legs akimbo inches from me and breathed, 'Fuck me Johnny doesn't any cunt go to school anymore?' I laughed out loud.

He leaned forward and whispered in my ear. He was wearing the same perfume as that last time I was close enough to smell him and I thought that I was going to pass out. 'Tell me Johnny, how come every time I see you your dick is hard?' As he said this he cupped my genitals in his hand and squeezed. I closed my eyes and let out another groan. 'You're a dirty little homo aren't you Johnny?' He sighed and he bit me gently on the ear. Then he cackled loudly, let go of my cock and balls and sauntered off down the street with an exaggerated sway of his hips. 'Be seeing you Johnny you naughty little poofter!' He shouted at me and flicked me a dismissive wave and then theatrically smacked himself on his arse. I looked down at the front of my jeans where a big wet patch was rapidly developing. 'Fuck it, I'll take it.' I said to myself, took off my jumper, tied it around my waste and skipped down the street, grinning like a mong and feeling on top of the fucking world. What a day.

Chapter eleven

I decided that there was fuck all now to do but go back home and see what carnage was there. I walked up the path expecting the worst. I opened the front door. Silence. I thought for one brief, terrifying moment that I could be walking into a trap. Mum and Dad could have seen me walking up the path and decided to jump me as I entered the living room. I suddenly felt very helpless without our Wayne. I picked up the heavy glass ashtray that was still on the floor from the last time my father had thrown it at me. Taking a deep breath I barged against the living room door with all my might. Unfortunately for me in my panic I had forgotten that it opened outwards into the hall and bounced back off it theatrically. Fortunately there didn't seem to be any witnesses. I quickly picked myself up off the floor and made my way into the living room. 'Hello? Anyone here? Julie? Dad? Satan?' Aww, Satan, 'I wonder whatever became of that sorry mutt' I suddenly thought to myself. We had had numerous pets over the years. My dad would bring them home from the pub. We had Satan the longest though and I suddenly missed the way that he would always greet me when I came home. He'd jump all over me and bark excitedly and lick my face and hands however much I told the dopey cunt to get the fuck off. He also loved to try and fuck the cats which was always entertaining.

The place seemed completely empty. I tentatively walked through the entire house in case it was indeed an ambush but it soon became clear that once again I was alone. I rolled a joint on our living room table, flopped down on the sofa and surveyed the damage. There were two sets of blood stains on our carpet and also a smattering of yellow teeth. It was real then. It had all actually happened. I wondered if anyone had actually died. Why didn't I care? It was true that I cared about not getting into trouble and going to prison but it honestly didn't bother me at all that both my mum and dad could now be dead. Neither did I care if the Oakhill Gang were all dead either. I pictured poor old Kenny still bent over that park bench out for the count with goodness only knows getting shoved up his arse by all and sundry. Maybe all the local down and outs were taking it in turns to roger his lifeless corpse as I sat here? Should I go back and de nail the cunt? Nah. Debbie could be getting it too maybe? If there was anything left of her to fuck that was. I tried not to dwell on it. Maybe they all simply dusted themselves down and then went back to Mickey's mum's to plot their revenge? I doubted that last scenario because we had left them pretty fucked up and I'd be surprised if they had wanted to do anything more than have a nice hot bath and an early night. Time would tell I guessed, and there was fuck all I could do until it did. I decided to clean up a bit in case our Wayne brought Candice back. It wouldn't do for her to see all this blood and teeth and goodness knew what else strewn all over the place. She may be an old whore on her last legs but she was Wayne's missus now so she had to be respected.

I put all the chip paper in the bin, picked up my dad's teeth and swilled the living room carpet with hot water and vim. The best thing so far, now that my dad was no longer in charge of this household, was that I could turn on the immersion heater with impunity. Hot water running through the taps was, up until now, an unheard of luxury. 'When in Rome' I said aloud, knowing that phrase was incorrect but not being able to think of a more apt one as I also turned on the radiators. I wasn't sure that they'd even work as I'd never known the fuckers ever to have been used before. I didn't even know what they did until I went round to my mate Billy's house one day. I walked in to the intoxicating smell of clean washing drying on these magical room heaters and I could have cried. All my life I'd been wearing clothes that smelled of damp because if on the rare occasions my mum actually did any washing she always just spread it all about the house to dry at room temperature. I decided there and then that one thing me and our Wayne needed above everything else was a washing machine. I also decided that our clothes would never smell damp ever again because to smell damp was a sure fire indicator of being poor. But on they came and after a short while the whole house felt completely different. It became what the rich call cosy. After a line of speed, within an hour I'd pretty much cleaned the whole house except mum and dad's room which would have to wait because that room was a proper shit hole. I'd filled five black bin liners with household waste and another five with me and our Wayne's dirty laundry. I had decided that if my parents were not dead they couldn't possibly come back and live here. A line had been crossed and there was now a regime change and those two cunts were not part of my new world order. Me and our Wayne were now in charge and I couldn't risk ever lapsing back into our old way of life. I was going to throw all my parent's stuff in the fucking bin. Years of dirt and grease and grime and

170

fuck knew what else I scrubbed away in a drug-fuelled frenzy and my new sense of domestic pride. Afterwards I sat back and surveyed my surroundings. It was in no way yet a palace but at least it no longer stank of neglect and despair. I'd also scrubbed away the smell of my parents. No more sickly stench of cheap aftershave and no more smell of cheap deodorant that tried and failed to mask the real stink of my parent's pitiful lives. I was once again buzzing off my tits and it wasn't just the drugs I'd recently taken. I had a new found sense of optimism for the future. It had been a busy day and collectively me and our Wayne had achieved a great deal. I needed to take stock and collect my thoughts so I decided to make a list of my immediate priorities.

1) Do not go to jail.

2) Lose virginity

3) Do not lose virginity in jail

4) Get a washing machine

5) Form a gang to protect self from revenge attacks and to begin building empire.

6) Make love to Sally from next door. (Priority)

7) Get Wayne some new clothes.

8) Get a hoover and other shit to keep the house clean and tidy. Also get paint and wallpaper, BBQ and patio furniture, and pot plants.

9) Discreetly try to find out if parents are dead without incriminating self

10) Get toilet roll (not the cheap shit) Purchase thick white, fluffy bath towels, and fluffy white cover for toilet seat.

11) Get Toilet seat.

12) Toothpaste and toothbrushes.

13) Everything else.

Toilet roll! That reminded me. I was in dire need of a wank. I unzipped my flies then thought about it and stopped in my tracks. No, from now on I was going to do it in one of the designated areas like a gentleman. I was going to start wanking in the bathroom.

Up until very recently my life could have been described as being fucking shit but one thing that I was always grateful for was being born a boy. My favourite hobby was wanking off and being a boy made it very easy to pursue that interest. As far as I could tell or care physically speaking it was a lot easier for boys to have a quick one off the wrist than girls. If I wanted a wank, which I pretty much did all the time, I could just get it out and start pulling it with impunity. Of course one would have to be discrete. I'm not trying to suggest that I could have a wank in broad daylight in the middle of town like our Wayne did. I mean that due to our anatomy – protruding cocks- for us lads it was just biologically more convenient. Of course I'd like to be a bird for a bit so I could play with my tits and stick things up my fanny and that but ultimately all things considered I'd always been thankful that I was born a boy because I could wank standing up. I'd always imagined that girls would always have to rub one out laying down on their backs because it would be too difficult and cumbersome to stand in front of a sink for example, have a quick tug, shoot ones load then swill it down the plug-hole. Job done. Then the mind was able to think about something else other than sex for a ten minutes. I knew that women could conceivably just let it all soak into their underwear but I knew from experience that after a bit that got very uncomfortable and started to chaff and after a while, especially during the summer months, started to stink the fucking place out. Men had spunk in their ball bags and in order to not go mental this spunk had to come out and when it was out we didn't want it hanging about. It was definitely a man who invented the sink because they are all cock height. I did see one lady have a wank into a sink once but that was in a porno. She put one leg up on the sink and after aggressively rubbing her minge for a good ten or so minutes she squirted liquid all over the place. I'd never seen a woman do this before and wasn't entirely sure if it was for me. It went everywhere for a start. When a man comes it goes pretty much in a straight line, two of three vertical arcs of decreasing velocity and volume and we're done.

It was pretty easy for me to predict how much jizz I was going to come out of me at any particular time. If I was laying down, with an educated guess, I could pretty much gauge how many pieces of bog roll I would have to put vertically along my belly and this spunk runway would only ever be one square across. The first wank of the day could easily be eight of nine pieces and as the day wore on these pieces would degrease until my tenth or eleventh whereby I would be down to one or maybe two just to be on the safe side. Whatever it was that came out of that porn bird's fanny it went all over the fucking place. One of the fundamental differences between watching pornography and engaging with the real thing is smell. If I could have had a quick whiff of what came out of her as she sloshed and sploshed her load every which way

172

then I would have been in a much better position to have a guess as to what the fuck it actually was. I'd smelled two female vaginas thus far and if I was going to have a punt as to what this puzzling mixture of viscous liquid consisted it could best be described as if someone had left a fish, possibly a herring, out in the sun, covered it in frogspawn, pissed on it and let the whole thing ferment for a good few weeks in a dark and dingy basement. I really hoped that this was an acquired taste like dark chocolate or cabbage and that eventually I would not just get used to it but actually like it. At the moment though even the thought of it made me want to vomit. I sorely hoped that by the time it came to lick out Sally I was used to it because I wouldn't like to hurl all over her and spoil the mood. 'Whoops! Oh dear, sorry my darling please pour yourself another glass of wine while I pull out these bits of carrot and tomato skins from your pubes.

Another difference between us lads and the fairer sex I now knew was that they took, ages to actually have an orgasm. I was proud to be a double figures a day kind of guy and thus did not have the time or inclination to take ages at it. I came quick and with the minimum of effort. It seemed to me that birds needed a lot more time and pre planning and they also made a fucking racket along the way. When I wanked off I was pretty much silent until I was about to come then as I was coming I might let out a little groan and even that was more to do with copying the guys I's seen in porn films than any real need to. Maybe I'd taught myself to be quiet during my formative wanking years? It had always been a solitary and guilt ridden action so I'd never felt the need to shout about it. 'Hey mum and dad and our Wayne I'm just popping upstairs for a wank!' 'Okay son have a good one!' Thanks mum will do!' For us Catholics wanking was shameful and a big fat sin. If my seed went down the sink then that was potentially one less catholic in the world. Not only that, due to our God being omnipotent I'd always felt rather self-conscious. Then we had all these guardian angels and dead relatives up in heaven relentlessly keeping an eye out. It was a wonder that I could get it up at all with all those fuckers watching me. I couldn't even take a piss in front of anyone else let alone crack one off. During a bout of self-love we Catholics had to try and conjure up a few raunchy thoughts while also trying to blot out the big man himself, all his crew, all our ancestors and any other passing spirits and try and get it done as quickly as possible.

'Hey guys put the harps down, climb down off your clouds our Johnny is having another wank!' I really hoped that they couldn't also see into my imagination too because if that was the case then I'd well and truly damned for all eternity. Christ only knew how all those priests got by without having a shag or a knuckle shuffle and it came as no surprise to me that so many of them ended up alcoholics, nut jobs and paedophiles. The first thing I had to do every morning was smash one out otherwise I wouldn't be able to concentrate on anything else. How could I think about what to eat for breakfast when my mind was rammed with sexual depravity? It was impossible. A quick one first thing would always allow me to get on with the more mundane aspects of life and stop me going crazy. I think the world would be a lot better place if every religion made it mandatory for their followers to bang one out every morning. In my humble opinion it seemed obvious to me that the membership of any religion which gave away a complimentary jazz mag with every copy of their religious text would certainly go through the roof. No, a life without ever being able to draw one off was not the life that I could live. As a young boy I'd often thought about becoming a priest as it seemed like a pretty cushy number. Sunday would be busy but after that it as far as I could tell it would be all sitting about getting drunk while people told me their dirty sins. Some hot mum would be in one side of the confessional telling me how she'd been sinning her arse off with the milk man while her husband was at work and I'd be on the other side having a wank about it. 'Not to worry Mrs O'Brian do ten hail Marys, five star jumps and show us your tits and you're good to go.' Piece of piss. This would all be fine and dandy until my day of reckoning when I'd stroll up to those pearly gates giving it the large one.

'Oi! Oi! Saint Pete me old china! How's it hanging?'

Saint Peter looks at me and then glances at his notes.

'Ahh Father McQueen! Not a fucking chance mate.'

'Oh come on Pete don't be like that!'

'Jesus, Mary and fucking Joseph Johnny it says here that you've sinned at least ten times a day by self-pollution since you first set eyes on a pair of tits back during that hot summer of 76! There's no way I can let you in here with that record. If I were you I'd be rubbing some of that factor fifty sun block into your Irish skin because it's pretty hot down there in the fiery depths of hell.'

'Let he who is without sin cast the first stone and all that eh Pete? I'm sure you must have had a few discretionary wanks while you were on earth. Good for the soul ain't it? I won't tell if you don't!'

'This ain't about me though is it and rules are rules Father McQueen so if you'd be so kind as to fuck off downstairs as quick as you can there's a tsunami due in Indonesia very shortly so it's going to get busy up here.'

'You need to calm the fuck down Peter, you're getting yourself at it. Yeah sure I've broken the no wanking rule but think of all the little boys I never fiddled! That's got to be worth something surely? Yes I enjoyed bashing the bishop on occasion but did I bum a child? No. Did I once seagull Sister Marie Christine in the vestry? Yes. Did I use my power as a priest to coerced innocent little children do sinful things to my bottom? No sir I did not. You know yourself how hard that was don't you Pete? If you look down at your notes, you'll see that my tally for child sodomy is a big fat zero and some of them at my church were absolutely gorgeous too! Whose idea was it to dress them up in those little dresses anyway?! You're asking for trouble if you ask me mate. Sometimes at the right angle on a sunny day you can see right through them and they leave nothing to the imagination I can tell you that! But did I ever scuttle even one? No Pete, I did not. And do you know why? Because my balls were always empty that's why. I can't tell you the number of times I was stood there at the front giving out the host with a massive boner under my cassocks! All those sexy woman and girls literally queueing up to kneel in front of me with their mouths wide open but did I abuse my position and take advantage? Nope. It was because of my constant meat beating that they received the body of Christ rather than a pearl necklace Peter. It was pure torture and I'd have to have been a right proper arse bandit- which as you know as well as I do is also a cardinal sin- not to wait for them all to fuck off and immediately and urgently smash one out into the font. And while I'm at it I know that they aren't all that but how many nuns did I shag? Go on have a look at your precious notes! Not one! And as they couldn't give themselves sticky fingers they were coming on to me all the time! Rubbing themselves up against me and trying to get me drunk on all that communion wine but I never succumbed because I made sure to keep the tanks empty. And what about some of the members of my congregation or them birds who come round to clean the place? Never even put even a hand on them except to bless them. How many times did I bend one over and give them one? Zero Pete. I

175

can't tell you the opportunities I had to blackmail some of the hotter women in my parish too! Some of the things they told me in confidence would make your bloody hair curl! But did I take advantage? No sir I did not. I just waited for them to finish, told them to do a few press-ups, absolved them of their sins and then had a nice long wank about it. The case for the defence rests Saint Peter. Now let me in you big pious twat or I'll get my brother to kick your fucking head in.'

'Oh fuck it come on in then Father McQueen you cheeky little scamp get yourself in.'

'Nice one Pete, now then what's the pussy like in here...?'

Saint Peter: (Putting his arm around my shoulder and walking me into paradise)

...You must come round to mine for a few drinks one evening and tell me in more detail about some of these confessionals you mentioned earlier. Any lesbian content?'

So yeah I'd decided that as I was the silver back of the house from now on I'd bang one out more discreetly and in a more civil fashion.

Ahh, having a wank in a clean environment. I suddenly felt very proud of myself. I liked the feeling of having a modicum of self-respect. I ran up the stairs two at a time and burst excitedly into the bathroom. The new smell of Vim and bleach that greeted my nostrils filled me with joy. I'd scrubbed the lino and the walls and the double layer of tiles around the bath and to my mind anyway it didn't look half bad. It was a real pleasure to empty my balls once again into the sink and then watch it all slip away majestically down the plug hole rather than congealing and sticking to the basin until my dad, and quite conceivably my mum too judging by her hairy old top lip, had come along and had a shave in it. The dirty bastards.One might have thought that their faces would have been a lot less lined and craggy what with all my spunk they'd been splashing over their faces ever since I was tall enough to crack one off into that basin. So with a mind full of Sally and Sandy and Aunty Joan and old June and to my utter shame and bemusement, Candice and big Ron's tits, it wasn't long before once again I'd emptied my bollocks.

I picked the worst of my family's public hairs off the soap, wet it under the tap and then rubbed it all over my cock and balls. It felt good to be clean. During my drug powered housework I'd thrown all the old towels we had into a bin liner so the only thing left to use before I had a chance to go to the shops was to dry off my cock using the bathroom curtains. I swore at that moment that would be the last time I would act

176

so crass. Well at least try not to anyway. Many of the vulgarities I'd indulged in up until this point I wasn't even aware were vulgarities. I wasn't conscious at the time that wanking into the sink or a sock or having a wank while watching Sally next door in the garden sunbathing was in any way wrong. I was just acting on instinct. I was a child and I didn't know the correct way to behave because I'd never been taught about morality. My dad, for example, never took the trouble to sit me and our Wayne down and say, 'look lads we are men and we all like a tug it's basically what we do, but you can't just get it out anytime you feel like it and start yanking away. A gentleman must be discreet. Now here's a copy of Razzle and a box of Kleenex so you don't keep ruining your mum's tights.' No, rather than being a guide and a mentor he was too busy being a selfish prick. We had to learn the hard way by trial and error. I thought to myself that when me and Sally had kids that I'd try my very best to be the perfect example of a father and learn by my dad's mistakes. My kids would be well fed, clean and polite and only wank off in the privacy of their rooms and if they did for any reason have to use the bathroom there would be lovely big white fluffy towels to dry themselves off with. And flannels. I made a mental note to try and remember to get a few flannels or wank rags to use the more precise term.

After my wank I came back down stairs, sat in my dad's old chair and surveyed my kingdom. I'd cleaned up as best I could with the cleaning utensils that I had to hand but it was still a shit hole. I would have been happy enough to have lived in a pig style like this forever had I not had seen Del and June's gaff. It felt so comfortable and warm and peaceful. I could have stayed in their lovely bathroom forever. The whole place was so well planned with so many classy touches here and there. There was even a knitted doll type thing that covered their shit tickets. Plus there was a can of something that you sprayed after you'd done a big smelly shit. I wanted to live in a house like that. If me and our Wayne were going to rise up in the world we needed a nice, safe, cosy place to come back to every night after a busy day becoming Mafia Dons. The thing I craved more than anything apart from Sally next door was respect and we wouldn't be getting any of that if my burgeoning Cosa Nostra where to ever see this fucking dump. I had three hundred odd quid in my pocket and to me that felt like a fortune but it wouldn't last forever. To maintain the lifestyle I had planned for myself I needed a steady income. Getting a proper job was obviously out of the question. For a start I was technically still at school and furthermore the thought of getting up atsix o'clock, working in some fucking factory or on a building site all day then coming home in the evening exhausted five days a week until I retired all fucked up and broken didn't appeal to me in the slightest. Maybe if my dad had been more of an upstanding citizen and earned an honest wage like I'd imagined the majority of normal fathers did then I might have felt differently but he wasn't and I didn't. Me and my brother Wayne had earned over three hundred quid today in less than an hour and the only tools we used were a couple of house bricks, a hammer a few nails and brute force. How long would it have taken us to make that kind of money legitimately? By my reckoning it would have been fucking ages.

It suddenly dawned on me that I had looted my parent's bedroom. That was a room I didn't like to spend much time in as it always filled me with fear and dread. Many wrong things had occurred in that room over the years and it made me shiver to even think about entering it even now that I was sure the coast was clear. The curtains were permanently closed and the windows always shut so it was perpetually dark and the air was fetid. It held sinister undertones and I thought twice about going in. I took a deep breath. If I was to dismantle the old regime and banish the past I had to step up to the plate and become a valiant and a brave, fearless warrior. I was no longer under the cosh of my parent's and only needed to keep reminding myself of this fact until all the ghosts had been exorcised. I slowly rose from my dad's old throne and climbed purposely back up the stairs and made my way to the room that used to be my parent's. I stood in front of the bedroom door, took a deep breath, held my nose and burst in. I headed straight to the window, drew back the curtains and opened all the windows as quickly as I was able. They hadn't been open in years and were caked in grime and mould and cobwebs and the skeletal remains of dead spiders and a whole host of questionable detritus but I managed to get them all open before I breathed out again. I stuck my head out of one of the windows, gasped and took a long and deep breath. In the cold light of day the room had already lost most of its mystique and general terror. I looked around at all the clutter and filthy disarray. Clothes were strewn everywhere. It smelled like a charity shop giving off an air of stifling decay and mustiness. Like dead people's clothes.

I briefly wondered if my parents were actually dead. I'd like to have thought so but what if when I'd actually found out that they were I felt differently? On some innate level weren't you predisposed to care for your parents unreservedly? I was pretty sure

178

that consciously I was sick to death of the cunts and was glad to see the back of them but what if on another level I'd be devastated? Fuck it, time would tell and I'd just have to cross that bridge if or when I came to the fucker. What about that Freud fella didn't he think that everyone wanted to kill their dads and fuck their mums? Well he'd got it half right. He'd obviously never set eyes on my old dear and if his mum looked remotely like mine and he did end up slipping here a length it would have been that cunt who'd ended up in therapy after trying to bite off his own eyes out.

I tried to imagine the first time Sigmund Fraud come out with that theory.

Mrs Fraud: 'Hey Sigmund you're quiet, whatcha thinking? '

Sigmund Fraud: 'Oh I was just thinking that every boy wants to fuck his mum and kill his dad.'

Mrs Fraud: 'I'm just nipping upstairs to put on some lippy before I pick up the boys from school.'

Awkward silence.

Looking at all the mess I quickly decided that I'd be fucked I was going to bag all their shit up like some kind of prize cunt so I tapped another little pile of whizz on to the side of my knuckle, snorted it, stood up straight, had a stretch and began frantically throwing all their shit out of the bedroom windows. I felt like one of those scorned woman you see in Italian films who has just found out that their lover had been cheating. Feverishly I start bunging all their gear outside but not before I searched for any money or drugs or anything else that I thought I could sell. Within a very short time I had pretty much cleared the room of its entire contents. I'd found about thirty quid in long forgotten fivers and change and also a few wraps. Mostly speed but one was good uncut coke which I stashed in the little pocket that I'd assumed was made for this exact purpose in the front of my jeans.

When I'd tossed out the last of their belongings I peered out of the window and looked down. Their whole lives were laid out amongst the unkempt wilderness that was our front garden. And what a sorry sight it was too. Even the starving Africans would have turned up their noses at that little lot. Jackets, trousers, jumpers, pants, socks, hats, gloves, ties, stockings and suspenders- I had briefly thought about letting big Ron have a look at some of my mum's stuff in case he fancied any of it but in the end decided that it was probably all too big and also too gaudy for his tastes. I just wanted all memories of them gone. I didn't want to be walking down the road one day

179

in the future to be greeted by big Ron wearing one of my mum's fucking frocks or a pair of her old tights. Especially the jizz stained ones. There was also an awful lot of fetish gear. Black leather rape masks and whips and chains and handcuffs and an assortment of plastic cocks and strap-ons and butt plugs and ball-gags. You name it if it was something that you could wear or stick up an orifice it was there. I wasn't even shocked by all that stuff as over the years I'd pretty much seen it all before anyway. One Sunday morning a few years ago my dad shuffled downstairs wearing a gimp mask and a studded leather G string. He walked right past me and our Wayne as we both sat about watching television without even saying good morning. Brazenly he went through to the kitchen and made himself a brew like that was the most normal thing in the world. Me and our Wayne didn't even comment. Such was the norm in our house. I gathered the whole lot up and put them in a black bin liner. I thought that maybe Doris might want them after they'd had a good scrub. I wouldn't even charge her anything for them because she'd put a smile on our Wayne's face and even though she was a rancid old troll I had to give her due.

'Phase one complete' I said out loud as I obsessively ground my teeth. I'd taken a hell of a lot of drugs that day and knew that sooner or later I had to crash so I pushed on quickly. Next I went through all the drawers. My dad's porn I was obviously going to keep. Apart from my favourite films and mags I thought that I'd give the rest of it to our Wayne to keep the fucker pacified when Dorothy was on rag week or with a client. He didn't take drugs so the only way I thought that I could control him was to keep his bollocks empty. I could no longer afford to have him looning off around town waving his cock about to any passing bit of crumpet that crossed his path anymore. I wanted to become respectable and respected and this wouldn't happen if our Wayne was forever sexually assaulting people.

I planned to move into my parent's old room and then he could have ours all to himself and wank away morning noon and night if he so wished.

Just as I was rifling through my dad's bedside cabinet I suddenly heard a familiar voice.

'Johnny you fucking little cunt what the fuck do you think your fucking doing you little cunt!?'

The unmistakable baritone voice of my dear old aunty Joan.

I poked my head out of the window.

180

'What the fuck do you want Aunty Joan?' I shouted down to her, even though I did have an inkling.

'You nearly killed your fucking mum you little cunt!' She shouted as she ran up to our front door, tried the handle, found that it was mercifully locked and started trying to break it down with her steroid enhanced body. I wasn't worried though because I knew that as my dad was a drug dealer and general all round scally wag that door could stand up to a nuclear blast.

'Nearly' I thought to myself. Shit the old bitch was still alive. And what did she mean by 'you' I never laid a fucking finger on her it was our Wayne that kneed her in the head. As I recalled all I'd done was thrown a chip in her general direction and was a tad sarcastic. Classic me.

She stood, legs astride beneath my parents' window. 'Get your fucking arse down here so I can kick your fucking head in!' Aunty Joan shouted up at me.

'I'm not going to do that aunty Joan' I replied. She was wearing a very tiny pair of Lycra shorts which was giving her an extremely pronounced camel toe and a crop top that was exposing her beautiful row of abdominal muscles. I knew that she wanted to kill me and I also knew that I really wanted to fuck her. I thought about saying, 'Listen aunty Joan never mind about old Julie why don't you come up here, I'll put a bin liner over your head and we can sort this out in the bedroom like men?' Then I remembered how badly her growler had stunk the last time so instead said, 'Fuck off Aunty Joan when my mum finds out what you did to me you're the one who is going to have the shit kicked out off. You dirty old nonce.'

Aunty Joan suddenly looked even more furious. 'You bloody little liar!' She shouted back at me all affronted. 'I never touched you! Who the fuck would go anywhere near you, ya ugly little poofter?!' I could tell by her tone that she was clearly shitting herself though. Nobody grassed around our way regardless of what it was and everyone kept their own and each other's secrets. There was always a ring of silence. Nobody had ever seen anything ever and it wasn't anybody's business anyway. Unless it was child abuse. Everyone was obsessed with the idea and if you got labelled a nonce then you were truly fucked guilty or not. Aunty Joan did not know that of course I was never going to tell my mum that she'd held me down using a half nelson or whatever the fuck it was and forced herself on me. One because I doubted that my mother would have given a shit and two, apart from seeing her ugly old boat

181

close-up and the smell of her breath and her nasty old rat, I'd very much enjoyed the whole thing.

'Don't be silly Johnny you know I'd never do that. 'She squirmed, looking furtively all around in case there were any witnesses. If Aunty Joan didn't play this right by the time she got back to see my mum word could quite easily spread that she'd done all sorts of sordid things to poor, innocent me. Around our bit you could beat the fuck out of your wife every Saturday night, neglect your kids, steal every fucking thing in sight and deal drugs openly in the street with total impunity but if anyone suspected that you were into kids you'd be strung up and lynched. Even having an air of nonce about you could get you killed by the baying mob. Any man who still lived with his mum over the age of thirty was a nonce. Any overweight scruffy loner was a nonce. Receding hair and glasses? Nonce. Train spotter? Nonce. Scout master? Nonce. Around here anyone male who wasn't married with kids by the time they were twenty might as well cut off their own genitals and top themselves just to get it over with. You were guilty until proven innocent by which time you'd be dead. Nobody bothered to phone the police around here. Everyone took the law into their own hands vigilantly style. It was like the Wild West and anyone breaking the host of unwritten rules would pay and pay dearly. The biggest insult anyone could throw at someone was the word nonce. Now if Aunty Joan had been a proper sort with a comely face and a beautiful womanly figure and demeanour then she'd be laughing. If I'd accused someone like that of sexually molesting me then I'd have just got fucking laughed at. Everyone knew that it was every school boy's sexual fantasy to be the willing 'victim' of a woman like that. We'd all read stories in the Sunday papers about older women who liked them young. These so called 'cougars,' prayed on us young lads and plied us with cheap alcohol and fags in order to seduce us and have their wicked way with us in any way in which they saw fit. Boys would bring these stories into school on Mondays and we'd all sit there poring over the pictures and reading these titillating tales aloud while dreaming that one day we would be one of their willing victims. We'd all sit there in class afterwards hoping that anyone of our female teachers would keep us behind after school, get us pissed and suck our cocks. I'd be walking home from school trying to catch the eye of any woman who looked anything like the birds in the papers in the forlorn hope that she might want to seduce a handsome rogue like my good self.

182

The trouble with Aunty Joan was that she looked like the polar opposite of these type of women. Not to put too fine a point on it she was a proper minger. She basically looked like a man with a vagina and not even a half decent looking man. It would have come as no surprise to anyone around here that she was suspect. I prided myself on having a very wide ranging and eclectic taste in birds and would pretty much fuck anything but not everyone threw their nets as wide as me. Aunty Joan was niche to say the least. Not everyone found bulging muscles on a bird as sexy as I did. Around here if you wanted to be accepted then you had to fit in to a very narrow and well established tradition of what was considered normal and what wasn't. If you didn't want to get ostracized or beaten to death you had to fit into the realms of what was considered the recognised British Kite mark standard. Classical femininity was the order of the day. The right amount of makeup, a nice hair do, a nice set of bangers, tight jeans that accentuated your arse however fat it was and a sexy pair of high heels. If you were a bird and you walked past a building site and the men started wolf whistling at you and telling how much they'd like to give you one you giggled and blushed and took it as a compliment. If you had the audacity to tell them to fuck off and not be so fucking sexist then you'd basically be broadcasting to the world how much of a big hairy dike you were. Unless they followed the well-trodden path of acceptable behaviour a young girl would very likely end up a sad and bitter, dried up old spinster who would die alone only to be found several weeks later when the meowing of her twenty odd cats would eventually alert the authorities to her decaying corpse. The face of which would inevitably be unrecognisable due to it having been eaten by her beloved pets. If you were actually a minority around our way the only way you could survive would be if you became a massive stereotype or if you made a mockery of yourself.

The only exception would be if you were hard as fuck like big Ron for example. You would be applauded by the majority for punching a suspected kiddy fiddler or shouting a racist remark at a dark skinned mum pushing a pram but you might as well pack up and fuck off if you got bitch slapped by a bloke wearing a micro skirt, crotch-less panties and boob tube. Aunty Joan was tolerated in our community because she was a friend of my mum and my mum was married to my dad and he was both respected and feared. She was different though and stuck out like a sore thumb. People around here did not celebrate difference and diversity what so ever and met it

183

with suspicion and contempt. Aunty Joan was true to herself and I admired that but she was walking across a high wire and it was a very precarious place to be. One unexpected gust of wind or a misplaced foot and she'd surely drop her pole and fall to her death.

 I felt a bit vulnerable without our Wayne around but decided that due to all the fucking drugs whirling around my body if push came to shove I might just about be able to take her. As I saw it, it was a win, win situation. Situation one, she calms the fuck down and fucks off or situation two we fight and she kicks my head in and I spend my recovery wanking off about the whole thing. I stared at her for a bit weighing up my options. The sun was beginning to set which threw off a beautiful reflection from her bulging arms as she was gathering up all my mum's stuff off the grass. Her whole body was pumped to perfection. When you use steroids you have to do three months on and three months off in order to give your liver and kidneys a fucking rest or something and Aunty Joan was clearly smack bang on them at the moment. When she wasn't on the gear her body shrank back to her normal size and she looked like a sun dried tomato. Not today though. As I watched her scrambling about on the floor my dick was getting harder and harder. Why did she have to take it all so seriously? I surmised. Mum was a cunt. Everyone knew that. So mum got what she deserved. It wasn't like it was an unwarranted attack. Aunty Joan was making my cock so hard and the old me would have cracked one off right there and then but if I was going to grow as a human and become a respected member of the community I'd have to wait until she's fucked off then done it into the bathroom sink like normal people.

I asked myself what a mafia Don would do in this situation. At the moment I did not have a machine gun so I couldn't spray her with bullets. For the neutral observer that would have looked fucking awesome but I didn't want her dead. Aunty Joan was one of a very select number of people that found my attractive enough to want to molest and I'd be cutting my nose off to spite my face if I killed her. I decided that damage limitation was my goal. I wanted the situation to be resolved diplomatically, peacefully and amicably so I tried reasoning with the bitch.

'Aunty John I don't want to fall out with you. Julie provoked us and paid the consequences. We will no longer take abuse from anyone. Those days are gone. You molested me on our couch because you are full of steroids and they've turned you in to a sexual predator that preys on the weak, the vulnerable… and yes, the sexy. Although I am clearly still sexy I am no longer weak and vulnerable. I'm a survivor and I will survive. You've always been a big part of my life and I've always loved you Aunty Joan but you took advantage of that love when you pinned me down and climbed onto my face while wearing those skin tight, tiny little shorts that left absolutely nothing to the imagination. You were grinding and writhing and gyrating and rubbing, rubbing and grinding and writhing as I lay there squirming helplessly on the sofa.' I said as I played back those events in my mind. I could already feel pre-cum seeping out.

'You've been more of a mother to me than my own mum over the years and I'll always love you for that.' I lied, trying to appeal to her nurturing side even though she patently didn't have one.

'I'm sure we can work this out without any more nastiness Aunty Joan. In fact I think this whole situation has brought both of us even closer together don't you?' My cock was throbbing like fuck so I started to sort of surreptitiously gyrate and bump myself against the edge of the window sill.

'I've always had a thing for older birds Aunty Joan and you in particular. I don't blame you for forcing yourself upon me as you're only human and if you do both of us a favour and calm the fuck down I'm sure we can come to some mutually beneficial arrangement.' I was desperately trying to think of a way of broaching the subject of her stinking fanny hole without upsetting her even more. I really wanted to slosh one up her but there was absolutely no way even a filthy little deviant such as I was ever going to stick my dick in her if her clopper was still as putrid smelling as earlier. I'd already decided that honesty in this scenario was probably not the best policy so I couldn't just ask her how badly her cunt stank. 'Hey Aunty Jean, just a quick one before we go any further, can we call a truce while I nip down and have a hasty sniff of your minge so I can decide on my next move please?' I pictured myself running out waving a white flag, skipping over to where she stood then getting down on my knees, sticking my nose between her legs, inhaling her crotch, nodding to myself as a scratched my chin, scribbling some notes into a small writing pad and then scurrying back in, up the stairs and back to the window. From there it could only go one of two ways. Either it's all good and I lure her in and fuck her brains out in all sorts of weird and wonderful ways or I tell her to fuck off to the nearest sheep dip and come back when her fanny didn't smell like it had died of the plague.

My train of thought was interrupted by a sudden outburst by Aunty Joan.

'You nearly killed your mum Johnny, she's up in our spare room in a right old state black and blue and missing her two front teeth! I should be me calling the police!' As she said, the word police, she looked around for any witnesses that might have heard her hint that she might be a fucking grass. I knew she wasn't going to call the fucking police and so did she.

'Fuck off Aunty Joan we both know that's not going to happen.'

However this was going to end it wasn't going to involve any legitimate authority, that was a given. We were at a stalemate. I couldn't think of any conceivable way of knowing what her old beaver smelled like so trying to calm her down enough to convince her that her best option was to let me fuck her wasn't a viable option right now. And from her point of view she couldn't get in to kick my head in so both our options were limited.

'Just fuck off and you won't get hurt Aunty Joan.' I told her, trying my best to sound intimidating.

Aunty Joan, rather rudely, burst out laughing. 'You fucking little weed Johnny who the fuck is going to hurt me? Certainly not a little bender like you that's for sure!'

'Bender!?' Bloody cheek. I don't know where she came up with bender because if I was a bender why did my cock get so hard when she was trying to rape me earlier? Why did I come in my pants while she was grinding herself against me? Why was my cock so fucking hard right now as I rubbed it along the window sill as I perved over her? No way was I a bender. I was a red blooded male and I liked birds that must have been demonstrably clear to her and everyone else. Yes It was true that I would dearly have loved to have a full on sexual relationship with all the trimmings with Andy from school but he dressed and acted like a bird so that didn't even count.

'I'm not a bender Aunty Joan!' I protested. 'If anyone is a bender around here it's you! You are to all intense and purposes basically a man! Look at all those muscles! That's hardly ladylike now is it? What are you trying to hide Aunty Joan? Who are you trying to kid eh? Well you're not fooling anyone! We all know that you're a fucking freak of nature Aunty Joan!' I was fucking furious that she'd questioned my sexuality and properly let her have it. 'You're a man trapped in a woman's body

186

Aunty Joan and you need to get help! You need therapy! You need to go to the doctor's right this minute and tell them that you want to change your sex! You can't live a lie anymore Aunty Joan because it's killing you! You've turned into a homosexual rapist Aunty Joan! Where will it end? Prison! If you don't get help now you'll end up in a woman's prison and be forced to eat minge all day! Twenty three hours locked up in a cell eating the fanny hole of the wing daddy or mummy or whatever she'd be called.' I got out my cock and started to frantically pull it. 'Chomp, chomp, chomp, all day long, morning, noon and night with just an hour's respite while you walked around the exercise yard just trying to get your breath back! They wouldn't tolerate a dirty snatch in there though Aunty Joan! No way! You'd be held down in the showers by big strong female inmates and they'd scrub your pussy clean so it didn't stink up the cell! Then they'd all be on you like sexy fucking locusts Aunty Joan! Pinning you down and licking your abs and thighs and biceps and eating out your lovely clean, hygienic, well-kept, beautifully trimmed fanny hole while a really fit one sat on your face and made you lick her minge to death! And bum hole! Then all the hotter female prison wardens will have their go Aunty Joan!' I rambled on like this in a frenetic stream of consciousness lesbian, prison fantasy way until my legs gave way as I came. After which I must have passed out.

Chapter thirteen

The next thing I recalled our Wayne was standing over me. I was soaking wet and my head hurt.

I came to my senses, looked up at our Wayne and asked him what the fuck was going on.

'Well I think you were having a wank out the window and must have fainted as you shot your bolt by the looks of things.' Wayne grinned.

'How the fuck would you know that Wayne? I asked incredulously.

'Well when we got here Aunty Joan was outside and she was very upset and said that you'd nearly killed mum and that you were wanking off like a fucking pervert while you were arguing about why you wouldn't let her in so she could kick your fucking head in. And then she said that you started telling her that she was a nonce and would end up in a women's prison getting fucked all day and night and then you must have shot your load because Aunty Joan said that she saw some spunk fly out the window and nearly hit her and then she heard a thudding sound and a groan and then it all went quiet and then we turned up and she said that we were going to get into real trouble and Brian the social worker was going to come and take us into care were we would both get beaten up every day and raped every night and I asked her to stop talking because she was upsetting me but she laughed at me and told me I was a stupid fucking retard so I head butted her and then Dorothy jumped on her back and hit her loads of times in the head with one of her stilettos. Then she fell to the ground and told us to get off her so we did then she ran off down the road and then she fell over and then got back up and started running again then she fell into the road again and then she turned into George Street and we didn't see her again after that. Then we came up here and found you laying on the floor and we couldn't wake you so Dorothy told me to throw a bucket of water over you and then give you a slap. We won't really get taken in care will we Johnny?' He rambled, looking all wide eyed and that wounded look that I knew so well had returned to his face.

'Wayne mate you're eighteen or nineteen or twenty or something so there's no way that you're going to be put into care so don't worry about that. Anyway how did that lying bitch know that I was wanking? Which I wasn't obviously. She's fucking sick in the head!' I replied to our Wayne as I looked up at him doing my best to look hurt and full of indignation.

'Well Johnny there's spunk all over the window sill and your little cock is hanging out of your jeans so you don't have to be ruddy lieutenant Kojak to work out what went on up here you filthy little bugger.' Dorothy chipped in delightedly.

'Oh hello Candice what the fuck are you doing here? The last time I saw you, you were fucking my brother in the arse with a big black strap-on penis. Pot, kettle and all that eh you old witch?' I said, as I quickly put my cock back into my pants and zipped up my jeans.

'That Aunty Joan of yours is old enough to be your mother Johnny you should be ashamed of yourself pulling your pudding over a woman like that it's not natural. And I use the term woman very loosely in her case, she looks like ruddy Geoff Capes!' She's a ruddy muff diver if ever I've seen one! You're wasting your time trying to get into her knickers Johnny because she bats for the other team. I'd put money on it. I've had clients like her in my time! Big butch, hairy dikes that are too afraid to admit their own sexuality and pay women like me to fulfil desires that they've tried to supress but couldn't. They're all the same! They pay whatever I ask and never try to haggle like you men always do and all they want to do is eat me out and then have cuddle. They're like pigs to a ruddy trough! Grunting and snorting down there with their fingers frigging away nineteen to the dozen at their own fanny holes until the alarm goes off and their time's up! Then it's a gargle with the Listerine a thank you very much and then back out the door. Full of shame they are but the truth will out you can't deny you're sexuality and if you do you'll have a life time of misery! It's not only sad and lonely men that come to us ladies of the night I've had the ruddy lot up me!'

'Fucking hell there Candice calm down or I'll be banging one out over you in a minute!' I said trying to sound sarcastic but in truth feeling a mixture of emotions the strongest being sick to my stomach. I had to admit that some of the things she said would be going into the wank bank but I'd obviously have to tweak it a bit and change the characters. The thought of old Dorothy being eaten out by Aunty Joan was a truly horrific image and one that I would find hard to erase. Maybe I could use it as my go to image if there was ever a time when I would be trying not to come too quickly. I could have done with that back in June's bathroom when I shot my load all over the taps rather than down her old gob like she'd wanted me to.

'Don't call Dorothy Candice when she's not working Johnny because she's my girlfriend and Candice is her prossy name. I told you before, me and Dorothy are in love.' Wayne suddenly piped up.

Oh yes I'd inexplicably wiped that information from my mind. Well fuck me that was shocking news to say the least. I had to use all of my mental strength to hold back all the thoughts that rushed to my brain after he had said those last few words. I shouldn't have been surprised I guess. That old bag of bones was the first person that had shown our Wayne any affection in any shape or form. Not only that she'd willingly let him stick his cock up her. I was sure that he wasn't the first person to confuse love with an intrinsic, burning desire to be wanted and cherished which manifested itself in being fucked in the arse with a plastic penis.

I had to be very careful what I said next because I didn't want to get on the wrong side of my brother now he'd found his strength. I also did not fancy getting bashed over the head with one of his bird's high heels. I could tell by their faces that they were expecting me to say something caustic and cutting and make a million jokes at their expense. I wasn't going to do that though because our Wayne was my brother and I loved him and if Dorothy made the soppy cunt happy then I was happy for them both. That was the truth. I was undeniably a massive cunt but I'd had a life time of people judging me and I hated it so who the fuck was I to judge them? The only trouble I had was getting them to believe me. I was perpetually sarcastic so being earnest didn't exactly come easy to me.

'That's fantastic news!' I cried. 'I'm over the moon for you both! Congratulations! I'm sure you'll be happy together for the rest of your lives! You make a really beautiful couple!' I was still on the floor so I sprang to my feet and shook them both heartily by the hand. I toyed with the idea of kissing Dorothy on both cheeks like the French did but thought better of it for many reasons the main one being that she looked like a fucking corpse and the thought of putting my face anywhere near hers filled me with horror.

Wayne looked blessed as punch with my reaction but Dorothy was eying me suspiciously and was clearly waiting for the punch line. I looked at her squarely in her wrinkly old cataract eyes, opened my arms out wide and said, 'Dorothy, welcome to
190

the family! You've made my brother very happy and for that I am in your debt. If there is anything that I can do for you then just say the word. Consider yourself at home! Consider yourself part of the furniture!' We've taken to you so strong, it's clear we're going to get along!' Before I knew what the fuck was going on, in my desire to please the old trout I'd done a medley of snippets from all the show tunes I knew including all the best bits from, My Fair Lady, Oliver, Mary Poppins, Seven Brides for Seven Brothers and Calamity bloody Jane. I was over compensating and as I sang, began theatrically twirling a reluctant Dorothy around the bedroom while giving her the full Dick Van Dike treatment until finally culminating with a mash up of We'll Meet Again, White cliffs of Dover and Boiled Beef and Carrots.

'This calls for a celebration!' I shouted trying my best to sound enthusiastic.

'You two crazy love birds make my heart veritably soar with delight!' I continued. Dorothy was still eying me suspiciously clearly not believing that I found her and Wayne's unlikely coupling anything other than fucking charming.

I took one of her bony old hands in mine and said, 'Come on Dorothy babe lighten up! Cupid's arrow has struck our Wayne right between the eyes and you're the lucky gal and there's fuck all I or anyone can do about that. It is what it is and I'm truly happy for the fucking pair of you. Now let's all getting rat arsed! Except for our Wayne obviously because he doesn't drink. Wayne, why don't you show Dorothy around the place while I nip to the shops and get some supplies okay?'

Dorothy looked at me and said, 'Okay Johnny I'll give you the benefit of the doubt for now but if I ever find out that you've been taking the ruddy piss out of me or disrespecting me I'll cut your ruddy ears off do you hear me? You're a sarcastic little shit and you always have been and I know that your parents didn't bring you up in what you might call the traditional way but that's still no excuse for walking around like a fucking crafty cunt thinking that you're cleverer than everyone else is it? I'm going to take you at your word Johnny but if I hear any snide remarks about me and Wayne's relationship I will bring a world of fucking pain to your door. You mark my words. I've been a whore for most of my life and in that time I've met and been fucked by some of the nastiest mother fuckers on God's green earth. It only takes one word from me and you'll find yourself nailed to the floor by your fucking bollocks son.'

Fuck me that was me told. Even though it was more likely Al Capone or Ned Kelly were her clients back in the day an image of the Kray twins spit roasting her popped into my head and it was all I could do not to burst out laughing. She certainly meant it though so if I was going to be emptying my nuts into Sally next door it wouldn't do to have them perforated by some underworld gangster that owed Dorothy a favour.

-Johnny darling, I have to ask, why are you leaking spunk out of your ball bag? 'Oh you noticed? Yeah sorry Sally that was my own fault for making a rude comment about my brother's sexual relationship with a ninety year old prostitute.-

'Well I appreciate your candour Dorothy. It's good to know where we stand. You can rest assured that I have taken your threats on board and you have nothing to worry about.' I replied dryly.

Dorothy then said, 'Well it's good to have cleared the air Johnny now let's put all that behind us and have this party shall we? It's been a while since I've had a proper knees up!'

Yeah probably D day. I thought to myself but thought best not to say it out loud.

I suddenly realised that I'd never held a party before or even been to one if I didn't include being in the same room as my mum and dad while they got off their nuts with their mates.

'I've got to admit Dorothy, me and our Wayne have never really organised a party before so I for one am a bit out of my depth here.' I told her and for the first time she looked at me with kind eyes and said, 'Well son there's no need to go overboard just get some beers and some spirits and a couple of bottles of wine, two red and two white, some crisps and some of them little pork pies, if they do them, and get some bread and butter, get real butter because I can't eat that fake stuff because it goes straight through me and gives me the ruddy shits. Get some slices of ham and pickled onions and some chutney and some cheese and pineapple and you'll need to get some cocktail sticks to put them on and fetch some peanuts too. You'd better get some soft drinks and some sweets for my Wayne. And see if they've got any vaginal lubricant because we used up all my supply earlier and I'm dry as a bone down there. Do you have any cocaine?'

Jesus was that all? Cocaine and vagina lubrication? I wish I'd never asked.

'Is that all?' I asked, trying not to sound sarcastic but failing. She ignored me and carried on babbling away.

192

'I used to love a bit of opium back in the day but you don't see it so much now. I don't mind a bit of toot though if it hasn't been cut all to buggery of course. I don't want to get a ruddy nose bleed snorting bloody baby powder! The good stuff gets me very randy though and I can go for hours on it. Or speed. That's a lot rougher but it was the drug of choice for many back when I was in me prime because it was so cheap. Blues we used to call them and everyone was on the buggers. For us girls it was a God send because it would keep the weight off too. The lads found it very difficult to get hard though. Whiz dick it was called. I don't know if that was the medical term but if you had a punter on that it was very frustrating for everyone. I didn't mind though because I was usually on the clock so the longer it took the more I'd get paid. I'd be sat there on the bed telling the poor lad not to worry and relax and he'd be sat there grinding his jaw and pulling furiously on his flaccid little chap getting all angry and frustrated. I'd be thinking, take as long as you like dear because I'm getting paid by the hour. It was money for old rope really. Usually they'd just give up but they still had to pay! If they started to get all shirty and argue the toss all I had to do was ring me bell and George, he was my pimp at the time, he would be down to knock seven bells of shit out of them. Although it seldom came to that because the punter would take one look at him and hold their hands up. George was a brute of a man. Big hands and often extremely and unnecessarily vicious. But he was good to me. Never took the piss or gave me a whack like some of them other ruddy cunts. His cock was massive. I've always preferred big men. I like to feel protected you see. You needed a good strong backup in my game because you never knew who would be coming through the door. I've had them all up me. All colours of the ruddy rainbow! I've had your blacks, your whites your browns, now your Asian fellas, they've only got little tiddlers usually and the Nips too but they don't care they just get on with it. Now your average white man if he's only got a small one he's usually very embarrassed and this embarrassment can turn to anger. In my experience if I pull down the trousers of a white man with a tiny little todger I expect trouble. I reckon Hitler had a small one. I bet many a war has been fought because of men with small cocks. Most of the rich men that have shagged me have had small knobs. That's just a fact. Even now if I see one of them fancy Rolls Royce cars coming down the street with the driver looking all pleased with himself I always think, aww bless, he's only got a little tiddler. They'd all give up their wealth for a few more inches on their John

193

Thomas and that's a ruddy fact lads. You've got a smashing cock Wayne so you've got nothing to worry.' Dorothy stopped babbling on for a moment before addressing me directly.

'Wayne has a nice, big, fat cock with a lot of girth too and that's unusual. He'll never have any problems pleasing a lady. I've had an awful lot of cock over my long and illustrious career as a brass and I can tell you right now that Wayne is a natural sword smith. Once he'd got the hang of it obviously. I didn't even charge you Wayne did I?' She glanced across at our Wayne who shook his head and grinned. Then she looked back at me.

'And we did the whole ruddy gambit! Things I hadn't done in ruddy years! I put your brother through his paces and he was more than a match for old Candice I should ruddy coco! He could be in the films! It's not easy for a man to be a porn star you know! I've done a bit of that myself and once you get a few people in a room even them lads with the big un's can get stage fright. It's one thing getting it up in front of your missus in the comfort of your own home but it's a whole new ball game when you've got to perform in front of a room full of people! And once the bugger is down it's a real cunt of a job getting it back up again! It's all in the mind you see lads? Once your head's gone it's over. Not Wayne though, he was as stiff as a ruddy broom the whole way through even after he'd popped a few times. He just kept on going Johnny! Time after time! And there's so much of it too! Pints and ruddy pints! My living room is absolutely covered in his spunk and it's not like I'm afraid to swallow either. I was full of the stuff before you could say Jack Robinson! I couldn't believe what I was seeing! The first time he came I felt like someone had tipped a full milk churn over me! I tried to get as much of it down my throat as I could but it was too much even for me! It was like being hit by a twelve bore shot gun full of nut butter! Every time I thought he'd finished out came another load of the stuff! Wave after ruddy wave of hot salty man fat covering me from head to ruddy toe. I've had come baths before obviously but nothing like that! Feel my skin Johnny I feel twenty years younger! He should bottle it and sell it to the beauty industry!' As she said this she came towards me and offered me her face to feel. I instinctively reeled back in horror. 'No, no it's okay Dorothy I can see from here how smooth it is. Quite a transformation! Not that you weren't pretty damned good for your age anyway of course.' I said, hoping that she hadn't seen my look of disgust.

194

Wayne was looking very pleased with himself and I did feel a bit envious at that point. If he could sustain an erection for hours while in the company of old Dorothy then imagine what he'd be like with an actual living woman? I found it hard not to gag just looking at her while she was fully dressed and the thought of her naked made me queasy to say the least. I now had so many horrifying images of our Wayne and Dorothy swirling around my head that no amount of therapy would ever be able to erase and so tried to focus on the extensive list of things I now had to get for the party. Fuck me so much for not going over overboard. What the fuck would be going overboard then? Champagne and lobsters with caviar stuffed up their arse holes? Our Wayne would be happy to have a family size packet of cheese and onion monster munch and a few balloons. I wished I'd never mentioned a party but it was too late. I could see on my brother's face that he was getting excited at the prospect and as he'd had a history of people letting him down so a fucking party he was going to get. 'Right then I'm off to the shops so don't do anything that I wouldn't do while I'm gone' I said, and winked at our Wayne.

'Okay Johnny we will try and behave!' he replied as he looked over at Dorothy, grinned and wiggled his big, fat tongue at her. Dorothy responded by miming giving him a blow job. I looked at the pair of them and if I'd had an appetite it would surely have vanished.

'Yeah well I'll see you in a thrice.' I said and left them to it glad to be going outside and into the fresh air.

Jesus I wasn't sure if I could eat in front of Dorothy. Old people gave me the creeps at the best of times. Especially really old fuckers like her. Whether they reminded me of my own mortality or just that they looked so fucking gross I wasn't sure but I did know that just the sight of her made me feel sick to my stomach. I'd definitely dodged a bullet by not fucking her that was for sure. Imagine if I hadn't been such a complete and utter bastard to her and she's let me give her one? Imagine if I'd lost my cheery to that old witch? And I'd paid for the privilege! Imagine if in my excitement I'd eaten her old snatch out. Imagine if it was me that had fallen in love with her instead of Wayne and it was me back at home right this very minute sunk to my nuts in her saggy old guts. I wanted to vomit just thinking about it but I was also somewhat surprised and also pleased with myself that I did actually have standards. Very low standards but standards never the less. I now knew that I drew the
195

line at necrophilia. Unless they were proper hot when they were alive. And only then if they'd fairly recently died. I was becoming discerning. Progress.

I ran down stairs and quickly racked up a line on the kitchen table before heading to the shops. The closest one was the local newsagents on the corner but Mr Patel, the owner, had banned me from there for shop lifting. This time I had money though so I decided to go there anyway and chance my luck. I open the door and the little bell rang.

Immediately I heard his distinctive voice. 'Bugger off Johnny you're barred you bloody little thieving little cunt bastard.'

'Ahh good evening Mr. Patel and what a fine evening it is don't you think? I reply ignoring this less than cordial greeting.

Mr. Patel came out from behind the counter and stood directly in front of me. 'I've told you before, everyone in your bloody family apart from your Wayne is bloody barred. So please do me the honour of bloody, fucking off you bloody little cunt.' Mr Patel had apparently come over from India during the seventies and he and his family didn't exactly receive a warm welcome when he arrived all bright eyed and bushy tailed into my town. Give the man his due though he persevered and with the exception of one or two people, namely my parents, he eventually became accepted as one of us. He'd certainly picked up the language.

'Now come on Mr, Patel, please don't be like that. That's all water under the bridge. I've seen the light. I'm a changed man. That was the old Johnny. I'm a respectable, upstanding citizen now, just like yourself. I pillow of the community.' I reply, trying to appear all wide eyed and innocent and indignant at the same time.

'I hear you almost killed your mother and father Johnny' He countered.

Fuck it my dad was also alive. The cunt. And why is everyone blaming me? It was Wayne for fuck's sake! I might have kicked him in the head a few times but that was well after he was already pretty much out for the count. Oh well I guessed that it wouldn't do my reputation as a hard man any harm but I needed an alibi just in case things got heated down the line. It only took one person to break ranks and grass and then that unspoken wall of silence could quite easily come tumbling down.

'Mr. Patel please don't spread vicious rumours. If you want the truth, in actual fact my dad fell down the stairs.' I replied, thinking fast.

'And your mother Johnny? Did she also fall down the same stairs?' Replied Mr Patel.

196

I thought for a moment before replying, 'Yes that's correct Mr Patel. My mother also fell down the stairs. She was on his back. It was a sex game gone wrong. It was tragic accident and absolutely nothing to do with me and our Wayne. We were miles away at the time and we have many witnesses ready and willing to testify to this should the need ever arise. Which it won't because, like I said, it was a tragic accident and absolutely nothing to do with Wayne or up to and including me. Me and our Wayne are beside ourselves with grief and are inconsolable and may I add on behalf of my brother and myself we wish them both a full and speedy recovery and our thoughts and prayers go out to this tragic couple and also to their grieving family, at this time.' I lowered my head and stood quietly for a bit trying to appear sombre and reflective.'

'Please leave my bloody shop Johnny and never come back.' Said Mr Patel.

Charming I thought to myself. Mr Patel clearly had a heart of stone.

'I thought you lot were all meant to be religious Mr Patel? Whatever happened to forgive and forget and turn the other cheek and all that? What's the point of having all these shrines and flowers and incense everywhere if you don't mean it?' I replied rather craftily I thought. Mr Patel was a Hindu and the place always had a sweet pungent smell about it that I'd always found rather intoxicating and a bit sexy.

'That's the words of your God not one of mine Johnny now fuck off please before I do something that I might bloody fucking regret. I'm trying to run a bloody business here and it's difficult to do that when bloody little gutter snipes like you are constantly bloody stealing from me.'

It was time to play my trump card.

'As I said Mr Patel sir, I've changed. I'm now a man of means, a man of substance if you will.' I said as I pulled out my wedge of cash.

Mr Patel stared at it. 'Where the bloody fuck did you get that Johnny? Actually I don't want t to know just tell me what you want and I'll get it for you but don't you bloody move from that spot. Do you hear me Johnny? Stay at all times where I can see your hands okay?'

'Absolutely Mr Patel, I shall not move. I'll shout out what I need from here and you can bring it to the counter, bag it all up and I will pay for it and be on my way. How does that sound?

'That's perfect Johnny you just stay there and put your hands in your pockets and don't move. I will get everything you need. Not a problem sir.'

197

Well he'd changed his tune, business was business I guessed and I couldn't blame him for trying to recoup some of his loses he'd made due to my family's light fingers over the years. Not our Wayne though. He may have been a sexual deviant but he was never a thief. Unlike me I fucking loved nicking stuff. I always got a proper buzz off it.

'Okay Johnny what would you like sir?'

I tried to recall what the old whore had said. 'Right then, beer, crisps, sweets, spirits, bread, real butter, cheese, pineapple, cocktail sticks, slices of ham, pickled onions, chutney, vagina lubrication … '

Mr Patel stopped me mid flow. 'Whoa there Johnny bloody slow down I cannot remember all of this at once!' He moved to the rear of the shop and shouted, 'Priti! Priti! Come down here for a moment will you please and help your father with a big order!'

Score. On hearing these words I automatically smoothed myself down and tried to make myself look presentable. Priti Patel was Mr Patel's daughter. She was in my year at school and she was one of the most beautiful girls I'd ever seen. She was also one of the sweetest people I'd ever met. She was nothing like those bitchy scrubbers in my year who thought that they were God's gift to men. I'd known her since we were in the first year together and for one blissful term we used to walk home together. Sometimes when I dropped her off her mum would give me food to take home. She always made it sound like it was me doing them a favour. 'Please take this and share it with your brother Johnny I'm such a silly old woman I've made too much food for us again and if you don't take it, I will have to throw it out and that will be a dreadful waste.' It would have be rude to have refused such kindness and besides it was for the pair of us and who was I to deprive our Wayne of a decent meal? If it wasn't for Mrs Patel we would probably have starved. The food was always hot and delicious too and I'd run home straight up into our bedroom to share it with our Wayne. We'd gobble it down as fast as we could and then sit back on our beds with full stomachs and belch and laugh and for a brief moment in time we'd feel okay. I had adored Priti because not only was she gorgeous but she also had kind heart. She had never taunted me or been cruel about our Wayne and she never swore or spat in the road or lifted up her skirt and flashed her knickers at passing motorists while calling the drivers fucking nonces like most of her peers. Of course I would have paid

198

good money to have seen her knickers but she was classy and I loved that about her. I only saw her lose her temper once and that was when Clifford Dunster had called her a fucking Paki. He'd just asked her out and when she'd politely declined, and quite rightly too because he was a big, ugly, ginger cunt and he'd got all angry and lost his temper. I think everyone at my school was a racist. Especially the teachers. But normally you'd only use an insult like that behind someone's back or from a safe distance. Clifford had said it right into her face and that was unprecedented. This happened in the school canteen and everyone had heard it. If I hadn't been such a scrawny little runt at the time and also a massive coward I might even have intervened myself because it was fucking shameful. I was raging at his vile audacity but before anyone else could make comment or react Priti had taken matters into her own hands and it became clear that she was in total control of the situation.

'What did you call me?' She asked Clifford. The whole place had gone very quiet by now and you could have heard a pin drop. Clifford already knew that he'd crossed a line but evidently he'd inexplicably and foolishly felt his best line of defence would now be to continue to attack. Maybe if he'd immediately apologised and fell to his knees and begged for forgiveness things might have turned out differently for him. But he didn't. He looked around that canteen at all the aghast faces desperately looking for backup and finding none. Priti was liked by all. She was polite and kind and respectful to everyone but more importantly, she was very easy on the eye. All of us boys and probably a high percentage of the girls, in my imagination anyway, desperately wanted to give her one. Clifford was on his fucking own. Any confidence that he may have had before quickly evaporated but he was like a rabbit caught in headlights and he pressed on.

'I called you a ...' He stammered and stopped.

'Go one Clifford, say it. It's okay. Just tell me again what you called me please.' Said Priti very calmly. Then she slowly pushed back her chair and stood up.

The tension in the room was now palpable. Everyone, including the teachers and dinner ladies waited expectantly to see how this would all pan out.

Clifford's face was bright red now and the sweat was dripping off his big freckly face. I didn't know about anyone else but I was trying my best to focus on anything but Priti. Her long, straight, shiny brown hair gleaming under the florescent lights and her beautiful, soft brown skin, and those slender hips, and her big brown eyes and her

199

perfect white teeth and her pert little tits that were poking through her blouse was very distracting to say the least. The last thing this situation needed was for me to whip out my cock and start furiously wanking off into the lumpy mashed potato that was in front of me. I had fucked a plate of warm instant mashed potato once before though and it felt great but I didn't want to steal the lime light. There would be plenty enough time for that afterwards anyway.

'Yes Clifford? Nearly there. You called me a fucking Pu... a pa ... pack... come on now Clifford we're almost there now aren't we? Priti exaggerated as she mouthed the letters of that awful slur. Then she suddenly stamped her foot and shouted at the top of her voice, 'JUST FUCKING TELL ME WHAT YOU FUCKING CALLED ME CLIFFORD YOU FUCKING UGLY GINGER CUNT!'

There was a brief moment of silence before Clifford buckled and shouted back, 'I FUCKING CALLED YOU A FUCKING PAKI!'

A right arm immediately shot out from Priti's shoulder and its attached fist thudded into Clifford's face. This was immediately followed by a right which did the same. Within seconds Priti must have punched Clifford in the face around ten times in quick succession and each blow was deadly accurate. She was like a sexy killer robot. Whack, whack, whack, whack, whack, whack. It was beautiful to watch. I had a perfect view of all this and within no time at all Clifford's face was reduced to a bloody pulp. He didn't even have time to plead for mercy or help because it was all over in a flash.

She grabbed him by his hair and snarled 'Now get up on the table and tell me and everyone else how sorry you are for calling me a fucking Paki Clifford.'

Clifford hesitated and I still don't know whether this was a pathetic attempt at bravado or that he was still disorientated by the beating he'd just received but regardless of why it didn't prove too pleasing to Priti who smashed his head into her own plate of food.

'Up you go Clifford.' Priti then calmly instructed. This time Clifford immediately did as he was told and clambered up on to the table. Priti looked up to where he stood and calmly said, 'You look like you've got something on your mind. Spit it out then Clifford.' Clifford's face was ruined. He was now sporting two swollen eyes and a broken nose and a split lip. He was also covered in mash potato and peas.

200

'I'm sorry that I called you a fucking Paki Priti.' He mumbled incoherently but this might have been because he was now missing some teeth.

'Let me help you down Clifford you don't look at all well' said Priti as she abruptly pulled him down from the table. Clifford landed on his knees and cried out in pain.

'Oh no Clifford look you've ruined my lunch! Please bring me some more.' She continued.

'What?' replied Clifford not now knowing what the fuck was happening.

'You ruined my lunch with your ugly ginger face so please bring me some more. It was fish fingers and mashed potatoes and peas. And don't you dare push in either just queue up for it like everyone else.'

Clifford, now a broken man, staggered over to the dinner line and patiently waited to get served. The whole place was still silent as we all watched his humiliation take place. All we could hear were the dinner ladies dishing up food, their ladles clanking against the big tin dishes.

'Yes son what would you like?' said one of them to Clifford dead pan. Playing her role beautifully.

'Please can I have the fish fingers, mashed potato and peas miss? Said Clifford very meekly. The dinner lady dished it all up onto a plate and then he carried along the line until he got to the lady at the till. Without being asked he paid for it out of his own pocket and then limped over to where Priti was now sitting.

'Here you are Priti.' Said Clifford and with trembling hand she placed it before her. She looked at it and then at Clifford.

'I don't want it now because you've touched it.' She replied. Then she picked up the plate and slowly tipped it over Clifford's head. 'Oh dear me Clifford what an awful mess you've made! Priti then pointed to the corner of the canteen. 'Right then Clifford I want you to go over to that big bin over there. The one that's full of scraps and I want you to climb inside it and stay there until I say you can come out. Clifford just stood there in a daze.

'Get in the bin Clifford.' She reiterated.

I love a bit of theatre and I didn't even do it to ingratiate myself with Priti but I found myself starting to slow clap while chanting, get in the bin! Get in the bin! In no time at all the whole of the canteen, including the teachers and dinner ladies, were gleefuly chanting along with me. It was a beautiful moment, especially when Priti caught my eye and winked. Clifford had no choice but to stumble over to that bin and climb inside it. After about five minutes of this Mr Hurt, the geography teacher jumped the queue and got Priti another plate of food which he paid for himself and presented it to her with a low bow. Priti smiled politely at him and accepted it. As she ate the rest of the pupils took delight in emptying there finished plates into the bin in which Clifford stood. Taking her own sweet time, Priti eventually finished her meal and skipped over to the bin and scraped off any remains into it. She then wiped her plate up and down Clifford's blazer and calmly put the plate on the pile with the rest.

'Fuck off now Clifford and don't ever come anywhere near me again or I will literally kill you.' She finally told him. Then she spat in his face. We never saw him again.

That incident was the most awe inspiring thing I'd ever seen and Priti became my hero and my inspiration. The way I'd debased Micky and his mob in the park was fundamentally down to her. Needless to say I think the whole school wanked off to that little episode until we were all red raw and if they were anything like me, they still did.

I think her parents must have gathered that we all wanted to bang her because apart from when our pathed crossed at school on the increasingly rare occasions when I actually attended. I hadn't really spoken to her in ages due to her dad now picking her up in his car.

'Hello Priti!' I breathed trying my best to sound all sexy and cool.

'Hello there Johnny long time no see! How are you? I hear your parents had an accident. I hope that they are okay! Poor you.it must be awful for you! She replied.

Hair down, no make-up, white baggy T-shirt, black leggings, and bare feet. I tried not to stare. I just wanted her to turn around just once so that I could see her little bum cheeks then I'd die happy. I could feel her dad's eyes burning into me hatefully and I knew that he was reading my mind.

'Yeah it was tragic really and incredibly upsetting but I'm sure they will both pull through. Least said soonest mended and all that. It's still all a bit raw so I'd rather not talk about it if you don't mind.' I had decided not to mention the sex gone wrong cover story.

'I heard that they fell down the stairs during a sex act that went wrong Johnny is that right? She giggled.

Fuck sake she must have been listening from upstairs.

'Uh yeah that is unfortunately correct Priti. Yes that is indeed so.' I was trying to figure out a way to try and wriggle out of this line of enquiry but was coming up blank.

'Yes even though they are really old and knackered out they still enjoy a healthy bout of sexual intercourse given half a chance. They are either fighting or fucking... don't cha know...' I blathered, not having any idea what was coming out of my mouth until I'd said it out loud.

'Stop talking all of this bloody sexy talk for bloody fucking goodness sake Johnny! You are not even at the age of bloody fucking consent! My daughter does not want to hear all your bloody fucking filth!' Mr Patel interjected.

He's a fine one to talk I thought to myself. Didn't all the birds get married at around eight years old where he came from and usually to some ninety year old tribal chef who already had ten wives? Or was that the other ones? If Priti hadn't been born over here she'd probably already be a grandmother by now. I wouldn't have been at all surprised if her dad wasn't planning on kidnapping her one night soon and flyher out to some tiny village in the middle of nowhere and marrying her off to some old goat herder who'd undoubtedly beat her and stick his gnarly old cock up her until she eventually produced a son. I bet he'd be her first cousin too or her uncle! Then she'd be thrown into the family yurt with all his other discarded wives and forced into hot, exotic lesbianism. The lucky cow. Good luck trying it on with Priti though. That old pikey nomad will be in for a big surprise on their wedding night I can tell you that. She'd kick the fucking shit out of him. I decided there and then that if this was indeed the case me and our Wayne would go over there and rescue her and maybe some of his hotter wives too and they'd be so grateful they'd all let me bang them. Up the bum.

'Hey Priti I'm having a party for our Wayne in a bit and you can come along if you like!? As the guest of honour! It's only a small affair just me and our Wayne and his new girlfriend.' I only really said this just to see if her dad would spontaneously combust. There would be no chance of her dad letting his beloved daughter be anywhere near the likes of me without armed guards.

'Wayne has a girlfriend!?' Priti replied, with genuine enthusiasm. Fuck me what a dame. If Sally and I ever split up I'd definitely ask her to be my second wife. Or my side bitch. That's if she wasn't living up a mountain with fifteen kids by then. I'd

203

heard that even one baby could destroy a bird's body so ten or so would obviously leave her with a fanny like an empty head lock and as much as loved her I didn't really fancy that. No way. Fuck that. Unless we just did it up the bum? Plenty to think about. It was always good to have a back-up plan.

'My daughter is certainly not going to attend your bloody fucking party Johnny! Now tell me what you want and fucking bloody fuck off.' Shouted Mr Patel. How his daughter ended up so sweet and demure and refined when her dad had such a potty mouth was beyond my comprehension.

Priti ignored him. 'How come I haven't seen you in school for so long Johnny? I thought for one horrible moment that you'd left.' Said Priti looking directly at me with her big almond eyes. I blushed.

'Yeah well I'm more of a business man these days. You know, wheeling and dealing and ducking and diving. This time next year I plan to be a millionaire actually.' I garbled as I attempted to casually lean against her dad's counter. I misjudged it though and toppled into all the crisps and chocolates that were stacked along the front, knocking most of them all over the floor.

'Oh golly gosh and fiddle sticks!' I exclaimed, well pleased with myself that I hadn't sworn. I was trying to be on my best behaviour in front of Priti and her dad even though there was virtually no chance of me being able to take her out ever in the history of the world I still hung on to the thought that anything was possible. Especially after a day like today.

Priti laughed and skipped towards me. 'Oh you silly sock don't worry I'll help you pick them up.' She laughed delightedly glorying in my discomfort.

As she crouched down to help me back to my feet I instinctively glanced up to meet her gaze and accidently looked down her top. She was wearing a red lace bra with little flowers all around the edge of it. I could also saw that her belly button was pierced. Oh my God all that caramel skin. I didn't even do it on purpose. I was just at the right place at the wrong time. However much I would have loved to have planned that in reality I would never have had the nerve to even have even attempted it. Jesus this really seemed to be a charmed day. I quickly averted my eyes and scrambled about on all fours picking up packets of Raiders and Wotsits and Curly fucking Wurlies. Thank fuck Mr Patel was behind the counter and didn't see that or he would surely have killed me and then set fire to her.

204

Mr Patel was starting to get really agitated. 'Why are you two bloody bastards taking so long? What are you doing? Please hurry up. Priti please come away from Johnny as he is a bad influence.' Mr Patel pleaded.

As he said this Priti looked at me and smiled mischievously, got to her knees and then quickly lifted up her T-shirt and flashed me. I thought that I was going to faint. My mouth dropped open and I just stared and stared trying to etch that sight into my mind forever. In reality it must have been a split second but at that moment time seemed to stand still. I was transfixed and mesmerised. Oh sweet baby Jesus. I saw her bra in all its full glory. I saw her tight little brown belly, her ribs, and the jewel in her belly button that seemed to be glistening seductively at me, the fine black hairs running down into her leggings. And I saw the perfect shape of her two little caramel coloured tits. A sudden smell of coconut oil radiated out from her. I saw the little V shape between her legs and then I felt the unmistakable sensation of my own rapidly hardening cock. All these things culminated into a heady maelstrom of wanton lust and desire. I was dumb struck and dizzy. The next thing I knew Priti pulled her t shirt back down, winked at me and stood up. It was easy for her to do. I was on all fours with an erection and I wasn't going anywhere very soon.

'What are you still doing down there Johnny? You'd better not be bloody fucking stealing!' Shouted Mr Patel.

'Yes come on Johnny stand up this instant! Why are you still on the floor you bloody fucking bastard' Priti gleeful shouted while imitating her dad which I couldn't help thinking was a bit racist.

There was no way that I could stand up without first adjusting myself and even then there was no way I was going to stand in front of Priti and her dad with a hard-on. I quickly tried to think of something gross so as to get rid of it. Our Wayne emptying his nuts over Dorothy's ropey old face? Dorothy eating out Wayne's ring piece? My mum sucking me off? Me sucking my dad off? Me and Wayne sucking each other off? I was digging deep into my depraved mind but if anything my dick was getting harder because that brief image of Priti I'd just seen kept burning through all of my gross thoughts. I briefly flirted with the idea of just whipping it out and power wanking until I came all over her while her dad beat me to death. It wasn't a bad way to go but I still had my whole life ahead of me so instead I pretended that the fall had put my back out.

'Oh crikey Mr Patel I think I've pulled a muscle in my back! I lied. 'If I can just rest here for a few moments I'm sure I'll be fine.' I continued pleadingly as I played for time.

'Oh you poor thing Johnny would you like me to rub it for you?' Said Priti with fake concern.

'No. No. please don't do that I'll be fine if I can just rest here for a couple more minutes I'll be able to stand up and then be on my way' I stammered. If Priti had even laid one of her beautiful fingers on me at that moment I would have ejaculated. My head was spinning. Why was she doing this to me? I wasn't about to start complaining though. If she wanted to tease me in order to get me all hot and bothered in front of her old man then that was fine by me. My embarrassment was a small price to pay. If I was a pawn in the mental game of chess that was being played out between Priti and her dad then so be it. I was more than content to be used by her in any way that she chose fit. Johnny stick your cock down my throat my dad would hate that! Johnny please pull down my leggings and put your tongue deep into my little, wet paper cut as that would really displease my father! No I will not marry my own grandfather! And to prove my displeasure Johnny will now fuck me in the bum! Not a problem Priti. Not a problem.

I decided to read the ingredients on the various packets of confectionary to take my mind off the last few minutes. Eventually that did the trick and I stood up.

'Right then down to business Mr Patel.' I said trying to maintain some kind of decorum. My face was beetroot red and I was sweating like a rapist.

'Ooh yes the party list! You shout it out and I'll run and get it!' Cried Priti with mock excitement as she bent down on all fours again this time she mimed an athlete on the starting blocks. A beautiful honey coloured athlete with a mischievous, devilish look in her eye. I immediately turned my head away from her. 'One your marks! Get set! Go Johnny Go! Go! Go! She yelled as she sprang gazelle like up from the floor. She then began to shadow box. 'Come on Johnny I'm waiting! Let's go! Trolley dash! She picked up a basket and looked up at me and turned her head to one side. 'First item please Mr McQueen sir. If you would be so kind?' I couldn't look at here. She was too beautiful and amazing. I knew that if I locked on to those big brown eyes I'd be lost forever. I didn't want to fall in love with her right now. I wanted to shag loads of women first. I wanted to shag Sally from next door. I wanted to shag June form the café. I wanted to shag the bird who worked for her whose name I'd forgotten and I even wanted to shag Aunty Joan. But I knew that if I'd looked into Priti's eyes at that exact moment I wouldn't ever want anyone else but her. Ever. So I stared hard up at the ceiling and pretended that I was thinking. The only problem was that all I could think about was Priti.

'Um… Crisps' I began.

Priti immediately replied. 'What flavour? How many? One? Ten? A box? Ten million? Come on! Come On!'

I decided to play along and lose myself in her game.

'Salt and vinegar, cheese and onion, prawn cocktail, Smokey bacon, chicken, ready salted!' A box of crisps? I didn't even know that you could buy crisps by the box.

'Give me two boxes stat! Over!' I shouted.

'Roger that Johnny!' Priti barked back as she saluted and started throwing packets of crisps into an empty box.

'Usually we don't make up variously flavoured packets of crisps but as you are a preferred customer I'm sure my father will not bloody fucking mind will you father?' She was off again taking the piss out of her dad's strong Indian accent. Honestly, I thought to myself if I'd done that I would have got a clip around the ear and quite rightly been called a fucking racist. Imagine if poor old Clifford had started giving it the old goodness gracious me shit back in the canteen? Priti would have surely killed the cunt stone dead. I was always doing impressions of my mum and dad and their thick Irish accents though and I also told Irish jokes so I was in no position to take the moral high ground. Right at that moment Priti could have called me a cunt and spat right into my face and I would have just giggled shyly and loved her even more.

Mr Patel just stood looking at me without saying anything and I realised that his focus was on me in case I started nicking stuff. Bloody cheek. I was hardly gong to pinch anything in front of Priti know was I? What would she think of me? I was behaving impeccably. I'd been polite. I hadn't sworn. I hadn't stolen anything. And up until now at least I hadn't come in my pants while looking at his incredible daughter.

'Next item please Mr Johnny bastard!'

I couldn't think of one more fucking thing on the list. I just wanted to frame Priti's face in my hands and kiss her mouth. I didn't even want to bend her over her dad's counter and bury my face between her arse cheeks and then fuck her brains out. It was

207

now more than pure lust. I'd moved on from the bass and animalistic to the love struck and romantic. I wanted to hold her hand and laugh with her and sing to her and write her poems and kiss her fingers and bathe her feet. I wanted to cut out my own heart and present it to her. Mr Patel always played Bollywood music in his shop and soon in my drug fuelled state me and Priti were whisked off into one of those elaborate films in full Technicolor. I was now chasing her through the woods. She was hiding and every now and then when I thought I'd lost her she'd poke her head out from behind a tree and giggle and the chase would resume. We were duetting to a love song about how we couldn't be together because she was a princess of high standing and I was just a lowly Irish thief. She was brown and I was white and our parents would never allow such a union. But we were in love and had run away together. I was wearing silk trousers and a shiny waste coat like Aladdin and she was wearing a colourful silk sari. She had rings on her fingers and bells on her toes and a nose ring which was attached by a golden chain to her ear. Her belly jewel glistened in the sun light and her charcoaled eyes, full of pathos, sparkled in the reflection of the crystal pools as we jumped across rivers and lakes and waterfalls, dancing on clouds as we escaped Priti's evil family. Eventually I caught up with her and pulled her to me. I tried to kiss her but she pulled away. Again I tried but to no avail. Please my darling Priti do not try and deny our fate! You are my destiny! I cup her face in my hands and she looks up at me shyly. Yes she says. Yes I am yours and you are mine! I kiss her soft pink lips as I slide my hand between her legs. Yes Johnny yes! I go down to my knees as I kiss her belly. Yes Johnny eat me! Eat my fucking pussy Johnny! She murmurs as she pushes my head forcibly between her legs. Johnny! Oh Johnny! Johnny!

'Johnny! Johnny! Wake up Johnny!'

I could hear a voice. A soft, sweet, tender voice. The voice became louder and louder and increasingly abrupt.

'Johnny for bloody fucking sake wake up! You cannot lay on my floor like this it's bad for bloody business! Please be getting up Johnny!'

It was Mr Patel. I must have passed out again. I quickly sat up praying to all the angels and saints that my cock wasn't out. Mercifully it wasn't. I must have got up too quickly though because I suddenly felt very dizzy.

'Don't move Johnny. Stay on the floor until you feel able to get up safely.'

208

It was Priti. She was behind me cradling me head.

'You fell Johnny. One minute you were talking and then you kind of drifted off and then you fell and hit your head but you're okay because you fell onto the bananas.'

I realised that I literally had my head in Priti's lap. It took all my strength not to inhale as deeply as I could.

'Oh my good gosh Priti, I'm so sorry.' I said. I didn't mention all the drugs I'd taken and blamed a lack of food.

'I haven't eaten all day that's why I must have passed out.'

'We were so worried about you weren't we dad?!'

Mr Patel just grunted.

'You will have to buy those bananas because you have damaged them. And now that you are okay will you kindly get up off my floor. Priti please get away from him.'

Oh dad don't be such a dick head! Johnny is not going to buy those fucking rotten old bananas!' Priti shouted at him.

I didn't give a fuck about paying for the bananas or anything else for that matter all I wanted to do was stay exactly where I was. Forever. Priti was absentmindedly stroking my hair and cradling me in her arms and I was in paradise.

Far too soon Priti said. Do you feel strong enough to be able to stand now Johnny'?

'I think so' I replied bravely. I made to get up and then pretended to come over all dizzy and fell back down into her lap. I felt her pubic bone with the back of my head. I was in love with Priti and there was nothing I or anyone else could do about it.

'I think I'd better just lay here for a while longer until my heart rate had returned to normal.' I said, doing my best impression of an invalid.

Suddenly out of nowhere I felt myself cruelly lifted out of Priti's loving embrace and into the burly arms of her dad.

'There you go Johnny let me have a good look at you' He looked into my eyes.

'Look left. Now look right. Now look up. Good, good. Now look down. Perfect. Everything seems to be in order. All back to normal. Good boy.' Said Mr Patel. Then, smiling, he patted me on the head while grinning at me sinisterly. All of which roughly translated into, there's fuck all wrong with you Johnny you bloody lying fucking bastard now take your head out from between the legs of my daughter.

Oh well it was good while it lasted but I knew when I'd outstayed my welcome.

Mr Patel then took a basket from the pile and started filling it expertly with everything I'd mentioned and more besides.

'So this party for your Wayne is for three people yes?'

'Well four including Priti Mr Patel.'

'So three peoples okay, okay'

He rushed around the shop and in no time he'd got most of the things Dorothy had asked for.

'We do not have any vaginal lubricant but we do have Vaseline which is just as good if not better okay Johnny?' Mr Patel looked at me and smiled.

I looked over at Priti who was giggling in the corner and I blushed from head to toe. 'It's not for me!' I stammered. 'It's for Wayne's girlfriend! She's a mature lady. Like a fine wine! A whisky that's been aged in an oak barrel!' I was desperate not to let them know that Dorothy was a ninety year old brass because Priti had been so genuinely pleased for him. Not that there was anything wrong with our Wayne having a girlfriend that was over seventy years older than him and one that other men paid to have sexual intercourse in but I didn't want to steal his thunder by telling everyone before he had a chance to do so himself.

'Is there anything else you need Johnny?' Said Mr Patel as he was bagging it all up and totting up the bill.

'Well as I said, Wayne's lady friend is a bit older than us and she did mention that she likes a small tipple on occasion and also a smoke so if you would be so kind and discrete as to include eight cans of Tenants Extra, four bottles of wine, two red, two white, a bottle of gin, a bottle of vodka, a bottle of Whiskey and forty Benson and hedges that'll be great.' I smiled trying my best to sound like this was the most natural thing in the world for a fifteen year old boy to be asking for.

'Well you know the law Johnny I can't possible let you have all that alcohol and tobacco without some sort of identification now can I? I could go to prison if I was caught selling any of those items to you!' He said this as he pulled out the various bottles from the shelves and bagged them up.

'And forty Benson and Hedges did you say?'

'Yes but I think you'd better make it sixty now I've thought about it.'

'As I said Johnny I cannot possible sell you tobacco as you are underage' He said as he took down three packets of B & H and put them into one of the bags.

210

Priti just looked at him with disgust and shook her head.

Mr Patel pressed frantically on to the keys of his till then with a great deal of satisfaction on his face he said, 'That'll be a grand total of £45.96 please Mr Johnny sir.'

I pulled out my notes and gave him two twenties and a ten., 'Here's fifty English pounds please put the four pence in the charity box and keep the rest.' I beamed

'Shall I give Johnny a hand taking all that to his house dad?' Asked Priti, although we all already knew the answer to that one.

'No! No! No! Johnny is a big strong young man and he is perfectly capable of carrying a few small bags just around the corner to his house can't you Johnny?' replied Mr Patel.

'Yes I'll be fine,' I reluctantly replied. There was absolutely no point in arguing the toss and I decided to play the long game. From now on Mr. Patel's would be my shop of choice.

'Please may I invite Johnny to my sixteenth birthday party father?' Priti suddenly cried.

'Absolutely no way Priti!' Mr Patel shouted back at her. Then he checked himself and said, 'No offence Johnny but it is a family affair you understand don't you?'

'Yes that's okay I understand perfectly Mr Patel.' I replied. And I did too. I wouldn't have invited me to my own party. I wasn't even annoyed. I was a despicable, retched individual and I suddenly saw myself as others saw me. My family were a laughing stock. We were poor, and feckless and rude with no social graces and we didn't give a fuck. In fact we were the complete opposite of Priti and her family. They were hard working and upstanding, decent people. If they found a wallet in the street the first thing they would do would be to hand it in to the police station rather than rifle through it and then jog happily to the nearest boozer. We were morally bankrupt. I felt embarrassed and shameful but things were about to change. I was determined to prove to everyone that given the right circumstances a boy from nowhere with limited means could make it to the top. I had fuck all except the money in my pocket, a quick wit and our Wayne and together we were going to build a fucking empire.

I gave Priti one last, lingering look, said cheerio to Mr Patel and fucked off home.

I opened the front door, walked straight down the hall and into the kitchen to dump the bags. I suddenly felt a new sensation. It was pride and this was brought about by providing for my family. Namely our Wayne.

'Wayne! Wayne! Come and look!' I shouted up the stairs.

Wayne immediately came thundering down the stairs.

He stared wide eyed at all the bags of goodies.

'Fucking hell Johnny look at all that!' He shouted.

Neither of us had ever seen anything like that before. We now had proper food in the house for the first time in our lives.

Get stuck in our Wayno!' I laughed, as we both tore into the bags.

'Crisps! Fucking loads of crisps!' gasped Wayne.

'Sweets! Sausage rolls! Ham! Cheese! More sweets!' We shouted out each individual item as we pulled it from the bag.

'Picked fucking onions!'

'Bog roll! The good stuff!' I laughed.

Tinned fucking pineapple?' We didn't even know that was even a thing.

'Vimto! Lilt! Coca fucking cola! Orange squash!'

'Cocktail sausages!

'Gin and beer and Vodka!' I cried.

 'Vaseline! Vaseline?' enquired our Wayne looking puzzled.

Yeah Mr Patel didn't have any proper fanny lube for your Dorothy's dried out old cunt hole so he suggested that. Give it a go and if it's no good I'll go into town tomorrow and nick you some proper stuff. No I'll fucking buy you some!' I replied.

'Oh Okay cheers.' He replied as he opened it, sniffed it, nodded to himself, put the lid back on and put the jar into his pocket.

I went to the bottom of the stairs and shouted up to Dorothy.

'Dorothy babe, are you hungry? Let's get this party started!'

Dorothy eventually tottered out from me and our Wayne's room and stood at the top of the stairs. She was smoking a long, filtered cigarette and wearing one of our Wayne's t shirts and nothing else. Not even her fucking wig. As much as I tried to redirect my gaze it was too late and I saw right between her legs. Her fanny resembled what I can only imagine Mick Jagger's lips would have looked like if they'd been repeatedly hit with a claw hammer. There was an unkempt wilderness of grey pubic hairs that reminded me of a furious Albert Einstein with bed hair and due to the plethora of varicose veins running up and down her spindly old pins they looked like an A to Z map of London that had been made out of cottage cheese.

I could feel puke rising up into my mouth. 'Fucking hell Dorothy put some fucking knickers on there's perishable food down here!' I shouted.

'Ooh you rude little bastard!' she shouted back indignantly.

'Oh come on Dorothy meet me half way! I don't care if you are Wayne's missus have some fucking self-respect for fuck's sake!' I replied, fucking livid. She could fuck right off with that shit. She may have gotten away with that eighty odd years ago but there was no fucking way I was going to have her running about the gaff like she was Samantha fucking Fox. I needed to nip this in the bud.

'Wayne your missus is standing at the top of the stairs showing me her gash and if you don't persuade her to put some proper fucking clothes on you can both fuck the fuck off out of this house!' I yelled at him. I was the fucking Don around here and that needed to be established fucking pronto.

Wayne came out of the kitchen carrying two half eaten induvial mini pork pies and had a mouthful of monster munch.

'Listen Wayne', I told him, 'I fucking love you, you know that but I can't put up with her and her fucking attitude anymore. I'm trying, I really am but she's doing my fucking nut in. She's your missus and beauty is in the eye of the beholder and all that and that's fucking great and I'm happy for you but somethings cannot go unseen. Her fucking rat for example. How am I going to be able to enjoy this party now that I've seen that? I'm going to have fucking nightmares Wayne. I've lost my appetite! If you don't tell her to fucking behave herself then you're going to have to make a choice between me and her because she is taking the fucking piss here. If you like you can go and live with her and there will be no more crisps and no more sweets and no more fizzy fucking pop and no more individual mother fucking mini pork fucking pies! … or pickled onion monster munch.'

Wayne looked at me and then at Dorothy.

Dorothy shouted at him, 'Are you going to let him speak about me like that Wayne?'

Wayne looked at her, then at me then down at his hands.

'Yes.' He said.

'Fucking what did you say Wayne? Bellowed Dorothy incredulous.

213

'I said yes Dorothy. I will let Johnny talk about you like that. Now either put on some clothes or fuck off. Please.' Answered Wayne as he grinned at me and winked. Well there we were then. Wayne preferred individual mini pork pies to his missus and I didn't blame the cunt.

Dorothy was fucking furious and fucked off back into our bedroom to sulk her fucking socks off.

'Thank you Wayne.' I said.

It had been an eventful day to say the least and I sorely needed to let my hair down. I grabbed a bottle of vodka and a couple of beers and took them into the living room. Wayne followed suit with as much food as he could carry and two big bottles of fizzy pop.

In no time we were having the time of our lives. If Dorothy was waiting for our Wayne to go up to her and apologise she was going to wait all fucking night. Me and our Wayne had never had the run of the place and we were making the most of it. It felt good just to hang out together with nobody in the way to ruin it. For the first time in our lives we didn't have to submit to other people's rules and regulations and unpredictable behaviour. When my parents threw parties they were rowdy and drug fuelled and often volatile. Sometimes it could be fun but a wrong look or word spoken could result in all hell breaking loose so everyone was always on edge. Not this night though. Everything was perfect. Yes it was just me and my brother but I wouldn't have wished for it any other way. We ate and danced and we sang and Wayne had his pop and I had my drugs and booze and it was magical. We played The Pogues and Elvis and Patsy Cline and The Clash and the Dubliners and every other piece of vinyl we had in the house that night and as I fell deeper and deeper into a narcotic stupor it all became a blur but the last thing I remembered was my brother laughing and dancing and singing at the top of his voice and I felt fucking incredible.

Chapter fourteen

The next morning I woke up fully clothed in my parent's bed. I felt sick to my stomach and my head was pounding. I pulled back the covers and looked about me. Thank fuck I hadn't shat myself. Score. My last memory was our Wayne jumping up and down singing Hi Ho Silver Lining. I remembered singing along with him to the line that went, 'It's fucking obvious!' but after that everything was blank. I still had my limbs and I wasn't dead so everything else was a bonus. I thought about the day before, mainly about Priti. I had a raging hangover and felt even hornier than usual so I pulled down my jeans and pants and was just about to have an angry wank when I suddenly heard someone banging very loudly on our front door.

'Come on Johnny open the fucking door son. This has gone on long enough. You can't hide in there forever. Let's get this over and done with so we can all move on eh?'

Shit, shit, shit it was my uncle Sean.

I decided to play it cool. I sauntered over to the window and looked out all bleary eyed into the bright sunshine of a rather beautifully crisp winter morning.

'How can I help you Uncle Sean?' I said, as if I was genuinely surprised to see the soppy cunt. To the best of my knowledge Uncle Sean had never really done me any harm but he was my dad's brother so he was now basically the enemy. At the moment he was standing in the way of me and Wayne's future as sole occupants of this house and also and more importantly, the wank I was just about to have. Some people like a coffee and a fag first thing of a mornig, others like to eat porridge while reading the morning paper but me, ever since the first time I was aware of my dick being hard and the pleasure I could get from pulling it, I liked a wank. And if that small pleasure was ever denied me I'd be a tad grumpy to say the least.

'Come on down and open the door Johnny. You're going to have to face the consequences at some time so let's just have it out now son.' Uncle Sean shouted up at me shielding his eyes from the glare of the sun.

'Listen uncle Sean before we go any further is there anything I could say or do to make you change your mind and not kick my head in?' I asked him directly.

'I'm afraid not Johnny, you nearly killed my brother and however much I like you son I've got no choice but to beat the fucking shit out of you. You know that.' My uncle Sean replied.

'So just to clarify, there's absolutely no point in discussing this matter and coming to an amicable arrangement?' I continued.

'I'm afraid not Johnny, you know how it is son I have to avenge me brother rightly or wrongly. It's just the law and it's not personal son.'

'Well if that's the way it's got to be then so be it. Hang on Uncle Sean stay there and don't move please. I'll be right down!' I shouted back.

'That's a good lad Johnny let's just get it all done and dusted and move on.'

I then took a chair from the corner of the room dragged it under the window, stood up on it unzipped my jeans, took out my cock and pissed all over him. By the time he had the good sense to move out of the way I had covered him from head to toe in piss. And that was my first piss of the day so it wasn't exactly the hay coloured stuff that the doctors say you should be doing if you're in rude health. This was dark orange and the consistency of sump oil and stank like fuck.

He screamed and shrieked like a little girl as he hopped about unsuccessfully trying to rid himself of his new cologne.

'I will fucking kill you Johnny so I will you dirty fecker!' He screamed.

I was on my own and had no audience but couldn't resist. I looked into my parents' vanity mirror and said to my reflection, 'Here's Johnny!' Then I quickly racked up and snorted a nice thick line of speed. I then sprang from the bedroom and ran down stairs. I prayed that our Wayne hadn't slept in his coat and was delighted to find that surprisingly it was hung up on the little wooden hooks by the front door. I frisked it and immediately found what I was looking for. The claw hammer that I used to nail Kenny to that park bench. Bingo. I unlocked the door and stepped outside. Uncle Sean was still on the front lawn trying to rid himself of my piss. He looked up at me and snarled. 'You fecking little cunt Johnny it's going to be a pleasure for me to kick your fecking head in now son.' As he was saying this he ran towards me and threw a right hook. I'm not a fighter but I'd had plenty of experiences of avoiding punches and instinctively dodged it and I reeled back on my heels. On missing his target he stumbled and fell forwards. I brought out the hammer from behind my back and stepped out into that bright blue day and promptly embedded it into the top of my

216

Uncle Sean's skull. Operation shock and awe was under way. Uncle Sean was a bit surprised at this to say the least. His legs buckled and instinctively his hands shot up to his head in order to shield himself from any further attacks. I prised the hammer out and the second blow hit him between his left shoulder blade and his neck. His head lopped to one side comically and I burst out laughing. 'For fuck sake Johnny stop son you're going to kill me! Have you lost your fecking mind son?' He screamed.

Well fucking duh I thought of course I'd lost my mind. Why else would I be hammering my uncle to death in broad day light?

'I was just about to have a wank Uncle Sean. You should have made an appointment.' I said as if somehow this was justification. This time I hit him directly in his mouth so he wouldn't be able to talk anymore. He was beginning to get on my fucking tits. When I pulled it back out I noticed that there were bits of bone and teeth stuck to the end because of all the blood. I wiped it clean using his shirt although by now that too was pretty well covered in blood and gristle. I looked at the black hole which was where his mouth had once been. He was trying to say something but I couldn't really make out what it was.

'I'm finding it very difficult to understand what you're trying to say Uncle Sean! Is it that you're sorry for coming around uninvited and making me postpone the fucking wank I was just about to have? Was that it? Because if it was anything else I'm going to hit you again. Did you think that if you came around I'd just hold up my hands and let you give me a good hiding? Is that what you thought? Then you could go back to my dad and be some kind of fucking hero for beating up a fifteen year old boy? Was that your plan uncle Sean? Well think again mother fucker because those days are over.' I screamed into his ear.

Then I dragged him over to our concrete pathway, threw him on his front and spread his arms out. 'This is the last time you are going to be doing my dad's dirty work Uncle Sean.' I said this as I brought the hammer down onto his left hand with all my might breaking every bone in it. 'Today you have officially retired from any hard man stuff.' I continued, as I brought down the hammer onto his right hand which had the same effect. 'If I were you I'd get a proper job. One with less risks because you're not really cut out for this type of game Uncle Sean are you?'

He was just panting on the ground by this point and trying his best not to die.

'Now then, I want you to go back to my dad and tell him that if I ever see him or you or mum or anyone else that wants to do me or our Wayne anymore harm I'm not going to be so lenient okay? I haven't killed you because up until today, unless you fiddled me as a child and I've suppressed it, as far as I know you've been okay to me and our Wayne and for that I thank you.' Something suddenly caught my attention. It was the watch he'd so kindly given me. 'Oh yes and I also thank you for the watch you gave me but you came here today to harm us and for that I cannot forgive you.' I suddenly felt a pang of guilt but if I was going to be a Don I was going to have to make difficult decisions and right now I had to make an example of my uncle Sean.

'Now then Uncle Sean you might notice a bit of swelling to your hands later but you may have also noticed that I've not touched your legs so in a minute, when you've got your breath back, I'm going to pull you up and you're going to get the fuck out of my front garden because you're making an awful fucking mess of it. And you might want someone to take a look at your head too because that's not looking too pretty at all if I'm being honest.'

I then dragged him to his feet and helped him into the road.

'Remember what I said Uncle Sean because if I even see anyone from the family ever again who isn't our Wayne I will kill them and I will kill you.' I threatened.

I then marched him down the road while kicking him up the arse so all our neighbours could see. 'Oh yeah Uncle Sean I've got a present for you! I nearly forgot.' As I said this I took off my watch and shoved it deep into his arse hole. Then I went back inside, washed my hands and had the wank that I was going to have before being so rudely interrupted. Shock and awe. Shock and awe.

Chapter fifteen

With all the excitement of the morning I must have fallen into a deep sleep after my wank because when I awoke it was dark. I got up and went into my old bedroom making sure to knock first in case old Dorothy was in there laying spread eagled on our Wayne's bed with a coke bottle up her arse or something equally fucking sordid. Thankfully the room was empty. I went down stairs to look for something to eat. I opened the fridge and found that it was still full of stuff. Oh happy day. The last time I opened that fridge the only thing that was in it was my mum's suppositories for her Nobbies and half a can of white lightening which turned out to have been full of dog ends.

I took out a couple of pork pies along with some cheese and ham and made myself a sandwich. I then took a couple of beers and went into the living room and turned on the TV. I was in the middle of watching a repeat of Dad's Army when I heard the door go. It was being unlocked rather than hammered on so I wasn't alarmed and a few seconds later in strolled our Wayne looking pleased as punch. Unfortunately old Dorothy was with him. I'd secretly hoped that after last night their mad affair may have come to an end but by the looks of the pair of them this was clearly not the case. 'Hello Johnny!' Said Wayne excitedly and he bounded over to me and ruffled my hair. 'Good evening Wayne.' I replied looking passed him to where Dorothy was hanging up her coat. 'Good evening Johnny.' She said and walked towards me holding out one of her bony old hands. 'I'm sorry about yesterday Johnny I was out of line and I apologise unreservedly. I got carried away by the whole me and Wayne thing and it went to my head. I realise that I'm no spring chicken anymore and from now on I'll act accordingly. Can you forgive a silly old woman for acting like a fool? My Wayne absolutely adores you and I want us to be friends. We've both acted at times like a couple of prize cunts but I say let's start again. What say you?' Fuck me it was still an odd thing to hear old Dorothy or any other pensioner use such profanities. I'd always assumed that turning the air blue was more of a young person's game. Who was I to judge the old hag though? I loved a good swear up. Fucking adored it. I used profanities like verbs and nouns and adjectives and I'd always loved to see how many I could fit into a sentence just for the fucking hell of it and for me Dorothy's potty mouth was one of her few plus points.

Well, well, well, would wonders ever cease? Old Dorothy had caved in and offered me an olive branch. What a turn up. It was less to do with her suddenly seeing the light and more to do with me putting a hammer to my Uncle Sean was my guess but I decided that life was too short to hold grudges and immediately stuck out my hand. 'I accept your apology Dorothy now let's not hear one more word about it.' I said, as I gave her hand a gentle shake just in case it came off or it snapped like a twig. I looked at our Wayne and winked at him and he grinned back at me. I glanced over again to Doris, looked her deep into her watery old eyes and finally said. 'If I ever do see that old growler of yours again or you talk to me like I'm some sort of cunt I'll cave in your fucking skull.' And everyone burst out laughing. Everyone except Dorothy. Shock and awe. Shock and awe.

Chapter sixteen

The next day I decided to go into school. I woke up bright an early, had a shower, put on my school uniform, had a bit of breakfast in front of the television, packed my school bag then hopped on my bike. This was a first for me. My normal school day routine was; wake up, have a wank, then a fag, then fuck it off and go back to sleep. I hated school and school most certainly hated me. A state school was not designed for the miss fits and the weirdos and the weak. If you stood out from the crowd in any way shape or form there would be a very high percentage of getting your fucking head kicked in. If you wanted to survive in that institution it was imperative that you slotted neatly into one of the few but well stablished moulds. If you were a boy for example, you needed to be either a certified nut job or more commonly, be a member of a gang. The real loons were pretty much left alone to do their own thing. Once the novelty had worn off bullying someone who was clearly mental it was a waste of time and there was no pleasure in it. Safety in numbers was the order of the day for the majority. Simple as that. This was fine for most of the kids but not for me. Due to its innate hierarchical nature, in order to be in a gang, unless you were the top dog you had to compromise yourself. I'd always found this a problem. Being someone else's little bitch had never sat well with me and from an early age I'd rather have continually run the gauntlet alone than have to metaphorically sucked dick to survive. From what I could see the same applied for girls but rather than being hard it helped their cause if they were hot. Or at least thought that they were. Confidence whether real or fake could get you a long way if you played it right. As far as I could tell a lot of school survival was smoke and mirror stuff. The Emperor's new clothes type of bullshit. Yes, confidence was key. If a lad gave the impression that he was nails convincingly enough then the other kids would meekly accept it and fall into line. This was all fine and dandy up until the inevitable point when they would be challenged of course. Once you'd gotten yourself a reputation as a hard man the clock was ticking and you were a marked man. Sooner or later the chances were that someone would want to take your title and all the rewards that went with it. And these rewards could be very great. Respect, prestige, fame, power, glory, not to mention all the protection money and all the other numerous kickbacks. All of these were worthy prizes but for me they all paled into insignificance in comparison with the greatest prize of all. Girls. If you were the school daddy then girls seemed to fall at your feet. I'd always done my best to keep my head down and the last thing I wanted to do was call attention to myself but I had to admit that the thought of unlimited minge did appeal to me. Our school had various different gangs within its perimeters but the biggest and most notorious was the Pound Hill Zombies. Their leader was Pete White aka Butch. I think he was supposed to have been named after the big, hard acting bull dog from the Tom and Jerry cartoons but to me the name Butch just sounded gay as fuck. Butch? Fuck off. I couldn't help myself from smirking behind my hand every time I saw the cunt. Anyway if a kid could get into the Pound Hill Zombies their life would become a lot easier. Affiliation would insure protection from the worst of the day to day casual brutality of school life. Unsurprisingly most of the other kids' were desperate to join up but the selection process was brutal. In order to even become considered an apprentice or 'prospect' you had to undertake numerous challenges that included, beating up and robbing other kids, running errands for the other more established, higher ranking members, petty theft and dealing eights. Once a prospect had proved themselves in these various disciplines the final hurdle would be to take a proper pasting from other gang members without dying. And then and only then would he or she finally be accepted. I was never interested in becoming a member of the Pound Hill Zombies but the gash that accompanied membership clearly did have its appeal. Butch himself was a real ugly cunt but he always had a string of hot girlfriends. I obviously knew that this had less to do with his charm and charismatic personality and more to do with his silver back status but it still ground my gears that he was banging all the best looking girls in our year when all I had was my imagination and left hand. So for an unprotected lone wolf such as myself with no social standing to speak off school was a place in which I found few pleasures.

On this day though, as I approached the school gates, rather than the habitual sense of fear and foreboding that I'd always felt deep inside my guts, I felt fucking great. A new feeling of optimism had enveloped me.

I smiled at Miss Clipson as I sped past her and thanked my lucky stars. My old art teacher was on inspection duty trying to make sure all of us pupils upheld the strict uniform guidelines. The usual fascist bollocks. Ties tied properly and top button done up, blazer on, no jeans or trainers, no drugs or knives or guns or explosives, no short skirts or jewellery or makeup for the girls. Nothing that might conceivably make us lads' cocks hard so we would hopefully spend more time learning and less time lusting. Miss Clipson was an artist though and therefore, thank fuck, above all those draconian rules she could not have cared less about how we looked so we all piled through unchecked.

My reason for attendance today was two-fold. To find and hangout with Priti and also to cause some fucking mayhem. Mayhem on an unimaginable scale. I needed to find out what all that flirting with me was about. My educated guess was that she just wanted to upset and antagonise her dad but I obviously wished that there might be more to it than that. Since I'd last seen her I'd prayed with all my might that maybe she really did fancy me for real. I knew that this was highly unlikely but until I'd spoken to her I could still hold onto a glimmer of hope. With this in mind I decided that rather than risk the day being conceivably ruined right from the start I wouldn't actively seek her out until at least after first break. I wasn't officially affiliated to any actual gangs but I did have a few friends that I would hang around with on the few occasions when I did actually attend school so I sought them out. I scanned the playground and fortuitously spied Billy, Diamond, Squint and Black Clint all huddled around the West block bins. I parked my chopper and strolled over to them arms out stretched and all smiles.

'Oi, oi bitches! Daddy is home who wants a cuddle?!' I shouted gleefully as I approached.

'Fucking hell you mental cunt!' replied Billy glancing around furtively.

'Good morning Billy I trust that this day finds you well you foul mouthed, little mother fucker!' I replied.

'They say you've gone fucking crazy and murdered both of your parents!' Diamond chimed in looking terrified.

'Fuck me boys they aren't even dead. Plus I never really laid a finger on either of the cunts really. Our Wayne did most of it. All I did was kick my dad in the head a few times I think.' I replied, trying to play the whole thing down.

'Howdy Johnny, folks around town be saying that you decimated the old Oakhill gang? We heard some pretty messed up rumours about them too. Yes sir we sure did. Yup.' Said Black Clint before spitting on the floor.

Black Clint was one of the few black kids in our school. He was adopted as a baby by this old couple who couldn't have children of their own. It transpired that they were

223

big country and Western music fans and did that line dancing and all kinds of other country and western themed shit like going to weekend conventions and dressing up and shooting guns and lassoing fucking cows and presumably re-enacting the wiping out of entire Native American civilisations. Well black Clint had taken to all this like a duck to water and could often been seen moseying down the high street in full cowboy kit including ten gallon hat, poncho and spurs on his boots. He could also play the guitar and did a very passable impression of Johnny Cash and Hank Williams and all his other Nashville heroes. His real name was Joseph but we all called him black Clint because of Clint Eastwood who'd starred in all those spaghetti westerns and because he was black.

'Howdy black Clint.' I always spoke to him in the same vein. I loved that he didn't give a fuck what anybody thought of him and delighted in playing along.

'Well you don't wana go listenin' to no crazy rumours now do you Mister?' Man could get himself into a mighty big heap O trouble spreadin' around lies and untruths now couldn't he?' I replied as I too spat on the ground and then said, 'ping'! As if I'd just spat into a saloon spittoon.

'Come on Johnny don't fuck around this is serious shit, Mickey is in the hospital on a life support machine and the rest of his gang are in intensive care! Did you really nail that Kenny kid to a park bench and fuck him in the arse? They say doctors found a dead squirrel up his arse and his colon had been ruptured and he will never walk again!' Squint burst out. 'No offence but you've got to fuck off we don't want to get mixed up in all that shit! Do the right thing and just leave us alone mate!'

Well fucking charming I thought. These pricks were supposed to be my friends. I couldn't really blame them for wanting to disassociate themselves from me though. If you were a none gang member the best thing to do in order to survive was to try and become as invisible as one could possibly be. By the sounds of it word of Wayne and I's recent shenanigan's had spread like wild fire and now I'd drawn attention to myself and these cunts evidently didn't want to be contaminated. A dead squirrel?

'Listen boys it was all a misunderstanding really' I replied, trying to act as if it wasn't really that big a deal. 'Micky and his crew were disrespectful to me and our Wayne so we had to act accordingly.' I continued.

'By raping one of them and putting them all in the hospital?' Inquired Boner.

Diamond was called Diamond because when he got over excited for any reason at all he immediately got a hard-on aka a diamond cutter.

'I never raped Kenny.' Let's get that straight. 'Kenny may or may not have been nailed to a park bench and brutally sodomised but what I can tell you guys is that it wasn't me that did the sodomising bit. In fact on that very same day I got wanked off twice by two separate older ladies and was very close to sloshing one up a very fit prostitute and that is the truth so you can all spread that around town if you like.' I protested.

I never mentioned the old bender in the public toilets or the fact that I came in my pants when Aunty Joan was grinding her old growler on me. Or the fact that the prostitute was a ninety year old on her last legs who had refused to let me anywhere near her wizened twat.

'What about your uncle and aunty then Johnny is that true, you mad cunt?' inquired Billy.

Jesus you couldn't do anything around here without the whole world knowing your business. I thought to myself.

'Why? What did you hear?' I replied, interested to know what the rumour mills had made of those petty little incidents.

They say your Aunty came round yours to plead with you not to try and kill your parents again and to call a truce and you pinned her down and wanked off in her face then beat the shit out of her!' replied Diamond looking at me like I was some kind of sexual deviant.

Squint then took up the reigns and said, 'And then when your Uncle Sean came around to plead with you to let him in so he could get your dad's pills he needed for his crippling depression you attacked him with a fucking hammer and rammed a stick up his arse!' A fucking stick up his arse? How did these Chinese whispers get so fucked up? I wondered who'd added that bit along the way. I wish I had stuck a fucking stick up his arse, the prick.

'That's only partly true!' I protested. 'The only thing I will say on this subject is that everyone who tried to fuck me and our Wayne up got what they deserved. All we did was defend ourselves. It is important that you know that I didn't pin down and wank off into my Aunty Joan's face. According to our Wayne and his young lady friend I wanked off out of the window and some of it may have landed on her but I can't be

225

sure because I passed out when I came. And furthermore I certainly did not push a stick up my Uncle Sean's dirt box. It was a digital watch that he'd previously given me.'

I needed everyone to know that because I didn't want those vicious rumours getting back to Priti or Sally in case they thought that I was some kind of fucking sex case or something. I did quite like the idea of pinning down Aunty Joan and wanking off over her face though. I'd hoped that she had started that particular rumour because that was what she'd wanted to happen. I was more than willing to do that if she desired, once everything had all blown over of course.

'Now then young Johnny boy if you don't mind obliging it would be awfully decent of you if you wouldn't mind getting the fuck outta Dodge before anything untoward happens around these here parts... Yup.' Said black Clint doing his best southern drawl.

'Well fucking so much for loyalty guys.' I say with mock incredulity. 'I've got two bottles of vodka and forty fags in my bag I thought that we could have a party but due to your innate cowardice you can all go fuck yourselves.'

'You got any sippin' whiskey in that bag of yours Johnny?' Drawled Clint.

'No black Clint I do not but if you swear allegiance to me right now I can categorically promise you that there will be whiskey galore.' I looked around at the others as I continued, 'There will also be drugs, money, fame and all the snatch you can eat.'

There was a moment of silence as they all just stared at me with that all too familiar look of pity, then Billy said, 'Look Johnny we know you and your brother have had it rough and no offence intended but I think your head has finally popped. Why don't you go home and get some rest? Come back to school in a few weeks and then we'll all club together have a few beers to celebrate leaving this shit hole. Get back on your bike and go home Johnny we don't want to get mixed up in all of this mess when we've survived this far. Do us all a favour and get the fuck out of here now. For our sakes if not your own. We just need to last a few more weeks and then we're out of here forever Johnny. You've made yourself a target and now you're in the firing line. Please don't involve us Johnny, we're nearly there mate.'

It was a heartfelt plea and the rest of them all nodded in agreement.

I had a beautiful plan though and if it was going to succeed then they were going to have to be a part of it whether they liked it or not. I needed to rally the troops.

'Listen guys I get it. I understand completely what you're saying. We've all been bullied and intimidated and kicked around since we were just little kids. I cannot remember the last time I had any dinner money or went a whole day without getting a dead arm or a dead leg or had to eat dog shit or not get farted on or not be forced to fight with another scrawny little nerd for the enjoyment of a few psychotic wankers or didn't wake up every morning and want to fucking die in order to be free from the purgatory of this fucking hell hole of a place and all the cunts within its walls. But if we don't make a stand right now we will be forever scarred. Do you want to be helpless victims forever guys? Or do you want to be able to hold your heads up high and say, 'I fought the cunts and the cunts lost?' All I need you to do is trust me and soon this nightmare will be over and we will be kings.'

Squint replied first. 'I'm more than happy to be a helpless victim Johnny. But thanks anyway.

Then Diamond joined in. 'Me too Johnny if we can keep our heads down for just a few more weeks than we will be free of this place forever and I'm more than willing to live with the consequences of never fighting back. I'm a coward and I can live with that. We all are. We can't all be alpha males. In order for a society to function properly there has to be a hierarchy and we are bottom feeders. It's social Darwinism Johnny and there's fuck all we can do about it. Cheers but it's a no from me.'

Black Clint spat on the floor and tipped me his invisible hat. 'Johnny son I sure would like to help you on your quest yes siree bob darned tootin' I would but yawl see I'm a gosh darned yella' bellied, lily- livered varmint like these here guys. I'm a black cowboy in a world of white folks and I need to keep me a low profile around these here parts. I'm mighty sorry Johnny but you're on your fuckin' own pilgrim'.

'And you Billy? Do you feel the same? Are you with me or against me?' I asked him.

'It's not a question of being with or against you Johnny it's a question of self-preservation. I just want to pass my exams and go to catering college and hopefully my life will improve and I can't do that if I've got brain damage due to having the shit kicked out of me because of my association with you. I'm out and I'm sorry to say that you're own your own here. It's just not our fight mate.'

I was ready for this and I'd already rehearsed what I was going to say.
227

'I fully appreciate your honestly guys and I hear loud and clear what you're telling me. If I was in your position I'd be saying the same kind of things but if you think your lives will improve once you've left this school then you are being very naïve. Do you think that there aren't bullies in the work place? On building sites and factory floors and garages and offices? There are tyrants everywhere.' I look at Billy, 'You will turn up at your beloved catering college all full of fucking Fanny Cradock dreams and optimism and I can guarantee you that by the end of the day you'll wish you were back here. We are all victims. You can spot us a mile away. We wear it like cloaks. If we don't act now we will spend the rest of our lives afraid to step out of line and truly live a fulfilling and rewarding life and then before we know it we will be laying on our death beds full of remorse and regret. Now swear your undying allegiance to me now and I will change the script of your lives forever! Now who is fucking with me!? Can I get a hell yeah!?'

'Nah you're alright Johnny I think we'll take our chances.' Billy meekly replied unable to look at me and the rest of them all muttered their agreement.

If I was being honest that didn't go as well as I'd hoped it would have. Just as I was trying to think of some more inspirational bollocks to inspire my spineless mates a little first year kid comes up to us and says, 'Which one of you cunts is Johnny McQueen?' Here we go, I thought to myself. It's on. I immediately knew what he wanted and was also pretty sure to whom the little arsehole belonged. I reached inside my blazer pocket and with the nail of my little finger I hooked out some of the coke and speed concoction I'd mixed up the night before and snorted it as discretely as I was able to given the circumstances.

'He is!' Said all my friends in unison as they pointed at me.

The old Johnny would have done the same and I wasn't even mad at them for this act of betrayal.

I looked down at this little kid and with as much contempt as I could muster I said, 'Who wants to know you fucking little prick?'

That threw him off balance for a split second because he wasn't used to being spoken to like that. He was a tiny cog in a big wheel but he was still a cog and still commanded respect from all those of us who weren't cogs. I was no longer living in fear and I now saw through this whole façade. To me he was just another scared little boy trying to protect himself. He was on the wrong side on this day though.

He stood to attention and clicked his heels and said, 'on behalf of the Pound Hill Zombies I need you to come with me.'

There was an audible gasp from the increasingly large crowd that had begun to gather. Perfect. Just as I'd hoped. He was a representative of the daddy of the daddy of all our school's various gangs.

'At ease sailor!' I said and kissed him on the cheek. He went bright red and didn't know what the fuck to do.

'Well lead the fucking way then shit cunt because I can't fucking wait to see what all this could possibly be about.' I replied with glee and I smacked him jovially but hard on his back which made him nearly shit himself.

'Oi fuck off do you know who the fuck I am?' He shouted in my face, all full of indignation but now consumed with wholesale embarrassment. The gang leaders always got the weediest little kids to do this sort of thing in order to humiliate the summoned knowing full well that they wouldn't be harmed due to their association with the gang. Unfortunately for this one he didn't know who the fuck he was dealing with. I whispered in his ear. 'When this is all over I am going to nail you to the nearest park bench and rape you with a dead squirrel...to death.' Then I ruffled his hair. I heard a dull like fart come from him as I said this and knew that this time he'd actually shat himself.

'Oh what's that fucking smell?' I shouted as loud as I could while theatrically holding my nose. 'Oh you dirty little cunt you've poo pooed! Is this how you represent your fucking firm? You're going to be in an awful lot of trouble when old Butch finds out you filled your nappy while on duty!'

The little kid was mortified and his humiliation was complete.

'Take me to your leader' I said in my best alien voice. 'Then I suggest that you go to the fucking nurse to get your diaper changed little boy.' As I said this I kicked him hard up the arse.

He fell over and everyone laughed.

I dragged him off the floor and gave him a push knocking him over again and said, 'Come on stinking bum let's go and see your master then shall we? See you later boys. Back in a jiffy!'

'More likely a body bag!' someone shouted from the crowd and got a big laugh.

The little kid picked himself up off the ground utterly distraught and led the way as best he could as I continued to kick his arse and throw him to the floor and pick him back up. I followed him and the crowd followed me.

Within no time at all we had reached our destination. The east block boys' shit house. This was the official offices of the Pound Hill Zombies. Nobody in their right mind would have gone into these bogs uninvited even if they had chronic diarrhoea or their life depended on it. As I stated earlier, I did though because if one of the hotter female teachers was on playground duty or the girls were playing netball it was a good place to spy on them and have a nice long wank straight into the communal trough. My need for sexual gratification had always outweighed my fear of having my head kicked in so it was like a home from home for me.

The little kid stopped at the door. 'Go in there.' He said. 'Say please.' I replied. He looked around at all the other kids and then at me not knowing how to respond. I took his head in my hands and pulled him towards me. 'I'm going to be in here for about five minutes and then when I come out I'm going to go to the woodwork department and get a hammer and some nails and then I'm coming for you so I suggest that you nip off to the showers and clean your little bum- bum because if there's one thing I can't stand it's getting shit all over my cock. Now be a good boy and say please.' 'Please.' He submissively replied. I slowly and purposely looked around at the gathered congregation. 'See you all in a minute.' Then I gave them all a cheeky wink, smashed the little kid's head against the brickwork and as he crumbled to the floor I walked in.

Pete White aka Butch sat at a table in the middle of the toilet and his two deputies, Kevin Westwood and Nigel Heath who stood either side of him. Also known unimaginatively as Westie and Nige these two were a couple of lumps and did the majority of Butch's dirty work. They were his two top boys and I couldn't help but feel a bit honoured that they'd felt the need to show such a display of strength. It seemed like I was already becoming a big deal.

'Alright Pete apparently you want a word. How can I help you mate?'

'The name is Butch you little cunt and I'm not your mate.' He sneered.

I looked at him up and down. Up until very recently I would be shitting myself in this situation. But not today. Today I was calm and full of anticipation. I'd never really appraised him before and I'd certainly never looked him in the eye. I'd always
230

thought of him as being a lot bigger than he actually was. He wasn't that big at all. In fact he was a rather diminutive figure. As Dorothy had quite rightly pointed out, it's always the tiny guys that cause all the trouble. They did seem to be perpetually angry and Butch here was no exception to the rule.

'Oh yeah sorry Pete that's right you're butch. My apologies. How can I be of assistance to you on this gorgeous morning? Isn't it great to be alive on such a day?' I grinned.

'Stop fucking talking McQueen!' He shouted as he banged his fists down hard on the table. He was used to kids cowering in his presence and he was finding it difficult to gauge me. I pressed on trying to push his buttons.

'Oooh Butch by name, Butch by nature!' I giggled, camping it up just for my own amusement. Acts of extreme so-called manliness always brought out the opposite effect on me.

Butch was now very red in the face and his two henchmen looked ready to pounce.

'You need to show me some fucking respect McQueen!' He shouted.

'Sorry Mr Butch it's just that I get very unpredictable when I'm nervous. I'll try and behave. Now then if you tell me what you want with me we can take it from there. How's that?'

'It's not mister fucking Butch it's just fucking Butch!' He yelled.

'Oops sorry Butch. As I said I'm very nervous and when I'm nervous anything could happen. Please forgive me Pete, shit I mean Mr Butch. Bollocks! Fucking Butch. Oh God I'm so sorry Butcho. The Butchstar... Butchy, Butch... Butch... Butch Cassidy and the Sundance cunt... MC Butch and the cookie collective... The butcher of Baghdad... Give me a B! ' I rambled as I watched him getting more and more irate. B! Shouted Westie excitedly before remembering where he was and going a deep red. Bless his heart.

'I will stab you to death if you don't stop talking McQueen.' Butch yelled, exasperated. I could only assume that this little interview wasn't going how he'd planned and to my glee he was getting increasingly agitated.

'I'm going to get straight to the point McQueen because you are already doing my fucking head in. Rumour has it that you and your retard brother and a load of other cunts managed somehow to nearly beat to death Micky Smith and the Oakhill gang. Is that correct?

231

'No it is not sir.'

'So it's not true?'

'Some of the story is indeed true Butch. Yay got it right! Well done me!'

'Which part is true McQueen?

'The part about me and our Wayne. Please don't call him a retard because he's not and plus that's a very disrespectful thing to say about anyone. Especially my brother. But in answer to your question the bit about nearly beating to death Micky and those other cunts it true.

'Watch your fucking mouth McQueen, Micky is a close associate of mine and I'm very upset that he is currently in intensive care in a fucking coma with a fucking brain haemorrhage.'

'Brain haemorrhage eh? That's great! I wonder if he'll ever be the same again. I fucking hope not because the last time I saw him he was a massive bell. You know they do say that in some cases a head trauma can actually change a person's character so you never know maybe if or when he does recover, God forbid, he might be less of a, an please excuse my language here, 'fucking cunt'.'

'This is your last warning McQueen you either shut your fucking mouth and speak only when I ask you to or these two will hold you down while I cut out your fucking tongue.'

'Okay, okay, you're absolutely right. I do tend to waffle on when I'm under a bit of stress but I will try and rein it in from now on. Just to clear everything up I need to quash any false rumours regarding the occurrence to which you are referring. Or is it, the occurrence to which you refer? Of which you refer? Fuck knows to be honest. Anyway that's beside the point. What you need are just the facts. Isn't that right? …Butch. I looked at him directly into his eyes when I said his name and then pouted and winked.

He stared back at my with a vacant, almost bored look on his face and said, 'Yes Johnny you tell us exactly what happened and then we will beat the shit out of you and then we can all get the fuck on with our lives. How's that McQueen?'

'Well with a few little tweaks here and there that sounds perfect to me.'

'Fucking fire away then.' He said, clearly by now irritated all to fuck.

I took a deep breath as a sudden wave of amphetamine coursed through my blood stream. 'Well the long and the short of it was this. Micky and his gang had been

232

humiliating, robbing and beating the shit out of me and our Wayne since before either of us could remember and then the other day we decided that enough was enough. We had this sort of epiphany you see? I wouldn't have said that it was particularly spiritual but it was kind of powerful in its own way. So yeah anyway after we'd had this what you might call an 'awakening' we ran down our stairs and before we knew it we had beat the fucking shit out of our dad and then we ran to the park because we knew that was where Micky and his gang hung out and besides that's where they were when they beat up my brother earlier in the day. So yeah, we found them and beat the fuck out of all of them and then we robbed them and then I nailed that Kenny one... You know the little bender one? Well I nailed him to the park bench that they all used to congregate on and then I think, well to be honest I'm pretty sure that our Wayne fucked him in the arse. Not because he's a bender. I must make that very clear. This wasn't some bigoted, homophobic attack it was more of a coincidence really. Kenny got fucked just because he was the one that our Wayne wanted to fuck. It could have just as easily been any of them apart from Debbie obviously. You really would have had to be retarded to have wanted to give her one up the tea towel holder am I right lads!?' Westie and Nige must have got caught up in the flow of it because they both laughed and nodded at that bit and high fived each other but abruptly stopped when they were glared at by Butch who was just sitting there looking irate as fuck. I carried on, 'So yeah I just left our Wayne and Kenny to it and after that I'm not really sure what happened because I fucked off. So in answer to your question we found them, we beat the shit out of them then we robbed them, and also humiliated them a bit too. Especially little Kenny. Between you and me Butch that Kenny really is an obnoxious little cunt and I'm not saying that because he's a homosexual, it's no skin off my nose what he or anybody else gets up to in the bedroom because it's none of my business but that boy is simply detestable. You do know he tried to make me suck his little cock right? And numerous other lads by all accounts. Apparently that's his thing. I must say though, and I'm not just sticking up for our Wayne because he's my brother, that out of all of those Oakhill chaps if you took away his personality and judged them all purely by looks alone, at a push I think if I had to, like to save my life or something I too would have chosen Kenny to be the one I would have scuttled over that bench. And furthermore and don't misunderstand me here because I'm not trying to condone what our Wayne did but you must ask yourself. Could it not have been

233

consensual? As they say, there's no smoke without fire and was it even burglary? It often takes two to tango and you know what guys? Looking back on it now I do remember little Kenny being a tad flirtatious towards our Wayne and he doesn't normally need to be asked twice. Come to think of it I think there had been a lot of pent up sexual tension between those two for ages and it was only going to be a matter of time before something had to give and unfortunately for little Kenny it was all the muscles around his ring piece.' Despite themselves, once again both Westie and Nige burst out laughing at that bit and were once again berated by Butch.

'Our Wayne is a gentle giant and I'm sure he didn't mean any harm. I mean it is the eighties after all and if two people of the same sex want to be together, if only briefly and viciously then who are we to judge? I'm certain that Wayne has a lot of respect for young Kenny and who knows what the future may hold for the pair of them. Stranger things have happened I'm sure you will all agree.' I couldn't stop talking and said whatever came into my head until that rush subsided. Finally I calmed the fuck down, took another deep breath and said, 'so yeah that's about the long and short of it Butch. It was like an avenging thing. Revenge for years of torment with a bit of buggery thrown in for good measure.'

Butch just stared at me without saying a word for what seemed an eternity.

Eventually, with a deep sigh he said, 'Fuck me gently.'

'What and die a cripple!?' I shot back gleefully but I don't think he really understood my joke.

'You are a deeply disturbed individual McQueen. Okay, okay, let's just press on, who else was involved in the revenge attack?' He asked.

'There was nobody else involved. It was just me and our Wayne.'

'So just the pair of you beat the fuck out of Micky and his bird and them other three?'

'Those other three... but yes, Mickey, Debbie, Mattie, Benny and little gay Kenny.'

'I've got to tell you boss, I've always suspected that Kenny kid was bent as a nine bob note. I was only saying that to one of the other lads just the other day.' Westie suddenly interrupted.

'I know right?!' I reply. 'I think the only person who doesn't know that Kenny is a raving egg is Kenny!' Talk about being in denial! I can't help but think he'd be much less of a prick if he just came out of the closet and got himself some fucking cock to munch on. Maybe that would calm the fucker down. He's always so angry isn't he?

234

Westie and Nige both laughed and agreed with me and for a moment I think we all forgot where the fuck we were and what was actually occurring. Everyone except Butch.

'Never mind who is or isn't a raving fucking egg! We keep getting off the fucking topic! When you three have stopped banging on about that Kenny cunt can we please get back to the matter at hand!?' shouted Butch. I held up my hands and shrugged. 'Sorry Butch yes let's crack on I don't know about you guys but I have a very full diary today.'

'Oh I don't think you'll feel like getting up to much after our little meeting McQueen.' Butch sneered.

'Well we will all just have to wait and see then won't we lads?' I replied and gave them all a little wink.

Butch took up proceedings again, 'Now then McQueen, Micky had some merchandise of mine that he was supposed to be selling on my behalf. Do you know what happened to it because when he was found he didn't have a thing on him and neither did any of the others.' Butch continued.

'Yeah I know what happened to it.' I replied.

'Well? Where the fuck is it?'

'I took it.'

'You took it?

'Yes. I took it. I took all his shit drugs and all his money. Next question.'

'You took my merchandise and my money?'

'Well as far as I was concerned at the time it was Micky's gear and money. I didn't know at that time that it was yours. But yes if it was yours then yes I took your merchandise and also your money. Oh well least said soonest mended eh? Boys will be boys and all that.'

'And why did you take it McQueen?'

'What do you mean?'

'What do I fucking mean you cunt? What do I fucking mean? I mean, why did you take all my fucking drugs and all my fucking money!? That's what I fucking mean! You fucking no mark muggy little shit cunt!'

'Well as I said just a moment ago, at the time I didn't know it was your stuff did I?' I replied.

235

'And if you'd known that it was my fucking gear would you have still fucking robbed it McQueen?'

'Almost certainly. You see I couldn't have given one flying fuck who the owners of that shit was because I figured that over the years I'd had a lot more than that taken from me and at the time thought that it was the least Mickey and his friends could do to make up for what they had done to me and my brother over the years you see?'

'Johnny, can I ask you a serious question?'

'Yes Butch you can ask me anything of course.'

'Do you have a death wish?'

'Now that is a very good question.' I replied. 'You know what Butch? I think I did have a bit of a death wish up until very recently. And do you know why Butch? I had a death wish because my life was so utterly shit. But you know what? You know what Butch? You know what boys? I think I've turned a corner. If you asked me right now if I was happy and wanted to live, if I was being honest, hand on heart I'd have to say yes.'

'Well that's fucking great McQueen. But unfortunately for you it's also bad fucking timing because if you don't tell me where all my fucking stuff is right this second I'm going to kill you. To death. And thinking about it even if you do tell me where it is and it's all there plus fucking interest and you've wrapped it all up in naked pictures of page three girls I think I'm still going to kill you because you've really got on my tits during this meeting.' Now where is my stuff McQueen?'

''Gotten' it's gotten on my tits, past tense you see? No? Anyway what you've done there Mr Butch is show all your cards too early. School boy error, if you'll excuse the pun.

'What?'

'School boy error, you know because you're a school boy. It's funny right? Well not exactly funny but apt.'

'Not that bit you cunt the other bit.'

'The bit about showing your cards too early?'

'Yes McQueen please explain to me what you mean by me showing my fucking cards too early. Please.' As he said this he slowly and methodically opened a drawer from under his desk top and pulled out an assortment of weapons. These included knives, hammers, a saw, a couple of bicycle chains, screw drivers and a pair of pliers all of which he laid out theatrically before him.

'You plaining a spot of DIY then Pete?' I said. 'To be honest this place could do with a makeover because, and I don't mean to be rude, your office looks like a fucking toilet.'

He was fucking furious that I wasn't fazed by his little display of torture equipment and shot out of his chair.

'Remember that day when you were crossing that playground out there and you suddenly felt a sharp pain in your fucking ear? Remember?' He snarled.

Oh this day was turning out to be just perfect I thought to myself.

'How could I forget Butch the pain was very intense to say the least. I'm assuming then that was your handy work?' I replied.

'It was indeed McQueen. And do you know why I did it? Simply because I just felt like it and also because I could. I didn't even hang around to watch your reaction. It was just a random and motiveless act of cruelty. It wasn't even personal and could have been directed at anyone. You were just in the wrong place at the wrong time.' He derided.

'Well you know what Butch? I'm very glad that you did that actually because you were the catalyst that set me free and for that I thank you.' I replied.

'I'm glad you've taken it so well McQueen. You really are a cowardly little mother fucker aren't you? You fucking little nerds make me sick. You never fight back and just take it and take it don't you? And then you go home to your mummies and daddies and cry your eyes out and they say, 'there, there my darling, don't cry mummy and daddy love you.' and then you get tucked up in your nice little beds you cunts! Well in a moment I am going to give you something to cry about because I'm going to pull your fucking ears off and shove them up your fucking ass. You sarcastic cunt!' He screamed, right into my face.

'Fuck me Butch it sounds like somebody needs a hug. Westie give Butch a hug and tell him that everything is going to be okay please.' I replied. Westie looked at Butch and held out his arms which I thought was a sweet gesture but Butch picked up a screw driver and pointed it at him threateningly while shaking his head.

'Pull off my ears Butch? Well I'd like to see that. Because that, my old friend, will be easier said than done.' I told him. I was cool as a fucking cucumber. 'Ears are mostly cartilage so they'll be all bendy and you'll have a really difficult job to shove them up an arse hole. I guess if you froze them it might work but you'd have to be quick. You got a freezer in here Butch? No? Well then if you want my advice the better thing to do would be to cut off my ears and then stuff them down my throat. That's got more of a flair about it. Plus it's that way has less homoerotic undertones. I think a lot of aggression stems from being a closeted bum bandit don't you think?' His face was so contorted with pent up rage by this stage I was worried that he might have a heart attack or a stroke. I waited for him to dramatically clutch at his chest or for half his face to drop but disappointingly it didn't so I changed tact.

'Please sit back down.' I said. 'There's no need for all this frightfulness and aggression now is there? Let's all just compose ourselves shall we? You're evidently upset and I don't blame you. You've lost your money and your drugs and your little pal and his mates are all in hospital and that's bound to have consequences further up the line. Am I right?'

For the first time in our conversation Butch looked a little bit unsettled. Butch was obviously leaning on me because someone higher up the food chain was leaning on him.

'I don't give a fuck about anyone else! I'm the fucking daddy around here and don't you fucking forget it!' He screamed at me. All these fucking Micky mouse wannabe gangsters came out with that line and I couldn't suppress my look of contempt.

'Something you want to say to me McQueen? You seem very fucking sure of yourself for someone who is in such deep shit. Do you have some kind of super power that you've been keeping to yourself all this time? Maybe you're secretly a fucking ninja? What have you got in that bag of yours then? A magic lamp? You planning to rub it and let out a genie who's going to grant you three wishes? Seems to me you're all on your own right now. I can't see your big retard brother coming to your rescue can you? Do you think that your sarcastic mouth is going to protect you from the stinging punches of my two generals here? I heard that bag of yours clinking as you walked in. You got any booze in there? Shall we have a little party in your honour? What you got in that bag Johnny?'

238

I was getting bored of the whole situation by now anyway and decided to speed things up.

'I was planning on having a party with my friends actually but one of your little bum boys came along so I had to postpone it. It really upset me actually. I've got an idea! Why don't we all have a drink and a smoke and see if we can come to a mutually beneficial arrangement? I would offer you some gear too but I've only got the stuff I nicked off Mickey and no offence but that's fucking shit. I wouldn't give that to my worst enemy. Don't you guys have any quality control? You'll lose all your customers if you're not careful. Now I'm not telling you how to run your business but with gear like that you won't get any repeat trade. Now I know it's still a bit early but who wants a cheeky slug of vodka and a spliff?'

I made to open my bag but before I could Butch lent over the table and snatched it from me.

'What goodies do we have in here then?' He exclaimed excitedly. He stuck his hand in and pulled out a bottle of vodka. He looked at me and winked. Not bad McQueen not bad.' He unscrewed the lid and took a big swig before passing it around to his mates.

He stuck his hand in again finding another bottle of vodka and a bottle of rum which he put on the table.

'Anything else you got in here McQueen?'

'No' I replied. 'It's just the booze and a can of hairspray for me mum. I'm going over to see her later and thought it might be a nice peace offering. She loves her hairspray does my dear old mum.'

'Hairspray you soft cunt? Is that all? Are you sure? Westie, do me a favour and punch Johnny hard in the face for me will you. See if we can't get him to stop telling porky pies.'

Westie immediately came towards me with his fists clenched.

'No, No, wait, wait your gear is in the side pockets of my bag but they are only a decoy for my own decent gear that I've got stashed down the front of my Jeans! Please don't hit me guys! I'll share that with you if you like!' I pleaded.

'I'm not really a sharing kind of person if I'm honest McQueen now put it all on the fucking table or one of my boys will smash your fucking head in.' He demanded as he took another slug of Vodka and passed it around.

239

I jumped up from my chair and shoved my hand inside the front of my jeans, delved about and then threw a handful of wraps onto the table.

'Oooh what have we here then McQueen?' says Butch while grinning and licking his lips.

'That's my own personal supply Butch. That's good gear let me rack us all up a line each and get this party started!' I said eagerly.

'No mate you're not having any I'm afraid because you are a cunt and a no mark nobody and you stole my gear and I don't fucking like you and you'll be dead soon so it will be a waste.' He replied.

'Come on Butch don't be like that. We could be partners in crime! I know where to get the good stuff and at a good price if you like I can cut you in?' I lied.

'No me old china what's going to happen is that you're going to give me the names of all your contacts and then these two are going to take you outside and kick you to death in front of the whole fucking school to be made an example of. How's that sound?'

As he was saying this he emptied two wraps onto the table, chopped them up expertly and then made it into one, big, fat line. He then took out a roll of notes, peeled off a twenty, rolled it up into a tube, bent forwards and sucked the line deep into his nose and up into his brain.

He then let out an ear piercing scream. Holding his head in his hands he leapt out of his chair screaming and crying and generally falling about the place in a blind panic.

'Arghhh! Fucking hell! Fucking hell! Fucking hell!' He screamed as he bounced around the toilets making a hell of a fucking song and dance. His two friends ran towards him. Westie looked around at me. 'What the fuck has he just put up his nose you cunt!?' He demanded.

'What? That white powder? Oh that was a combination of Vim and rat poison. He'll be dead in less than five minutes.' I had no idea if this was true or not but it certainly put the wind up them. They all looked at me in horror. Well Westie and Nige did. Poor old Butch was too busy staggering about the place in agony to bother with me anymore.

'Yeah and that bottle of vodka you three idiots have been swigging back also contains rat poison and enough bleach to kill a fucking bull so you two might well die before

240

him. If you're lucky! Just be thankful that you didn't start on the rum because that's petrol.'

They both looked at each other fearfully and then began franticly sticking their fingers down their throats trying to throw it all back up.

'I bet you wish you'd all been a bit more cordial towards me now don't you lads? We could have been a great team but no you wouldn't have it would you? To quote your leader, 'you're not sharing kind of guys'. Now look at the state of you. Look at Butch over there all frothing at the mouth like he's got fucking rabies!' I shouted at them gleefully.

'Oh yeah I nearly forgot! I've got another little surprise for you guys! Who wants it first?' I was talking but I don't think at this stage any of them was really listening. Butch was running around like Groucho Marx and the other two were now both curled up on the piss stained floor coughing up blood.' It was pretty much a done deal by now but I had to put on a bit of a show for the baying crowd outside.

'I was only going to use this as a last resort boys but I've got to say that you've been very rude to me during our meeting today and I didn't like the way you were talking about our Wayne either. For the last time Wayne is not a fucking retard. He was just a very sad young man who had lost the will to live. You should see him now though lads, totally transformed! Even going steady with a nice young lady! Hang on where was I? Line! Oh yes so with that in mind regrettably I'm going to have to do something I really didn't want to.'

I then opened the inside pocket of my coat and pulled out a tin of lighter fuel.

'Who wants to be first? I asked them, but all I could hear now was screaming and retching. I might as well have been talking to myself but I was having a good time so carried on regardless.

'Butch, you're supposed to be the Daddy so I suggest you lead from the front.'

I walked over to where he was now flailing about in one of the cubicles literally tearing his hair out. I quickly frisked him for valuables and found the roll of notes and also about a quarter of hashish. When I was satisfied that I had anything of any value off him I squirted him in the face and body with the lighter fuel. I then moved over to the other two. Nige looked up at me and was trying to say something or other but it was just a load of garbled nonsense to me so I squirted him in the mouth to see how lighter fuel reacted with blood and vomit. It was less impressive than I'd imagined

241

though so I quickly frisked him, found another roll of notes and a bit of change plus a few small bags of weed. Westie looked up at me pleadingly. I wondered how many kids had given him that same look just before he gave them a slap or kicked them in the nuts or slammed their heads against a wall. I Stepped back from him, took a little run up and kicked him hard in his bollocks. Then I stamped on his head a few times, robbed him of more rolled up bank notes and a few more baggies and then I squirted him a few times in the face with the lighter fuel. I then turned back to Nige and kicked him in the head and threw him into the urinal trough.

'It doesn't feel too good to be on the receiving end does it boys?' In retrospect I should have said all the revenge type stuff earlier on when they were more focused because by now they were in so much pain it wouldn't have mattered what I'd said or done to them. I said it anyway and was glad that I was getting it out of my system. I then went over to the table and picked up a pair of pliers and walked over to Butch. I took the pliers and clamped them on his nose then twisted them in a clockwise direction to around 180 degrees. Pleasingly he screamed out, clearly still able to feel pain. I wished I'd planned this a bit more thoroughly because I was basically making it up as I'd went along. I could have tortured them for a lot longer and been a lot more creative if I'd really thought it through beforehand. I was having a good time though and by the looks of them they were definitely beginning to look a lot less self-assured. I let go of the pliers around Butch's nose and cupped his head in my hands.

'Shit mate you look fucking awful.' I told him. This was true. His face was all contorted and his skin was now a pale blue colour. He also didn't really have much of a nose left.

'I'll tell you what might make you look a bit better Butch.' I said to him. 'If I cut off your ears!' He didn't react well to this at all. He started to thrash about wildly and I had to subdue him with a hammer. Luckily I'd spotted a neat little hacksaw that he'd produced from the drawer earlier. I had planned to do some James Bond villain type material but to be honest I was getting a bit bored with it all and all that screaming was starting to grate on my nerves. I pulled one of Butch's ears away from his head and started sawing away. It was a new blade and felt quite satisfying as I sliced through the cartilage and in no time at all it came away in my hand. Then I did the same to the other one. I took a few steps back and brought his severed ears up to my mouth.

242

'Can you hear me Butch?' I whispered into them. 'Or should I say, can you 'ear' me!? Butch! Butch! Pete! Peter! Butch! Butch mate! Are you deaf?'

Butch was clearly not paying any attention because he didn't laugh at that.

The romantic in me wanted to shove these ears right up Butch's arse hole but as he'd evidently shat himself I decided instead to shove them down his throat. He looked hilarious running about with no ears or nose and chocking to death and it was a shame nobody else was witnessing this marvellous spectacle. Westie and Nige were still writhing and lurching all over the toilet floor now covered in their own piss and shit and a surprising amount of blood too. It was quite a satisfying sight and I knew that our Wayne would have loved to have been witness to it but regrettably it was time to wrap things up.

'Now guys I know we've all had a good time and it was great to have touched base but sadly all good things must come to an end. I think I speak for everyone here when I say that it's been an absolute pleasure to spend some quality time with you all and I really do feel that we've all got to know each other a little better. I do hope that after today you can appreciate what it feels like to be on the receiving end of all this bullying lark. Hopefully I've given you a little insight into how it feels to be receivers rather than givers.' At this point it would have been great if our Wayne had been hanging out the back of one of them but alas it wasn't to be. I'd flirted with the idea of sodomising Butch as I was doing my final speech but he was such an ugly cunt and seeing him lying there on the toilet floor all mashed up and covered in his own juices didn't really make me feel all that sexy. That was our Wayne's bag anyway and I didn't want to be seen as a copycat. It was time for the big finish.

'Right then boys meeting adjourned! I'm off now but before I go I've got one last surprise! Although I think that the more astute of you may already have guessed what it is. Anyone have an inkling? Hmmm? No? Okay I'll put you out of your misery. Drrrrrrrrrrrrrrum- roll please! I tapped my hands on the table in quick succession.

'I'm going to set you all alight!' This last sentence did actually get a bit of a response because they all suddenly tried desperately to get up off the floor but kept falling over and slipping in their own bodily fluids.

'Okay guys listen up just so we are all nice and clear I'm going to run through with you the next proceedings. First, as I've already stated, I'm going to set the three of you on fire.' There was more groaning and screaming at this point and I could barely

243

here myself think. 'Then I'm going to light these Molotov cocktails that I've made.' I opened my bag and held them aloft for all to see. 'Seriously guys your security is absolute pants. Nobody even frisked me on the way in or checked my bag or anything. Now look at yourselves. It's bloody shameful. You clearly underestimated me boys and as you can see you've paid a pretty high price. If I'd at least been patted down at the beginning poor old Butch may still have his ears and his nose. Oh well never mind we live and learn I guess. Well not you three because you'll be dead in a minute but there you go. Butch did you catch all that?' I shouted.

I suddenly wondered if Butch could still actually hear without his ears.

'You don't really look very butch at the moment mate! I shouted at him and exaggerated my words. 'In fact I would go as far as to say that you looked like a pathetic little no mark shit cunt!' I wasn't sure if he got that reference but I was pleased with myself and that was what mattered the most to me.

'It's the end game boys! The grand finale! The final countdown! I need you to pay attention now lads because this bit is very important. Westie and Nige I'm going to set you two on fire at the same time because you're the deputies and you come as a team okay?' No response but I pressed on. '

Then I'm going to push you both out of these toilet doors and into the playground. There's going to be a big crowd out there and they are going to be expecting a big performance from you guys so please don't let them down. When I kick you out of those doors I would like you to both run out screaming and waving your arms about like you really are on fire. This shouldn't be too much of a stretch because you will be. After that you can pretty much do what you like. Free style or whatever. If I were you at that stage I'd probably be looking for a damp tea towel or a fire extinguisher. I don't mean to be rude lads but once your part is over I don't really give a fuck. After that it's the big man. Butch mate it's basically the same thing for you but you go out alone. You can really ham it up if you like because the stage will be all yours. Try and really put on a good show for the kids okay? You've only got one chance so make it count. Please don't get too stressed about it though because I've pretty much done all the hard work for you haven't I? If you could just focus on trying to get to the other end of the playground without dying then that would be perfect. I know it's easy for me to say because I won't be the one burning with two screw drivers stuck in my eye sockets but just do your best that's all I ask.'

Butch started to whimper and it was hard to tell by this stage but I think he shit himself again. Happily he'd definitely pissed himself. Butch pissing himself actually helped because I only wanted the top half of them to burn so that they could run properly. I didn't want them to ruin the spectacle by just limping out the door and dying. I wanted them to run about for a bit and really put on a spectacular performance.

All that I needed to do now was get them into position.

'Right boys it's show time. Now then the only way that you have a chance of living is to get through those doors and into the fresh morning air. Who knows? Maybe some of your gang might be out there and when they see you all ablaze I'm pretty positive that they'll come running to your rescue. So let's get you up and out without any more fuss shall we? I'll tell you what lads as I've had such a good time I'm going to throw you all a bone. Instead of just setting fire to you and shoving you out like I said earlier I'm going to give you a ten second head start. How does that sound lads? If you can get through those doors within that time you'll be free as birds I promise. Are you up for it?'

I walked over to them and squirted the remainder of the lighter fluid all over their top halves.

'Butch you stay where you are for now. Let's get these lads out safe and sound first.'

I then began to count down from ten.

'Ten!'

Nige and Westie tried their best to scramble to their feet, slipping and sliding in all the blood and piss and shit and puke.

'Nine!'

They were pushing and pulling each other and frantically trying to get up and out of the door first.

'Eight!' Considering the fucking state they were in I couldn't help but be impressed at their speed and dexterity and within no time they'd got themselves within a few feet of the toilet entrance.

'Seven, six, five, four, three, two, one!'

Just as they got to the doors and swung them open I took out a handful of matches from my pocket, struck them against the side of the wall, and with one swift movement, threw them at dear old Nige and Westie. Right on cue they both burst into

245

flames. It was fucking beautiful to watch. I'll give them their due, those boys played a fucking blinder. They did everything I'd asked and more. With the help of my boot in their backs they burst through those doors with their whole top halves all lit up exactly as I'd pictured it. Out they ran, hair ablaze, waving their arms about like I'd asked them and running blindly around amidst all the other kids' screams and howling and chaos and confusion. I thought it was quite a sweet moment as they naively ran towards the crowd seeking help. Everyone ran screaming and wailing in the opposite direction though and the two boys just ran around the playground recklessly and looking at one stage very much like actual zombies which was a nice touch. They didn't last long though and within a few minutes poor old Nige had crumpled to the ground and didn't look at all well. Westie was the best though because in his blind panic he ran straight into one of the west block walls and knocked himself out. Doink! It was fucking hilarious and I was extremely pleased with their performance.

I went back in and walked up to where Butch was now sat on one of the toilet seats. 'Come on little fella you're up now!' I said to him excitedly as I smacked his face a few times to wake him up. 'You would have been very proud of Nige and Westie just then because they put on a fantastic show! You'll have a difficult job following that but no need to worry mate because I'll be with you. Now then let's get you ready Peter.'

I walked back over to the table, picked up two screw drivers and with a flourish turned on my heels and like a Spanish matador raised my arms theatrically into the air. I caught my reflection in the big toilet mirror, waited for a split second, stamped my foot like a flamenco dancer, gave myself a proud nod of recognition and then brought them down majestically and into Butch's eye sockets.

'Olay!'

It was a bit of a shame that Butch was now blind because I'm sure he would have appreciated how fucking cool all this must have looked. He immediately howled, fell to his knees and made a noise I'd never really heard before. It was the kind of sound that your soul might make as it was wrenched from your body against its will.

'Come on Pete, I can't help but think that you're more of a Pete than a Butch in my opinion I'm afraid to say. Anyway nearly there! Just one more thing I would like you to do if you don't mind.' I asked I dragged him out of the toilet cubicle and up to the entrance. I knew it was childish and pretty much pointless saying it but he looked so

246

much like a Dalek as I pushed him towards the doors I couldn't stop myself from saying 'Exterminate! Exterminate! Resistance is futile! Your vision is impaired! You cannot see!'

It was a crying shame that there were no witnesses to this except fucking Butch because it was completely lost on the prick. I thought it was inspired though.

I propped the cunt up against a wall and took out my Molotov cocktails. I then marched swiftly into all three toilet cubicles and placed one on each of the toilet seats. I then lit the rags that were sticking out of them and went back to Butch.

'Right then pal time is now of the essence. I think we've got about two minutes before these fucking bogs go boom so let's crack on. I've got to be honest with you Butch, this is the first time I've done this sort of thing so those fuckers could explode at any moment so best not drag your feet eh?'

He was very unresponsive by now and was barely alive but I had to get him through those doors and into the playground. I took the bottle of vodka that was laced with the rat poison, the one that the boys had been drinking earlier, and poured the rest of its contents all over him. I wasn't sure if vodka was flammable but was soon going to find out.

'Now then Peter I need you to apologise to me.' I'd said this because it was in the script but I'd gone too far too soon and he was just a mess of blood and gore and I didn't even get mad that he didn't respond. Plan B. I took his jaw in my hand and manually moved it up and down.

'Sorry Johnny! Sorry for everything! Sorry for all the beatings and bullying and for causing so many kids to live in fear and self-loathing! If I wasn't just about to be burned to death I'd certainly change my ways and spend the rest of my life only doing good things… like charity and that!' I said, trying to do my best Lord Charles impression.

'Okay I forgive you because I'm an old softy I guess. I forgive you Butch. I forgive you and absolve you of all your sins by the cleansing nature of fire.' I said this as I kicked his arse through the doors while at the same time setting him ablaze using the can of hairspray as a blow torch.

I was delighted to find out that vodka was very flammable indeed and he went up in flames in a spectacular fashion. I'd kicked him with such force that after falling through the doors he disappointingly simply fell straight to the ground. Luckily for me

247

and the spectators though he obviously had some kind of innate showman inside him because he managed to get himself up to one knee and with arms outstretched and head pointing skyward he suddenly looked like he was going to burst into song. The best moment was when the crowd noticed the two screw drivers sticking in his eye balls. First there was a brief moment of dead silence. This was followed by a collective gasp. Then the screaming started. I looked around at the absolute carnage I'd created. It was so beautiful to witness. Kids were fainting and puking and crying and holding each other for support. One kid was in absolute hysterics just laughing and pointing at poor old Butch kneeling there on the playground tar mac. Butch was getting all of the attention now but it was my special day so I dramatically pushed open the toilet doors, stepped out and stood feet astride and with one hand on my hip. I'd planned to come out full super hero mode and stand there triumphantly with both hands on my hips but I was still holding the can of hairspray that I'd used to set fire to Butch and that made it a bit awkward. The crowd now all turned and faced me. I looked at them and they looked back at me, puzzled. I looked down at myself and saw what they saw. A dishevelled looking school boy with one hand on his hip holding a can of hairspray. I also had an erection. It was damage limitation time so thinking on my feet I quickly sprayed the can into the air and lit the vapour. It give off a very satisfying flame along with an audible whooshing sound. A collective 'Ahhh' rose up from the crowd. I'd pulled it back. I walked out into the playground and as I passed Butch I gave him a nudge and as he fell over sideways and his head hit the ground, his ears fell out of his mouth.

He smelled like barbeque chicken. I glanced around at all the faces that had once ridiculed and harangued me. Or even worse, didn't know or care who the fuck I was. 'There's been a regime change boys and girls. The Pound Hill Zombies are no more!' As I said those words I threw all the money I'd taken off Butch and Nige and Westie up into the air. 'Here's all your dinner money!' I shouted. And as all those notes rained down and fluttered about on the morning breeze, right on cue, the east block boys' toilets blew up.

I strolled over to where Billy and the others still sat and said, 'Shock and awe boys. Shock and awe. Right then who now wants to be in my fucking gang?'

'Yes please Johnny.' They all said in unison.

'Good boys. Welcome aboard mother fuckers. Is anyone else fucking starving?'

248

Sexy Six inch part two teaser alert...

Hang on a minute before you get stuck into chapter one of the sequel would you be so kind as to leave a review? You would? Awesome. I've made it easy for you... click, click, click, five stars, laugh out loud, poignant, deep and life changing etc. etc. http://www.amzn.com/dp/B08WBF87R

Thanks in advance. Okay you may now crack on. Oh and thanks for taking the time to read my words.

Kind regards,

Dom

Six More Inches for the Holy Spirit

Chapter one

My cock was so hard. I put my hand inside my pants and freed it from between my balls, sat on my designated bin, rolled a joint and surveyed my surroundings. It became clear to me that when the shit hits the fan all self-respect goes out the window. We all like to think that we would be cool in a crisis but from what I was witnessing the opposite was true. Watching all those boys and girls scrambling about the playground chasing after all the money I'd just thrown into the air, I couldn't help thinking how fickle people were. When I'd walked into those toilets The Pound Hill Zombies had ruled our school with an iron fist for generations and by the time I'd walked back out they were well and truly fucked. I'd done Butch and his two deputies and I knew for sure that the gang would disintegrate leaving a power vacuum that I would need to fill as soon as possible. I glanced down at my watch to see how long the whole thing had taken and seeing only an empty wrist remembered that I'd recently shunted it up my Uncle Sean's arse hole and for all I knew it was still be up there.

'Hey Billy, how long do you think I was in those bogs?'

Billy was staring into space. He was obviously still in shock. I'd forgotten that for Billy and the rest of my mates this was rather a lot to process. The last time they'd seen me I was like them, just another terrified miss fit keeping my head down and trying to do my time at school with the minimum of aggravation and fuss. Now I was suddenly the Daddy. The King Pin. The Boss. The Guvnor. Numeral Uno. El Johnny.

I wondered if maybe I should give myself a new title to match my new position. When Pete White, the recently deceased leader of the Pound Hill Zombies, had taken over the reins, somewhere along the line of his ascension he changed his name to Butch as he clearly thought that this would make him appear harder. The irony for me though had always been that every time I heard the word Butch I couldn't help but immediately think of women tennis players. One had to think carefully when choosing a new identity because one didn't want to end up looking like a prize cunt. Traditionally your peers chose a nick name for you anyway and regardless of what it was, you were stuck with it. Forever. As for my mates, Diamond, for example, was called Diamond because every time he felt anxious his dick got hard thus giving him a 'diamond cutter' in his pants. Black Clint was called black Clint because he was black and liked to dress up as a cowboy and you didn't need to be Sherlock Holmes to figure out why Squint was called Squint. Billy was 'Billy the Willy' because he was hung but I was just plain Johnny. As far as I was aware anyway.

Sometimes you could have a nick name that you were unaware of. They were the best ones. One of the kids in my year, for example, was called Jeremy King but behind his back we all called him Wan. Wan King. Wanking. School boy humour at its finest. Simple, undermining and beautifully cruel. Perfection. I don't think he ever found out that was what he was known as because he was hard as fuck and would undoubtedly have reacted badly. He used to strut about the place giving it the large one obviously thinking that he was the dollars when in reality we were all laughing at him behind his back. For us mere mortals these small victories helped to get us through the day.

Like every other school I guess the place was awash with alternative names for the lucky or more likely, unlucky few. They could be funny, apt, harsh and spiteful or just downright ridiculous. We had a maths teacher called Bruno Hare and we all used to call him, the German. I loved that one because it didn't really make any sense. I often wondered if he ever questioned why kids perpetually goose-stepped into his class room giving Hitler salutes, pushing the Jewish kids around and attempting to annex the class next door. Some of our more established teachers had nicknames that had been passed down through the generations. Miss Bullen had taught English to Billy's mum and even back then she'd been known as, old wooden tit. The rumour was that she'd had one of her real tits cut off, reason unspecified, and replaced by a wooden one. She was head of the upper school and every time she led our assembly I'd spend the whole time staring at them and trying to figure out which one was which. It had never occurred to any of us to question the authenticity of this rumour either. 'Hey miss have you got a wooden tit?' Only a mental case would have asked such an impertinent question. So I was surprised that nobody had so far.

We'd all inherited these rumours and nicknames and never questioned their origin or authenticity at the time. Mr Hart, who taught Geography, was said to have killed a man with his bare hands and then shot his wife in the cunt after he'd come home early from work one afternoon and caught the former hanging out the back of the latter. Mr and Mrs Clipson were brother and sister and they both taught art. They were alleged to be at it with each other. Miss Topping and Miss Lilly taught auto engineering. The gossip here was that they were hard core feminists and even harder core lesbians, constantly on the lookout for hot school girls to recruit into

251

both causes. That was my favourite one. Dave Swann. He was our science teacher. He was rumoured to be a prolific sex case who sucked off boys in his lab during break. This last rumour started when he'd asked if any of the third year boys wanted to stay behind after their lesson and wank off into a petri dish and then look at their wrigglers through a microscope. The guy was a scientist and I suppose that could have been just an invitation to participate in a rather cool scientific experiment but in no time word spread like wild fire and before you knew it the whole school was calling him Paedo Dave. Paedo Dave didn't really look like your average nonce though in fact he was quite the hunk. Especially for a science teacher. He could have wanked me off if he'd asked but he never asked which was typical of my luck. I would have let anyone wank me off just to break up the monotony of doing it myself. I've never thought that it was gay to let someone of the same sex wank you off. Or even wank someone off for that matter. With very few exceptions that I could think of, regardless of sex or gender, if someone wanted to touch my cock who the fuck was I to say no? A wank is a wank is a wank. I'd have let anyone suck me off too. Especially paedo Dave.

Apart from Billy the Willy's, I'd never known a nickname to have ever been complimentary. Up until now I was yet to have one and was therefore vulnerable. Given my recently acquired status as top dog around here I couldn't risk the possibility of being undermined by some moody fucking moniker. What I needed to do was give myself a cool name and make sure that it got around. I decided to seek some inspiration. Drug fuelled inspiration. I licked my finger and then pushed it deep into the little baggie I'd secreted in the inside pocket of my school blazer, pulled it back out and popped the finger into my mouth. It tasted rank so I quickly dug into my bag and took a big swig from the last uncontaminated bottle of vodka I had therein. Seconds later I felt a euphoric rush. A wet finger of a speed ball washed down with a vodka shot was just what I'd needed at that moment. My brain fired up.

Less than a week ago I was a nonentity, a fucking nobody, an also ran. But now as I looked out across the playground at the mayhem I'd single handily caused everyone now knew that I was somebody to fucking reckon with. A bad mother fucker. The main man. 8 Ball. The Ace of Spades. Pretty Boy McQueen. The Mad Hatter. Death Row Johnny. Ole Snake eyes. The Enforcer. The Cardinal. The Duke. Fuck it, when I'd burst out of that East block shit house I should have shouted, 'Heeeear's Johnny!' while grinning manically. That would really have put the wind up all these stupid pricks and a cool nickname would have surely followed.

'Fuck me it's Mad Dog McQueen! Run for you fucking lives!'

That would have done me. Burning three cunts alive and blowing up the east block boys' toilets was still a good strong statement of intent though so I decided not to beat myself up about it too much. Oh well, I thought, it was too late now and anyway I was sure that there would be more opportunities to say cool stuff like that in the future. I had to maintain the momentum. There was no going back and I couldn't help thinking that it would be a backward step to just stroll into double maths and act like nothing had happened.

'Hey Johnny saw what you did out there. Nice job. The part when Butch coughed up his own ears was priceless. Hey guys! What about when Westie's head burst into flames?! I nearly shat myself! Anyway if you'd all now like to turn to page 55. Diophantine Equations.'

No, I had to up the ante even more and make it clear to everyone that I was someone not to fuck with. Figuratively speaking anyway. After my little show of strength I figured that it would only be a matter of time before I was drowning in prime snatch. Age appropriate snatch obviously. With my previous track record I'd be happy with anyone under sixty with their own teeth and hair and a minge that didn't take the paint off the doors as they passed by.

'Anybody need a livener?' I asked.

'Fuck sake it's not even first bell Johnny!' said Diamond, also clearly still in shock.

'Diamond me old mate, I've just single handily wiped out the biggest and most notorious gang this school has ever seen and that is a cause for a celebration so stop being such a little protestant and drink up mother fucker because you're a long time dead.' I replied.

'We'll all be dead soon anyway thanks to you Johnny.' Squint chipped in.

'Don't be so negative Squint! For fuck's sake I'm the daddy around here now and you lot are my henchmen. My deputies. My right hand men. My Generals. We run this fucking school now so let's just enjoy it shall we? Let's all do a line and have a drink and work out where we go from here. What do you say boys?'

'Well I think what we should do first is put out Butch and those other two lads because I didn't have any breakfast and they're making me hungry for barbeque ribs.' Replied Billy.

'See!? That's the spirit! A bit of gallows humour!' I said, well pleased with Billy's apparent changed attitude to the situation.

We all looked over to where the charred remains of the Pound Hill Zombie's top brass were smouldering away. Those three pricks were once feared by everyone at our school. Including the teachers. They'd been able to act with total impunity; Extortion, intimidation, torture, you name it these mother fuckers and their minions had done it and got away with it. They had once been the stars of the show but fame is a fickle mistress. I'd given them a good send off and they'd certainly be remembered that was for sure. They'd be forever known as the three cunts who came up against Johnny McQueen and ended up melted into the playground tarmac. Thanks to me their swan song had been spectacular and I was sure that they would have been pleased with the effort I'd put in giving them a bloody good send off.

Let's just get the facts straight here. They had started on me. I was minding my own business chilling with my mates when I'd been summoned by their leader, Billy Jean King aka Butch. They'd heard about my previous exploits and tried to make an example of me but they'd underestimated my ability to defend myself. I knew that they'd come for me and I was prepared. It was always going to be a fight to the death and a less creative man would have simply brought a knife along to the meet and stabbed the fuckers in the throat or used some other clichéd method. But not me. They'd been poisoned, beaten, tortured, humiliated, set on fire and then paraded in front of the whole school for everyone to see. This was all accompanied by top class banter along the way. It was an unforgettable performance and I'd choreographed it to perfection. It was certainly more than they'd deserved. But I was a showman.

When those boys came out of the east block toilets all ablaze, at first there was absolute mayhem. Kids were screaming and puking and generally getting themselves at it but that all changed when the money started raining down. I must have thrown around three hundred quid into the air and suddenly the same kids who were screaming in terror where now stepping over the lads' corpses and fighting with each other in their rush to get to as much cash as they could lay their grubby little hands on. And who could blame them? We'd all been skint since the first day of the first term of the first year thanks to those cunts.

I could still vividly recall my first day at Copthorne Comprehensive. I was all wide eyed and optimistic. I'd been to a Catholic primary school and thoroughly enjoyed it. Good food, good company and we'd all had a collective and burning desire to learn. I thought that everyone felt like me and couldn't wait to be filled with more intoxicating knowledge. I'd set my sights high and wanted to be nothing less than either the prime minister or the fucking Pope. By the end of that day I'd been beaten and robbed and demoralised to such an extent any academic ambitions I'd previously dreamt about had been well and truly kicked into touch forever.

Primary school had been a sanctuary for me. My home life was fucking horrible to say the least but primary school was awesome. I was a good Catholic boy and the nuns who ran the place fucking loved me. I could get away with murder because however much of a cunt I was I would never be as bad as those Protestant, holy

255

roller, jaffa, soup taking Proddywhoddy, orange mother fuckers. They were all going to burn in the fiery depths of hell whereas however much of a cunt I was as long as I confessed it all on a Sunday morning I was destined for paradise. The food was great too. At that time I'd imagined school would always be brilliant. How naïve I was.

For the rest of my school days I had to focus less and less on learning anything from the curriculum and more on rudimental survival techniques. Most kids took the Italian option and immediately capitulated before any shots were fired. For the more adventurous, if you were willing to compromise, any self-respect you might have had then you could try and join a gang. Joining a gang would afford you some protection but there's no such thing as a free meal and this option also came with its dangers. Now that their King had been dethroned and the royal guard wiped out, any of the remaining members of the Pound Hill Zombies would now be well and truly fucked. Old scores would be settled and it was all going to get very messy around here very soon. Nobody would be coming for me anymore though because hopefully I'd proved too formidable a force. I'd not only met fire with fire but I brought rat poison and a hacksaw and screwdrivers and Molotov cocktails and also I'd like to think, a wry wit, along with me. I was pretty confident that nobody would question my being the new ruler of this small but significant kingdom. Not in the short term anyway. I knew enough about history to be fully aware that all empire's will eventually collapse but until that day came I was determined to make the fucking most of it.

Suddenly I spotted the little cunt who had summoned me to the meeting with Virginia Wade.

'Oi Shit cunt' I shouted over to him. He was fucking terrified to say the least. I'd put the fear of God up him earlier and now I could see that he was visibly bricking it. 'Get over here now you little bitch.' I shouted again.

He knew that unless he fancied changing his whole identity and fucking off to Spain or somewhere he had no option but to do as he was told.

'What the fuck are you wearing?' I asked him.
256

'I had to get these shorts out of the lost property because …'

'Because what? Because you … you shat yourself earlier didn't you?'

'Yes.'

'You'll think twice about trying to play the big man now won't you shitty pants?' I said trying to lumber him with a nickname that he would hopefully have until laying on his fucking death bed.

'Yes Johnny.'

'Good boy shitty pants. Now what did I say was going to happen to you after I came out of those fucking bogs?' I asked him.

'You said that you were going to rape me.' He meekly replied.

My mates all looked up at me in horror and disgust.

'I wasn't really going to rape him guys it was just a figure of speech!' I protested.

'You raped ole Kenny.' Drawled black Clint, as he theatrically spat on the floor.

'How many more fucking times?! I did not rape Kenny! Our Wayne raped Kenny! All I did was nail the cunt to a park bench to facilitate his sodomisation!' I yelled, not wanting my new nickname to be, 'homosexual rapist.'

The little kid looked as if he was just about to faint.

'Listen shitty pants I'm not going to rape you I promise. I just got caught up in the moment back there. It was just a bit of banter. I'm only going to finger bang you and lick you out.'

A look of abject horror enveloped his face.

'I'm just fucking with your head mate. I'm hardly going to rape you or even finger bang you am I? And how would I even begin to lick you out for goodness sake? Especially as you've so very recently just shat yourself. All I want you to do is tell everyone who needs to know exactly what happened here today.'

'Okay I'll do that Johnny. Thanks Johnny. I'll make sure that everyone knows exactly what you did to Butch and Westie and Nige and the east block boys' toilets. Not a problem. I'll get right on that this minute.' He replied as he tried to make his leave.

I grabbed him by his lapels and pulled him close to me. 'Not so fast shitty pants!' I said. 'I don't want you to tell every cunt what really happened! I want you to tell them my particular version of events. I don't want to end up in borstal now do I? Because if I do I'll make sure that I take you along with me. And a pretty little thing like you will not last a minute in that environment. It wouldn't just be me raping you then shitty pants it would be every mother fucker and within no time your nickname will have changed from shitty pants to, massive, gaping arse hole boy formally known as shitty pants, so you'd better listen very carefully for I shall only say this once.'

'Okay! Okay!' he pleaded.

As I pulled him close I couldn't help but feel his genitals pressing up against me through his lost property shorts. I didn't know if it was the sensation of his cock and balls rubbing against my leg or the power I had over him as I held this little cunt against his will but for whatever reason my dick was starting to get hard. The last thing I wanted was to undermine myself by getting an erection at this point in the proceedings.

'What's that in your pocket?' Please don't stab me Johnny. I'll say whatever you want me to!' He cried.

I released my grip and pushed him away while trying to think unsexy thoughts.

'You make it known to anyone that needs to know that I was the innocent party here today. I was summoned to a meeting with Butch and they tried to torture me but it all went horribly wrong for them and they ended up on the receiving end. They had tried to set me on fire but due to their incompetence and general fuckwittery they blew themselves up. I managed to escape unscathed and even, at my own peril and risking my own life, tried to save those three cunts from the explosion by dragging them out but tragically it was too late for them. Tell everyone that I am a hero and I'll let you live. Also refer to me as, The Showman.'' I then clipped him around the ear and said, 'Okay, now you can fuck off.'

He didn't need telling twice and immediately ran off back into the crowd. As I watched him go I couldn't help myself from thinking that his arse did look pretty damned sexy in those ill-fitting shorts.

'Why is your dick hard Johnny?' Asked Billy nonchalantly.

'What?' I replied incredulously.

'I said, why, after pulling that kid up against you, has your penis gone hard?' He repeated dryly.

'Um... well I obviously made my dick hard on purpose in order to frighten and intimidate him didn't I? It's an old power game tactic. Al Capone used to do it. And the Kray brothers.' I replied, desperately clutching at straws.

'Oh is that right? I thought it was because you are a raving nonce Johnny.' Replied Billy.

'I will fucking set fire to your fucking face if you ever say anything like that to me ever again Billy!' I screamed.

'No you won't Johnny.' He replied.

'I might do Billy because, the showman, is a fucking nut case! Heeeeeear's Johnny! I shouted and then grinned at them all manically.

'We aren't going to start calling you the fucking Showman Johnny and furthermore referring to yourself in the third person is just lame as fuck and makes you look like a cunt.' Billy sighed.

Those cunts. Hadn't they seen what I'd just done? I'd ripped a large hole into the very fabric of civilisation as they knew it but all I got from them was sneers and insinuations that I was into little boys.

To be fair to me if anyone at all had rubbed themselves up against me at the point my dick would have got hard. I was buzzing off my fucking tits. Adrenaline was coursing through my veins and so was the speed and coke I'd just snorted. I'd read somewhere that after you've killed someone you get horny as fuck and even though I was pretty much horny most of the time anyway this had indeed seemed to be the case. I couldn't even go to the boys' toilets and crack one off to relieve the tension because I'd just destroyed it.

'Anyone mind if I have a quick wank into one of these bins?' I enquired.

'Jesus Johnny you really are one sick individual aren't you? This playground looks like a bomb has hit it and all you can think about is self-gratification. Why didn't you have one this morning like the rest of us? Said Squint.

'Well duh I obviously did have a wank this morning didn't I Squint? When do I ever not have a wank in the morning? You know that I'm at least a six to ten a day man. We all are! We've discussed this many times. Why do you think our gang is called, the magnificent Six for fuck's sake? The clue is in the title! We all love a wank and if it wasn't for black Clint and his low libido bringing down the mean average we would be called The Magnificent ten or even fifteen! The Magnificent Twenty if Diamond was in the gang all on his fucking own! '

'Now lookee here young Johnny I've told you many a time that there's nothing wrong with ole Clint's libido. Yawl know this. The only reason I only beat ma meat six or so times a day is because of ma maw and paw. They're mighty old folks and God fearin' Christians and they sayin' that masturbation be the devil's work so I have to be mighty sly around them when it comes to crackin' one off the wrist yawl here?! They're forever checkin' ma room and under ma bed for evidence of any vile devilish self pollutin see? And furthermore I would really appreciate it if you would refrain from bashin' one out into one of these here dust bins Johnny as I don't want to risk getting' any of your man milk on ma suede jacket because it's a real son of a bitch to get off. Believe me. Darned tootin' it is!' Drawled black Clint in his God awful fake cowboy accent.

What I needed at that moment was for one of the fifth year slags to come over and offer to suck my dick.

'Hey Johnny, or should I call you, the Showman? How did you know that extreme violence makes my gash soaking wet? On behalf of all the hot sluts at this school please give me the pleasure of feeling your load down the back of my throat.'

That didn't look very likely at the moment though. Everyone who wasn't dead was still chasing after money.

'Why the fuck did you throw all that money in the air Johnny?' Asked Diamond.

'Pure theatre darling. It was Le Grand gesture wasn't it?' I replied. 'In doing that I was telling everyone that yes I was the new boss around here but rather than ruling with an iron fist like all those previous cunts, please accept this gift. It was as if to say, I am a benign dictator but I will get spiteful should the need ever arise.

Just then I saw a girl try to peel off a tenner from the charred face of Butch but it ripped as she pulled it away and she kicked him and called him a cunt. How the mighty fall.

'I need to see Priti' I said to nobody in particular.

'What the fuck would somebody as hot as Priti want to see you for Johnny?' enquired Diamond.

'I want to take her on a date.' Then I want to walk her home and kiss her on the cheek and say 'goodnight Priti, I've had a lovely time. And she'll say, 'me too Johnny. We really must do this again sometime.' And I'll say, 'well I'm free tomorrow as it happens and she'll say, well then that's a date. And we will go on date after date after date and fall in love and have babies and grow old together and die in each other's arms.'

Everyone burst out laughing.

Squint said, 'I thought you might marry that little kid who just gave you a hard-on.'

'Or Andy I've always imagined that you'd end up with her. Diamond continued dryly. 'Sandy has always made your dick hard too.''

'Fuck me gently first of all I had that hard-on before that kid came over so bollocks and Sandy is basically a girl with a cock anyway so that's not even gay so you can all fuck off! Sandy, as she likes to be known, was born in the wrong body and has to live every day in turmoil until she can have hormone treatment and get tits and a fanny you heartless cunts! Stop making fun of her pain!' I replied furious with embarrassment and at their crassness and how well they knew me.

'Is that why you love her because you're trapped in the body of a homosexual?' Replied Diamond.

'I bet he'd like to be trapped in the body of that little kid.' Squint continued.

'Maybe when Sandy has her cock chopped off she could give it to you and then you'd always have something to suck and stick up your arse while you're married to Priti? You know like on weekends and special occasions?' Said Diamond.

262

'How's about if yawl all got married? That way you could have sexual relations with all three of them, Priti, Andy and that little ole boy that keeps making your cock so gosh darned hard Johnny'? Black Clint said, as he spat on the floor, whacked himself on the thigh and shouted, 'Yeehaw!'

'For fuck's sake that little shit doesn't 'keep' giving me a hard-on! He gave me one fucking hard-on that I probably had anyway! I was full of adrenaline after killing fucking Butch and fucking Nige and cunting Westie! If any of you had rubbed yourselves against me at that time the same thing would have fucking happened! I replied exasperated.

'Maybe we should rub ourselves up against you and see if the same thing happens!' exclaimed Squint.

They then all jumped up in unison and gleefully started trying to rub their cocks up and down my legs. 'Get the fuck off you bunch of fucking perverts that's sexual assault!' I protested.

After what seemed like an eternity but was probably only half a minute or so they stopped and stood back and all started staring at my genitals for any signs of movement.

'Nope. I can't see no hard-on eeeerection young Johnny!' said Black Clint while staring at my crotch like I was some sort of livestock.

My one chance of redemption was Diamond. If Diamond had a hard-on, which he pretty much did all the time anyway then I could deflect all of this unwanted attention on to him. I looked down at his cock and balls but inexplicably there was no obvious movement. He had just rubbed his knob all over me which was most definitely the closest thing he'd ever had to sexual intercourse yet not even a murmur. The cheeky cunt. It seemed like I was the only person ever not to give him a hard-on.

263

'Well it's a scientific fact that the only thing that gets your penis hard is little boys Johnny.' He laughed.

'And transvestites.' Chimed in Squint.

'Transsexual for fuck's sake! Sandy is a pre-op transsexual! Listen you bunch of cunts the truth is I'd bang anything and anyone except you ugly fuckers because I'm a nymphomaniac pan sexual!' I replied, exasperated by this point and sick to death of the whole situation by now. I'd just murdered three school kids in front of their very eyes yet five minutes later my own gang were still humiliating me just as they'd always done. It was true that the power I knew I had over that little prick who'd tried to fuck with me did make my dick hard but it didn't have anything to do with me being sexually attracted to him and even if it did there was nothing I could do about it was there? If grownups didn't want their kids to be objectified then why did they insist on putting us all in sexy school uniforms?

'Anyone or anything except us eh? So you'd bang your own mum then Johnny? Or a dead pig?' Or a baby? A little tiny, innocent baby Johnny?' enquired Diamond cross examining me.

'What about an old timer Johnny? An old woman? An old man? Would you bum an old man Johnny and then suck his wrinkly old cock Johnny? Do you think you should see a doctor Johnny because sucking off an old timer and having sexual liaisons with a new born baby is not in any way normal in my humble opinion.' Drawled black Clint with a glint in his eye.

These fucking arse holes knew that they had me on the ropes and were revelling in my mortification. Ever since we had all first met the only thing we ever did was to take the piss out of each other mercilessly and when you were on the receiving end of it you just had to roll with the punches until it was someone else's turn. The whole point was to wind someone up enough that they bit and lost their shit completely.

'You fucking cunts you know what I mean! I'd fuck anything fucking normal! Normal women with tits and fanny holes!' I pleaded.

'And?' said Diamond.

'And your fucking mum Diamond you cunt!' I replied.

Diamond wasn't at all phased by that comment because he'd heard it all before because even he had to concede that his mum was hot as fuck.

'And?' he continued.

'And fucking Squint's mum too! … Right up the fucking arse!' I shouted.

This was also old news to everyone because we'd all agreed that Squint's mum was also hot as fuck and also looked to us anyway that she liked it up the bum. Apart from Squint obviously.

'And?' Diamond continued.

'No offence Black Clint but not your mum.' I replied.

Black Clint's mum was old as fuck and looked more like someone's Nan and even I wouldn't have fucked her unless I'd had at least three pints and an E

'None taken pilgrim.' Replied Black Clint nonchalantly.

'And?' Persisted Diamond.

'Okay! Okay! I'd fuck my own mum, a dead pig, a tiny innocent baby, Sandy the tranny all of you cunts and that little fucking kid who shat his fucking pants!' I screamed at them.

'Good morning Johnny. Lovely day for a slaughter. Well at least I know your standards I suppose. Your own mum eh? That's the only surprise.'

It was Priti.

Perfect timing.

'I didn't even make the list. I can't pretend that I'm not a tad disappointed.'

'Hello Priti!' I replied trying to appear all bright and breezy and failing miserably. I could have really done with Diamond's distraction boner right then but as I glanced over at his cock, inexplicably, just to spite me, there was nothing going on. I made a mental note to change his name to 'Bastard.'

'How did you know that murder got my tiny, little, silk panties wet Johnny?' she said.

And just like that, when it was too late to come to my rescue my gang produced four boners all at once.

'Lucky for you I don't get sarcasm Priti so I'm going to take that statement at face value. Would you like to watch as I chop up my friend Diamond here into little pieces? You could masturbate at the same time if you like?' I replied. I figured that I had nothing to lose now anyway so I might as well give myself and my gang something to wank off about later.

With a sweep of her hand directed at all of us and aimed at crotch height Priti then said. 'Oooh look at all those little bulges in your trousers! How sweet! Are they all in honour of me? How delightful! Nom, nom, nom what a treat!' Right then who's first up for a lovely blow job!?'

She was a sarcastic bitch but none of us at this point cared.

Priti walked over to Black Clint, glanced down at his throbbing dick and staring directly into his terrified eyes said, in what I thought anyway, was a very passable impression of a Texan cowgirl, 'My oh My Mister Clint sir that sure do look like a mighty fine weapon you've got there now don't it?? Why I bet you'd like to just whip that thang out and stick it right down my purdy little throat now wouldn't you... cowboy?'

Black Clint was shaking like a leaf but I'll give him his due he did eventually respond and even kept in character and replied, 'Why yes I would mam... that would be mighty fine.' And with a trembling hand he tipped his hat.

The next thing we heard was a groan as Diamond came in his pants. Thank fuck for that. Diamond had finally came through and the heat was now off me to some extent.

'Oh you dirty little boy Diamond!' said Priti with a look of mock horror.

This interruption to proceedings had cooled down the rest of us and we all started pointing and laughing at the ever increasing wet patch developing on the front of his trousers. Diamond was mortified and we all glorified in his misery.

'I think somebody needs their little bottom spanked.' She continued, with a look of exaggerated outrage.

'Is it me? Is it me that needs to be spanked on the bottom?' I asked her. Trying desperately to shoe horn myself back into the conversation.

'Oh I think that you're beyond a spanking Johnny.' She replied.

'Maybe if you let me take you out on a date? I think that would teach me a damned good lesson and hopefully one that I would never forget.' I replied, with what I'd hoped would come across as both cheeky and charming.

'Ooh that sounds like heaven Johnny but you know us Asian girls. I'd have to ask my father's permission but if he says yes then I'd definitely go on a date with you! He's always dreamed about me dating a psychopath! ' she replied with a wink.

Oh well at least she'd let me down gently and it wasn't too humiliating in front of my gang. It was clearly a no but she'd made it look like it was her father's fault and not the fact that I was a despicable low life mental case. Well apart from the psychopath bit obviously. I wasn't even that disheartened. Back in her dad's shop she was certainly flirting with me but even then I realised it was only because she wanted to wind him up. Her dad hated me and my family and I couldn't blame him. Between us we'd been robbing him hand over fist for years. Our Wayne was no thief but he was a bit of a pervert to say the least what with always getting his knob out in public and that. Killing Butch and his mates probably didn't help me cause either if I was being honest. The other factor, and the one I would cling on to with both hands, was that realistically even if I wasn't such a horrible bastard I would still have stood no chance of being Priti's boyfriend because I wasn't Indian. Or more specifically a Hindu. I was a white working class little knob head and there was fuck all I could do about so I decided to put Priti's rejection of my offer down to simple racism

'If I was brown do you think I'd stand more of a chance Priti?' I asked.

'Well you'd still be a twat Johnny.' She replied. Then for one beautiful, brief moment in time she caught my eye. I looked at her and she looked at me and I swear to God that her pupils dilated. I'd read somewhere that when this happens it's a sign of sexual attraction and I couldn't help but grin. That broke the spell and Priti literally stumbled. It was now her turn to be on the back foot but I didn't play it to my advantage. That look was a sign of hope and I was elated. Within seconds Priti regained her composure and glanced around flicking her eyes onto all of us.

'Well I must say that I'm very upset with all of you except Diamond. At least he had the decency to prematurely ejaculate into his pants at the sight of me. The rest of you should be thoroughly ashamed of yourselves for disrespecting me. Either I'm losing my touch or you lot are all bloody fucking racists. I bet if I was some blonde white girl with a fat arse and a fag hanging out of my mouth you lot would have exploded your loads all over her! Unless of course you are all homosexuals in which case you are forgiven.' She said, trying to look hurt. Fuck me who says that kind of thing? No wonder I was so in love with her she was awesome. Furthermore by the look on their faces it was patently obvious that my gang were now also under her spell.

'Well Johnny is definitely a homosexual paedo' quipped Diamond. 'I bet if you were a little boy he would have shoot his bolt.'

Fuck me he had a lot of nerve to say anything at all sat there with spunk seeping through his trousers. What has a boy got to do to get any loyalty around here? I thought to myself. Diamond was trying, in his own fucked up way, to hit on her right in front of me! Unfortunately the law clearly states that your mates have to try and belittle you and humiliate you to within an inch of your life and you have to do the same back. That's just the way it is and there was fuck all anyone could do about it. They are just the rules of friendship. Anyway I loved it and so did they. I had to admire the cunt's balls but surely even I was a better bet than a boy whose response to any social interaction was to get an erection?

'I'm not actually a homosexual paedophile at all Priti, spunky pants is just trying to be amusing to distract from the fact that he's jizzed himself in front of you. And if it makes you feel any better at the first opportunity I'm going to wank myself into a fucking coma and you will be the sole protagonist in said wank.' I told her. I wasn't even lying.

'Me too Priti, Ah gotta say that you're a mighty fine looking lady and I too will be having a good ole yank on ma big black anaconda all about you as soon as the first opportunity arises. Darned tootin I will young missy!' drawled Black Clint.

The cheeky cunt. Of course he had to get in that he was hung didn't he? White people always assume that black guys have massive knobs and Black Clint was never shy about perpetuating this myth. I'd assumed that it was a myth anyway. Not that I'd seen many black cocks up until that point obviously. I couldn't help noticing the bulge in his trousers earlier though and it did seem to be bigger than the rest of ours.

269

The lucky bastard. Maybe that was why Black Clint took all the racism he suffered on a day today basis with such good grace? Who cares about bigotry when you're hung?

Then Squint piped up. 'I concur. Touché. Forsooth, at my first opportunity I shall also be partaking in an act of self-pollution while thinking about your good self ma lady.'

The treacherous bastards.

'Ditto.' Said Billy.

'That's good to hear boys. I feel a lot better. Thank you all for your kind words. I feel both honoured and humbled. Right then you little scum bags I can't stand here all day chit chatting to you bunch of wankers as all that burning flesh is starting to make me quite queasy. Laters bitches.'

 Then she turned on her heels and sauntered off across the playground oozing an innate self-assurance that made me fall so deeply in love with her that my soul began to ache for hers to such an extent that I involuntarily groaned out loud. We all watched Priti walk away in silence. I was in love with her and even though I would definitely be going to wank myself half to death about her as soon as possible it would be respectful and reverent this time. A homage to the most fantastic and awesome person I'd ever had the privilege to have met. She knew my name. I actually knew her. She'd even spoken directly to me. On numerous occasions. We could legibly be called friends. Well we were once. Her dad owned our local corner shop and we used to walk home together but at that time it was just platonic. Before my balls dropped she was just a girl who was kind to me and talked to me as if I was just another normal kid. This was very refreshing at the time because, due to my parents being arses holes most people kept their distance or looked down on me, assuming that I was as bad as them. Which I was. My family had nicked so much stuff from their family's shop it was amazing that they hadn't gone broke years ago. Despite that fact, on numerous occasions, and to the dismay of her dad, Priti's mum would often give me food to take home for me and my brother Wayne, which may well have saved our lives. It was this sense of decency and morality that ironically I found so appealing in Priti herself and her family. That and her beautiful caramel skin and perky little tits and pert little bum. Maybe it was opposites being attracted? Due to my Irish heritage I was pasty and ill looking most of the time. I could get blistering sun burn just by turning on the living room light and it wasn't like my mother to ever think about slathering me in sun cream either. In the summer you just burnt, peeled and then burnt again until it was winter and nobody gave it a second thought. My parents were rank and I hated them. At the time I didn't know how bad they were. It was ages before I found out that not everyone's parents fought each other and hit their kids and stole things and didn't work and took drugs and got drunk all the time. It was my normal. Anyway they got what they deserved and now me and our Wayne had the house to ourselves and as far as I cared they might as well be dead. Fuck the pair of them.

I decided that I'd had enough of school for one day so decided to fuck off home.

'Listen guys I'm off home, I might come in tomorrow and then we can start to build our new empire.' I said, but those degenerates were still watching Priti cross the playground, etching her deep into their filthy overflowing wank banks.

'Jesus you perverts for fuck's sake stop objectify Priti!' I pleaded, but it fell on deaf ears. I only said it because in my head she was already my girlfriend and I couldn't bear the thought of that lot beating their meat while thinking about her. That was what I was going home to do obviously but it was different for me. My wank would be full of romance and love and emotion there's would be no doubt sordid and depraved.

Suddenly Billy came out of his trance and said, 'Right then lads I think I'm going to go home I'm not feeling too good.'

Diamond then piped up, 'Me too guys. That was a lot of excitement for one day and I think I'm going to go home and have a lie down actually.'

Squint then looked at black Clint and said, 'Mum and dad will both be at work by now do you want to come home with me? Stacey is at college so you can have a wank in her room if you like ... Just make sure that you clean up this time and don't leave any evidence. She still thinks that was me.'

'Why that sounds like a mighty fine idea sir thank ya kindly.' Replied Clint and then they all fucked off leaving me on my own and looking like a prize prick. 'Charming' I said out loud, I then surveyed my handy work for the final time, got on my bike, cycled home and had one of the most satisfying and frenzied power wanks I'd had since my uncle Sean had taught me how to do it all those years ago.

Please don't forget to leave an honest review. We writers are needy.
http://www.amzn.com/dp/B08WBF87R

Printed in Great Britain
by Amazon

66503264R10159